Refractions of Bob

Manchester University Press

Refractions of Bob Dylan

Cultural appropriations of an American icon

Edited by Eugen Banauch

Manchester University Press

Published by Manchester University Press
Altrincham Street, Manchester M1 7JA

www.manchesteruniversitypress.co.uk

British Library Cataloguing-in-Publication Data
A catalogue record for this book is available from the British Library

Library of Congress Cataloging-in-Publication Data applied for

ISBN 978 07190 9174 2 hardback

ISBN 978 07190 9716 4 paperback

First published 2015

Typeset in Swift Neue and Camphor by R. J. Footring Ltd, Derby
Printed in Great Britain
by Bell & Bain Ltd, Glasgow

Contents

Contents

Contributors

Eugen Banauch gained his PhD in American and Canadian literary and cultural studies in 2007 at the University of Vienna. He has since taught literary and cultural studies at the University of Vienna and at Hebrew University, Jerusalem. He has edited and authored a few books, among them *Fluid Exile* (Heidelberg: Winter, 2009) and (with A. Ganser and M. Blumenau) a popular book in German on Bob Dylan and Austria, *Austrobob: Österreichische Aneignungen von Bob Dylans Poesie und Musik* (Vienna: Falter-Verlag, 2014). In 2011, he organised the 'Refractions of Bob Dylan' conference in Vienna (http://www.dylanvienna.at).

John Frederick Bell is a doctoral candidate at Harvard University, where he is pursuing a PhD in the history of American civilisation. His research explores the politics of subculture across American history. His dissertation project will examine the relationship between religion, social reform and higher education through a study of the earliest co-educational, racially integrated colleges. He received a BA in history and religious studies from the College of William and Mary in 2007 and an AM in US history from Harvard in 2013.

Jean-Martin Büttner works as a reporter and music critic for the *Tages-Anzeiger* in Zurich, Switzerland. He studied psychology, psychopathology and English literature at the University of Zurich and wrote his doctoral dissertation about the psychoanalysis of rock'n'roll. It was published as *Sänger, Songs und triebhafte Rede: Rock als Erzählweise* (Frankfurt am Main: Stroemfeld, 1997).

Rob Coley is a lecturer in media theory and practice at the University of Lincoln. He is the author (with Dean Lockwood) of *Cloud Time: The Inception of* *the Future* (London: Zero Books, 2012) and *Photography in the Middle: Dispatches on Media Ecologies and Aesthetics* (Brooklyn, NY: Punctum Books, forthcoming), the latter of which commends the collective reappropriation and 'fabulatory function' of photography. He is a member of the Society for Ontofabulatory Research, a group dedicated to experimenting with new rhythms of collective enunciation.

Andrea Cossu currently teaches sociology of culture at the University of Trento and at the University of Bologna. He has a PhD in sociology from the University of Trento and has held visiting positions at Yale University, the University of New Haven and the University of Padova. He is the author of *It Ain't Me, Babe: Bob Dylan and the Performance of Authenticity* (Boulder, CO: Paradigm, 2012).

Michelle Engert is a scholar-in-residence at American University in justice, law and criminology and in history. She is also an attorney advisor for the Defender Services Office in Washington, DC, where she supports the constitutional right to counsel for indigent people charged with federal crimes. Previously, she taught at the America Institute at Ludwig Maximilian University in Munich. In her life outside of the law, she teaches and speaks about Bob Dylan's cultural significance and live performances.

Paul Fagan is a lecturer at the University of Vienna. He is the co-founder and co-president of the International Flann O'Brien Society, chief editor of the *International Flann O'Brien Society Brian O'Nolan Bibliography* and co-general editor of the official society journal *The Parish Review*. He has published articles in *Joyce Studies in Italy*, book chapters in edited collections from Syracuse University Press, Cork University Press and Rodopi, and is a primary co-editor of the edited collection *Flann O'Brien: Contesting Legacies* (Cork: Cork University Press, 2014).

Ben Giamo is an associate professor of American studies at the University of Notre Dame. His interests include economic inequality, homelessness and literary/cultural studies. His book *Kerouac, the Word and the Way* (Carbondale, IL: Southern Illinois University Press, 2000) examines Jack's prose art as the expression of an ever-shifting spiritual quest. His most recent book is entitled *Homeless Come Home: An Advocate, the Riverbank, and Murder in Topeka, Kansas* (Notre Dame, IN: University of Notre Dame Press, 2011). He is now working on a manuscript that deals with the novelist William Kennedy and his celebrated Albany Cycle.

Michael Gray wrote the first critical book ever published on Dylan's work, *Song and Dance Man: The Art of Bob Dylan* (London: Continuum, 1972), updated as *The Art of Bob Dylan: Song and Dance Man* (London: Continuum, 1981).

With John Bauldie he co-edited *All Across the Telegraph: A Bob Dylan Handbook* (London: Sphere, 1987) and in 1999 published his monumental third and final edition, *Song and Dance Man III: The Art of Bob Dylan*. In 2006 came his vast *Bob Dylan Encyclopedia* (London: Bloomsbury), followed by *Hand Me My Travelin' Shoes: In Search of Blind Willie McTell* (London: Bloomsbury, 2007, 2009). Michael is British and lives in France.

Leighton Grist is reader in media and film studies at the University of Winchester. The writer of numerous articles published in edited collections and journals, his output has included work on classical and post-classical Hollywood, genre, film and cultural theory, psychoanalysis, gender and popular music. He is as well the author of two books on the filmmaking of Martin Scorsese: *The Films of Martin Scorsese, 1963–77: Authorship and Context* (London: Macmillan, 2000) and *The Films of Martin Scorsese, 1978–99: Authorship and Context II* (London: Palgrave Macmillan, 2013).

Susanne Hamscha teaches American studies at the University of Göttingen. Currently, she is a visiting scholar at Columbia University, where she is working on her postdoctoral project on the American freak show tradition. Her publications include the monograph *The Fiction of America: Performance and the Cultural Imaginary in Literature and Film* (Frankfurt am Main: Campus, 2013) and the co-edited volume *Is It 'Cause It's Cool? Affective Encounters With American Culture* (Münster: LIT-Verlag, 2014).

John Heath gained his PhD from the University of Cambridge in 2004, with a thesis entitled *Behind the Legends: The Cult of Personality and Self-Presentation in the Literary Works of Stefan Heym*. He has been a lecturer at the Institute of English and American Studies, Vienna, since 2004, a lecturer at the Institute of German Studies, Vienna, since 2008, and was also a lecturer at the Centre for Translation Studies, Vienna, over 2004–08. Although his main focus is writing under socialism, other research projects cover various aspects of literature from 1600 to the present day.

Clinton Heylin is recognised as a leading Bob Dylan scholar, as well as an authority on folk music and popular music in general. His books on Bob Dylan include *Revolution in the Air: The Songs of Bob Dylan, Vol. 1: 1957–73* (London: Constable, 2009), *Still on the Road: Songs of Bob Dylan, Vol. 2: 1974–2009* (London: Constable, 2010), *Behind the Shades: The 20th Anniversary Edition* (London: Faber and Faber, 2011), *Dylan Day By Day: A Life in Stolen Moments* (London: Music Sales; New York: Schirmer, 1996) and *Bob Dylan: The Recording Sessions 1960–94* (New York: St Martin's Press, 1995). The last was nominated for the Ralph J. Gleason Award in 1996. He is also known for his acclaimed studies of American punk in *From the Velvets to the Voidoids* (New York: Penguin, 1993) and bootlegging in *Bootleg! The Secret History of the Other Recording Industry* (New

York: St Martin's Press, 1994), which was *Record Collector*'s book of the year in 1994. He edited *The Penguin Book of Rock and Roll Writing* (London: Viking, 1992) and is the general editor of Schirmer's 'Classic Rock Albums' series. He has written on topics outside of popular music, including *So Long as Men Can Breathe: The Untold Story of Shakespeare's Sonnets* (Cambridge, MA: Da Capo Press, 2009) and *Despite the System: Orson Welles Versus the Hollywood Studios* (Chicago, IL: Chicago Review Press, 2006).

Paul Keckeis is a research assistant at the Department of German at the University of Salzburg. He is currently working on his dissertation on notions of genre in the works of Robert Walser. He studied German literature and history in Vienna, Cambridge and Zurich and from 2011 to 2013 received a Junior Fellowship from the International Research Centre for Cultural Studies (IFK), Vienna.

Robert McColl received his doctorate from the University of Liverpool in 2006, following a thesis on the historical romance in Byron and Scott, to be published shortly. From 2008 to 2010, he was Assistant Professor of English at Alfaisal University, Riyadh, Saudi Arabia, and from 2010 to 2014, Lecturer in English at Ruhr University, Bochum, Germany. He continues to research Byron and Scott, and has further research interests in Bob Dylan, folk and blues. He is also the author of an inexorable romance.

Martin Schäfer received his PhD from the University of Basel in 1977 and has been a producer for Swiss Public Radio for thirty-seven years. He writes for *Neue Zürcher Zeitung* and teaches at the University of St Gallen and the Hochschule für Musik in Basel. He was responsible for the special Dylan issue of the Swiss cultural magazine *Du* (*Bob Dylan – Der Fremde*, 2001) and has published a biography of Johnny Cash in German, *Johnny Cash – Leben, Werk, Wirkung* (Frankfurt am Main: Suhrkamp, 2008).

Stephen Scobie, born in Scotland and now living in Canada, is an award-winning poet and critic. He has published widely on both Bob Dylan and Leonard Cohen. His major works on Dylan are *Alias Bob Dylan: Revisited* (Markham: Red Deer Press, 2003) and *And Forget My Name* (Victoria: Ekstasis Editions, 1999).

Mark Shanahan is an undergraduate student of English and sociology at the National University of Ireland, Galway. His areas of academic interest include the work of Bob Dylan and the poetry of Michael Hartnett. He lives in County Longford, Ireland, with his wife, Emma, and children, Elizabeth and Teddy.

Acknowledgements

I would like to thank all contributors, both for their chapters and their collaboration, and also for their patience during the editing process. I would also like to thank the anonymous readers of the manuscript for their commendation, encouragement, suggestions and criticism, all of which helped to make this a better collection.

A very warm thank you goes out to the 'Refractions of Bob Dylan' conference administration team: Martina Rössler, Helen Kopetzky, Ranthild Salzer, Brigitte Petritsch, Leopold Valenta, Klaus Heissenberger, Bettina Thurner, Alexandra Hauke, Julia Schüller and Daniel Schwarz. My thanks go out to Rainer Vesely for sharing his expertise on all things Dylan.

I would like to thank the sponsors of the conference, especially the US Embassy in Austria (in particular Karin Schmid-Gerlich and Roland Fuchs), the University of Vienna, its Department of English and American Studies, and the City of Vienna.

I would like to thank Robert McColl for his indispensable help with proof-reading, especially for those chapters written by authors who do not have English as their first language. Special thanks go to Ralph Footring, the copy-editor of this volume.

A thank you to Callie Gladman and Special Rider Music for granting permission to quote from Bob Dylan's song lyrics. In accordance with this permission, Dylan's lyrics are quoted from http://www.bobdylan.com throughout the book. Thank you to S. Fischer Verlage and Dagmar Schreiber for granting permission to use an extensive quote from Ilse Aichinger's 'Journal des Verschwindens'. Thank you to Wes Daily from Glad Music Co. and Jack Music, Inc., for granting permission to quote from George Jones's 'She Thinks I Still Care'.

I would like to dedicate this book to my wonderful wife and my two beautiful daughters. May you stay forever young and: euch solls geb'n, solang's die Welt gibt/und die Welt soll's immer geb'n.

Eugen Banauch
Vienna, Austria

Part I

Intro

1

Refractions of Bob Dylan: an introduction

Eugen Banauch

This book is a re/fraction. I made the title before we made the book.

Those two sentences are mine, but are also close to a spoken intro Dylan used (in different variations) in 1964 to introduce his song 'Love Minus Zero/No Limit'.[1] Although it is an almost direct Bob Dylan quotation (just a few words have been changed), its new context makes its meaning an entirely different one; the appropriation becomes a mere allusion, still, however, carrying its origin, like a shadow. Here, it serves as an example, in a very condensed form, to illustrate the general focus of *Refractions of Bob Dylan*: it is the processes in-between – allusion, borrowings, the complex mechanisms of appropriation, the losses and gains inscribed in cultural and literal translation – which are at the core of this publication and the chapters collected here.

Both the key terms in the title and subtitle of this publication – that is, *refractions* and *appropriations* – were used when I asked for submissions for a conference in Vienna celebrating the seventieth birthday of Bob Dylan in 2011. They were used as signposts, partly because of their potential for different, even diverging meanings. 'Appropriations' is deliberately used in a broad sense, encompassing categories such as reception, influence, adaptation and translation, as well as quotation, plagiarism and intermedial exchange.

There is, of course, a conscious ambivalence in the notion of cultural appropriation in relation to the work of Bob Dylan. On the one hand, a number of the chapters in this book investigate how both Dylan's texts and what may be called the 'formation Dylan' – that is, his image, myth, stardom, created independently from and partly, even largely, outside the control of the person Bob Dylan – have been appropriated in culturally and regionally divergent spheres. When the focus is on Dylan appropriated, translated and refigured, the perspective is less on Dylan than on *how* and *for which purposes* he has been used, depending on divergent cultural and regional contexts. On the other hand, some chapters look into Dylan's own appropriations and fusions within his work, image or projection, such as the accusations of plagiarism in his 2001 album *"Love and Theft"*, his memoir, *Chronicles*, or the paintings of his 'Asia Series'. Related to both approaches, some chapters are interested in Dylan's strategies to regain a certain degree of autonomy over the signifier Dylan, or to evade appropriations by others.

Appropriation comes in various guises, of which the attempt at interpretational sovereignty over someone else is one. When Dylan appeared at half time during the 2014 Super Bowl – not as a performing artist, but in a television advertisement for Chrysler, proclaiming 'we [i.e. the American working class] will build your car' – the interpretations put forth in the blogosphere, in online discussions, newspaper articles and media commentaries in the aftermath of its airing described Dylan in divergent ways: as working-class hero and fighter for a lost cause, but also as sellout (remember 1965?), as partaking in large-scale capitalism, even as cynically endorsing the horrible working conditions of Asian ancillary industries and, finally, as the unfathomable trickster, constantly defying any categorisations (and thus reproducing the Dylan of myth, the epitome of entirely self-determined agency and authenticity). Even in Austria – where this book was edited – the headlines in the commercial press were mostly scathing, denouncing the protest singer's fall from grace and, for example, glossing over the fact that this was only one of many commercials Dylan had done or lent his songs to since the Victoria's Secret ad from 2004 (and, for that matter, glossing over the fact that the description of Dylan as a protest singer stopped making sense half a century ago). Rather than invest in the futile and ultimately unanswerable task of assessing Dylan's involvement in this commercial, the divergent reactions point towards a relevant issue for this book: the ongoing productivity and global scale of the many divergent meanings that have been and are still being invested in the 'formation Dylan'.

Dylan's cultural production in the second half of the twentieth century, his songs but also his changing images and self-fashionings, has productively informed cultural appropriations of Bob Dylan in different cultural, regional and political contexts. Dylan emerged as a star in 1962 and since then, with temporal delays and widely differing intensity in various parts of the world, Dylan has been a worldwide phenomenon. Reactions to and receptions of him can be perceived on individual, but also on regional, national and global levels. Marshall (2007: 11) points out that 'how a particular star is portrayed and understood depends on a relationship between media and audiences that is completely independent of the star's control'. And putting Dylan to the fore, chiefly as a public figure in whom, over decades, multiple meanings have been invested, it is obvious that the meaning of 'Bob Dylan' is not (solely) under the control of Bob Dylan himself.

This volume is, thus, especially interested in the social, political and cultural functions of appropriations of Dylan. Various possibilities of 'metamorphoses' of Dylan are explored: How have Dylan's texts and the text 'Dylan' been translated, adapted and re/constructed? How and to what ends were they appropriated, and how did they become relevant for cultural or social productions, mainly in non-American cultures? And how do these appropriations inform more general debates about the appropriation of popular culture and the issue of Americanisation in general, especially when Americanisation is envisioned not predominantly as cultural imperialism but as a 'liberating form of expression' (Kooijman, 2008: 11) for other cultures, as a tool for active cultural agency. How are certain 'structures of feelings' (Williams, 1977: 128) translated and relocated in divergent cultural, regional and social settings?

Refractions of Bob Dylan is a collection of essays by experts on the life and work of Bob Dylan and scholars from fields such as cultural studies, literary studies (American, German, comparative), history, the arts, film studies, music and musicology studies, and folk studies. It incorporates topics such as Dylan and Europe; the reception of Dylan in Britain, Switzerland, Italy and Germany; the influence on and possible transformative powers of trans/regional (youth) cultures, with Dylan 'performing' America; and fan cultures of Dylan. Accordingly, *Refractions* collects contributions by writers from the United States, Canada and various European countries.

Many of the chapters, thus, do not focus on Dylan's songs and lyrics and their adaptations, but on aspects of cultural appropriations of (and by) Bob Dylan, his re/presentations of self and autobiography outside his songs, as in *Chronicles*, and on deliberate representations of Dylan's persona/e, most prominently in Todd Haynes's 2007 film *I'm Not There*, an especially fertile ground, both for exploring visual and musical de- and reconstructions of Dylan and for processes of cultural appropriation beyond Dylan – for example the movie's closeness to the work of Jean-Luc Godard, with which it shares a similar poetics of cultural appropriation, as shown in Stephen Scobie's chapter. Rather than explore the Dylan myth or attempt to pinpoint him as a universal genius, in this collection Dylan becomes a case study for cultural appropriation, an entry point into the function and appropriation of popular culture: How and to what ends have Dylan, his songs, his appearance, his media image, his 'Americanness' (or deviation from a mainstream perception of it) been appropriated at different times and in different countries? And how and what did the singer, writer and painter Dylan quote, misquote and appropriate himself?

The volume is divided into six parts (four main parts, an 'Intro' and an 'Outro'), but various chapters have thematical and methodological links that transcend this structure. Michael Gray's 'Dylan's Americanness in 1960s Britain' (Chapter 2), located next in the 'Intro' (Part I), acts as a prelude to the book, especially to Part II, which explores adaptations and translations of Dylan's work in divergent cultural and national contexts. In his essayistic contribution from the perspective of the eyewitness, Gray, the author of the seminal study on Dylan, *Song and Dance Man*, focuses on how Dylan was perceived in mid-1960s Britain. In this transcultural encounter, Gray delineates a unique kind of cool in Dylan that was not only far from a projection of prevalent ideas held about mainstream America in Europe but that was also already a composite of various transatlantic cultural forms, with its fusion of, for example, French avant-garde movie looks, rock'n'roll and European literature. The chapters in Part II, 'Dylan abroad', investigate Dylan's reception in different European countries. The case studies collected here include Switzerland, Italy and literary versions of Dylan in Austria and Germany: Martin Schäfer's 'Bob Dylan in Switzerland: a classic case of "love and theft"' (Chapter 3) investigates the reception of Dylan's music in Switzerland by commenting on the history of Dylan covers, but also on Dylan's performances in Switzerland and the attention Dylan has received in Swiss media. Schäfer's comprehensive approach uncovers early Dylan translations into Swiss dialect and dialect rock – as early as 1973, five years earlier than Wolfgang Ambros's seminal album *Wie im Schlaf*, the first album of Dylan translations into German. In a similar vein, Andrea Cossu in Chapter 4 looks at the ways Dylan was received and appropriated in Italy, albeit employing a decidedly sociological perspective. In Italy, a reversal of the Dylan chronology of roles becomes apparent, where the 'electric Dylan' was adopted (and frequently covered) first, with the 'topical Dylan' becoming considerably more focused upon in later years. Cossu uncovers the coalition of forces behind this peculiar reverse movement in appropriation and the specific forces at work in the imagined/desired Dylan that was regarded as appropriate to local or regional needs. Lastly in Part II, John Heath's contribution investigates Dylan's traces in German-speaking literature, especially in Wolf Biermann, the 'GDR's Bob Dylan'. His Dylan translations, but also the short prose piece by the Austrian poet Ilse Aichinger, form the core of this chapter. In the way Dylan is negotiated in the works of both these authors, Heath delineates a poetics of absence, prevalent long before this was to become a more widespread approach to thinking about Dylan, arguably most prominent in Haynes's *I'm Not There*. Whether an anti-climactic personal encounter with Dylan is narrated by Aichinger or Dylan's '11 outlined epitaphs' are translated by Biermann, what we see are deliberate non-representations. These texts display an awareness of the constructedness of any portrayal and thus deny any form of make-believe authenticity. 'And when Biermann and Aichinger hide Dylan, they expose themselves' – their Dylan refractions put the gaze, and the process of reflection, at the centre.

Todd Haynes's grand biopic of absence, *I'm Not There*, works as an entry point for three of the four chapters in Part III, 'Who is not there', with the intention of productive tension: it contrasts two decidedly Derridean/deconstructive and Deleuzian/postmodern readings with its two other chapters, one of which reclaims Dylan as investing in a modernist project, the other finding potential weakness in Haynes's movie in its omission of the very changes in Dylan whose various outcomes it so forcefully depicts with the help of six impersonators of the one who is *not there*. The latter of these contributions, Ben Giamo's 'Bob Dylan's protean style' (Chapter 6), opens Part III by focusing on the different guises of Dylan and contextualising Haynes's movie with Dylan's central dictum of the artist's position as always being in a constant state of becoming. Different or, rather, complementary to Haynes's approach, he is interested in this very process, the liminal spaces of metamorphosis, so to speak, and its causalities. The focus on the protean flags various points of crisis in Dylan's career, some of which are identified as advancements of Dylan's reinventions. Whereas the protean mode is unarguably an existential one and thus partakes in a modernist project in which, to quote Sartre, existence precedes essence, in Susanne Hamscha's 'The ghost of Bob Dylan' (Chapter 8) it is performance that precedes essence, by use of the ghost, in the sense of Derrida, as a 'spectre'. Dylan is read as an open-ended signifier realised only temporarily in its appropriations. By this, Hamscha deconstructs the concept of shape-shifting or mask-wearing as the prevalent (even hegemonic) narration of a Dylan chronology and challenges its presupposition of an underlying ontology. Rob Coley's Deleuzian reading, 'I don't believe you … you're a liar: the fabulatory function of Bob Dylan' (Chapter 7) joins forces and constitutes a complementary reading in its interest in the non-representational image of Dylan, in which fans and critics are equal players, but also in what he calls Dylan's 'ontology of "untruth"', a lie that is less an attempt to mask or hide but rather to create. The chapter discards finding a stable framework to encounter Dylan, productively pointing to a 'multiplicity of cultural and temporal entry points' instead, enabling all cultural agents to partake. The last chapter in Part III, 'Mr Pound, Mr Eliot and Mr Dylan: the United States and Europe, modernity and modernism', by Leighton Grist, starts with Dylan's (ironic) allusion to the godfathers of modernism, Ezra Pound and T. S. Eliot, in 'Desolation Row', to develop his assessment of Dylan as someone who 'formally and epistemologically' invested from the beginning and throughout his career – or at least including his constant touring commonly dubbed his Never Ending Tour – in a decidedly modernist project. This is, of course, in both a provocative and productive way, quite disconsonant with the two preceding contributions of postmodern analysis. Grist's chapter can also be linked to Gray's introductory contribution, deepening the analysis of the clash of the 'two different worlds' in the mid-1960s, Britain and the United States, and to Scobie's contribution (Chapter 15), with its references to Godard and *cinema verité* towards the end of the volume.

Part IV, 'Dylan critics', charts the productive space opened up in dialogue with critics, as in John Frederick Bell's chapter, 'Time out of mind: Bob Dylan and Paul Nelson transformed', and through the critics' representations, as in Jean-Martin Büttner's chapter, 'Greil Marcus and Bob Dylan: the writer and his singer', in which, by drawing from an extensive personal interview with Marcus, the relationship between Dylan and one of his most renowned critics is explored. Bell's contribution centres on Paul Nelson, one of the early critics of Bob Dylan, and his formative, if largely overlooked, influence on Bob Dylan's career. Nelson was one of the first to recognise Dylan's potential as a folk artist, but almost singularly also supported and helped promote his move away from that designation.

The chapters in Part V, 'Dylan appropriated', are linked by their interest in exploring, even if in quite different ways, communicative modes of Dylan and Dylan's song-writing. Questions of appropriations by Dylan are investigated but so too are his strategies not to be appropriated easily – and how these modes sometimes appear intertwined. Common strategies of Dylan's appropriations are investigated and also how interpretive categories and labels are put on Dylan. The chapters discuss examples of appropriation within Dylan's work, such as his adaptation of song-writing tools and his ways of subverting appropriations. Notably, Stephen Scobie's chapter, 'Plagiarism, Bob, Jean-Luc and me' discusses the related and much-debated question of plagiarism in Dylan's work.

In Paul Fagan and Mark Shanahan's 'Tell-tale signs' (Chapter 12), the trope of self-deception is explored in a number of Dylan's love-lost songs by close readings of Dylan songs of the mid-1960s and mid-1970s and comparisons with earlier country and blues standards. It shows how Dylan initially appropriated earlier song-writing strategies but soon significantly adapted them in songs such as 'Don't Think Twice' and further developed them, using them with increased sensibility and variation in his 1975 album *Blood on the Tracks*. Fagan and Shanahan also link Dylan's song-writing approach investigated here to a modernist aesthetics, which opens up interrelations with other chapters, such as Grist's 'Mr Pound, Mr Eliot and Mr Dylan'. Paul Keckeis in Chapter 13 is interested in Dylan's spoken intros during his performances in the 1964 shows, notably during the concert at the Philharmonic Hall in New York, known as the Halloween Show. Keckeis shows Dylan's attempts to use spoken words on stage between the songs as a space of agency to regain control of his image and defy then-prevalent projections of him as a spearhead of the folk movement. Besides centring on a communicative device in performance less focused upon, it is also a link to Giamo's 'Bob Dylan's protean style' (Chapter 6) in its interest in a transitory phase of Dylan, in which his trickster mode is in full swing. Robert McColl in Chapter 14 ('Surplus and demand') focuses on a different phase of Dylan's creative *oeuvre* – late Dylan. The explosion and 'superfluousness' of language in his 2001 album *"Love and Theft"* are read as a linguistic strategy of inflation, deliberately used to evade appropriation not by restricting access but by quite a contrary strategy – that of surplus, of 'too much'. McColl touches upon the often repeated charge of plagiarism in Dylan's approach, a topic central to the following chapter, Stephen Scobie's 'Plagiarism, Bob, Jean-Luc and me'. Scobie, the writer of *Alias Bob Dylan* and Canadian poet who has won the Governor General's Award, sets out from the commonly known territory of Dylan's own appropriations from the folk tradition to chart Dylan's work within the framework of the drifting terms 'quotation', 'appropriation', 'assimilation', 'adaptation' and 'plagiarism'. Exemplarily, he looks at the sources that are being drawn from, taking into account the contexts in which the respective borrowings are situated and at what stages in Dylan's career they happened, which are often, but not always, the 'deliberate and sophisticated appropriations of a well read and highly self-conscious mind'. This is illustrated with the help of contrastive and complementary looks at Godard's movie work, but also at Scobie's own poetical work and contextualised with a historiography of appropriation from Seneca to T. S. Eliot's dictum 'Immature poets imitate; mature poets steal'.

As a sort of coda, the volume closes with a transcription of Clinton Heylin's and Michelle Engert's personal evening lecture given during the Refractions of Bob Dylan conference, which fittingly focuses on the development and changes within Dylan fan culture during the Never Ending Tour from its beginnings in 1988.

It is a hope that this book succeeds in transcending its immediate object of investigation and also makes a case for more concerted attempts at the transnational study of popular culture by using Dylan as a showcase and by following and inspecting traces rather than the idea/l of an original. After all, if there is one common trait within Dylan's work it is that it ever so often eludes interpretation, and suggests divergent levels of meaning, inviting, certainly, multiple listenings but more often than not resisting ultimate signification. As Adorno once said about Kafka: 'Jeder Satz spricht: deute mich, doch keiner will es dulden' ('Each sentence says interpret me, but none wants to put up with it'; my translation) – it is this quality of open signification in Dylan's work which also makes an investigation of Dylan refractions especially worthwhile.

Note

1   'The name of this song is a fraction. Love minus zero is on the top and underneath no limit. I made the title before I made the song' (Bob Dylan, introducing the song at the Manchester Free Trade Hall concert, 1964).

References

Kooijman, J. (2008) *Fabricating the Absolute Fake* (Amsterdam: Amsterdam University Press).
Marshall, L. (2007) *Bob Dylan: The Never Ending Star* (Cambridge: Polity).
Williams, R. (1977) *Marxism and Literature* (Oxford: Oxford University Press).

2

Dylan's Americanness in 1960s Britain

Michael Gray

If we are as much fans as scholars, and our purpose is to look at some of the very many ways in which Bob Dylan has seeped into our lives, and into the consciousness of many countries, then I must start by trying to recall the way that Britain was shortly before Bob Dylan left Minnesota in 1960 – before he had come to the outside world's attention.

The pre-Bob Dylan Britain that I recall was, first of all, Merseyside, in the English north-west, and especially the city of Liverpool, which I encountered as a child in the early 1950s, when people from all over Africa would sail there, many departing from Mombasa, to start a new life in the cold grey unwelcome of England.

Liverpool thrived then. You could still ride the world's oldest electric-powered overhead railway all along the vast dock road, looking down at huge ships in every dock. A black steam train hissed on every platform of the big metropolitan Lime Street terminus. Trams, vying with the buses, sliced their way along the main roads and down the city streets. Smoke and industry and cloth caps and sailors and business people and smartly dressed, glamorous secretaries were everywhere. The Pier Head down on the waterfront was the headquarters of many international shipping companies; Liverpool had its own stock exchange. And the Mersey Tunnel, like a great overflow pipe, fed in and out its stream of lorries and vans and black cars: Morris 8s, Ford Prefects, Austin 12s, Triumph Mayflowers, Wolseleys and Rileys and Rovers.

But this, the end of the 1950s, the start of the 1960s, was also the world of the working-class bicycle. As Iain Sinclair wrote in the *London Review of Books* in 2011:

> The industrial worker, as represented by Albert Finney in Karel Reisz's film of Alan Sillitoe's *Saturday Night and Sunday Morning*.... The most exciting young actor of his generation tracked across the Nottingham

cobbles [enjoyed the] liberation of moving through a city independently … no bus queues, weaving around pedestrians, doing the banter, in English weather.

Sleeves rolled, Finney turns out parts for Raleigh bicycles in the industrial heartlands: 1960…. Foremen in dun coveralls. Cigarettes smoked in cupped fists. The bikes streaming from the factory gates are aspirational, bought at a discount, like the cars of workers on the Ford assembly line at Dagenham. The first episode of the initially realist soap opera *Coronation Street*, also screened in 1960, used a bicycle as a symbol of class division. Ken Barlow, a living at home student, paralysed by pretension, is outraged when his father and brother mend a puncture on the carpet, in front of the living-room fire. Cilla Black's memory of watching the launch of *Coronation Street* involved peering at the screen, to witness the Barlow inner-tube wrestle, over the back of her father, who was carrying out the same operation in the parlour [of their house in] … Scotland Road, Liverpool. (Sinclair, 2011)

Some of this grimy, Victorian-terraced north-west of England can be seen in the glimpses of street urchins and fans in the documentary films *Dont Look Back* and *Bob Dylan 65 Revisited* as Dylan descends upon this England like a being from another planet, and as he rides across it, surveying it impassively, from a carriage pulled by one of those steam trains.[1]

Things came through slowly. News about records and records themselves. There was often a gap between when a record was released in America and in Britain, and often, until the second half of the 1960s, another gap between when it might be available in London and in the small provincial record shops of the north. In most towns, you could buy discs only at hardware and electrical-goods shops with a small record section somewhere behind the vacuum cleaners, washing machines and lampshades; and the manager would be a tweed-jacketed, middle-aged man barely familiar with the name Elvis Presley, let alone Bob Dylan. The upshot was, for years, that if a record was in the top ten the shop had sold out of it and if it was not, the staff had never heard of it. And of course almost all music on the radio came via the BBC, whose policy was to repress anything American unless it was pre-rock'n'roll. Under these conditions, news was a matter of leisurely paced rumour.

The old and the newer coexisted. *Coronation Street* in Manchester and the Beatles in Liverpool both began in 1960. So did the legal right to publish D. H. Lawrence's 1928 novel *Lady Chatterley's Lover*, after a month-long trial brought against Penguin Books by the Director of Public Prosecutions in which the prosecution not only lost but was ridiculed for being out of touch when the chief prosecutor asked the jury: 'Is this the kind of book you would wish your wife or servants to read?'

The great British poet Philip Larkin famously summed up this antiquated Britain in his 1974 poem 'Annus mirabilis', writing that 'Sexual intercourse began/in nineteen sixty three/Between the end of the *Chatterley* ban/and the Beatles' first LP' (Larkin, 1974).

The Beatles made nearly 300 appearances at the Cavern Club between 1961 and 1963. The great preponderance of their repertoire was cover versions – interpretations, if you prefer – of American records drawn as much from 1950s rock'n'roll as from the contemporary early 1960s. These records were by artists who, while repugnant to those who ran the arts columns of newspapers, declamatory politicians, the BBC and the middle aged in general, nevertheless exemplified and celebrated a kind of Americanness that was entirely conventional and widely familiar to us in Britain. We who were young regarded them as embodying the glamour of America itself. Chuck Berry sang in untroubled celebration in his 1959 hit 'Back in the USA' of a country where hamburgers sizzled on open grills, jukeboxes were jumping and every wish could be fulfilled: 'Yes, I'm so glad I'm livin' in the USA'. 'Back in the USA' was a belated British top ten hit in 1963.

After Bob Dylan, the Beatles could write 'Back in the USSR' – but before Dylan they were happy to sing Chuck Berry's anthem. Dylan himself, years later, would offer his own succinct yet more ambivalent take on this in 'When I Paint My Masterpiece' (1971): 'Sailin' round the world in a dirty gondola/Oh, to be back in the land of Coca-Cola!' Back before the 1960s, Coca-Cola (with ice!) was as glamorous to us in tea-drinking Britain as a drive-in movie. Chuck Berry was on the money.

Decades later, I was given a copy of a letter written by the great sax player from the Dave Brubeck Quartet, Paul Desmond. Writing in 1958 he described, among other things, a visit to England while the group was touring Europe. He wrote this:

> Enjoyed England pretty much, possibly because I sympathize with their desire to live in the past. Outside of a few minor problems (finding food after midnite, or coffee anytime. And heat), very pleasant. Two Sunday afternoons in London, which makes Philadelphia seem like Mardi Gras.... Walked around the streets for awhile, came presently to huge throng. 'Groovy,' I thought, 'At least the day hasn't been a total loss. Some unique British Sunday-afternoon diversion. Bear-baiting, perhaps, or street-corner debate....' Gradually pushed way thru crowd. Turned out to be a Lincoln Continental. (Desmond, 1958)

Along with all this American modernity – the equipment, the plenty, the cheerful and confident squandering, all of which enthralled us – we in Britain were naturally both envious and resentful of the kind of individuals Americans so often were: the gum-chewing, crew-cut Americans who knew nothing about the rest of the world even when they were stationed there in army or air force bases – the Americans who imported their gorgeous fin-tailed automobiles to Europe however briefly they were going to be there.

If they did not look like Charles Atlas, they looked like John F. Kennedy: a president like a film star, shining with entitlement and money, and with a glamorous wife, while in Britain our aristocratic prime ministers – who in the early 1960s included Lord Home, son of Lord Dunglass and Lady Lilian Lambton, the daughter of the 4th Earl of Durham – gave way to Harold Wilson, a small, pipe-smoking man in a Gannex mackintosh.

Of course, some Americans wore raincoats too, and emanated a more cynical attitude to the paraphernalia of US consumerist culture. But these Sam Spade/Humphrey Bogart types, while less glossy, were still romantically, archetypally American: they were hard-boiled reporters and detectives, cigarettes hanging from their mouths, talking of 'dolls' and 'broads', toting big cameras and snatching sodium-flare photographs of dead bodies or Hollywood hunks. One such reporter was Horace Judson, the man from *Time* magazine who comes up against Bob Dylan in *Dont Look Back*. Do look back to that riveting scene. What this shows us is the culture clash between two very different kinds of American – between one of the old, familiar sorts and one of the new, excitingly different kind of American that the twenty-three-year-old Bob Dylan was then.

There he was, with the world of celebrity and glamour kissing his feet and cooing in his ear: the most perfectly hip creature on earth. Imagine how you would have coped with that. Even 10 per cent of it would have turned your head. But Bob Dylan did cope, telling the man from *Time* magazine: 'I'm saying that you're going to die, and you're gonna go off the earth, you're gonna be dead. Man, it could be, you know, twenty years, it could be tomorrow, anytime, so am I. I mean, we're just gonna be gone. The world's going to go on without us.... Alright now, you do your job in the face of that and how seriously you take yourself, you decide for yourself' (Pennebaker, 2006: 128).

Dylan wasn't only the opposite of Horace Judson. He was also the opposite of those gung-ho, pudgy, anti-Communist, overfed Americans we knew about. Bob Dylan was as thin as a wire, contemptuously unconcerned to be 'manly', flaunting an androgynous look (so much so that it made perfect sense when Todd Haynes chose Cate Blanchett to impersonate this Bob Dylan in his 2007 film *I'm Not There*) and, as he has always been, replete with the implication that he knew something we did not. He would soon sing 'Why must I fall into this sadness?/Do I look like Charles Atlas?' – and this was funny not only for the outrageous rhyme but because Bob Dylan was, of course, as unlike Charles Atlas and that America as possible. This young, infinitely cool Bob Dylan's knowingness stemmed, no doubt, from a distinctly American self-confidence, yet it was so sharply observant – it was completely different from the oblivious self-confidence of the pampered all-American boy. He was serious.

When Bob revisited Britain in 1965, he knew quite well that European literature mattered, and he had read a fair amount of it. He knew enough to have made his personal style one that implied a radical internationalism. Think of that wonderful photograph of Bob and an elderly European lady in 1966, the two regarding each other across the room and looking uncannily similar (Pickering, 1971).[2]

He embodied his own novel kind of cool that, while partly *modelled* on a French avant-garde movie look, was *based* upon sharp and restless intelligence, a clear conviction that everything had to *earn* our respect, that time was short and impatience justified, that everything the grown-ups had organised was *not* necessarily acceptable, that cultural stuffiness was over. In these ways, he rewrote our ideas of Americanness – and his impact on British culture was forcefully to encourage everyone, particularly a younger generation, to want to stir everything up.

Of course, it was not mere personal style. It was his songs, his powerfully successful work – not least his hit singles. In Britain, Bob charted for the first time in March 1965, with 'The Times They Are A-Changin'', which was still climbing when 'Subterranean Homesick Blues' entered the charts a month later; both reached the top ten while Carnaby Street Bob toured England with his giant lightbulb, dark glasses, Chelsea boots and acoustic guitar. (That giant lightbulb: what an audacious symbolic flourish that was. 'I am the way and the light'. Or at least, 'I bring you some enlightenment…'.)

Two months after that, 'Maggie's Farm' arrived in the lower reaches of the chart and on 19 August 'Like a Rolling Stone', which gave Dylan his first top five hit record in Britain. At the end of October, the scathing lilt of 'Positively 4th Street' charted, soon becoming another top ten hit. Within four weeks of New Year's Day 1966, Bob's next single, 'Can You Please Crawl Out Your Window?', would join the hit parade, too.

It was all go for Bob, the folk singer who had 'gone pop'. Except that it was obvious he had not. He was on his way somewhere else. Pop was all the others. The Beatles in 1965 were still mop-tops; their hit singles in Britain that year were 'I Feel Fine', 'Ticket to Ride', 'Help!' and 'Day Tripper' combined with 'We Can Work It Out': all number one smash hits and only just beginning to hint at something less vacuous than 'She Loves You'. To put the contrast most strongly, we might note that in 1964 the Beatles were singing 'I Want to Hold Your Hand' and Bob Dylan was writing 'To dance beneath the diamond sky with one hand waving free/Silhouetted by the sea, circled by the circus sands/With all memory and fate driven deep beneath the waves…'.

It took many of us a while to get used to his voice, but once we could hear that within it lay such riches of expressive thought and feeling, such resources of intelligence, such clear-sighted, uncompromising purpose, we were hooked. He was a most exotic American: unique. It is impossible, now, to describe the thrill of being there then, hearing these seminal records when they were new – and when each one was so different from the last – and when Bob's voice, or rather, voices offered so subtly nuanced and yet so direct a communication that he seemed to be expanding your mind when he opened his mouth.

He was crucial, the authentic contemporary heavyweight, primarily an agent of the radical future – not, as now, a guardian of the past. He had cultural clout, not mere celebrity.

He began to become an ever-present, formative influence. From 1965 onwards, people's diaries and letters (people still wrote letters) began to alight more and more on moments and incidents for which a Dylan aphorism came as the natural *bon mot* – and they were all the more *bon* for their freshness. It was sparky then to throw off a line from 'Desolation Row' or 'To Ramona'.[3] These records were almost new. Student newspapers, too, began to feature Dylanisms, sown among their headlines and sub-heads.

Where Bob Dylan was going, nobody knew. Where the 1960s were going, nobody knew. It is as the original generation of rock'n'rollers always said. At the time, it was not experienced as history in the making; at the time, it was just how things are.

And the world of music Dylan brought to our attention was itself both old and new. On the one hand, for most people in Britain his early records, and the repertoire he would explore in *The Basement Tapes* album (1975), brought into the light of day the music of what Greil Marcus (1997) has memorably called the 'Old, Weird America' and the 'Invisible Republic'. And on the other hand, the radical, experimental rock music he was hurling at us in the mid-1960s, when he was having his hits in the pop charts, was a big part of the shock of the new – while incorporating Dylan's own rarefied knowledge of both the pre-war blues and the post-war work of the Beat poets.

There were small minorities of folk-club members in provincial Britain who knew the 'Old, Weird' American folk music, and there were small minorities on the London scene who had read and followed the work of the Beats (indeed, there were enough of the latter to fill the Royal Albert Hall in 1965, less than two months after Dylan filled it, for the rapturous event that was the International Poetry Incarnation, when 5,000 people unexpectedly occupied a hall built to symbolise the might of Victorian rectitude, to listen to Beat poets mostly from America).

But these were esoteric coteries alongside the large, nationwide populace who knew of literature only what they had been forced to read in school, whose knowledge of music was shaped mostly by the hit parade and whose idea of America was mainstream America's own idea of itself: that is, the innocently Philistine suburban America of big refrigerators, big guys, drive-in movies and eggs-over-easy.

Bob Dylan brought the other Americas into the mainstream for us. And since he fused so much of poetry and of music into his own commercially successful work, and thereby knocked down the walls of song, he liberated us all, planting those chimes of freedom in our heads.

Notes

1 Both films directed by D. A. Pennebaker, with footage shot in 1965. *Dont Look Back* was released in 1967, *65 Revisited* in 2007, with out-takes from the former film.
2 The photograph is unattributed but is by Barry Feinstein. It is captioned as being taken in Paris, but was actually taken in Birmingham, England. It is reproduced (without caption) in Pickering (1971: 44).
3 'Desolation Row' from *Highway 61 Revisited* (1965) and 'To Ramona' from *Another Side of Bob Dylan* (1964).

References

Desmond, P. (1958) Letter, undated, in the Paul Desmond Archive, part of the Brubeck Collection in the Special Collections, Library of the University of the Pacific, Stockton, CA, USA.
Larkin, P. (1974) 'Annus mirabilis', in *High Windows* (London: Faber and Faber). 167.
Marcus, G. (1997) *Invisible Republic: Bob Dylan's Basement Tapes* (Basingstoke: Picador/Pan Macmillan).
Pennebaker, D. A. (2006) *Dont Look Back* companion book, in the DVD release *Dont Look Back* (65 tour deluxe edition) (Sony BMG Music Entertainment).
Pickering, S. (1971) *Praxis: One* (Santa Cruz, CA: No Limit Publications).
Sinclair, I. (2011) 'The raging peloton', *London Review of Books*, 33:2 (20 January). Available at http://www.lrb.co.uk/v33/n02/iain-sinclair/the-raging-peloton (accessed 8 November 2014).

Part II

Dylan abroad

3

Bob Dylan in Switzerland: a classic case of 'love and theft'

Martin Schäfer

Dylan's work has been 'refracted' in Switzerland on three distinct levels: in cover versions by Swiss singers and musicians, often (and most interestingly) in their own language(s); by the Swiss public as record buyers and concert audiences; and by the Swiss media, constructing their own versions of Dylan, mainly in radio programmes and the printed press.

The aim of this chapter is to produce a composite image of Bob Dylan as seen and heard in Switzerland, starting with the first magazine articles and cover versions by local 'beat bands' in 1965 and 1966. Special notice is given to the Swiss-German translations by artists such as Franz Hohler, Toni Vescoli and Polo Hofer, but also to his less obvious but still distinct influence on younger artists, from Stephan Eicher to Sophie Hunger.

Additionally, we will view the emergence of a highly controversial Dylan persona through the impact and critical reception of his Swiss concerts from 1981 onwards, with particular emphasis on Locarno 1987, depicted as a crucial moment by Dylan himself in his 2004 memoir *Chronicles*, and Montreux 1990, the first Swiss date on the Never Ending Tour.

Finally, the image of Dylan in the Swiss media is discussed through a closer look at his journalistic fans and detractors. Here, the starting point must be the almost incidental, but highly telling, reportage of the 1966 Paris Olympia concert in a very early issue of the first Swiss youth magazine, *Pop*, the first in a long line of major articles and even whole issues of magazines, leading to the 2001 'Dylan edition' of Switzerland's celebrated *Kulturmagazin Du*.

As an amusing (but still quite telling) prelude, we will review Bob Dylan's performance in the Swiss record charts.

19

Dylan's performance in the Swiss hit parade

In contrast to the situation in the United States and Britain, there was no officially recognised Swiss 'hit parade' before 1968.[1] The sales performance of Bob Dylan's records in the preceding years, therefore, is anyone's guess. The first major magazine article on Dylan appeared in February 1966, in the liberal weekly *Die Weltwoche*: a report by its New York correspondent, Heinz Pächter[2] (1966: 25), announced on the cover as 'Bob Dylan – Der Politische Troubadour'. Compared with Dylan's reception in the German-speaking world in general, this was still quite early: the very first mention of 'America's highly-paid folk music troubadour' ('Amerikas hochbezahltem Volksmusiktroubadour') in Germany's leading news magazine, *Der Spiegel*, is to be found a few months earlier, in June 1965, in a short review of the album *Odetta Sings Dylan* (1965, by the US singer Odetta).[3] The fact that even the liberal media took a long time to notice the new pop culture contributed to the emergence of a specialised, sometimes underground, pop press, which included the commercial, market-oriented *Pop* magazine (comparable to Germany's *Bravo*, but with a clearer music bias) and the self-declared underground magazine *Hotcha!*, whose founder, the surrealist poet Urban Gwerder, became quite important for the critical awareness of Bob Dylan in Switzerland: he was to reprint (illegally) the very first excerpts from Dylan's then still unpublished novel *Tarantula*.

Another special feature of the Swiss situation has to be mentioned here: since Swiss-German public broadcasting (by the radio station Radio der deutschen und rätoromanischen Schweiz, called Landessender Beromünster up to 1967) at first hardly acknowledged the new beat and pop music coming out of America and Britain, Swiss youth turned to the English service of Radio Luxembourg and commercial French long-wave stations, such as Europe No. 1 and its celebrated *yé-yé* programme *Salut Les Copains*,[4] in order to keep up. This French influence, reinforced through the French-speaking parts of Switzerland, ensured that the first Dylan songs may have been heard in Switzerland in early French cover versions: 'Don't Think Twice' as 'N'y Pense Plus, Tout Est Bien' by Hugues Aufray (still today the most important of Dylan's French interpreters), 'Blowin' in the Wind' as 'Ecoute Dans Le Vent' by Richard Anthony, Marie Laforêt and others. The importance of the French pop and chanson scene for Switzerland can be gauged by the fact that the first successful Swiss beat group gave itself a French name: Les Sauterelles (the Grasshoppers) – even though they sang in English. Also known as 'the Swiss Beatles', they were probably the first Swiss band to cover several Dylan songs: 'Desolation Row' and 'She Belongs to Me' on their first album *Les Sauterelles* (1966), then 'It's All Over Now, Baby Blue' on their second (*View to Heaven*, 1968) and finally 'I Threw It All Away' as a B-side to a 1969 single. Their main singer was Toni Vescoli, later to record the first Dylan cover album in Swiss-German.[5] Les Sauterelles had a number one single ('Heavenly Club') in the so-called Swiss Radio Hit Parade in the very first year these charts were published (starting in January 1968 in the form of a weekly top ten programme). The first Dylan song to enter this list was 'Mighty Quinn' in its British cover version by Manfred Mann (which was number two for eleven weeks).[6] The other big Dylan hit of 1968, 'All Along the Watchtower', by the Jimi Hendrix Experience, although very popular in everybody's memory, strangely enough did not make the Swiss top ten. In other words, it did not register at all officially, since only the top ten singles were considered. (There would not be an official album chart before 1983!) Even more curiously, not even 'Lay Lady Lay', Dylan's own big single of the following year, managed to reach the Swiss charts; in fact, the only Dylan single ever to enter the top ten came exactly one year later: it was 'Wigwam', that ironic semi-instrumental from *Self-Portrait* (which for four weeks was number nine in the charts). And that, as far as singles are concerned, is almost all: the only Dylan songs ever to make the Swiss singles charts since then are 'Knockin' on Heaven's Door' by Guns N' Roses (1990, which had thirty weeks in the charts and reached number five) and 'I'll Be Your Baby Tonight' by Robert Palmer and UB40 (1990, which had nineteen weeks and reached number five).

Now, it is well known that Dylan never wanted to be a singles artist – at least not from the moment that 'Can You Please Crawl out of Your Window?' flopped in 1965. So this sad state of (Swiss) affairs should not worry him – or us – unduly. But what about his albums? A so-called LP 'hit parade' was not officially introduced in Switzerland until November 1983, when Swiss public radio inaugurated its pop channel DRS 3. Good for Dylan: this was exactly when *Infidels* was released, and it made the album top ten at once (reaching number nine and spending fourteen weeks in the charts). *Empire Burlesque* even managed to reach number six in 1985 (eleven weeks). But subsequently, Dylan's shaky performances of the later 1980s affected his Swiss chart showings as well. He finally redeemed himself in 1989, with *Oh Mercy* (number four, eleven weeks), but his first number one album was not the universally acclaimed *Time Out Of Mind* (1997, number twelve, seven weeks) nor even *"Love and Theft"* (number three, nine weeks), but *Modern Times* (2006, eleven weeks) – which, by then, might be read as the sign of a general drop in CD sales, leading to the renewed importance of a committed fan base.[7] Remarkably, *Together Through Life* almost matched that feat three years later, by reaching number two (nine weeks).

It has often been said that Dylan's importance cannot be explained (or demonstrated) by his record sales, much less his charts performance. Of course, the commercial charts, although often treated as an objective measure of an artists' success, cannot really be taken as a serious historical record. On the contrary, they remain an obvious example of rather incidental (and accidental) data gaining credence purely by the passage of time and the lack of more reliable information.[8] However doubtful, the Swiss example

21

still gives us an indication of Dylan's status in the pop market: never an idol of the first order, to be sure, but nevertheless, as Lee Marshall has put it, a 'never ending star' (Marshall, 2007).

Bob Dylan's Swiss interpreters: some notable Swiss-German song translations[9]

The Swiss history of Dylan's songs begins, as noted, with some early cover versions in the mid to late 1960s. The example of the Byrds' 'Mr. Tambourine Man' was certainly influential here: Swiss beat groups such as Les Sauterelles or Polo Hofer's Pop Tales gladly helped themselves to selected Dylan songs. At the same time, it may be surmised that the Swiss folk movement (as documented by the annual festivals at Schloss Lenzburg from 1972 to 1980) also produced its fair share of Dylan covers, although no such recordings are readily available. Indeed, there was even a popular Swiss-German singer–songwriter (singing in the Bernese dialect, *Bärndütsch*, and so termed *Bärner Rock*) whose songs and influence could usefully be compared to Dylan's: Mani Matter (1936–72), who modelled himself on French *chansonniers* like Georges Brassens, but also on the American satirist Tom Lehrer. Although Matter never considered a transition to rock for himself and did not obviously make any references to Dylan, it remains interesting to speculate what he might have gone on to do, had he not died in a car crash at age thirty-six. In any case, he was to become a huge inspiration for some of the very same Swiss rock singers who had originally styled themselves after Dylan.[10] Matter could even be said to have been, although indirectly, at the root of the Swiss-German folk rock movement which started, after his death, with the so-called *Bärner Rock* bands such as Rumpelstilz (with singer Polo Hofer) and Span. But the first important Swiss-German translation of a Dylan song, in 1973, came out of the very same literary folksy *Kleinkunst* scene, of which Matter and his colleagues, the so-called 'Berner Troubadours', were such an important part.

'Dr Liebgott Isch Derby' ('With God on Our Side', translated and sung by Franz Hohler)[11]

It is a clear indication of Bob Dylan's special status among rock stars that it was an established writer and poet, Franz Hohler (born 1943), who became the first artist to sing a Dylan song in Swiss-German. That this was seen as a risky but worthwhile undertaking may be illustrated by the reaction of his friend Mani Matter when informed of Hohler's plan: 'Söicheib' (son of a bitch) was his comment, according to Hohler himself (Hohler, 2011). Awarded prestigious literary prizes by such institutions as the C. F.

Meyer-Stiftung and the Deutscher Kleinkunstpreis, Hohler moved in a quite different sphere from that of the earlier Swiss Dylan cover artists, as he was neither a rock nor even a folk singer, but rather a wholly original practitioner of that literary musical *Kleinkunst* genre which, in the German theatre world, is known as *Kabarett* and could be compared, among Dylan's other interpreters, to the work of the Austrian artist–singer André Heller, who once claimed that Dylan himself called him 'a strong poetic muscle'.[12] Hohler's fourth album, *I glaub jetz hock i ab*, released in 1973 (coincidentally on the same record label as Dylan's earlier albums, CBS/Columbia), contains Swiss-German versions of songs by Woody Guthrie, Frank Zappa, the Beatles, Boris Vian, Wolf Biermann (who still likes to think of himself as the German Dylan[13]) – and by Dylan: 'With God on Our Side' (as 'Dr Liebgott Isch Derby') and 'Blowin' in the Wind' (as 'Dr Einzig, Wo Das Weis'). Again, the choice of songs can be taken as a sign that Dylan (as well as the Beatles and Frank Zappa) had by now been elevated to the status of that respectable department of high culture called *Kleinkunst*; that Hohler used Toni Vescoli (formerly of Les Sauterelles) as a guitarist for the latter song confirmed, in a way, that folk, pop and *Kleinkunst* had begun to meet under the auspices of the so-called counter-culture. Of the two songs, it is 'Dr Liebgott' which can be considered a definite artistic success: Hohler manages to transform the lyrics into a satirical commentary on Swiss history quite comparable to Dylan's view of the American past (with specific reference to Swiss immigration policy during the Second World War), while adding a special musical touch by evoking, on his cello, the sound of an alphorn.[14]

'Warehuus Blues' (based on 'Just Like Tom Thumb's Blues', performed by Rumpelstilz, 1973)[15]

The second famous instance of a Swiss-German Dylan cover song followed in the same year (1973); it was equally typical of its times, but of an entirely other kind – one might say a classic case of 'love and theft'. This time, it was a rock group who tackled a Dylan number, Polo Hofer's Rumpelstilz, the first (or one of the first) of the above-mentioned *Bärner Rock* bands that started the trend towards singing in Swiss-German instead of English. This so-called 'Mundart-Rock' (dialect rock) movement had its origin especially in British (and subsequently German) folk rock, with its love for traditional ballads; indeed, Rumpelstilz would, a few years later, be the first Swiss rock group to cover such an old Swiss ballad ('Stets i Truure', from the famous *Röseligarte* collection edited by Otto von Greyerz, 6 vols, 1908–25). Another important inspiration came from German *krautrock* bands singing in their own language (Ihre Kinder, Udo Lindenberg, Floh de Cologne, Rio Reiser's Ton Steine Scherben). For their very first single, Rumpelstilz chose to adapt Dylan's 'Just Like Tom Thumb's Blues', although 'Warehuus Blues'

(Department Store Blues) was not quite a cover version: the lyrics were not a translation of the original at all and, indeed, Dylan was not credited for the song in any way. Musically, though, 'Warehuus Blues' was not just identical to Dylan's composition but even to a precise version of it, the 1966 live recording from Liverpool which had graced the B-side of the single 'I Want You' and was, for many years, the only officially released example of Dylan's rock sound with his band the Hawks. (It was, for that very reason, quite commonly heard on Swiss jukeboxes at the time.) The resemblance between these two recordings was so striking that it was immediately commented upon in the Swiss media, although Hofer and his group were usually excused from any charges of plagiarism for the good reason that the process of clearing an American song for translation was held to be too lengthy and expensive for a fledgling band such as Rumpelstilz. It must be added, however, that this continued to be Polo Hofer's modus operandi for several years, one of his biggest hits ('Kiosk', 1976) even being an undeclared version of Little Feat's 'Dixie Chicken'.

'Schlangelädergurt' (based on 'Leopard-Skin Pill-Box Hat', performed by Polo Hofer's SchmetterDing, 1978)[16]

No wonder, then, that Hofer compounded his crime, if crime it was, with his next band and his second famous Dylan adaptation, in 1978.[17] 'Schlangelädergurt' was closely based on 'Leopard-Skin Pill-Box Hat', not just musically, but also in its lyrics, the only major difference being that Dylan's object of desire was replaced by a 'snakeskin belt'. Nevertheless, Hofer got away with it once more – the Swiss market probably being too small to bother for a big US company such as Columbia or Dylan's publishing representatives. Still, the success of Hofer's new band was great enough to warrant a *Hochdeutsch* (standard German) version of the album, from which a single was released, with the Dylan adaptation on the flip side – and the connection made even more obvious by a new title: 'Schlangenlederhut' (snakeskin hat)![18]

'So Wie Ne Frou' ('Just Like a Woman', Polos SchmetterDing, 1982)[19]

By 1982, however, Polo Hofer (soon nicknamed Polo National) had become so prominent and successful, as the very figurehead of an ever broader Dialekt-Rock scene, that he could no longer rely on the tolerance even of the Swiss publishing rights authorities, especially as his next Dylan adaptation concerned one of the Minnesota bard's best-known compositions: 'Just Like a Woman'. Thus came 'So Wie Ne Frou', on his fourth SchmetterDing album, *Papper-La-Papp*, the first of Hofer's official Dylan covers, later to be included on the monumental tribute *Polo Hofer Singt Bob Dylan 1981–2011*, along with such later highlights as 'Maa Im Schwarze Chleid' ('Man in the Long Black Coat') or 'Dr Blind Willie McTell'.[20] This was not, to be sure, the first Swiss-German album entirely devoted to Dylan songs – here, too, Zurich's own *Liedermacher* Toni Vescoli (of Les Sauterelles fame) had been first, with *Bob Dylan Songs Mundart* (1993), which, by the way, did not even contain all of Vescoli's Dylan dialect versions, a notable example being his 1983 recording of 'Mr Chnochemaa' ('Mr. Tambourine Man').[21] When Dylan played the Frauenfeld festival in 1998, Vescoli managed to offer the album to his idol, and later claimed to have influenced the set-list by his song choices – although there were no more than a few correspondences. Again, in 2011, Polo Hofer originally hoped to open Dylan's Sursee concert and thereby arrange a meeting, but this did not come to pass because Hofer was unable to dodge a previous commitment.

'We D Se Gsehsch' ('If You See Her, Say Hello', translated and sung by Martin Hauzenberger, 1985)[22] / 'Hesch Du Mi Gärn' ('Is Your Love in Vain?', translated and sung by Tinu Heiniger, 1986)[23]

Apart from Hofer and Vescoli, there have been other notable appropriators of Dylan among Switzerland's singer–songwriters, the most successful being Martin Hauzenberger and Tinu Heiniger, both coming out of the tradition of the Berner Troubadours. In 1985, Hauzenberger recorded an excellent dialect version of 'If You See Her, Say Hello', entitled 'We D Se Gsehsch', on his album *Verreise*. The following year, Heiniger followed suit with 'Hesch Du Mi Gärn', his take on 'Is Your Love in Vain?'[24] It may be interesting to note that both were known mainly for their biting political lyrics but, as Dylan fans, they preferred rather private and emotional songs, thereby confirming that even among Switzerland's leftist opposition, Dylan was not admired solely or even principally as the 'protest singer' he had long ceased to be.

'Intercity' (Stiller Has, 1994)[25] / 'Like a Rolling Stone' (Stephan Eicher and Sophie Hunger, unreleased live performance on French television)

There is no denying, however, that the Dylan influence was no longer quite as overwhelming for the Swiss pop generation of the 1980s and 1990s. A new wave of younger Mundart-Rock bands obviously did not feel the need to translate Dylan anymore – perhaps in a conscious attempt to distance themselves from their immediate predecessors – sometimes preferring to do Bruce Springsteen or Elvis Costello songs (like Züri West), sometimes choosing to practically forego such versions altogether (like Patent Ochsner, whose only important cover was a moving, bluesy, not to say Dylanesque, adaptation of

Brahms's 'Ich Hab Die Nacht Geträumet', reminding some listeners of 'St James Infirmary', not to mention 'Blind Willie McTell').[26] Nevertheless, the Dylan style and voice remained present as a crucial point of reference, not least thanks to Stephan Eicher and Endo Anaconda, possibly the two most inspired Swiss rock singers coming from the 'new wave' era.

Eicher started out with a punkish techno sound (first with the band Grauzone, then solo) and went on to craft his own songs in three to four languages: English, French, German and Swiss-German. He, too, eschewed any direct Dylan covers, but he did sing Chuck Berry ('Johnny B. Goode') and Hank Williams ('I'm So Lonesome I Could Cry'), thus paying tribute to Dylan's own roots. As he kept returning to his folk and blues origins, Eicher succeeded in reviving the original folk rock formula – earlier perfected by Hofer's Rumpelstilz – by transforming the famously nostalgic 'Guggisbärglied', one of Switzerland's greatest folk classics, into a bona fide chart buster.[27] Along with Züri West, who covered Mani Matter's 'Dynamit' even earlier, Eicher then was among the first to rediscover the songs of Berne's most celebrated *chansonnier*, even managing to turn Matter's 'Hemmige' into a hit in neighbouring France in 1991 – sung in the original Bernese dialect! The closeness of his vocals to Dylan's has often been noticed; and by 1995, he came around to recording 'I Shall Be Released' for the celebrated French television show *Taratata*, as a duet with Scottish singer Sharleen Spiteri from the group Texas.[28]

In a similar way, Endo Anaconda (born Andreas Flückiger), with his adventurous group Stiller Has, hardly ever turned to the Dylan songbook directly, but referred to it again and again, most conspicuously in 'Intercity', a train song on his fourth album, *Landjäger* (1994), which on close listening sounds like yet another adaptation of 'Just Like Tom Thumb's Blues' (which Polo Hofer had famously stolen some twenty years before). Anaconda's own speciality remains denouncing the false Swiss *Gemütlichkeit* in an operatic baritone but, as this example shows, he likes to use a Dylanesque blues voice, so to speak, as his default mode.

Finally, the circle closes with young Zurich songstress Sophie Hunger, who clearly modelled herself on Joni Mitchell, but was never afraid to talk about her admiration for Dylan, too.[29] Writing and singing in English and German, her finest hour came when she played Glastonbury in 2010, with 'Like a Rolling Stone' part of the set-list; a spirited version can be seen on French television show *Taratata*, as a duet with fellow Dylan fan Stephan Eicher.[30]

Old faithful: Dylan's Swiss concerts, 1981 to 2011

It is not known whether Bob Dylan ever visited Switzerland before his first Basel show in 1981. The first Dylan concert that received a measure of attention in the Swiss media was certainly the famous Paris Olympia date on

26

his twenty-fifth birthday, 24 May 1966. In fact, it was reviewed at length in an illustrated five-page feature article in the fifth issue of the newly founded *Pop* magazine, by its co-editor Beat Hirt (1966: 8–12), who also reported on the notorious press conference at the Hotel George V.[31] In 1969, Dylan's appearance at the Isle of Wight festival was also widely reported and a recording could even be heard, late one night, on a Dutch radio station, but this may have been a pirated (bootleg) transmission. For many Swiss fans, the famous first Dylan concert, then, was either Nuremberg (the site of the infamous *Reichsparteitagsgelände*, now known as Zeppelinfeld) or one of the Paris concerts in July 1978, both cities being near enough to Switzerland to be easily reached.

When Dylan, at last, did come to Switzerland, he had, in the meantime, made his most controversial (and still, to some, most foolish) move, by publicly converting to evangelical Christianity. This may have been part of the reason why the local promoter, Good News, chose to hold the concert in Basel, at its smaller St Jakobshalle, instead of Zurich,with its big Hallenstadion, where Dylan would not play until ten years later. Why, in fact, the first three Swiss Dylan shows were all held in Basel remains a puzzle, but it may have to do with Dylan's contested status as a rock star: was he, in business terms, a big draw at all? Even the second Basel concert, held at the larger, open-air, St Jakob football stadium on the 1984 tour with Santana, was not considered an unqualified success, drawing only about 40,000 people, compared with the 50,000–60,000 that the Rolling Stones, Bruce Springsteen or U2 managed at the same venue.

But Dylan's Swiss premiere on 23 July 1981 is memorable for the very reason that it was part of his last gospel (or at least semi-gospel) tour, starting with an impressive (but loudly contested) opening set by the backing singers, later to be known as Queens of Rhythm, then leading into the by then usual mixture of older and newer material and featuring no less than four songs from *Shot of Love*, which would be released in August that year.[32]

The so-called Open Air concert in 1984 was not quite as controversial: opened by the esteemed Willy De Ville (or rather his band, Mink De Ville) and culminating in Dylan's very first performance of Willie Nelson's 'Why Do I Have to Choose?' (as an encore, with Carlos Santana on guitar), it was quite well received by the public and by the press.

The opposite must be said of Dylan's third Basel concert (10 September 1987): coming immediately after his first concerts in Jerusalem and Tel Aviv, this was, at the same time, only the third show on the infamous Temples in Flames tour with Tom Petty and the Heartbreakers. Among *cognoscenti*, it is famous for making clear Dylan's then completely new format: in these three shows, he did not sing a single song twice; in Basel, he even performed 'The Ballad of Frankie Lee and Judas Priest', which he had never done live before his concerts with the Grateful Dead in the previous summer. Not that too many among the audience noticed: the sound was so bad, and the amount of improvising on Dylan's part so reckless, that it took all of Petty's (and the Heartbreakers') musical experience to keep the concert from descending into a complete shambles. A local Swiss-French paper even entitled its review 'Comme une bière qui coule' ('Like a beer that spills'), a rather cruel word play on 'Comme une Pierre qui Roule' ('Like a Rolling Stone')![33] Was Dylan, in fact, drunk? At least, he *was* noticed to totter and sway in a way that reminded some of an overenthusiastic Hasid, but the opinion among fans, to this day, remains sharply divided: to some, 'Basel III' was utterly thrilling; to others, an absolute disaster.

Bob Dylan's fourth Swiss concert, a few weeks after playing in Germany, Scandinavia and Italy on the same tour, has the special distinction of being remembered as a turning point by the artist himself, not least in his official memoir *Chronicles* (Dylan, 2004: 152–3). In a certain sense, the Locarno show (5 October 1987) could even be considered as the real start to the fabled Never Ending Tour which Dylan undertook from June 1988. Why Dylan chose Locarno of all places for this honour must remain a mystery: one might suppose that, from the Temples in Flames tour, it would, rather, be his first appearance in Jerusalem that would stick in his memory – or even the Berlin concert, transferred at rather short notice from West to East and remembered, in East Germany, as an occasion of quite traumatic public disillusion.[34] Listening to bootleg recordings of Locarno, the difference with other shows does not become immediately obvious: acoustic opening set by Roger McGuinn of the Byrds, first main part by Petty and the Heartbreakers, joined, after a short intermission, by Dylan, still supported on this tour, for the last time, by the Queens of Rhythm. Why, then, is he overcome on this very evening by the realisation that the audience is here for him and him alone? What was remarkable, certainly, was the dream-like setting of Locarno's Piazza Grande, by the lovely Lago Maggiore, first impaired by heavy rain, then enhanced by the appearance of the full moon. Was Dylan, as a movie freak, conscious of the fact that this was the setting, too, of Locarno's renowned Film Festival every summer? Was he dreaming of one day triumphing *there*? Or was he really moved, after the fact, by memories of Jerusalem or East Berlin, where much more had been at stake from the public's side? The recordings, at least, do confirm that a certain change in mood took place with the semi-acoustic songs in the middle of Dylan's set ('Simple Twist of Fate' and a very lovely 'Tomorrow Is a Long Time') but did this, indeed, happen only in Locarno on this tour? 'Don't trust the artist, trust the tale': one might speculate that his Locarno memory, psychoanalytically speaking, really hides another moment of decision at this time of (self-admitted) crisis, but that, of course, is pure guess work.

Then again, not a few Swiss Dylan followers might remember quite another concert as just such a decisive moment: namely, the first and possibly – as regards media attention – most important Swiss date on the Never Ending Tour, taking place at the Montreux Jazz Festival on 9 July 1990.

In the course of that very special evening, featuring the Tex-Mex band of Flaco Jiménez (of Texas Tornados fame), the incredible two-man string band of Ry Cooder and David Lindley and – as a late addition to the line-up – the Dylan band with G. E. Smith on guitars, something extraordinary happened. Dylan started off in a rather surly mood, but then, apparently galvanised by a number of younger fans standing close to the stage and cheering him on, suddenly changed gears and delivered what may well have been his best Swiss show up to then, graced by a rare performance of Ry Cooder's (and John Hiatt's) beautiful 'Across the Borderline', with Flaco on accordion.[35] That this was Dylan's first Swiss Never Ending Tour date (after two years and a quite extensive European stint in 1989) again goes to show that, even with his 1989 album *Oh Mercy* behind him, he was still not considered a safe draw by Switzerland's big promoter, Good News, which brought him to its main venue (the Hallenstadion in Zurich, in January 1991) only after the successful Montreux experience. Indeed, Dylan himself must have felt something special that evening – after the show, he asked Festival boss, Claude Nobs, for a recording, even though he (or his people) had expressly forbidden one![36]

Dylan's fifth Swiss show was the first of many at Zurich's Hallenstadion; it remains memorable mainly because it took place a few days after the outbreak of the first Gulf War. Many American acts then cancelled their European tours but not so Dylan. By now, G. E. Smith had left the band, replaced temporarily by celebrated guitar technician César Díaz. One more thing deserves mention: the first performance of his song 'Bob Dylan's Dream' since 1963. What nobody could have imagined, at the time, was that Dylan would become such a regular guest on Swiss stages since then, performing practically every summer at festivals (Leysin 1992, Gurten 1993, Montreux again in 1994 and 1998, and so on) as well as in concert halls in Zurich, Basel and Geneva. The only gigs planned but cancelled were those in June 1997, at the Zurich benefit festival Rock gegen Hass and (once more) Locarno – when Dylan was in hospital with histoplasmosis. A few months later, after the release of his album *Time Out of Mind*, his standing with critics and the general public took a well deserved turn for the better, and his concerts from 1998 onwards were usually quite well received, the best, possibly, being the one in Zurich in 1999, with Graham Parker as a solo opening act and, according to rumour, Elvis Costello in the wings (who had a show of his own in town, later that evening). Or was it the 2011 Sursee Summer Sound festival? Anyone wishing to go through a complete list of Dylan's Swiss concerts and even their set-lists can do so now by simply selecting from the complete yearly tour lists on his official website.[37]

During the course of his so-called Never Ending Tour, that is, ever since Montreux 1990, Bob Dylan thus quite unexpectedly turned into one of the most faithful visitors of Swiss rock festivals and concert stages. But the best-known incident involving a Swiss Dylan fan happened in Eindhoven (the

29

Netherlands) in 1993, when Liz Souissi, also known as 'Swiss Liz', managed to join Dylan on stage and was allowed to sing along on 'The Times They Are A-Changin''.[38]

Dylan in the mirror of Swiss media attention (1966 to the present)

As we have seen, serious Swiss media attention to Bob Dylan started in 1966, with Heinz Pächter's *Weltwoche* piece in February and Beat Hirt's Paris reportage in the youth music magazine *Pop*.[39] A sort of running commentary on Dylan's further doings, from 1968 on, may be found in numerous issues of Urban Gwerder's underground magazine *Hotcha!*[40] Although Gwerder's main focus was on the music of Frank Zappa, he featured Dylan-related reprints from the American underground press such as the first bootlegged excerpts from Dylan's quasi-novel *Tarantula* (not officially published until 1971). The first critical overview of Dylan's career up to 1971 was featured in the weekend supplement of one of Switzerland's major newspapers, the left-liberal *National-Zeitung* in Basel, in 1972 (see Schäfer, 1972); this was followed, in 1974, by coverage of Dylan's comeback tour with the Band in *Neue Zürcher Zeitung* (Figlestahler, 1974: 59) and, shortly afterwards, by a closer look at the officially released *The Basement Tapes*, again in *National-Zeitung* (Schäfer, 1976).

Nevertheless, there was hardly any continuous discussion of Dylan in Swiss media before 1978, when his concerts in Germany and France generated what was probably Switzerland's first Dylan cover story in a major magazine, the prestigious *Tages-Anzeiger Magazin* (Schäfer, 1978).[41]

During the 1980s, at last, prompted by Dylan's first Swiss concerts, there came the beginnings of what, since then, has come to be regarded as the normal state of affairs for Dylan's public perception in Switzerland. Albert Kuhn, one of our wittiest pop writers (and a singer–songwriter himself, for Swiss new wave band Frostschutz), has defined this cheekily as 'Kniefall vor St. Bob' (genuflection before St Bob) (Kuhn, 2007). 'Unerträglicher als Bob Dylans Stimme und Mundharmonika sind nur seine Apologeten', Kuhn wrote in 2007, cleverly remarking that 'Der reflexartige Kniefall vor Sankt Bob ist für Journalisten über dreissig sozusagen der global gültige Presseausweis. Keine Redaktion ohne berufsmässigen Dylan-Exegeten mit dem Hang zur vollen Zeitungsseite' ('Only his apologists are more unbearable than Bob Dylan's voice and harmonica ... the knee-jerk genuflection before Saint Bob being, for journalists over thirty, their globally valid press credentials. No editorial staff [is] without its professional Dylanologist, with a tendency towards a full-page analysis).

An obvious case of throwing stones from a glass house, of course: Kuhn himself then went on to fill more than a full page with highly pertinent observations of what had been going on between Dylan, his public and his critics at least since the beginning of the Never Ending Tour. In this way,

Kuhn's article managed to represent all currents of Switzerland's Dylan debate at the same time: the jaded scepticism (not to say cynicism) of many media and business circles, the sometimes understandable disillusion of simple fans and concert-goers *and* the passionate yet critical commitment of a number of writers such as Jean-Martin Büttner[42] of Zurich's *Tages-Anzeiger* or Manfred Papst of *NZZ am Sonntag*. An important voice repeatedly joining that debate was that of German sociologist Günter Amendt (1939–2011), who lived in Zurich himself for many years and wrote – about sex, drugs and Dylan – for the Swiss weekly *Die Wochenzeitung* (*WOZ*), as well as its long-established German counterpart, the monthly *Konkret*.[43] The most remarkable journalistic product of this Swiss Dylan scene was certainly the special issue of *Du* magazine (May 2001), subtitled 'Bob Dylan. Der Fremde' ('the stranger'), which honoured Dylan on the occasion of his sixtieth birthday.[44] In recent years, there has also been a Swiss Dylan book, by Guido Bieri, that has earned considerable praise from British and American *cognoscenti*, *Life on the Tracks: Bob Dylan's Songs*, published in German and English (Bieri, 2008).[45]

Still, in all fairness, it must be said that many Swiss people may love Dylan, but all do not necessarily like him.[46] For some, he has remained *Der Fremde* indeed, a version of Albert Camus's *Stranger*, instead of, maybe, *Der amerikanische Freund*.[47] Unlike Bruce Springsteen or Tom Petty (or even Leonard Cohen), Dylan is obviously not just a nice guy, sharing a beer with promoters, media people or fans; his shyness, his diffidence or simply his need for privacy have not endeared him to everyone; nor has his obstinate refusal to please the public with easily recognisable versions of his hits – or routinely kind words from the stage like 'Great to be in Sweden' (as country star George Hamilton IV once famously did). And – as in Germany – there have been, at times, quite ugly hints about financial greediness, which might easily be construed as veiled anti-Semitic jibes.[48] But then, this uneasy position on the margins of popular rock culture may indeed befit an artist who, again and again, has proclaimed that 'It Ain't Me, Babe' and asked that the badge of counter-culture hero be taken off him.

Notes

1 Quite apart from the often dubious methodology of all record charts, the very term 'Swiss hit parade' was (and remains) doubtful: for many years, only the German-speaking part of Switzerland was represented.

2 The author, known in the United States as Henry M. Pachter (1907–80), was an interesting man himself: a German-Jewish emigrant and a professor of history at the New School of Social Research, where Theodor W. Adorno had been teaching.

3 'Odetta sings Dylan', *Der Spiegel*, issue 26 (23 June 1965). Available at http://www.spiegel.de/spiegel/print/d-46273163.html (accessed 2 April 2014).

4 *Salut Les Copains* was the invention of photographer Daniel Filipacchi, who went on to

found the music-oriented youth magazine of the same name, which in turn became the inspiration for the Swiss magazine *Pop*.

5   That album was *Bob Dylan Songs Mundart* (1993), which reached number 29 in the Swiss album charts. There is a famous story of how Vescoli was sold his first Dylan album (*Freewheelin'*) in 1964 or 1965 by one of his rivals, Hardy Hepp, then working in a record store. For an excellent history of the Swiss beat bands, see Mumenthaler (2001).

6   This song remains a classic in Switzerland, although most rock fans don't know (or care) that it was written by Dylan. It was covered, famously, in 1996, by Swiss hard rock band Gotthard on *G.*, their third album.

7   The same phenomenon, by the way, made it easier for many worthy local heroes to reach the top of the charts, one case in point being the ever better results achieved by Dylan's other big fan among Swiss rock stars, Polo Hofer, who has reached number one three times since 1990, and, in 2011, reached number four with his own Dylan tribute in *Bärndeutsch* (the Bernese dialect), *Polo Hofer singt Bob Dylan*.

8   For many years, historical Swiss charts records, from 1968 on, were documented by private fans and collectors only. Since the advent of the internet, around 1995, they can be easily accessed through the official website of the company now entrusted with compiling the charts, Media Control AG, http://hitparade.ch.

9   See also Vigne (1991).

10 Matter's later influence became obvious when 'new wave' artists like Züri West and Stephan Eicher began to cover his songs in the 1980s and 1990s. A fine tribute album, *Matter-Rock: Hommage à Mani Matter*, made it to number one in 1992, featuring several Dylan fans, like Polo Hofer and Stephan Eicher.

11 Originally published on the album *I glaub jetz hock i ab* (CBS S 65794, 1973) and subsequently live on the album *Iss dys Gmües* (Image U 780-012, 1978).

12 On the cover of Heller's 1971 album *Platte* (Amadeo): 'andré heller: ein starker poetischer muskel'. The quote, however, was invented, as Heller himself later admitted (see Stöger and Miessgang, 2012). Heller recorded Dylan's 'You Angel You' in Austrian dialect as 'Du Engel Du' for his 1975 album *Bei lebendigem Leib* (Intercord).

13 See Biermann's interview in *Der Spiegel* (Hage and Höbel, 2003).

14 For a less sympathetic view of Hohler's attempt, see the disparaging comments made by the Swiss pop singer Hardy Hepp, reported by Mumenthaler (2005: 102–3). Hepp, himself vacillating between pop and rock all through his controversial career, had his own moment of fame with progressive blues rock band Krokodil from 1969 to 1973.

15 Sinus Records PU-5/2000, 1973; re-released in 1991 on the CD *Musig Wo's Bringt* (Schnoutz SCD 4).

16 Released on the album *Polo Hofer SchmetterDing* (Schnoutz Records SCD 6, 1978).

17 Dylan himself, of course, is famous for many similar borrowings. It may be interesting to note that this procedure, although frowned upon in a pop context, is quite usual in most folk traditions – and is equally accepted in classical music, where it is referred to as *Kontrafaktur* (contrafact).

18 In 1995, the same song, in another translation, became the title track of Wolfgang Niedecken's album of Dylan songs in *Kölsch*, the dialect of the city of Cologne: *Leopardefell* (leopard-skin).

19 From the album *Papper-La-Papp* (Schnoutz Records SCD 9, 1982).

20 On Hofer's life-long obsession with Dylan, see Mumenthaler (2005: 106ff.).

21 But Vescoli, again, was not the first to record an entire Dylan cover album in a German dialect: the Austrian singer–songwriter Wolfgang Ambros had been there before, in 1978, with the album *Wie im Schlaf* (Bellaphon).

22 Originally on the album *Verreise* (1985), re-released on the CD *Früecher Hütt Gäng* (Zytglogge ZYT 4309, 2008).

23 Originally on the album *Füf Liebeslieder und ei Tango*, now on the CD *Mängisch Fägts No & Füf Liebeslieder Und Ei Tango* (Zytglogge ZYT 4041, 1992).

24 In 1977, Heiniger had recorded his own version of 'Blowin' in the Wind', apparently without knowing Hohler's earlier translation, under the title 'Fridenswuchelied'. See Vigne (1991: 35).

25 On the CD *Landjäger* (Sound Service 394-2, 1994).

26 Included on the CD *Gmües* (BMG Ariola 74321 22117 2, 1994), Patent Ochsner's second number one album.

27 To be heard on Eicher's third album, *My Place* from 1989 (Barclay 841 025-2). Matter's 'Hemmige' followed, together with the Hank Williams tune, on Eicher's first number one album, *Engelberg* (1991, Barclay 849 389-2).

28 Featured on the compilation CD *Duos Taratata, Vol. 1* (Barclay 529 509-2). On Eicher as a Dylanesque singer, his hard rock colleague Chris von Rohr (of Krokus fame) commented: 'Stephan Eicher to me is the Swiss Bob Dylan. Like him, he has a medicine voice. By that, I don't mean huge pipes covering three octaves, but a broken, melancholic timbre. Singers with such a voice don't need to work on expression, everything's there already' ('Stephan Eicher ist für mich der Schweizer Bob Dylan. Wie dieser hat er eine Medizinstimme. Damit meine ich nicht etwa ein gewaltiges Organ, das über drei Oktaven reicht, sondern ein gebrochenes, melancholisches Timbre. Sänger mit einer solchen Stimme brauchen nicht an ihrem Ausdruck zu arbeiten, bei ihnen ist einfach alles da') (Frischknecht, 2006).

29 For Sophie Hunger on Dylan, see Hunger (2009).

30 The performance can be found online.

31 The photographs of the concert and press conference were taken by Beat Hirt himself. The concert was supposed to be broadcast on the following Sunday by Radio Europe No. 1, which had a weekly programme of Olympia concerts called *Musicorama*, but this one was cancelled, apparently for technical reasons.

32 Between 'Mr. Tambourine Man' and 'Solid Rock', the concert also featured an unknown instrumental, later claimed, by some, to be a film theme from a Brigitte Bardot movie, Bardot allegedly having been seen among the audience.

33 If my memory serves me well, the newspaper in question was *Le Démocrate* in Delémont.

34 This was most cogently analysed by Annette Simon in her contribution to the Frankfurt Dylan congress in 2006. Her lecture was based on an earlier publication in a psycho-analytical journal (Simon, 1996).

35 Dylan's sudden good mood was evidenced by his introductory comment to this song, which, not incidentally, was played for the second time that evening: 'We're gonna play a song you already heard once tonight – it's so good!'

36 And, as Nobs has repeatedly confirmed, dutifully (but unfortunately) none was made!

37 See http://www.bobdylan.com/us/home#us/events.

38 For details see http://expectingrain.com/dok/who/s/swissliz.html or http://johannas visions.com/bob-dylan-swiss-liz-the-times-they-are-a-changin-eindhoven-17-february-1993-video.

39 See notes 2 and 31.

40 Published in Zurich, sixty-two issues appeared between 1968 and 1971, most of which are reprinted in Gwerder (1998).

41 See also Zingg (1978). A second Dylan cover (indeed, almost a whole Dylan issue) of the same newspaper supplement, now simply called *Das Magazin*, was published on the occasion of Dylan's first Zurich gig: 'Spiel mir das Lied vom Wind. Bob Dylan, ein Dossier' (*Das Magazin*, 25/26 January 1991: 17–32). A third cover story in *Das Magazin* followed in 2011 to commemorate Dylan's seventieth birthday: 'Der Alte', an exclusive interview with Greil Marcus conducted by Jean-Martin Büttner (Büttner, 2011).

42 For Büttner's highly original take on Dylan and rock story-telling in general, see his doctoral dissertation (Büttner, 1997: esp. 545ff.).

43 For an appreciation of Amendt's role, see Schäfer (2011: 23). A complete version can be found at http://guenteramendt.de/nachrufe/schaefer.html.

44 *Du, Die Zeitschrift der Kultur*, 176 (May 2001). Contributors included Günter Amendt, Jean-Martin Büttner, Manfred Papst, but also Greil Marcus, Stephen Scobie and Klaus Theweleit.
45 See http://home.datacomm.ch/gbieri/index.html. Bieri has also contributed to English and American fan publications such as *On The Tracks*, *Judas!* and *The Bridge*.
46 Interestingly, there has never been any kind of Swiss fan convention, although a number of Swiss fans and writers have attended Austria's legendary Burg Plankenstein meetings over the years – and contributed to its late-lamented *Parking Meter* magazine.
47 Director Wim Wenders ended his 1977 film *Der amerikanische Freund* (*The American Friend*) with a Dylan quote. In fact he has referred to Dylan on more than one occasion in his films.
48 Of all Dylan followers, Günter Amendt has been most attentive to this tendency. See Amendt (2001: 141ff.) but also Siegfried (2006: 587–8).

References

Amendt, G. (2001) *Back to the Sixties. Bob Dylan zum Sechzigsten* (Hamburg: Konkret Literatur Verlag).
Bieri, G. (2008) *Life on the Tracks: Bob Dylan's Songs* (revised English version) (Basel: self-published).
Büttner, J.-M. (1997) *Sänger, Songs und triebhafte Rede: Rock als Erzählweise* (Basel: Stroemfeld/ Nexus).
Büttner, J.-M. (2011) 'Der Alte', *Das Magazin*, 20 (21 May). 16–26.
Dylan, B. (2004) *Chronicles: Volume One* (New York: Simon and Schuster).
Figlestahler, P. (1974) 'Bob Dylan: Comeback und Abschied eines Aussenseiters', *Neue Zürcher Zeitung* (10 February). 59.
Frischknecht, M. (2006) 'Chris von Rohr – seine stille Seite', *Spuren*, 78 (winter 2006). Available at spuren.ch/content/magazin/single-ansicht-nachrichten/datum////chris-von-rohr-seine-stille-seite.html (accessed 2 April 2014).
Gwerder, U. (1998) *Im Zeichen des magischen Affen* (Zürich: WOA Verlag).
Hage, V. and Höbel, W. (2003) 'Das habe ich ihm reingeschoben', *Der Spiegel*, 42 (13 October). Available at http://www.spiegel.de/spiegel/print/d-28859791.html (accessed 2 April 2014).
Hirt, B. (1966) 'Bob Dylan: Fast ein Poet', *Pop*, 5 (1 July).
Hohler, F. (2011) Email from Franz Hohler to the author, 29 June.
Hunger, S. (2009) 'Ich liebe Dylan – und weiss nicht wer er ist', *Tages-Anzeiger* (14 April). Available at http://www.tagesanzeiger.ch/kultur/pop-und-jazz/Ich-liebe-Dylan–und-weiss-nicht-wer-er-ist/story/17965247 (accessed 3 April 2014).
Kuhn, A. (2007) 'Kniefall vor St. Bob', *Die Weltwoche*, 18 (3 May). Available at http://www.welt woche.ch/ausgaben/2007-18/artikel-2007-18-kniefall-vor-san.html (accessed 8 November 2014).
Marshall, L. (2007) *Bob Dylan: The Never Ending Star* (Cambridge: Polity Press).
Mumenthaler, S. (2001) *Beat Pop Protest: Der Sound der Schweizer Sixties* (Lausanne: Verlag Editions Plus).
Mumenthaler, S. (2005) *Polo: Eine Oral History* (Zürich: Editions Plus).
Pächter, H. (1966) 'Die Gitarre als politisches Instrument', *Die Weltwoche*, 34:1864 (18 February). 25.
Schäfer, M. (1972) 'Das Spiel durchschaut: Bob Dylan und die Kommerzialisierung der Musik', *National-Zeitung, NZ am Wochenende* (4 November). 3.
Schäfer, M. (1976) 'Es war fast zu spät für ihn', *National-Zeitung, NZ am Wochenende* (17 January). 3.
Schäfer, M. (1978) 'Dylan ist walisisch und heisst Meer', *Tages-Anzeiger Magazin*, 47 (25 November). 6–11.

Schäfer, M. (2011) 'Günter & Dylan – die grosse Liebe', WOZ (Die Wochenzeitung), 15 (14 April). 23.

Siegfried, D. (2006) Time is on My Side. Konsum und Politik in der westdeutschen Jugendkultur der 60er Jahre (Göttingen: Wallstein Verlag).

Simon, A. (1996) 'The Times They Are A-Changin' – Bob Dylan als Identifikationsobjekt in Ost-West-Phantasien', Werkblatt – Zeitschrift für Psychoanalyse und Gesellschaftskritik (Berlin), 36:2.

Stöger, G. and Miessgang, T. (2012) 'Von meinem Ideal bin ich noch entfernt', Falter, 11 (March). Available at http://www.falter.at/falter/2012/03/13/von-meinem-ideal-bin-ich-noch-entfernt (accessed 3 April 2014).

Vigne, B. (1991) 'Bob Dylan auf Mundart: S isch hüt aues angers', Züritipp (25 January). 34–5.

Zingg, M. (1978) 'Dylan was here!', Basler Zeitung (5 July). 31.

Internet sources

http://hitparade.ch (accessed 2 April 2014).
http://www.bobdylan.com/us/home#us/events (accessed 2 April 2014).
http://expectingrain.com/dok/who/s/swissliz.html (accessed 2 April 2014).
http://johannasvisions.com/bob-dylan-swiss-liz-the-times-they-are-a-changin-eindhoven-17-february-1993-video (accessed 2 April 2014).
http://home.datacomm.ch/gbieri/index.html (accessed 2 April 2014).

4

Localising Dylan: political and musical narratives in Italy

Andrea Cossu

In the age of global celebrity, cultural icons are the result of processes that take place at different levels, and which involve not only the production of representations by cultural centres, but also their translations in geographical, ideological and political peripheries. Even the most revered figures – those for whom we assume a high degree of homogeneity – are subject to these multiple projects, which may result in very different representations in local contexts.

Bob Dylan is no exception. As many scholars have noted (and as the recent 'revisionist' turn in Dylan studies suggests), Dylan's figure and his reputation as an artist are tightly connected to a cultural centre, America, which is at the same time a centre of production and an imagined ideal. On the other side, however, Dylan's influence has been able to cross times and spaces, reaching peripheries that have produced their own discourses about both America and the artist. These local representations are often selective, in that they focus on particular aspects of Dylan's career, but they are also adaptive, because local contexts constrain the production as well as the reception of artistic reputation.

Drawing on ideas developed within the sociology of reputations (Becker, 1982; DeNora, 1997; Fine, 2001, 2011), in this chapter I first expand the arguments on artistic reputation and authenticity that I have explored in my recent work (Cossu, 2012) and focus on the reception of Bob Dylan in Italy and its specificity. While it is true that writing about Bob Dylan today means, to a large extent, writing about a project of star-making (Marshall, 2007) that involves a vision of America as a cultural centre (even though this vision of America is itself decentred, because Dylan's America is peripheral, as are its vernacular culture and its roots music), the relation between Dylan, cultural peripheries and national contexts remains largely unexplored. Neglecting this more decentralised dimension obliterates the local dynamics at work in the reception of an artist, as well as the peculiar alignment of the narratives of the centre to local conditions, which always have a certain degree of autonomy. An analysis of the Italian reception of Dylan's music and figure is helpful to understand this interaction between different centres of production and reception, both in terms of the history of popular music and in terms of its sociology. Dylan's reputation in the country is still dependent (more than in other contexts) on the 1960s and the 'topical' Dylan. Yet, when Dylan was first 'imported' to Italy, politics played a very small role, because he was appropriated by a coalition of agents positioned at the institutional centre of the music field. It was the 'electric' Dylan, rather than the 'folk troubadour', who came first. However, in the context of social change and internal changes in the Italian music field (with the rise of a peculiar tradition of singer–song-writing and the centrality of political discourse in the field), these images soon changed valence and relevance. In this chapter, I will elucidate the long-term consequences of this shift in the perception of Dylan, which have largely influenced his reception in Italy. I will pay particular attention to the coalitions which have supported Dylan and to the main 'reputational entrepreneurs' (Fine, 2001) who have filtered his image for the large Italian public at the intersection of music production and criticism. In the following sections of this chapter, I will focus particularly on the reception of Dylan's appearances in Italy, and highlight the peculiar traits of the 'narrative of authenticity' that is at work in the Italian context.

The context of representation: Dylan's absence

Reportedly, Dylan took the stage for the first time in Italy sometime in January 1963, on a visit from London, while in search of his girlfriend of the time, Suze Rotolo. As a young and, at least in Italy, unknown folk singer, he made an impromptu visit to Rome's Folk Studio, a club that was founded by an American painter and which became, for a while, a glorious venue where many of Italy's young songwriters made the symbolic passage from amateur to professional. Then, in 1984, he returned, but this time as 'Bob Dylan' the star, the myth, the icon, the game-changer and, ultimately, according to one reviewer of his first shows in Italy, a 'Great Master' and 'the most beloved prophet of the new music' (Castaldo, 1984). This 'official' debut was a let-down, the occasion for just another of his many rehearsals on stage, and yet it was perceived as an 'event', simultaneously an epiphany and a comeback.

It was a comeback because Dylan was slowly but steadily emerging from his religious phase, the gospel trilogy with its promise of fire and Armageddon, with a subtler 'religious' album, *Infidels*. And it was an epiphany of sorts because, by 1984, Bob Dylan had become so elusive for the Italian public that a whole new Bob Dylan had been created. It was an 'imagined' and 'desired' Bob Dylan, on whom fans, critics and other actors in the Italian music field attached meanings, feelings and visions.

Dylan's absence from Italy had indeed produced a stereotyped 'Bob Dylan', whose image was not fuelled by presence and visibility, but rather by absence and longing. It was, most of all, a mediated visibility, which paved the way for the creation of a myth, where external narratives (produced in the United States or in England) merged, albeit not seamlessly, with representations and ideas that had an unequivocally Italian origin and which made sense (or acquired one) when put in the cultural, political and musical context of the country.

To the Italian public, Dylan was a poet, a prophet, a troubadour; but these images did not necessarily carry the same exact meaning they had elsewhere, and certainly they had not come to the surface from the moment Dylan's figure appeared in Italy. Rather, Dylan's trajectory in the country had been peculiar. Dylan appeared rather out of the blue, only in the mid-1960s, at the peak of his success as a 'rock' singer, with a handful of singles (long-play records were expensive) and, most importantly, thanks to the mediation of a composite coalition that was trying to change the rules of Italian popular music from within, rather than from the periphery. The work of these cultural entrepreneurs, musicians and songwriters, embedded in the institutional logic and in the system of production of Italian popular music, produced a counterintuitive outcome: Dylan, contrary to what happened in the United States or in England, was perceived from the beginning as a 'rock' star on the same level as the Beatles (and with their endorsement). As I will show in the next section, at some point the narrative changed, and aligned itself to the commonly perceived trajectory of Dylan's transition from folk, to folk rock, to rock music. In this process, the stereotypes (political as well as aesthetic) became fixed in a narrative that has shaped readings of Dylan for the past forty years.

Importing Dylan

By 1966, Dylan was world famous and he had successfully accomplished many transitions. Not only had he contributed to changing the audience of folk music but also he had created a public for 'rock', still in its infancy as a genre. He had been able to acquire a central position and considerable status first in the folk revival and then by leading the 'folk rock' revolution with his songs. In both cases, he had been able to find strong and powerful allies, not only among record executives, producers and critics, but also among fellow artists. The success of Peter, Paul and Mary's version of 'Blowin' in the Wind' and the Byrds' 'Mr. Tambourine Man' accompanied Dylan's transition and marked (together with the Beatles' endorsement) Dylan's rise to great success as a songwriter and a performer. His work became more and more a valuable resource that artists could use to get a position in a competitive field, increasing Dylan's status and legitimacy as a successful songwriter.

It was the central position that Dylan had reached as a best-selling artist and songwriter that caught the attention of the Italian music industry. Save for a few mentions in newspapers, Dylan had been – and would be for a long time – a marginal figure for the Italian folk revival (but see, for an appreciation, Marini, 1981). But then Dylan's commercial success, and the sudden appearance of his songs in the American and British charts, ensured the availability of his music to the Italian public.

It was, however, through cover versions of his songs that the Italian audience first experienced Dylan, and not through expensive import singles and LPs. As Dylan's songs were flooding the charts in 1965 and 1966, they were soon translated and covered by Italian groups. These covers were often faithful to the folk rock arrangements that had been more successful abroad. Thus, the Minstrels' 'Mister Tamburino' is a jingle-jangle, less crafted cover of the Byrds' 'Mr. Tambourine Man'; the Kings sang 'Bambina Non Sono Io', modelled on the Turtles' 'It Ain't Me, Babe'; even more famous groups and singers covered Dylan as well as other folk rock numbers, most notably I Nomadi ('Ti Voglio', that is, 'I Want You'), Elvis clone Bobby Solo ('Addio Angelina') and Ricky Gianco ('Come una Donna', 'Just Like a Woman'). Even 'Like a Rolling Stone' was quickly covered, in possibly the most awful version of a Dylan song to appear in Italy, by one-hit wonder singer Gianni Pettenati ('Come una Pietra che Rotola', which was also done by the Wretched). The guitarist from I Campioni, Lucio Battisti (who would become, by the end of the 1960s, the best-selling singer in Italy), released 'Ciò che Voglio', a faithful rendition of Sonny and Cher's version of the Dylan song 'All I Really Want To Do'. Dylan's earlier songs were remarkably underrepresented, with the exception of a non-charting version of 'Blowin' in the Wind' by the Kings. The song, however, proved popular beyond expectations in later years, when Dylan's image aligned with political visions and with the offspring of the Vatican Council, becoming a favourite campfire song for Catholic groups. An unreleased attempt at 'La Risposta Nel Vento' was recorded also by Luigi Tenco, who, after his suicide in 1967, quickly rose to the iconic centre of the singer–songwriters field (Santoro, 2010).

Dylan's popularity through covers of his songs, while Italian CBS was releasing his records, needs further explanation, not only in terms of the game of 'authentication' that Italian songwriters and bands were playing in order to achieve legitimacy in a field under formation, but also because they reveal the context in which his figure was originally perceived.

Unlike some later Dylan covers, rewritten by singer–songwriters like Fabrizio De André, Francesco De Gregori or Massimo Bubola, these early attempts were almost passed off (and certainly were perceived by many audience members) as original tracks coming from a movement, Italian 'beat', that was struggling for authenticity. Dylan, in other words, was absorbed by an industrial infrastructure that was scouting for foreign sounds, acquiring publishing rights, listening incessantly to Radio Luxembourg and skimming the American and British charts for new songs. It was in this context that he became a valuable artist, for he had proven himself able to provide songs that entered the charts and that could be adapted to the Italian market. A young lyricist – Giulio Rapetti, who was writing under the *nom de plume* Mogol – provided most of these translations, taking advantage of his position as record label Ricordi's most accomplished young author and as the son of the head of the label's publishing company (which had licensed some of Dylan's songs with the goal of making some covers in Italian).

While this 'versioning practice' was not uncommon in the Italian music field, it reached a high degree of routinised efficiency following the 'British invasion' (the earliest covers of Beatles' songs date from 1963 and their first Italian single was released shortly after). Record labels could work quickly, with the aid of session musicians and trained songwriters, while in many cases earning full publishing rights for the covers or giving a credit to the author of the original song. As a side-effect, record labels could also supply a steady flow of songs to groups and artists who could not write enough original material, while disciplining the sound and the lyrics in accordance to the aesthetic standards held by label executives and writers.

Dylan, thus, first came to Italy through adaptation and mediation by entrepreneurs who were situated at the centre of the music business, and who downplayed his role in the transformation of the folk scene and in the creation of a public for rock music. Rather, the emergence of the 'old' Dylan came slightly later, triggered by the interplay of three factors that were going to have enormous influence on the coming of age of Italian popular music in the 1960s and beyond: the internal differentiation of the 'Italian beat' field; the new prominence of political song and Italy's own 'folk revival'; and, finally, the emergence of the singer–songwriter as a paramount figure in the field.

The politics of authorship

Dylan had, to a certain degree, to be introduced to the Italian public. However, the first profiles appeared only after Dylan had already 'gone electric' and information was – to say the least – sketchy or plain wrong, derived from sleeve notes and some of Dylan's notoriously misleading interviews. The first problem was to provide an answer to the question 'Who is Bob Dylan?' and to trace some coordinates that could be understood by the Italian audience. The mediators in the music industry had put Dylan on the map, but Dylan as an artist was himself quite invisible, transfigured by covers. The daily newspaper *La Stampa* attempted to give a tentative answer, reproducing the perceived traits of Dylan's originality, describing him as a singer who 'comes from the mass of American folksingers, and we really have nothing to share with them.... Bob is an angry young man. He never cuts his hair, and his clothes look like he has lived on a boxcar' (Donaggio, 1965; present author's translation here and below). In October 1965, this was hardly the image that Dylan was projecting, and possibly the album Donaggio was describing was *The Freewheelin' Bob Dylan* (there are a few mentions of the song 'A Hard Rain's A-Gonna Fall'). Most importantly, though, the article was about the Beatles' endorsement of Dylan's work: 'The Beatles, too, are crazy about Bob, and "I'm a Loser" is written in his style and dedicated to him: "He shows us the way", they say' (Donaggio, 1965). The Beatles were indeed instrumental in creating a wider audience for Dylan, in England as well as in Italy, where their success allowed them to lend authority to other figures. In some respects, their endorsement did much to put Dylan in their camp, that of popular music, and to draw him away from the folk revival. At the same time, Dylan's older image was resurfacing and it had to be accounted for. The communist daily *L'Unità* (and its music critic Leonardo Settimelli in particular) were more aware of Dylan's original trajectory (especially because it touched for a moment the American left) and praised Dylan as a voice of protest: 'Beside "Blowin' in the Wind", rapidly assimilated by the industry and by pop singers (who are considered the antithesis of folk), he is also the author of "Masters of War", a song that hits like a punch those who send the youth to war and which contains a clear proposal. Seeger is enthusiastic about Dylan, although he fears that his big success will draw him out of the right way' (Settimelli, 1965).

These two profiles indicate the tensions of reading 'Bob Dylan' from the periphery. There were indeed temporal lags, but there were also alternative projects, usually conditioned by politics and cultural affiliations, that contributed to the complex shape of the network of his supporters. The mediators of Dylan's figure, positioned in different sectors of the Italian music field, were indeed facing a dilemma. The moment Dylan acquired a central position in popular music, there was an urge to rediscover his previous work. But this meant a clash between the present and the immediate past, and a conflation of images of Bob Dylan that belonged to different phases of his trajectory. There were also, however, more structural, and internal, factors that affected the timing and the staying power of narratives about Dylan.

In 1966 and 1967, the Italian 'beat' scene was changing (Tarli, 2007) and Dylan played a role in shaping directions and tastes, together with other folk rock artists (even inauthentic ones, if we consider the prominence of US singer Barry McGuire in the Italian debate). 'Italian beat' was for some time a loose category, in which both local bands and British and American artists seemed to fit. Moreover, the scene was artificially divided by operations of categorisation that distinguished between 'progressive' beat, with a political message, and pop music, with no existential or political implications. A

41

debate emerged in magazines, with songwriters taking sides, between an unpolitical 'yellow line' (from the name of the popular radio show *Bandiera Gialla*, 'yellow flag') and a 'green line' (which symbolised hope and social change). Naïve as it was, this debate highlighted the fractures that were present in the field of music and which led, as is evident in retrospect, to a reconfiguration of the role of singers and songwriters in the decade to come.

Politics was introduced to the Italian beat scene from the centre as well as from the periphery. The emergence of the 'green line', championed by Mogol, always a great observer of tastes and trends, had somehow brought to the surface the concern for the politicisation of music that had been up to that point confined to militant circles, closer to the traditional 'politics of style' of the folk revival, and which coalesced around the music collective Cantacronache and the Ernesto de Martino Institute, a private research centre with close ties to the Italian Socialist Party (Straniero and Rovello, 2008). From this milieu, and from the experience of Rome's Folk Studio (where Dylan allegedly performed in 1963), rose a more politically conscious, albeit marginal, vision (the so-called 'red line'). However, the presence of the supporters of the green line in the centre of the music field, with a coalition of songwriters, radio personalities and performers, meant a broadcasting of 'protest' songs to a wider audience of teenagers. The debate, despite its artificiality, was harsh, because it aligned to available representations about justice and freedom rooted in Italy's great political cultures, Catholicism and socialism/communism.

As an advocate of a more politically moderate vision, Mogol argued that 'the ideals of protest have not disappeared from the minds of the young. However, that discourse cannot be repeated always in the same way'. His self-defence called Dylan to his aid, although in an ambivalent way: 'It is not true that I condemn [Bob Dylan]. I have not hidden a certain feeling of surprise for the phases he has gone through.... It seems like Dylan, today, has nothing to do with the Dylan of the past. I believe that he doesn't want to be seen as a protest person but, rather, as an artist' (Mogol, 1967).

As Mogol was on his way to becoming one of the most acclaimed lyricists in Italian popular music, he intercepted the trajectory of other singer–songwriters who had been influenced more by the tradition of the French *chansonniers* and for whom Dylan played a very small role as a source of legitimacy. However, as a new breed of songwriters, who had been born in the late 1940s and who had been more influenced by American music, came of age and made their recording debuts, the problem of the Americanisation (and hence 'Dylanisation') of Italian song-writing came to the fore.

The Italian discovery of Dylan in the 1970s was less influenced by the early representations as a rock star and bore more resemblance to the American narrative about Dylan the 'poet', although the political reading could never be silenced. In this regard, he entered the debate about Italian singer–songwriters (see Santoro, 2010) as a disembodied, largely mythic figure, to whom singers could be compared (as in the case of Francesco De Gregori), whose work could be appropriated with the goal of providing covers of poetical standard (Fabrizio De André), or who could be analysed and dissected, often with reference to the 'other America' that was becoming a strong cultural representation in intellectual circles (see especially Portelli, 1977). It was at this time, indeed, that critics and scholars paid more and more attention to Dylan's work, with the publication of histories of rock and folk for the large public of young leftists, with appraisals (Ala, 1981) and even with scathing criticisms that were closer, as far as their political charges went, to the idea of Dylan as a sellout (Stampa Alternativa, 1978). The discourse of rock criticism and the Americanisation of Italian singer–songwriters were parallel processes that played with the idea of a national tradition and its connection to external influences. In some sense, it was the consequence of the opening of Italian popular music to what was coming from abroad. But, as it happened, it was also a process of differentiation, that involved at the same time the internal context (leading to the creation of the singer–songwriter as a dominant figure in the intellectual discourse of music and to the fixation of *canzone d'autore* as a 'genre': see Fabbri, 1982; Santoro, 2010) and the external context (which was categorised with more accuracy than in the easy categories of the mid-1960s). In this process, Dylan emerged as an autonomous figure, both as a reference and as an artist. The three major narratives (the poet, the political prophet and the rock star) became more interconnected, while at the same time providing legitimacy to those who aligned themselves to those representations, especially the poetic frame.

Dylan's reception in Italy has been guided by these symbolic templates, which became powerful constraints as Dylan, after more than twenty years, became a visible and recurrent presence in Italy, not mediated by records and articles anymore, but as a touring artist. In the next section, I will focus especially on the reception of Dylan's concerts in Italy, and on the emergence of a new trend of writing about Dylan by Italian authors.

Dylan's visibility after 1984

Back to 1984, and Dylan's (official) debut in Italy. Despite all the efforts by music critics, who were willing to see Dylan as an artist rooted in the present rather than as a relic of a past that was becoming distant enough to trigger nostalgia, Dylan's wane in popularity seemed hard to stop, especially in a country where he was never a bestselling artist. It would take Dylan three years to come back, in the middle of the Temple in Flames tour, which, after the publication of *Chronicles*, we can read as the seed of a project that would, with the full realisation of the Never Ending Tour, defeat nostalgia. Dylan performed this change of attitude on stage, in five shows that immediately followed the 'epiphany of Locarno' (on which see Dylan, 2004;

Williams, 2004; and Martin Schäfer in this volume, Chapter 3). The music press and newspapers covered the shows enthusiastically, contrasting Dylan's projected authenticity with the plastic pop of Madonna, who had just toured Italy.

To the eyes of critics, however, it was a type of authenticity that was still rooted in the 1960s: 'Dylan has taught us how to grow up, and he has been with us until today, through the utopia of the 1960s, in the social deflagrations of the 1970s, and today, in a world so much different from the one in which he became the folk hero able to embody an era – he has still got something to say' (Castaldo, 1987). Despite this prophetic role for Dylan, as a guide and as a companion, Castaldo's hagiography touched themes common in the representation of Dylan: he was an 'ageless minstrel', whose voice 'allows us to have no regret about the past, old dreams, but rather to find a continuity between what we were and what we are now, to reconstruct a link with the very roots of youth culture' (Castaldo, 1987). The link between Dylan and the 1960s was reproduced in other articles, notably the profile in the same issue of *La Repubblica*, which spoke of Dylan as a singer whose poetry was 'his only weapon' (Assante, 1987). Reporting from Turin, Laura Putti exploited the nostalgia frame by giving voice to a fan who she argued was a representative of Dylan's world: 'Dylan [said the fan] remains in our hearts, as do the songs he sang. He has been our chronicler, the one who saw things the way the youth of that generation saw them. Things could have been something else entirely, but we saw them that way' (Putti, 1987). The fan was probably disappointed by the adventurous set-list, with 'new music and lyrics, which did not prevent the disappointment of those who had gone to the show in order to cry on the shore of memories' (Tropea, 1987: 27).

After 1987, Dylan returned to Italy almost yearly, and thus the Italian audience began to be exposed to the logic of the Never Ending Tour, a project that played with the past and the present, tradition and modernity, and with many images of Bob Dylan. Nevertheless, older images of Bob Dylan resurfaced periodically, only marginally opposed by the visibility of Dylan on stage. Therefore, the comparison with the past was always there to frame the words of critics, as in this review of the 1989 show in Milan (certainly one of the best Dylan ever played in Italy): 'Dylan sings as if his songs were brand new, without the aura of nostalgia, without the triumphalism that generally accompanies the performances of the protagonists of popular music'. And, again, Dylan was described as a poet, a 'beaten' but also 'brave, and determined poet' (Castaldo, 1989).

These narrative templates constrained public representations of Dylan and tried to sustain his present relevance through the exploitation of the mythic narrative centred on poetry, charisma and political influence. It was, to some extent, a facet of the increasing memorialisation of Dylan's figure and work, which started to get momentum in the early 1990s (with the celebration of his thirtieth anniversary and the release of *The Bootleg Series* box set of albums) and which saw the publication of the first 'official' Italian edition of *The Lyrics* (on Italian translation of Dylan's work, see Carrera, 2009).

This narrative silenced the present, while at the same time mediators like critics and scholars were busy challenging the threat of nostalgia. While reviewers often focused on the present and on the 'demolition of his own myth' that Dylan was pursuing on stage (Castaldo, 1992a), they could not silence reservations about the results of this deconstructive approach: 'every show is an unpredictable surprise. You cannot know what's going to happen, because Dylan is not willing to celebrate himself, even when the result is disappointing' (Castaldo, 1992a). The past was seen by critics as both a burden and a resource that Dylan tried to escape on stage: 'Dylan is above all a complex artist of high literary and musical value who, thanks to the unrepeatable set of circumstances in that explosive crossroads of the Sixties, has become one of the most powerful mass myths of our era.... Dylan keeps on living uncomfortably, with irritation, his mythic role, and he makes this clear every time he takes the stage' (Castaldo, 1992b).

Perhaps unwillingly, these critics were unable to escape the use of such categorisations, and they continued to link Dylan's authenticity to the past, rather than seeing it as a new project in the redefinition of the artist's role: 'Dylan remains the last, among the founding fathers of popular music's modernity, to keep on touring as a tormented and unpredictable minstrel. His refusal of celebrations guarantees a passionate, authentic, and poetically alive show' (Castaldo, 1993a; see also the interview with Dylan in Castaldo, 1993b). Dylan was thus perceived as the 1960s troubadour, and received more praise for his ability to rework the songs from that age than for his present efforts, even the albums that brought him back to the folk tradition – *Good as I Been to You* (1992) and *World Gone Wrong* (1993).

The climax of this past-oriented narrative was probably reached in 1997, the year Dylan released *Time Out of Mind*, was hospitalised and played in Bologna, Italy, for the Pope. That show, broadcast on national television, turned out a huge media event, with an on-site attendance of 300,000. Newspapers of all sectors of the cultural and political spectrum seized the opportunity to frame Dylan's participation in terms of the old political narrative, focusing more on his cultural relevance than on the performance.

Controversy came both from the left and from within the Catholic field. From the mid-1960s, following the Vatican Council, Italy witnessed the emergence of a peculiar version of contemporary Christian music, with obvious Catholic themes that proved to be especially popular among adherents to new Christian movements. While often not able to cross over to larger audiences, these singers and songwriters nonetheless created a lively underground scene, performing mostly in parishes, meetings and dedicated festivals. They were, however, excluded from the Bologna show, and one of them (Giuseppe Cionfoli, probably the only one who had been able to cross over and reach the top of the charts) voiced his contempt for the choice to invite Dylan and other singers: 'They have built golden bridges to a communist like Dylan...' (Manin and Cappelli, 1997). Others, like influential Catholic writer Vittorio Messori, adopted the past-oriented representations of Dylan to criticise the detachment between the Church and modernity. By taking Dylan on board, the Church showed that it was coping with the ghosts of the past rather than with the challenges of the present: 'the American songwriter is the prophet of 1968. Does [the Church] really want to catch up with modern times through a singer of thirty years ago?' (Rocca, 1997).

Criticism came from the left as well, and Dylan became the *casus belli* for just another symbolic battle between the nation's two major cultures. Thus, *L'Unità*, which covered the show extensively, asked almost rhetorically: 'What is Dylan doing here – we think – together with these Catholic people; what have his lyrics and the poetry of his songs got to do with it; where has that feeling of protest and detachment from conventional society gone, with its eternal injustices, that we read in Dylan's sound?' (Menduni, 1997). And again: 'Dylan is meaningful most of all for those who remember [the struggle for] civil rights and the Tet offensive [a major event in the Vietnam War], a generation torn by political contrapositions and by the division of a world in which they were born, a division they did not want' (Menduni, 1997).

The controversy was both religious and political, but it testified to the centrality of the 1960s in Italian society, and the power that the mythic narrative of the past had in shaping contemporary representations of Dylan. Not surprisingly, charges of selling out came from other singers, like Zucchero (Adelmo Fornaciari), who had previously declined to perform for the Pope: 'Dylan goes everywhere. He follows the money! I'd call him Bob "Pila" [a vernacular term for "bucks"].... There's no divine message in rock' (see Farkas, 1997). On the other hand, in one of the most explicit homages by an Italian songwriter, Francesco De Gregori praised Dylan's role and his attitude, while arguing that Dylan had been often misunderstood and betrayed in Italy, both by translators (like Mogol) and by the public: 'I discovered Dylan at the beginning of the 1960s, when I was eighteen. A version of "Blowin' in the Wind" by Peter, Paul and Mary: watered-down, white country music. My brother [Luigi Grechi, a songwriter with a cult following in Italy] brought home Dylan's original version. The sticky sweetness was converted into a rough vocality, that of a mountaineer. I was petrified' (Cappelli and Farkas, 1997).

Interestingly, De Gregori's praise was for Dylan's musical authenticity, far from both political implications and nostalgia. Around the same time, he composed the Italian version of 'If You See Her Say Hello' ('Non Dirle Che Non È Così'), which later appeared in the 2003 film *Masked and Anonymous* (directed by Larry Charles and co-written with Bob Dylan).

The symbolic conflict over different interpretations of Bob Dylan reached a point of condensation in 1997, the year of Dylan's comeback and also the year of a much publicised performance in Italy. The traditional mediators of Dylan's reputation in Italy (singers and critics) were busy exploiting two facets of Dylan's authenticity, the political and the musical, and in doing so they were reproducing the narrative coming from the past, or trying to adapt it to the present (as in De Gregori's case) to point out Dylan's contemporary relevance. Around the same time, the glowing reviews of *Time Out of Mind* produced a strident juxtaposition, with the Dylan of the past, as he had been portrayed by the press that covered his performance for the Pope, looming over his present achievements as an artist (Sisti, 1997; Susanna, 1997a, 1997b).

Compared with the controversy of 1997, Dylan's presence in the 2000s has been more subdued. However, there have been several changes that have brought us to a more nuanced – and at the same time accurate – vision of Dylan. In particular, there has been the attempt to align the representation of Dylan to the current development of 'Dylan studies' abroad, especially with regard to the creation of a counter-narrative aligned to the new trend of studies that links Dylan and America. Second, there has been a de-centralisation of criticism, with the web becoming more and more an arena for the discussion of Dylan and for grassroots cultural entrepreneurship. Third, Dylan's position has been more and more safe as a cultural reference for Italian music, which has led to the fixation of his reputation as a 'poet' at the expense of the political narrative.

As mentioned, in Dylan studies there has been a shift in focus whereby Dylan is more and more understood in the context of American culture, rather than within the boundaries of 'rock' culture (see especially Carrera, 2001). Not only have the major biographies been translated in Italy, as well as new editions of Dylan's work, but critical essays (with authors ranging from Sean Wilentz to Greil Marcus) have contributed to a wider understanding of Dylan's roots. In this context, a new coalition of reputational entrepreneurs has emerged, linking the academic world to the realm of fandom. Some collections of critical essays have been translated by Alessandro Carrera (2008), and some books have followed on specific aspects, presenting an innovative vision of Dylan in comparison with the traditional narrative that was exploited in the 1970s and 1980s.

This new criticism was somehow reflected in the reviews that praised the albums *"Love and Theft"* (2001) and *Modern Times* (2006), where the references to an imagined, and largely imaginary, militant Dylan were replaced by the now usual frame of Dylan the founding father of popular music, with more weight accorded to the reworking of American tradition.

These two processes, the emergence of a new Dylan criticism and its link with an active fan community, have deeply changed the form of the field of Dylan's supporters, even though the bond with the 1970s is still quite strong. While in the 1960s Dylan was championed by actors situated in the production side of the field of popular music, the emergence of critics and songwriters in the 1970s led to a reframing of his role and new claims about

47

his status. Many of the protagonists of that age are still around, but what we have witnessed is a shift in focus, which has stressed both his autonomy as an artist (in terms of a dialectic between individualism and collectivism) and his relation to Italian popular music.

Conclusions

Dylan's work in the new millennium has been characterised by the explicit project of developing a geography of desire and belonging which assumes a romanticised, and populist, vision of America and its vernacular tradition at its very centre. This revisionist project is still in the making in Italy, not only because of a cultural and temporal lag, but also because it has to confront the long-term consequences of the narratives about Bob Dylan that have been developed since the late 1960s. I have shown here that some of the reasons for the permanence of the older narrative about Dylan lie in the long-term consequences of the process of institutionalisation of the field of singer–songwriter in Italy, which involved the incorporation (and justification) of American influences by the new wave of singer–songwriters during the 1970s, the emergence of a new generation of professional critics and the politicisation of the field as a distinct practice.

The aggregate effect of these dynamics has been a prolonged reproduction of Dylan's image as a political figure, despite the many attempts to promote (both professionally and within the fan community) a new discourse, aligned to the revisionist project. That Dylan is still today portrayed as a 'minstrel' (with a more direct reference to folk minstrelsy than to the new thread of analysis that followed the release of *"Love and Theft"*), as a folk hero, a troubadour, needs to be analysed less with reference to the presumed sloppiness of critics and more as the result of a discourse of differentiation and legitimisation of the field of song-writing in Italy. Given, as I have shown, that Dylan burst on to the Italian music scene as late as 1965–66, at the peak of his influence as a rock star (a chart-topping, commercially viable artist on a par with the Beatles), the power and durability of this image are somehow counterintuitive. As I have shown, the rock-star image was in fact short-lived because of the rapid transformations in the field of Italian popular music that took place in the second half of the 1960s.

The loose coalition that supported Dylan (mostly as a mythic reference) brought together critics, writers, singers and the later generation of singer–songwriters. In that context, the loose allegiance between the 'beat' movement in music (promoted at the centre of the music field) and social movements fostered Dylan's centrality but prevented the circulation of plural narratives. In the 1970s, the flirtation with politics on the songwriters' side – some of them took Dylan as a reference, like De Gregori and Fabrizio De André – helped reproduce this vision without questions arising about its accuracy. To a large extent, thus, Dylan's reputation in Italy was a fabricated fantasy, where the imagined 'Bob Dylan' became an object of desire and the representative of the 'other America'. This vision of America had more explicit political implications than it ever had in the United States and it was reproduced as Dylan – as a performing artist – became more and more available for the Italian public.

By the 1990s, with Dylan disappearing from public view and playing to smaller audiences in Italy, there was a chance for a reappraisal – and a critical repositioning – of Dylan's image, which was pursued by another coalition of writers, fan critics, bloggers and scholars. In this case, audiences and critics, less than musicians and executives, played a role in shaping the new vision of Dylan, with books, blogs and translations. For the public at large, this vision, aligned to the revisionist image that Dylan was acquiring in the United States, remained largely unavailable. It served, however, the function of producing an alternative discourse to which fans could align and to which new 'followers' could be socialised.

The image of the 'old' Dylan looms over this process, largely because it is one of the legitimising discourses of Italian popular music, especially in the tradition of singer–songwriters who are still best-selling artists who regularly tour and perform.

Local conditions produced both this vision of Dylan and the delay in the development of the reputation of Dylan that has occurred in other countries since *Time Out of Mind* and *"Love and Theft"*. Local processes of celebrity making are, indeed, less a mirror of what happens in the centre or at the global level, and more a selective outcome of contingent dynamics at the local level. The timing of the establishment of Dylan's reputation in Italy was crucial in the determination of the way he and his work are generally represented by the press and by fans' accounts, with a centrality of his 'poetic' self that challenges the master narrative of Dylan as a rock star. Dylan the protest singer is still a very powerful image in the public representation of the artist, and represents a relevant point of entry for the production of any discourse about his figure, role and status in the music field. It is, however, not the product of a circuit of nostalgia that is centred around his figure; rather, it testifies of the long legacy of the 1960s in Italian politics and in the cultural sphere, and of the power of ideas, and imagined representations, about Dylan in the authentication and the creation of the music field.

References

Ala, N. (1981) *Bob Dylan* (Rome: Savelli).
Assante, E. (1987) 'Poesia, la sua unica arma', *La Repubblica* (12 September). 21.
Becker, H. S. (1982) *Art Worlds* (Chicago, IL: University of Chicago Press).
Cappelli, V. and Farkas, A. (1997) 'De Gregori: Adesso canto come Dylan', *Corriere della Sera* (11 August). 23.

Carrera, A. (2001) *La voce di Bob Dylan. Una spiegazione dell'America* (Milan: Feltrinelli).

Carrera, A. (ed.) (2008) *Parole nel vento. I migliori saggi critici su Bob Dylan* (Novara: Interlinea).

Carrera, A. (2009) 'Oh, the streets of Rome: Dylan in Italy', in C. J. Sheehy and T. Swiss (eds), *Highway 61 Revisited: Bob Dylan from Minnesota to the World* (Minneapolis, MN: University of Minnesota Press). 84–105.

Castaldo, G. (1984) 'Benvenuto Bob Dylan poeta della folla', *La Repubblica* (30 May). 23.

Castaldo, G. (1987) 'L'Utopia di Dylan e il Luna Park di Madonna', *La Repubblica* (12 September). 1.

Castaldo, G. (1989) 'Dylan, poeta severo', *La Repubblica* (21 June). 22.

Castaldo, G. (1992a) 'Bob Dylan, un mito senza miti', *La Repubblica* (4 July). 25.

Castaldo, G. (1992b) 'Bob Dylan, irriducibile per sempre', *La Repubblica* (7 July). 25.

Castaldo, G. (1993a) 'Il menestrello canta la fuga dalle ovvieta', *La Repubblica* (27 June). 41.

Castaldo, G. (1993b) 'Pronto? Sono Bob Dylan', *La Repubblica* (24 June). 34.

Cossu, A. (2012) *It Ain't Me, Babe: Bob Dylan and the Performance of Authenticity* (Boulder, CO: Paradigm).

DeNora, T. (1997) *Beethoven and the Construction of Genius: Musical Politics in Vienna 1792–1803* (Berkeley, CA: University of California Press).

Donaggio, E. (1965) 'I Beatles cambiano stile e si ispirano a Bob Dylan', *Stampa Sera* (24 October). 13.

Dylan, B. (2004) *Chronicles: Volume One* (New York: Simon and Schuster).

Fabbri, F. (1982) 'A theory of music genres: two applications', in P. Tagg and D. Horn (eds), *Popular Music Perspectives* (Göteborg: International Association for the Study of Popular Music).

Farkas, A. (1997) 'Io col Papa? Se lo dice il Vaticano', *Corriere della Sera* (28 August). 35.

Fine, G. A. (2001) *Difficult Reputations: Collective Memories of the Evil, Inept, and Controversial* (Chicago, IL: University of Chicago Press).

Fine, G. A. (2011) *Sticky Reputations: The Politics of Collective Memory in Twentieth Century America* (London: Routledge).

Manin, G. and V. Cappelli (1997) 'Bologna, rivolta dei "cantanti di Dio"', *Corriere della Sera* (25 September). 15.

Marini, G. (1981) 'Curiosita' e delusioni', in E. Assante and E. Capua (eds), *Le strade del Folk* (Milan: Savelli). 16–24.

Marshall, L. (2007) *Bob Dylan: The Never Ending Star* (Oxford: Polity).

Menduni, E. (1997) 'Bob Dylan. Alle radici della musica contro l'ingiustizia', *L'Unità* (28 September). 8.

Mogol (1967) 'Cosa dice Mogol', *L'Unità* (2 April). 12.

Portelli, A. (1977) *La canzone popolare in America: la rivoluzione musicale di Woody Guthrie* (Bari: De Donato).

Putti, L. (1987) 'La magia si ripete', *La Repubblica* (15 September). 27.

Rocca, E. (1997)'Messori e Cavalieri litigano per Dylan', *La Repubblica* (17 September). 40.

Santoro, M. (2010) *Effetto tenco: genealogia della canzone d'autore* (Bologna: Il Mulino).

Settimelli, L. (1965) 'Cantano le canzoni dell'Altra America', *L'Unità* (28 October). 11.

Sisti, E. (1997) 'Il ritorno di Dylan: Undici canzoni di rabbia', *La Repubblica* (31 July). 39.

Stampa Alternativa (1978) *Dylan S.p.A.* (Verona: Bertani/Stampa Alternativa).

Straniero, G. and Rovello, C. (eds) (2008) *Cantacronache. I 50 anni della canzone ribelle* (Civitella Val di Chiana: Editrice Zona).

Susanna, G. (1997a) 'Provato ma ancora capace di amare. Ecco il Dylan alle soglie del Duemila', *L'Unità* (24 September). 9.

Susanna, G. (1997b) 'E' lui l'unico davvero indispensabile', *L'Unità* (24 September). 9.

Tarli, T. (2007) *Beat Italiano. Dai cappelloni a bandiera gialla* (Rome: Castelvecchi).

Tropea, S. (1987) 'E tra il pubblico tanti giovani vip', *La Repubblica* (15 September). 27.

Williams, P. (2004) *Bob Dylan. Performing Artist: 1986–1990 and Beyond* (London: Omnibus).

5

Not there: the poetics of absence in portrayals of Bob Dylan by Wolf Biermann and Ilse Aichinger

John Heath

German literature has proven to be a subtle recipient of Bob Dylan, even if his reception in German-speaking countries has not always been the most sympathetic. The German response to his songs was marked from its very beginning by a pronounced time lag; the 1968 reformists drew inspiration from a Dylan who was already three phases further on in his musical development, if one believes in phases as such (Anderson, 1981: 87, 135). And in 1978 his Berlin audience, expecting older material, was so aggravated by his performance with gospel backing singers that an obituary appeared soon thereafter (Biermann, 2003: 137). Perhaps a more celebrated case of the German Dylan reception is the esteem he is held in by Joschka Fischer, who claimed he had had more influence on his political development than Marx and Engels (Fischer, 2002: 33). The revolutionary student who was to become minister for foreign affairs was thus indebted to a poet who had already distanced himself from political activities before Fischer could have begun to listen to his songs. The title of Todd Haynes's 2007 film is, then, quite fitting for German-speaking Bob Dylan reception: *I'm Not There*.

Others have examined Dylan's playfulness regarding his public image and the question of the artist's identity (Klein, 2011; Schimank, 2002: 87–10); my focus lies, rather, with a related concept first evoked in the title of the Hollywood biopic. While Dylan's own film *Masked and Anonymous* points to the concept of identity,[1] Haynes's title *I'm Not There* signals the systematic denial of authenticity in portraying characters who are inspired by the singer's public persona but are expressly claimed to be anyone other than Bob Dylan. It is this treatment of the Dylan legend that is also characteristic of the more subtle examination of the figure in German literature: the very absence of Bob Dylan.

This absence first came to light as a dramatic principle in a radio play by the Austrian writer Michael Köhlmeier, *Like Bob Dylan* (Köhlmeier, 1975),

51

examining a Dylan aficionado's frustration with his life and employment. Köhlmeier was to return to this theme in a short story published in 1999, in which the most intriguing events take place once Dylan and the chess master Bobby Fisher abandon the scene for a private conversation, leaving the reader to construct their encounter (Köhlmeier, 1999). And in 1980 Thomas Brasch used a German audience's vitriolic rejection of Dylan in 1978 as the basis for a poem examining the latent nationalism and hatred displayed by the so-called left wing (Brasch, 1980). A mere four verses (and the title) mention Dylan; the larger part of the poem portrays the crowd. Whereas in Köhlmeier's play the singer's absence allows for reflection on the futility of imitation and, indeed, admiration, Brasch's poem deals with a lack of genuine political progress since the war; Dylan is swiftly abandoned. This principle of absence lies at the heart of two more recent texts which form the focus of this chapter: Wolf Biermann's 2003 Dylan translation and a short piece of prose narrative by Ilse Aichinger published in book form the same year.[2] It is significant that across genres there remains a consistent interest in playing peek-a-boo with Dylan.

For Biermann, whose protest songs were renowned contraband in the German Democratic Republic (GDR) and who was finally expatriated from that country in 1976, Dylan represents both an artistic figure with whom to identify and an opportunity to reflect on the political and intellectual development of his earlier self. Interestingly, Biermann chose to translate not a song, but Dylan's poetry, '11 outlined epitaphs', or, in Biermann's extended translation, *Elf Entwürfe für meinen Grabspruch*.[3] Four of Dylan's verses, composed in 1963, appeared on the back cover of Dylan's 1964 album *The Times They Are A-Changin'*. Biermann's translation was greeted with quite scathing criticism; this dismissive reception, along with the remarkable common ground it shares with Aichinger's prose piece, makes a re-examination of both texts somewhat overdue. None other than the German Dylan expert Heinrich Detering commented in the *Frankfurter Allgemeine Zeitung*: 'One could not have treated Dylan's poetry more roughly' (Detering, 2003)[4] and Willi Winkler was no more complimentary in the *Süddeutsche Zeitung*: 'When Dylan is too brief for him, Biermann makes additions, runs his own hobby horses into the ground'. Winkler claims Dylan has been abused and hollowed out as Biermann's 'ventriloquist's dummy' (Winkler, 2003: 19). The critical consensus is, then, that Biermann has not produced a faithful translation. In sum: Dylan is not there.

The Bob Dylan of the GDR

Some of Biermann's stylistic alterations certainly seem rather arbitrary, most obviously his arrangement of strophes: he renders Dylan's first with three of his own. His treatment of verse length is similarly headstrong:

whereas Dylan's long strophes consisting of short verses suggest a stream of consciousness, the German inexplicably employs long, numbered songs. However, on the micro level Biermann has retained the use of alliteration and sporadic rhyme. While they might not be found at corresponding junctures, they are there. While it is difficult to disagree with Detering and Winkler entirely, if we examine Biermann's poetics, there is no reason to be surprised at his departure from the original. Even a superficial reading of Biermann's theory of poetry – or, more precisely, and equally unsurprisingly, of his *own* poetry – or indeed his comments in the appendix to *Elf* prepares the reader for plenty of reference to Biermann himself.

This self-reference results from biographical similarities between the author and the translator. The singer poets share artistic predecessors and role models: both were strongly influenced by François Villon and Bertolt Brecht. But it is not only shared heritage that unites parallel careers in opposing societies: there are also similarities regarding reception. *The Times They Are A-Changin'* was Dylan's last album of an overtly political nature, at least for a number of years. Particularly towards the end of the 1960s, as protest in relation to the war in Vietnam intensified, dissatisfaction with Dylan's work grew. Biermann, too, encountered similar criticism in his half of the world. In one of his poetics lectures in Düsseldorf in the mid-1990s, he explained: 'I've encountered the cringeworthy question of whether my songs are political enough for thirty years'.[5] The authorities in the GDR were often disappointed: 'In the eyes of the rulers, a conversation about trees was still a crime'; love poetry was, for Stalinist theorists, 'a lapse into petit bourgeois weakness' (VL 23). In the 'free world', this opinion was shared by many of Dylan's listeners.

Biermann's poetics emphasise the personal, although a withdrawal from the political is by no means the aim: 'I am always interested in a poem's position in the political and social coordinate system too' (VL 150). For Biermann, aesthetics and social circumstances stand in a reciprocal relationship. Nevertheless, the private is uppermost in his reception of a poem: 'Ultimately I am most interested in myself' (VL 41). He wants to compare the experiences of the poet with his own (VL 41). The same holds for his theory of translation: it is not familiarity with the source language that is the most important consideration, but one's ability to express oneself in one's own language (VL 150). He has a similar stance when it comes to the question of loyalty to the source text: 'don't just do it well … make it at least better than the original!' (VL 153). A point of criticism was, of course, that he had not achieved that.

It is significant that Biermann did not attempt to translate a song, but a poem. For Biermann, the appropriation and surpassing of a poem is a 'labour of love'; if the translator – or, more accurately, the German *Nachdichter*, suggesting someone who writes a poem 'after' another – cannot create something better, he or she should refrain from trying, out of respect for the original (*VL* 153). This reticence to tackle a Dylan song can also be explained by Biermann's programme of making songs in the German tradition rather than as a poor parodist (*VL* 201), but his respect for Dylan's work did not stand in the way of his attempt to surpass the poetry of 'the poet of our age' (*Elf* 99). And in order to write a better poem than the original, his poetics decree that he has to write about himself.

'I' in poetry

For Biermann, the most essential element of poetry is the first person. Lyrical I, lyrical subject, narrator, author: here we have, of course, a theoretical problem. And when it comes to works by GDR writers, too often it is neglected. In Biermann's poetics, however, the lyrical subject and he himself are identical where it suits him – where it suits my argument, I will reflect his usage. The poetical value the presence of the lyrical subject holds for him becomes clear in his criticism in a Düsseldorf lecture of his GDR colleague Volker Braun. Braun wrote a cryptic poem, 'Schauspiel' (Braun, 1990a), and showed it to Biermann, telling him he was in it. Biermann considered the poem *too* cryptic however: he failed to recognise himself in the figure of a banjo player, since he played the guitar, and in his lecture he complained of Braun's code: 'then the final, precious word FREEDOM is just an eight-letter blabla, and every four-letter word of Bob Dylan's like *love* or *fuck* has more dignity and a higher degree of freedom' (*VL* 90). Biermann does not object to the vague description of his own person *per se*; rather, he argues that if the very person the poem depicts cannot find himself, the poem's 'I' is absent too (*VL* 90).

Since Biermann seldom distinguishes between the lyrical subject and the poet – although, as we shall see later, in some situations he *does* make the distinction – he considers writing poems such as 'Schauspiel' a literary betrayal of oneself. The significance for his 'Transportarbeit' (transport work) cannot escape our attention: quite apart from the long-established poetological insistence that poetry is or should be a subjective genre, if Biermann holds this view, then we must expect him to be present in his translations.

It is also significant that his discussion of Braun's poem is one of the few instances in which he mentions Dylan, despite the esteem in which he holds him. For the Dylan text to which he refers, 'Love is just a four-letter word', comes from a time when Dylan intensified his retreat from the political to the surreal. During this period Dylan is vague, opaque, but for Biermann fully present in his art as an artist, through the use of the personal – although the complex question of Dylan's presence is an area to which we will return.

But Biermann's selection of '11 outlined epitaphs' is also significant. For Detering, the final strophe of '11 outlined epitaphs' represents 'a strophe that lays the foundation [for Dylan's] later work. It is the first time that the apparent retreat into the individual and artistic, into the intimate and private becomes the precondition for an emancipation [...] the political explosiveness of which will surpass everything that could be achieved by the most pointed of finger-pointing songs' (Detering, 2007: 43). Biermann too combined the political and the private and in his poetics lectures he went out of his way to explain the rejection with which such works are met.

The private nature of poetry was considered suspect not only by the Party, but also by Biermann's audience in both East and West Germany, for 'it stinks a bit of betrayal [...]. A poet with the stigma of the private always appeared to the left-wing tastes of the day to be a thief' (VL 11). He then ventures into etymology: the Latin *privare* means *berauben*, and 'whoever makes private songs lays a lyrical claim to everything that he has stolen from the masses, everything he has taken from the collective property, all the pleasure and all the intellectual fodder and power of disposition' (VL 11). Dylan himself steals from a collective corpus of music and poetry – as early as the '11 outlined epitaphs' the subject concedes: 'yes I am a thief of thoughts' (Eleven 83). (In his rendering Biermann places the thief in a respected tradition: 'Copyright Brecht, tja!' (Elf 26).) A complete list of works plundered by Dylan would be too ambitious for this chapter, but a brief list would include Robert Burns, Arthur Koestler, Lewis Carroll, Mark Twain, Junichi Saga, Robert Johnson, John Lee Hooker, Gene Austin, Merle Haggard, Henry Timrod (Detering, 2007: 159–60, 166–71), Walt Whitman (Price, 2006: 170, note 18) and, not least, the Bible.

Despite claims of plagiarism that followed the appearance of Dylan's 2006 album *Modern Times* (Detering, 2007: 167), the stolen art remains public property: from the common body of American popular music Dylan creates equally public texts. In his Dylan study, Detering writes of the 1970 album entitled, of all things, *Self-Portrait* – on which Dylan sings hardly any of his own songs and has his latest offering sung only by a choir – that Dylan's presence is to be considered an absence in the tradition of American song (ibid.: 100), recognising the 'polyphony, anonymity and at times the speechlessness of American popular culture' (ibid.: 101). (Here Detering anticipates a more recent Dylan song: 'Some people they tell me/I got the blood of the land in my voice' – 'I Feel a Change Comin' On', from the 2009 album *Together Through Life*.) The most personal of songs remain public property – we might be tempted to rehabilitate a comment of a television presenter which incurs the mirth of Dylanologists: 'You know him, he's yours' (seen in Scorsese, 2005: disc 2, 00:14:14).

One might conclude that if Dylan steals in order to become public property, he can also receive gifts – and for Biermann, it would appear there are few works that wouldn't benefit from his donations; in his poetics lectures he declares that in Goethe's *Faust* someone sings a song in Auerbach's cellar 'als wärs ein Stück von mir' (VL 8). If we accept Biermann's explanation of the private in art, then the personalisation of someone else's text, even if it is meant to improve it, must be considered an act of theft. Those who give a translation a private colouring commit theft, even if they do so out of love for the original. For Biermann, the personal is also, however, a precondition of a good poetic text.

Biermann's donations: love and theft[6]

Biermann's donations to Dylan's text include more than references to himself however. If the poem is to function in his own German tradition, and if he is to retain the intertextual characteristic of Dylan's style and invoke the common property of an artistic tradition, then he must pilfer from German works. And so we encounter Hölderlin: where Dylan writes of walls, Biermann describes them as 'sprachlos und kalt' (VL 16). The compulsory education Dylan rejects is rendered as 'Ding-an-sich-Wissen' (VL 33), and Biermann further laces his work with a sprinkling of allusions to Dante, Heine and Brecht (VL 25–6). A – first-person – offering of Volker Braun's is also included: 'Wir! und nicht sie' (Elf 45; cf. Braun, 1990b) – itself a reference to Klopstock (see Gronemeyer and Hurlebusch, 2010: 468–9). Ultimately, we must not forget Biermann, who cites a song of his own: 'so soll's sein, – so wird's sein' (VL 27). And when he translates Dylan's – or his subject's – concession 'I am a thief of thoughts' ('Ob ich was abgeschrieben hab von andern?/na logo! An die hunderttausendmal'), he is also commenting on his own poetic intentions: 'Ich geb ja auch immer mal andern was ab' (Elf 44).

Whose 'I'?

In his poetics lectures, Biermann describes how all his renderings have to take on a North German flavour: when he translated a Cuban song, he found that the subject's claim to be an honest man would arouse the suspicion of a German audience: 'Of course the whole audience knows that the North German fish-head Biermann doesn't mean himself; it's a song about Cuba after all. Nevertheless, there is no northern country in which such a line can be tolerated' (VL 167). As his audience is also German, he must sing from their perspective on the exotic (VL 168). Who then is the subject of his translations? If the new 'I' is to be convincing as an 'I', Biermann has to be convincing in his own voice, hence the donations from his own culture. When one considers that Biermann is quite aware that an old Biermann is translating a young Dylan (Elf 108), it comes as no surprise that some passages of the translation necessarily diverge from the original.

Biermann's text is characterised, for example, by anachronisms: Dylan's 'blast' (Eleven 66) is rendered as 'so'n Fegefeuer-Sound' (Elf 10). Biermann's blast is suggestive of the change to electronic music and thus points to later developments in Dylan's career. Similarly, Biermann's 'Flowerpower' (Elf 11) was not a common slogan in 1963 – and he is well aware of the fact. In keeping with his perspective on the 'exotic', he also adds images of the United States of the early 1960s absent from Dylan's text: the Ku Klux Klan (*Elf* 11) and McDonald's (*Elf* 23). These America-themed additions are joined by German donations: Dylan's gentle 'the candles of sundown' (*Eleven* 67) become a 'Himmelsbrand' (sky on/of/from fire) (*Elf* 13) reminiscent of the bombing of Biermann's native Hamburg, and in the description of the town of Hibbing, divided into North and South Hibbing by the railway line, Biermann evokes Berlin: 'Wo der ganze Ort durchschnitten wird von Gleisen' (where the whole town is cut in two by tracks) (*Elf* 15). The original has merely 'cuts the ground' (*Eleven* 68); the partitioning of the *town* is not explicitly mentioned. A more faithful rendering might have had more socialist overtones however, reflecting the line of the GDR minister for culture and poet Johannes R. Becher on the death of Stalin: 'Und durch die Erde ein Riß' (and the earth/ground is torn) (Becher, 1954). But socialism is certainly permitted in the translation: Dylan's 'Billboard' (*Eleven* 72) becomes a propaganda placard complete with Marx quotation (*Elf* 22). (On the other hand, in the original there is a greater emphasis on absence here: 'There's nobody home / all have moved out': *Elf* 72.) Biermann's Germany is combined, then, with Dylan's America – further instances are Dylan's 'roads' (*Eleven* 77), in Biermann 'Straßen / Chausseen, per Anhalter Highways' (streets / avenues, hitchhiking highways) (*Elf* 32), reminiscent of his own flat in Berlin's Chausseestraße – and of the poetry of Peter Huchel (*Chausseen, Chausseen*; Huchel, 1963).

Biermann readily admits, in the afterword to *Elf Entwürfe*, to the interest in himself he outlined in his lectures: he translates out of 'self-interest', sees in the original 'elements of an image of myself alienated through America' (*Elf* 103). The extent to which the 'I' must change becomes clear when lyrical third parties appear with greater specificity than in the original. Dylan's poem asks 'who to fight?' (*Eleven* 65) – Biermann's subject knows precisely who and how: whom should he 'mit Spottgesängen niedersingen?' (sing down with ridiculing songs – put or bring down through song), 'Wie zeigen wir's dem etablierten Pack?' (How shall we stick it up the establishment mob?) (*Elf* 9). Biermann protests against the anti-Americanism of many Europeans (*Elf* 40) and Dylan's description of the landscape of the Great Lakes becomes a crusade against 'Industrieabwässer' (industrial effluent) around Cleveland. Dylan does not even mention this: at this juncture of Biermann's translation the neo-beat poet is reduced to a Monika Maron.

Yet while Biermann's 'I' often imposes itself on Dylan's, there are passages in which Biermann's Dylan figure is more present than in the original: 'Vor meiner Zeit in Minneapolis kam ich nach Hibbing / wo ich allmählich wurde, der ich noch nicht bin' (Before my time in Minneapolis I came to Hibbing / where I gradually became he who I am yet to be) (*Elf* 14). This is quite lacking from a Dylan who in 1963 was departing from his public's projection of a messianic figure and who would surely not have used such a biblical formulation in reference to himself. (Also in Biermann: 'ich wandel nicht abgeklärt auf Erden' (I walk this earth not serenely/aloof/worldly-wise), 'verbring meine Zeit, die auf Erden mir/gegeben ist' (spend my time that has been given to me on this earth) (*Elf* 17). In both lines, the use of 'Erden' instead of 'Erde' has a biblical quality.) Nevertheless, Biermann presents an image of the artist marked by an implicit constructedness, by an absence: 'der ich *noch nicht* bin' (who I am yet to be) (my emphasis). Biermann's afterword suggests that he sees Dylan's identity during this period as far from complete: he writes of a 'Robert Zimmerman als er gerade on the way war, um Bob Dylan zu werden' (Robert Zimmerman when he was on the way to becoming Bob Dylan) (*Elf* 99). For Biermann, Dylan was not yet present, indeed not yet *existent*; his construction was, however, a clear, defined goal: 'on the way [...] *um* Bob Dylan zu werden' (my emphasis; the German 'um', which Biermann certainly could have omitted, suggests a deliberateness which might be rendered by 'in order to become Bob Dylan'). Hence, for Biermann, the Bob Dylan of the original is both absent and present.

Absence intensifies presence. This becomes clear through one of Biermann's more subtle renderings. While Dylan's 'stranger' (*Eleven* 73) becomes Biermann's 'Ich ich ich' (*Elf* 24), Biermann can also refrain from such references. For three whole pages the 'Ich' is not used (*Elf* 14–17), until a new strophe is launched with 'Ich aber [...]'. But it is not just the subtlety of this intensification that represents a paradox: the heightened presence of Bob Dylan or an 'ich' that could be considered his is best explained by Biermann's interest in himself. The passages in which Dylan examines his existence as a singer are among those selected for expansion in the translation. Four lines by Dylan (*Eleven* 71) on the trades unions of the 1930s, marked by an economical sarcasm – 'come now! can you see 'em/needin' me/for a song/or two' – become sixteen lines in Biermann (*Elf* 20). But here the theme is the presence of Bob Dylan as an artist, representative of song-writing and the status of the singer.

On the one hand, Biermann rejects the enigmatic in poetry – as in the example of Volker Braun – yet, on the other hand, he grapples with one of the first of Dylan's decidedly enigmatic texts. But a writer who refuses to permit his texts to take on an enigmatic character has to take care of exegesis himself. Thus Biermann has his justification for a form of self-reception that can only lead to self-presentation – and the vehicle for such self-presentation is the parallel with Dylan. Even when Dylan is there, his presence serves Biermann's self-understanding.

Absence, presence, presence through absence

Dylan's tendency to play hide and seek with his audience draws comment from Biermann in his afterword. He writes of a Dylan concert he witnessed in 1997: 'Dylan seemed absent, almost as if immersed in other worlds' (*Elf* 135); 'He stood beside his songs, like the classical Brechtian actor at the Berliner Ensemble beside his role' (*Elf* 134). Biermann considers Dylan's songs in concert a 'Sparversion', a more economical or budget version: 'Our own little computer in our skulls delivered to the ear from within that which the artist out there on the stage chose not to deliver via his microphone, or wasn't able to – how should I know' (*Elf* 134). A performer's observations on performance are worth careful consideration. I described Biermann as a subtle recipient: when he reflected on Dylan in concert, he could not know what Dylan would write a year later in his memoir, *Chronicles* (Dylan, 2004: 159). There he explained his performance was linked to his technique of playing music: he employs a 'bone structure' which allows the audience to construct a work for themselves: '[you] trust that the listeners make their own connections'. This structure replaces 'passion and enthusiasm', which he considers unnecessary, since they are unreliable: 'Ideally, I would have liked to have taken a song, played it more than a few times for a musicologist who would then write the basic parts for an orchestrated version. The orchestra could even play the vocal line. I wouldn't even have to be there' (Dylan, 2004: 159). Again, the enigmatic: shortly thereafter he observes that the strength of this system is that 'With a new incantation code to infuse my vocals with manifest presence I could ride high' (Dylan, 2004: 161). This technique displays, then, a tension between absence and presence. But lest we take Dylan's inconsistency too seriously, let us return to Biermann. The songs, indeed the entire performance, exist only in the head of the member of the audience. Biermann considers Dylan's presence to lie in the very absence that permits a construction – or a reconstruction – whereby everyone constructs, like the translator of the '11 outlined epitaphs', whatever they want.

Biermann is not concerned, then, with the person of Bob Dylan; he is concerned with art – his own art. Dylan stands for the possibilities of poetic creation. If Dylan is absent, this absence serves as a balance to the absence of a public stage Biermann felt so keenly.

Biermann's early career was marked by enforced privacy: he was banned from performing before his expatriation from the GDR in 1976 and suffered a lack of subject matter in the years immediately thereafter. The absence of Dylan is compensated for by his substitution by a poet who wrote and played for eleven years *in absentia*, as an unperson in his Chausseestraße flat, and whose public reception was also restricted to the private sphere by the threat of arrest. But in working on Dylan, Biermann joins a choir: in his afterword, the absent Dylan is replaced by formerly absent singers, singers sharing a similar tradition of 'protest' but who were forced by circumstance to remain in their own milieus. The Portuguese José Afonso, the Argentine Atahualpa Yupanqui – the unpersons step out of the shadows and fill the spotlight that he does not permit to shine on Dylan alone. And yet to a large extent Biermann writes of their protracted absence. Absence (Bob Dylan's) gives way to absence (that of the oppressed artists).

Neither *there* nor *me*: Ilse Aichinger

Absence and a merely fleeting presence are also central motives behind Ilse Aichinger's 'Journal des Verschwindens', a newspaper column in *Der Standard* in which she uses films, photographs or events as a point of departure for reflection on the disappearance of members of her family in the Holocaust, but also on her own wish that she could disappear. The articles were collected in the volume *Film und Verhängnis. Blitzlichter auf ein Leben*. Two of these texts refer to Bob Dylan. While in one he is mentioned only in passing, the focus being on the Beatles film *A Hard Day's Night*, the other takes its title from an interview Dylan gave in the 1960s: 'I'm glad, I'm not me – Bob Dylan'.

In the latter short text, a reading tour takes her to the United States. She has but two motivations for crossing the Atlantic: the Atlantic itself, which she misses due to seasickness, and Bob Dylan, whose autograph she has promised her son, who, together with his left-wing friends, listens to Dylan songs from morning till night in their house in Großgmain. Armed with a picture book of the star, she travels to the Catskill mountains and finds his house:

> 'No, no, no', sagte seine Frau, als sie das Buch sah. – 'Give it to me', sagte die Vierjährige hinter ihr und warf sich gegen eine Holztür, die ich übersehen hatte: Dylan kam im Halbdunkel in den Flur, hatte eine halbe Bratkartoffel in der Hand, kaute an der anderen Hälfte, hielt den Band gegen die Wand und schrieb eine Zeile auf den Deckel, die der Regen gleich auf dem Weg zum Auto rasch löschte.
>
> Die verwischte Tinte blieb. Es ließ sich nicht mehr herausfinden, ob er seinen eigenen Text geschrieben hatte wie *I'm glad, I'm not me*. Das einzige Wort, das nach den Winterstürmen auf dem Atlantik in Großgmain noch zu lesen war, hieß *Dylan*. (FV 138–9)

> 'No, no, no,' said his wife when she saw the book. – 'Give it to me,' said the four-year-old girl behind her and threw herself against a wooden door which I had overlooked: Dylan came in the semi-darkness into the hall, had half a roast potato in his hand, chewed the other half, held the volume against the wall and wrote a line on the cover which the rain quickly washed away on the way to the car.
>
> The smudged ink remained. It remained unclear whether he had written his own text like *I'm glad, I'm not me*. The only word that could still be read in Großgmain after the winter storms on the Atlantic was *Dylan*.

The text culminates, then, in the dedication disappearing and the name, or part of it, remaining. Aichinger is interested in disappearing, hiding. Veronika

Fehle has demonstrated in great detail how Aichinger writes of disappearance while herself disappearing in her own text (Fehle, 2006: 176). Fehle examines this aspect in the context of theoretical discourse on memory: the 'Journal des Verschwindens' is all about the fleeting nature of memory – and hence it is also about the fleeting nature of the object of memory, and indeed that of the person doing the remembering (Fehle, 2006: 141).

To be fleeting is ultimately to become absent. In a journal piece on Laurel and Hardy, Aichinger sums up the concept when she states she is interested in the otherwise inexistent possibility of not being there: 'nicht da zu sein' (FV 95). Samuel Moser observes that in her earlier texts she is also concerned with her own absence, and in these memoir pieces she is present only in passing; the text is her hiding place (Moser, 1996: 9). That Aichinger's texts should feature the word 'ich' only in passing can be traced back to an experience she had in her youth; in the preface to the 'Journal des Verschwindens', she writes: 'ich sagte ich bald und empfand es ebenso bald als daneben' (FV 65) ('I said I quickly and just as quickly it felt wrong'). The question of identity is raised in similar fashion in the title of her Dylan text: 'I'm glad, I'm not me' (FV 138). Is it significant that her Dylan quotation features a comma? In the film *I'm Not There*, the line is also used, but without the comma, without a caesura. The figure reminiscent of the Dylan of the mid-1960s intonates thus: 'I'm glad I'm not me'. If we may assume that the Anglophile Aichinger is familiar with English punctuation after her time in England, then instead of emphasising that Dylan is glad to have nothing to do with the media image of himself, in Aichinger's version he insists on an identity outside of himself – and is happy about that. It may, of course, be an editorial or authorial error, but this alienation from the self is also to be found in Dylan's '11 outlined epitaphs' ('It's as though my mind ain't mine to make up anymore': *Eleven* 91), or in Biermann, even closer to Aichinger's formulation: 'Ich steh als ein anderer fremd neben mir' (*Elf* 55).

Biermann's observations on Dylan's live performance of his songs are of great relevance for Aichinger's text too – vastly reduced, the songs permit or require reconstruction on the part of the audience. ('You know him, he's yours.') Regarding memory in Aichinger, Fehle notes, surprisingly similarly: 'Das Verschwinden schlägt Lücken in die chronologisch angeordnete Bedeutungskette der Erinnerung und setzt so das zeitlich orientierte Erinnerungsmodell. In diesen Leerstellen, die auf die Existenz eines verschwundenen Erinnerungsgegenstandes hinweisen, liegt die ständige Möglichkeit, das Verschwundene immer neu zu formulieren' (Fehle, 2006: 40) ('The act of disappearing knocks holes in memory's chain of meaning and in so doing establishes the temporally oriented model of memory. These empty spaces pointing to the existence of an object of memory that has disappeared play host to the permanent possibility of forever formulating anew that which has disappeared.') And thus Aichinger creates an image of Dylan in which Dylan himself is fleeting. She seeks Dylan in his retreat, in his hiding place in the country. The encounter with Dylan could be an encounter with anyone chewing a potato; this one just happens to be called Dylan. It is the wife, the daughter who speak, not Dylan. Bob Dylan's only words in this text are those Aichinger has retained from fragments of interviews – the aggressive interviews of the mid-1960s, in which Dylan, as in the interview scenario portrayed in the '11 outlined epitaphs' (*Eleven* 86–7), refuses to give information, or provides provocatively vague answers. Then the door closes, in the end most of the ink has run. The physical encounter and the thoughts Dylan writes – which need not have been his own, as Aichinger emphasises – are immediately gone. Again the parallel with Biermann: 'verbring meine Zeit, die auf Erden mir/gegeben ist, als extremer Flüchter/im Geiste wie im Fleische' ('I spend my time me on earth as an extreme fleer [i.e. person who flees], in spirit as in flesh') (*Elf* 17). It is not just the fleeting nature of the mind and the body that represents a marked similarity to Aichinger's account: Dylan uses the term 'Refugee', but while Biermann uses the equivalent 'Flüchtling' in the next verse, he first generalises with 'Flüchter' and thus emphasises the quality of fleetingness.

It is not only the fleeting nature of the identity Bob Dylan that interests Biermann, but also the fleetingness of memory. (Perhaps less consciously, but if I may be permitted to force the link, I believe it will prove justified.) In the course of his poetics lectures he provides an example of the artistically beautiful arising from the naturally vile: Brecht's poem 'Erinnerung an die Marie A.'. He employs this example to demonstrate that an attitude that is far from noble, namely the lyrical subject's almost completely forgetting the girl he has loved under a tree, can become beautiful in the hands of a masterly poet. Let us leap from here to Dylan – for if Brecht's 'I' is the perpetrator of forgetting, Dylan's is once the victim: in the 1964 song 'I Don't Believe You (She Acts Like We Never Have Met)'. The song is an exception in Dylan's early work, in which often the lyrical subject himself has, as in the song 'I'm Not There', long departed – for example 'Restless Farewell', 'Boots of Spanish Leather', 'Don't Think Twice, It's Alright', 'It Ain't Me, Babe', 'Mama, You Been on My Mind'. We have already seen that in Biermann and Aichinger one can construct what one wants. That also means, of course, that one can arbitrarily omit: 'Though we kissed through the wild blazing nighttime/She said she would never forget/But now mornin's clear/It's like I ain't here/She just acts like we never have met' ('I Don't Believe You (She Acts Like We Never Have Met)', from the album *Another Side of Bob Dylan*). The 'I' is treated by the 'she' as if it were nonexistent. Hence the conclusion: 'An' if anybody asks me/"Is it easy to forget?"/I'll say, "It's easily done/You just pick anyone/An' pretend that you never have met!"' This conscious and demonstrative forgetting can also be read in Biermann's revered Brecht: the subject is only reminded of Marie A. by a cloud: 'Und auch den Kuß, ich hätt ihn längst vergessen/Wenn nicht die Wolke da gewesen wär' (Brecht, 1988: 92–3, lines 17–18) ('And the kiss, I would have forgotten it,/Had it not been for the cloud'). But the cloud too is soon gone: 'Doch jene Wolke blühte nur Minuten/Und als ich aufsah, schwand sie schon im Wind' (*ibid.*: lines 23–4) ('But that cloud bloomed for mere minutes/And when I looked up, it was already disappearing in the wind'). The same might be said of Bob Dylan's autograph in Aichinger: 'Das einzige Wort, das nach den Winterstürmen auf dem Atlantik in Großgmain noch zu lesen war, hieß *Dylan*' (*FV* 139) ('The only word that could be read in Großgmain after the winter storms on the Atlantic was *Dylan*'). Only the legend, the pseudonym, the mask remains.

We may presume that Aichinger would not have forgotten the event had the Catskills or the potato not been there, but it is significant that we experience little else – despite the private setting, she encounters only the designation 'Dylan'. Aichinger's readers have to imagine the famous figure for themselves, just as the readers of 'Marie A.' have to construct 'die junge Liebe' if she is not to remain an empty label. Aichinger, too, presents, then, a tension between absence and presence. The name, the image remains, admittedly only as a hiding place, but although Dylan's intellectual gift to Aichinger's son disappears, his art remains: the music in the house in Großgmain. (One can of course see art as the artist's hiding place, as has been observed of Aichinger's writing.) And while Dylan retreats into the Catskill mountains, the mountains in Großgmain retreat from Dylan: 'Seine ziemlich helle und aggressive Stimme hatte schon jahrelang das Haus unter dem dunklen Waldrücken beherrscht, hinter dem sich der Untersberg tarnte' (*FV* 137) ('His somewhat high and aggressive voice had already dominated the house under the forest ridge behind which the Untersberg hid'). In the United States, Dylan is hidden by the landscape, but in Aichinger's home Dylan the artist is acutely present: it is the mountains that hide behind the woods, while the house stands before them and is *dominated* by Dylan's art – by his voice. But Aichinger herself hides from this art: she disappears into the upper floor of the house: 'Ich war bis gegen Abend Bob Dylan entgangen' (*FV* 138) ('I had escaped Bob Dylan until the evening'). Whereas in Biermann the tension is rather between the presence of the 'ich' and the figure of Dylan – they give each other plenty of room, as the spotlight does not allow both to be present – in Aichinger the autobiographical subject and the other artist share at the very most the flashes, the *Blitzlichter*, both preferring the shadows. 'Dylan kam im Halbdunkel in den Flur' ('Dylan came in the semi-darkness into the hall') – that applies just as well to Aichinger. Dylan and Aichinger escape each other. Biermann is ultimately right, however: the poetic examination of the world is, at least here, an examination of oneself. If Dylan's absence serves Biermann's presence, it also provides Aichinger with opportunities to be absent, opportunities to be neither 'me' nor 'there'.

And yet both writers are extremely present. In the '11 outlined epitaphs' Dylan portrays the action of an artist: 'I "expose" myself/every time I step out/on the stage' (*Eleven* 88). A textual hiding place may be a hiding place, but the handwriting never runs completely, just as Dylan, despite all the techniques of alienation, exposes himself with every performance – through his art. And when Biermann and Aichinger hide Dylan, they expose themselves.

But we are concerned with Bob Dylan – not with Dylan himself, but the image of Dylan in these works pre-dating the mainstream film. Biermann and Aichinger portray Dylan using the technique Biermann ascribes to Dylan himself: in all of these portrayals the presence of Bob Dylan can manifest itself only as a very conscious construction that permits an equally constructed absence.

Notes

1 *Masked and Anonymous* (2003) was directed by Larry Charles and co-written with Bob Dylan.
2 Ilse Aichinger, 'I'm glad, I'm not me – Bob Dylan', in Ilse Aichinger, *Film und Verhängnis. Blitzlichter auf ein Leben* (Frankfurt am Main: S. Fischer Taschenbuch Verlag, 2003). 137–9. Further references to this (and other journal pieces in the same collection) appear in the text as *FV* plus page number.
3 Dylan's 1964 *The Times They Are A-Changin'* presented '11 outlined epitaphs by Bob Dylan' on the back of the album cover with a continuation on an insert. Wolf Biermann translated these as *Elf Entwürfe für meinen Grabspruch* (Cologne: Kiepenheuer und Witsch, 2003). Further references to Dylan's original as it appears in Biermann's *Elf* and to Biermann's translation appear in the text as *Eleven* and *Elf*, respectively, plus page number in Biermann (2003).
4 All German-language sources appear in my English translation, with the exception of Biermann's translations from English into German and where the German wording is significant.
5 W. Biermann, *Wie man Verse macht und Lieder. Eine Poetik in acht Gängen* (Cologne: Kiepenheuer und Witsch, 1997). 11. Further references to this source appear in the text as '*VL*' plus page number.
6 My allusion is also stolen: see Wilentz (2011: 251–64; Wilentz's article first appeared in 2001 at http://www.bobdylan.com but is no longer available there). Like Detering (2007: 158–64), I am taking it for myself; after all, it comes from Dylan himself, or Eric Lott (Lott, 2009: 167–73), or someone or other.

References

Aichinger, I. (2003) 'I'm glad, I'm not me – Bob Dylan', in I. Aichinger, *Film und Verhängnis. Blitzlichter auf ein Leben* (Frankfurt am Main: S. Fischer Taschenbuch Verlag). 137–9.
Anderson, D. (1981) *The Hollow Horn: Bob Dylan's Reception in the United States and Germany* (Munich: Hobo).
Becher, J. R. (1954) 'Stalin, du Welt im Licht', in G. Caspar (ed.), *Du Welt im Licht. J. W. Stalin im Werk deutscher Schriftsteller* (Berlin (East): Aufbau). 353–5.
Biermann, W. (1997) *Wie man Verse macht und Lieder. Eine Poetik in acht Gängen* (Cologne: Kiepenheuer und Witsch).
Biermann, W. (trans.) (2003) *Elf Entwürfe für meinen Grabspruch* (Cologne: Kiepenheuer und Witsch).

Brasch, T. (1980) 'Und der Sänger Dylan in der Deutschlandhalle', in T. Brasch, *Der schöne 27. September. Gedichte* (Frankfurt am Main: Suhrkamp). 39.

Braun, V. (1990a) 'Schauspiel', in V. Braun, *Texte in zeitlicher Folge (Bd. 2. Der Hörsaal. Wir und nicht sie. Hinze und Kunze. Notate)* (Halle: Mitteldeutscher Verlag). 67.

Braun, V. (1990b) 'Wir und nicht sie', in V. Braun, *Texte in zeitlicher Folge (Bd. 2. Der Hörsaal. Wir und nicht sie. Hinze und Kunze. Notate)* (Halle: Mitteldeutscher Verlag). 70–1.

Brecht, B. (1988) 'Erinnerung an die Marie A.', in B. Brecht, *Große kommentierte Berliner und Frankfurter Ausgabe*, ed. W. Knecht, J. Knopf, W. Mittenzwei, K.-D. Müller (Bd. 11. Gedichte 1. Sammlungen 1918–38) (Frankfurt am Main: Suhrkamp/Aufbau). 92–3.

Detering, H. (2003) 'Wüste Winde heulen kalt. Transportschäden: Wolf Biermann vergreift sich an Bob Dylan', *Frankfurter Allgemeine Zeitung* (25 October). 46.

Detering, H. (2007) *Bob Dylan* (Stuttgart: Reclam).

Dylan, B. (2004) *Chronicles: Volume One* (London: Simon and Schuster).

Fehle, V. (2006) 'Blitzlichter auf ein Leben. Ilse Aichingers Erinnerungsystem der Leerstellen am Beispiel der Texte des "Journal des Verschwindens"' (Diploma thesis, University of Vienna).

Fischer, J. (2002) '"Ein unheimliches Gefühl". Außenminister Joschka Fischer über amerikanische Besatzungssoldaten und Bob Dylan, den Vietnamkrieg und seine Visionen vom künftigen Verhältnis zwischen den USA und Europa', *Der Spiegel*, issue 21 (18 May). 32–5.

Gronemeyer, H. and Hurlebusch, K. (2010) 'Sie, und nicht Wir', in *Friedrich Gottlieb Klopstock: Werke und Briefe* (Historisch-kritische Ausgabe. Abteilung Werke 1/1. Oden. Bd. 1. Texte) (Berlin: de Gruyter). 468–9.

Huchel, P. (1963) *Chausseen, Chausseen. Gedichte* (Frankfurt am Main: Fischer).

Klein, R. (2011) 'Über Sinn und Unsinn der Rede von Dylans "Masken"', in K. Theweleit (ed.), *How Does It Feel. Das Bob-Dylan-Lesebuch* (Berlin: Rowohlt). 269–74.

Köhlmeier, M. (1975) '*Like Bob Dylan*. Einakter (1973)', in M. Köhlmeier, *Like Bob Dylan. Drei im Cafe spielen. Das Anhörungsverfahren* (Bregenz: Fink's Verlag). 5–34.

Köhlmeier, M. (1999) 'Königsschach', in M. Köhlmeier, *Der traurige Blick in die Weite. Geschichten von Heimatlosen* (Vienna: Deuticke). 78–82.

Lott, E. (2009) '"Love and Theft" (2001)', in K. J. H. Dettmar (ed.), *The Cambridge Companion to Bob Dylan* (Cambridge: Cambridge University Press). 167–73.

Moser, S. (1996) 'Ein leiser Wind. Über die Gegenwart Ilse Aichingers', in F. Cercignani and E. Agazzi (eds), *Studia Austriaca. Ilse Aichinger* (Milan: Editione Minute). 9–20.

Nüchtern, K. (2010) 'Die Schrammeln, der Jazz und die Neue Musik. Über Musikalisches in "Abendland"', in U. Längle and J. Thaler (eds), *Michael Köhlmeiers 'Abendland'. Fünf Studien* (Innsbruck: Studienverlag). 53–66.

Price, K. M. (2006) *To Walt Whitman, America* (Chapel Hill, NC: University of North Carolina Press).

Schimank, U. (2002) *Das zwiespältige Individuum. Zum Person-Gesellschaft-Arrangement der Moderne* (Opladen: Leske und Budrich).

Scorsese, M. (2005) *No Direction Home* (Paramount), DVD-Video.

Wilentz, S. (2011) 'American Recordings: Über Love and Theft und die Figur des "Minstrel Boy"', in K. Theweleit (ed.), *How Does It Feel. Das Bob-Dylan-Lesebuch* (Berlin: Rowohlt). 251–64.

Winkler, W. (2003) 'Poetenbestialisch berauscht. Wolf Biermann schleppt Bob Dylans Grabsteine ins Deutsche', *Süddeutsche Zeitung* (Literatur) (6 October). 19.

Part III

Who is not there

6

Bob Dylan's protean style

Ben Giamo

Here, there and elsewhere

In Martin Scorsese's 2005 documentary film *No Direction Home*, Dylan, in present time, likens his career to an odyssey undertaken by a 'musical expeditionary'. 'I was born very far from where I'm supposed to be, and so I'm on my way home'. For Dylan, home was never a fixed place that existed back in time. The vacancy of the upper mid-west of the United States and, in particular, the rural remoteness of Hibbing, Minnesota, where Dylan was raised, served as a point of departure. Dylan's odyssey never called him back to reclaim lost time. If he returns anywhere, it is to an abiding sense of openness and indeterminacy, a return not to what is stable and familiar – a homecoming – but to possibility, to reinvention, to the contention between being and becoming. In part, Dylan's quest has been an existential one – wilful, uncanny, wondrous.

Todd Haynes's 2007 film *I'm Not There* is very much attuned to the transformations in Dylan's odyssey. To foreground Dylan's protean style as an artist and performer, six actors portray various personas over the course of his career. This postmodern construction, employed willy-nilly throughout the film through intensive cross-cutting, privileges fluidity, rupture and multiplicity in order to refract the breadth and flux of a long creative life. The cinema viewer, somewhat unhinged by such kaleidoscopic time-tripping, leaves the theatre with a renewed appreciation for Dylan's many selves, stylistic innovations and remarkable knack for turning his work and image into a compelling aesthetic object, time and again.

The existential struggle between being and becoming is unwittingly signalled in the very opening of Haynes's film. As the credits roll, Dylan's 'Stuck Inside of Mobile with the Memphis Blues Again' plays off-screen. It seems like the perfect road song to accompany the jumbled, chopped-up narrative and chaotic structure of the film. But, as the title indicates, one is stuck inside the very medium of mobility. To complicate matters, the song begins and ends on the Bowery – Skid Row – the very symbol of entrapment. This circular structure signals repetition, defeat, the *alpha* and *omega* of the self's surrealistic rambling, which occurs in parenthesis. As much as Haynes is attuned to Dylan's transformations, his movie does not provide a commentary to this dialectic, nor to the undertow of Dylan's *oeuvre*, and so we get only the surface appeal of the shape-shifting artist. We get the myth and mobility of Dylan unstuck in time and place. We get his penchant for seeking freedom and liberation without any nod to constraint, that is, to the notion that 'but for the sky there are no fences facin'' (Dylan, 2004a: 152).

The result is not without its entertainment. Marcus Carl Franklin, a youthful black minstrel in the guise of Woody Guthrie, starts the mythology rolling, hopping freight trains, befriending hobos and working the carny circuit. It is the late 1950s but this vagabond harkens back to the Dust Bowl and Great Depression. Haynes treats this embodiment of Woody imaginatively, effectively symbolising Dylan's pattern of death and rebirth by a scene in which the kid gets pushed off a box car and falls underwater; a whale appears and swallows him whole. He will never be the same again. From the Guthrie persona to folk protest singer to amplified popular artist (in the best sense) to country western balladeer to born-again Christian to infidel to celebrity to mystic drifter, the film moves back and forth among all these varied personas.

Like the Woody segments, Ben Whishaw, who plays Dylan à la Rimbaud, serves as the go-to man in the film, seated in an interrogation room, answering questions with poetic wit and wisdom. The grainy black and white film used during these exchanges heightens the atmosphere and sense of Dylan as trickster artiste. It also cleverly presents Dylan's own sense of theatre in re-enacting Rimbaud's aesthetic proposition 'Je est un autre', or 'I is another'. To round out the successful portrayals, Richard Gere plays Mr B, a popular Western outlaw modelled after Billy the Kid, thus evoking Dylan's music from the late 1960s to the early 1970s (*John Wesley Harding, Nashville Skyline, New Morning, The Basement Tapes*) and his minor role as Alias in Sam Peckinpah's *Pat Garrett and Billy the Kid* (1973).

Dylan's protean style appears most effective when cast imaginatively. For instance, Mr B lives in a new frontier that conflates the vanquished Wild West with a contemporary rural town faced with the problem of an impending six-lane highway tearing through the countryside. On occasion, the forested hillsides flash with the firestorms raging in the jungles of Vietnam to bring us back to the formative late 1960s. In Fellini style, the characters from Dylan's songs come to life – yes, even a man on stilts, a camel and circus freaks like the sword swallower. Mr B is locked up for his opposition to the road plan but, of course, he is eventually sprung from the jailhouse of identity and regains his freedom.

The less effective aspects of the style are those that attempt verisimilitude to Dylan and his times. Christian Bale plays Jack Rollins to capture Dylan in his initial public role as folk protest singer. Later, he will morph into Pastor John to characterise Dylan's born-again Christian period. Neither simulacrum adds anything to what we already know about Dylan. Similarly, Heath Ledger plays an actor named Robbie, though Robbie is a stand-in for Dylan as celebrity rock star. This leaves us with Jude Quinn, portrayed brilliantly by Cate Blanchett, who represents Dylan during his appearance at Newport in 1965 and throughout his 1966 European tour, when he launched an aesthetic revolt by turning on the juice. Jude is the most iconic image of Dylan presented in the film, and Blanchett incarnates this surreal phase of Dylan perfectly, including the look, mannerisms, gestures and animated performance style.

Haynes does not really account for Dylan's dictum that an artist is always in a state of becoming. Postmodern ethics trump any genuine attempt to account for a particular transition, which always contains a measure of visionary crisis. The soundtrack to the film, comprising Dylan's own renditions and covers by contemporary musicians, never really points to development. The music simply reflects what has been attained. For instance, by pairing 'Where Are You Tonight? (Journey Through Dark Heat)' – the last track from *Street-Legal* (1978) – with 'Precious Angel' – the second cut from Dylan's next recording, *Slow Train Coming* (1979) – one would hear the very process of change (and profound spiritual awakening) experienced by Dylan. In the former song, Dylan sings in desperation, wondering not only about the whereabouts of his beloved but, through her, about the loss of his grip on the divine itself. The song and his pleading voice register his forlornness. In contrast, the latter song reveals regeneration, which you can hear clearly both in the content of the song and in his rejuvenated sound (music and voice). (Between the two songs, and their respective albums, Dylan converted to Christianity and joined the New Age evangelical Vineyard Christian Fellowship in California.) According to Robert Jay Lifton, proteanism

> involves a quest for authenticity and meaning, a form-seeking assertion of self.... The protean self seeks to be both fluid and grounded, however tenuous that combination. There is nothing automatic about the enterprise, no 'greening of the self', but rather a continuous effort without clear termination. Proteanism, then, is a balancing act between responsive shapeshifting, on the one hand, and efforts to consolidate and cohere, on the other. (Lifton, 1993: 9)

Haynes may present Dylan's various personas and fractured artistic selves to viewers, but he never seriously explains the disorientation that is part and parcel of Dylan's own self-process. Transformation is not simply killing off one Dylan and then moving on to the next. It is a dialectical art that includes a sense of reintegration as well, 'a lifetime burning in every moment', to borrow a line from T. S. Eliot – an art Dylan practices to this very day in his tireless expedition to find out where he is supposed to be. Perhaps this is why the most riveting moment in the film is the final image, in which the actual Dylan is shown, circa 1965, playing the long, rapturous harmonica solo to 'Mr. Tambourine Man'. It is a fitting ending, for it shows the musical poet under the spell of his own trance, at one with the muse, being transported – being there.

A new template

Dylan has made many decisive moves throughout his musical career. The first was right after arriving in Dinkytown, the campus district surrounding the University of Minnesota in Minneapolis, when he traded in his electric guitar for a double-O Martin acoustic. (He would soon add the harmonica mounted on a rack around his neck.) Rather than making any statement about radical individualism, this exchange simply signalled Dylan's youthful pragmatism. The trade removed the need for cumbersome equipment and band members. While a teenager at Hibbing High School, Dylan had formed several bands, such as the Golden Chords, which played early rock'n'roll music. (Picture a young Bobby Zimmerman pounding on the piano like Little Richard.) Playing electric rock music involved a costly investment. And, to make matters worse, band members were always leaving him to form other groups. It was not a practical enterprise. In a 1965 interview with Joseph Hass for the *Chicago Daily News*, Dylan replied that he didn't go into the folk music venue because it offered a better vehicle for 'making it': 'You couldn't make it livable back then with rock'n'roll. You couldn't carry around an amplifier and electric guitar and expect to survive, it was just too much of a hangup.... I didn't go into folk music to make any money, but because it was easy. You could be by yourself, you didn't need anybody. All you needed was a guitar' (see Cott, 2006: 56).

Stripped down to the essentials, he landed in Dinkytown's folk scene in 1959. The first time someone asked him his name, he responded without hesitation: 'Bob Dylan'. At eighteen years old, the initial reinvention was underway. Soon, the formative folk influences began to pile up: Odetta, Leadbelly, the New Lost City Ramblers, rural blues – precursors to Muddy Waters and Howlin' Wolf, John Jacob Niles and, most notably, Woody Guthrie, whose work Dylan would inhabit for a couple of years until he worked through him. Upon arriving in the Bohemian enclave of Manhattan's Greenwich Village in late January 1961, a few months before turning twenty, Dylan visited Guthrie on a regular basis at Greystone Hospital in Morristown, New Jersey. At this time, Dylan was struggling to distinguish himself as an interpreter and stylist of traditional music amid the competitive Village folk-revival circuit of clubs, coffee shops and basket houses. He was not yet a singer–songwriter, but simply a folk singer who transported himself to other eras, such as the Great Depression, and into a mythic realm of archetypal figures – in his own words, 'a culture with outlaw women, super thugs, demon lovers and gospel truths ... streets and valleys, rich peaty swamps, with landowners and oilmen, Stagger Lees, Pretty Pollys and John Henrys' (Dylan, 2004b: 236). Soon after landing in New York City, and for a good while afterward, it did not even occur to him to write his own songs, nor to reflect upon the realities of his own times.

Dylan hints at the process of self-discovery in his memoir, *Chronicles*. At a farewell party hosted by Camilla Adams for terminally ill Cisco Houston, who had been part of the Weavers with Pete Seeger, Dylan spots Mike Seeger, Pete's half-brother, standing among the crowd – a virtual who's who of the folk movement. It was a defining moment for Dylan as he recalled previously hearing Mike play at Alan Lomax's loft on a couple of occasions. Dylan refers to Mike Seeger as being an accomplished and gifted musician.

> He played all the instruments, whatever the song called for – the banjo, the fiddle, mandolin, autoharp, and the guitar, even harmonica in the rack.... He played ... the full index of the old-time styles, played in all the genres and had the idioms mastered – Delta blues, ragtime, minstrel songs, buck-and-wing, dance reels, play party, hymns and gospel – being there and seeing him up close, something hit me. It's not as if he played these songs well, he played these songs as good as it was possible to play them. (Dylan, 2004b: 70)

Awed, Dylan realised that Mike Seeger had the whole folk music world in the very structure of his DNA. How does one compete with genetic inheritance? 'Before he was even born', Dylan remarks, 'this music had to be in his blood. Nobody could just learn this stuff' (Dylan, 2004b: 71). But rather than incite resignation, or misguided rivalry, this led to an epiphany. Dylan glimpsed right then and there that he might have to change tracks and do something entirely different rather than try to emulate what he simply could not, and it 'dawned on me that I might have to change my inner thought patterns ... that I would have to start believing in possibilities that I wouldn't have allowed before, that I had been closing my creativity down to a very narrow, controllable scale ... that things had become too familiar and I might have to disorientate myself' (Dylan, 2004b: 71).

What Dylan perceived intuitively at that moment when he glimpsed a 'jump into the unknown' might be construed as defamiliarisation, a deliberate and reflective process of leading one self to the end of the line and bringing another self into being – a new beginning. In 'It's Alright, Ma', his scathing critique of American consumer society and its conformist strictures, Dylan would sing the lyric: 'He not busy being born is busy dying' (Dylan, 2004a: 156). In 1976, Jimmy Carter would quote that line during his acceptance speech after being elected the thirty-ninth president of the United States, thus turning the very mantra of proteanism from a personal claim to the task of renewing the nation itself after Vietnam and Watergate. Back in 1961, however, this was all unknown, but the seed had been planted. 'The thought occurred to me', Dylan recalls, 'that maybe I'd have to write my own folk songs, ones that Mike didn't know. That was a startling thought' (Dylan, 2004b: 71). It is startling precisely because of the uncertainty as well as the possibilities surrounding it. Dylan likens this process to opening a door into a dark room that has been rearranged, and you do not know what you are going to find until you actually step inside. Dylan comments: 'If I wanted to stay playing music ... I would have to claim a larger part of myself.... My consciousness was beginning to change ... change and stretch. One thing for sure, if I wanted to compose folk songs I would need some kind of new template, some philosophical identity that wouldn't burn out.... Without knowing it in so many words, it was beginning to happen' (Dylan, 2004b: 72–3). Dylan had unwittingly stumbled upon a generative template to confer multiple identities – the protean style – and he has employed it ever since without outstaying his welcome.

It did not take long for Dylan to amass a body of work. By the summer of 1962, he had nearly two dozen songs composed. Some of his earliest compositions were in the Guthrie talking blues style, such as the sardonic 'Talkin' Bear Mountain Picnic Massacre Blues' and the humorous 'Talkin' New York', as well as the wistful tribute to his mentor, 'Song to Woody'. The last two songs would be the only originals on Dylan's first eponymous album, recorded in November 1961, which consisted mainly of folk interpretations. In fact, on his debut album Dylan is introduced to the public as 'one of the most compelling white blues singers ever recorded' (sleeve notes to the *Bob Dylan* album, 1962). His placement as a new voice in the country blues tradition highlights his knack for assimilation and ability to breathe new life into tried and true forms. The blues verge to black, as Dylan's somewhat melodramatic and highly mannered world weariness resonates strongly in such songs as 'In My Time of Dyin'', 'Man of Constant Sorrow', 'Fixin' to Die' and 'See That My Grave Is Kept Clean'. These were all impressive renditions, especially his appropriation of Dave Van Ronk's arrangement of 'House of the Risin' Sun'.

As a folk interpreter, Dylan attained a mastery of his craft between April and October 1962. At the Gaslight, the premier folk club in New York City, he performed first drafts of his own songs, such as 'A Hard Rain's A-Gonna Fall' and 'Don't Think Twice, It's All Right', humming in places to fill in the void of lines yet to be written, along with rural blues and Anglo-American ballads like 'Rocks and Gravel', 'The Cuckoo', 'Moonshiner' and 'Barbara Allen'. He was emerging into a folk singer–songwriter. His second album, *The Freewheelin' Bob Dylan*, comprised all original songs except for one. This remarkable album, released in 1963, brought the young Dylan (at twenty-two years of age) both popularity and critical acclaim. In a very short time, he had managed to 'change and stretch', adopting the new template to achieve astonishing results.

The blend of civil rights and anti-war songs on *Freewheelin'* (continued on his third album, *The Times They Are A-Changin'*, 1964) announced Dylan to America as a protest singer and folk prophet. The integration of voice, lyrics and music in the recording gives ample proof of this rebellious artistic and cultural position, reinforced by the James Dean-like image of cool on the album cover. However, as indicated by the liner notes to the album, penned by journalist Nat Hentoff, the imprint of this persona captured in song and image is at best provisional. If proteanism is an existential mandate – a personal way of life – it is also a branding mechanism, a means to further ends, enticing listeners to stay tuned for future developments. The notes state: 'In these performances, there is already a marked change from his first album ... and there will surely be many further dimensions of Dylan to come.... This album, in sum, is the protean Bob Dylan as of the time of the recording. By the next recording, there will be more new songs and insights and experiences. Dylan can't stop searching and looking and reflecting upon what he sees and hears'. Authenticity and novelty appear to go hand in hand, reminding us that the artistic value and moralistic merits of the work are embedded within a matrix of consumption. Accordingly, reinvention is both the process and product required to rise above the din in the marketplace of cultural expression. Thus it is that cultural radicalism and consumer capitalism meet up in uneasy yet mutually beneficial congress.

This is not to suggest that Dylan's brand of proteanism is a facile manipulation. Clearly, it is not. Dylan has repeatedly immersed himself in the flux of experience throughout his career, and like Charlie Chaplin's tireless worker in his 1936 film *Modern Times*, Dylan keeps entering the inner workings of the machine, always coming out at the other end, landing on his feet to sing the tale – to 'tell it and speak it and think it and breathe it'. And though Dylan prefers to 'reflect from the mountain so all souls can see it' (Dylan, 2004a: 60), the fact is that, however noble and prophetic such a stance is artistically, the result is pressed in vinyl and sold in stores. In short, what we are dealing with is an empowered romantic vision rendered variously over the years, operating culturally at the level of rebel fantasy world, managed by a savvy business enterprise, contracted to a record company and turned into a cultural product that's sold internationally. This is the course of art, protean or otherwise, in an age of mass-mediated mechanical (and electronic) reproduction. Any blue-eyed son today would have to abide by the same conditions and make the best of it, working within the matrix to reach a mass audience.

Cultural radicalism

Dylan's knowledge of traditional music and his knack for juggling with new combinations, the hallmark of proteanism, enabled him to make the breakthrough with *Freewheelin'*. As he recalled in *Chronicles*, 'What I did to break away was to take simple folk changes and put new imagery and attitude to them, use catchphrase and metaphor combined with a new set of ordinances that evolved into something different that had not been heard before' (Dylan, 2004b: 67). In doing so, his songs expressed both an insistent individualism and a collective awareness. Dylan advanced his persona as prophetic folk rebel, the voice of social conscience and the incarnation of dissent, in his next album – *The Times They Are A-Changin'* (released in 1964). Clearly aligning himself with the oppressed in this recording, Dylan aimed to capture the *Zeitgeist* of the movement and sound the alarm by gathering listeners around his songs, drawing boundaries between generations, con- textualising racism in the South, decrying social and economic injustice, and signalling hope and triumph. In the poetic liner notes to the album, which Dylan titled '11 outlined epitaphs', he states frankly, 'I am on the side of the hurt feelings'. And, adhering to his prophetic role, he admits: 'yes it is I/who is poundin' at your door'. Together, *Freewheelin'* and *The Times* stoked Dylan's early persona as protest singer and moral witness, an artist in a line extending back to Pete Seeger and Woody Guthrie, remnants of the Old Left and Cultural Front of the 1930s.

No singer–songwriter was more relevant to the times than Dylan in the early to mid-1960s. As the times changed, so did his persona, lyric, style and sound. Turning against his previous moral absolutism, and refusing to be a poster boy for the Old Left for very long, he produced another album in 1964, entitled *Another Side of Bob Dylan*. This was a transitional album that paved the way for his transformation from folk protest singer to confrontational rock poet. (Evidently, he had entered another dark room, feeling his way around the signs of personal meaning and value.) Rather than acting out mythic allegories on a political landscape, he employed *Another Side* to register a wholesale 'mutiny from stern to bow'. Accordingly, most of the songs on this recording take a momentary reading of his restless palms. As Ellen Willis so rightly observed, 'For Guthrie, the road was habitat; for Dylan, metaphor' (Willis, 1972: 227). Dylan mines the metaphors of personal authenticity in this album with a more expansive poetic language, finally shedding Guthrie's activist anxiety of influence and opting instead for the stance of artist, pure and simple. Most of the songs here are by turn witty, ironic, plaintive, wary, confessional and introspective. And the liner notes that accompany the album, advertised as 'some other kinds of songs – poems by Bob Dylan', appear more elliptical, suggesting that a new persona is in the making.

Concluding his notes for *Freewheelin'*, Hentoff stated that Dylan was a 'young man growing free rather than absurd'. Ironically, in 1965 and 1966

Dylan would blend freedom and absurdity into the romantic nihilism of *Bringing It All Back Home*, *Highway 61 Revisited* and *Blonde on Blonde*. The electric trilogy, embracing the escalating absurdity and chaos of America, encapsulated a sense of cultural displacement associated with the transition from JFK's New Frontier to LBJ's Great Society, the latter undermined by assassinations, a divisive war, race riots, student unrest and the burgeoning counter-culture. Dylan's metamorphosis from folk protest singer to amplified popular artist underscored the values of personal liberation and empowerment. As such, his new urban hipster persona not only embodied cultural change but also functioned as the avant-garde for an entire youth culture that would follow in his wake. Dylan turns up the volume and experiments with ambiguity, paradox, confusion, the pop netherworld and the dramatic complexity of the self. In the liner notes to *Bringing It All Back Home*, Dylan tips off his audience: 'I accept chaos. I am not sure whether it accepts me.' The chaos of the era formed the very music, voice and subject matter of Dylan's art, which in the liner notes he likens to poems 'written in a rhythm of unpoetic distortion/divided by pierced ears. false eyelashes/subtracted by people constantly torturing each other. with a melodic purring line of descriptive hollowness – seen at times through dark sunglasses an' other forms of psychic explosion. a song is anything that can walk by itself/i am called a songwriter. a poem is a naked person … some people say that i am a poet'. With this complete change in image and sound, Dylan charted a new course. Through the marriage of Western modernism, poetry and folk rock – ever attuned to the vibrations of the times – he created an altered state for both himself and the 1960s.

Bringing It All Back Home propels Dylan into his new, more self-reflexive persona and style. On the album cover, Dylan, sporting a dark jacket and a high-collared shirt with French cuffs, appears seated in the foreground of a couch in a cramped living room like the Rimbaud of American pop art. Holding a cat, and surrounded by record albums and magazines – the contemporary signs of popular culture (including a cover of *Time* featuring LBJ), he stares serious and sullen into the lens of Daniel Kramer's camera. In the background, right in front of the fireplace, the lady in red reclines on the same divan, mimicking the posture of a goddess in plaster relief on the decorative mantelpiece. She provides colour and contrast, and along with her upheld cigarette, angular posture and blank stare, seems the very image of impervious beauty. Kramer's photograph is carefully composed and aesthetically wrought, an apt visual suggestion of the musical artefacts to be found on the album.

Dylan's voice, so prominent during his folk period, now emerges from within the revved up sound itself. In the amplified tracks such as 'Subterranean Homesick Blues', 'Maggie's Farm', 'Outlaw Blues' and 'On the Road Again', the listener hears a popping electric guitar, pronounced drumbeat, strong bass line and strident harmonica in rollicking counterpoise.

The voice itself – rapid, witty and sarcastic – seems like another instrument integrated into the music. Throughout, Dylan exchanges the communitarian and egalitarian values of folk revival for the heightened posture of radical individualism. Embracing the role of oppositional artist, the lyrics are more cynical and nihilistic – the synthesis of myriad influences, including Jean Genet's theatre of the absurd, the alienating effects of Bertolt Brecht's epic theatre and Arthur Rimbaud's dense symbolism. Clearly, and in combination with the acoustic tracks, such as 'Mr. Tambourine Man', 'Gates of Eden' and 'It's Alright, Ma (I'm Only Bleeding)', Dylan raises innovation and rebellion to a new level, pushing nonconformity to an extreme that leaves its high-water mark in the album *Highway 61 Revisited* (especially in songs such as 'Like a Rolling Stone' and 'Desolation Row').

The Beats also seem to be under the eaves of *Bringing It All Back Home*. Kerouac provides the speed – the breathless spontaneous prosody – and Ginsberg furnishes the spectre of post-war social critique embodied in the biblical god Moloch. Dylan runs with it, incorporating the Beats' submerged and subversive perspective, setting his vision and sound against a broader social canvas updated for the turbulent 1960s. In both his electric and acoustic songs, Dylan derails conventional viewpoints, constructing a notion of 'home' as refuge for the self. The change in persona and style is complete, and so too the morphing of direct topical protest into broad social critique. Though the form has changed, becoming more complex and discordant, the underlying structure remains the same: the strident sound of dissent.

The vivid, telltale signs of personal change are apparent in the last cut of the album, 'It's All Over Now, Baby Blue'. On one level, the song can be viewed as a form of self-address that expresses the dislocation accompanying the process of change (deconstructing and reconstructing the self). In that liminal stage, where one is truly neither here nor there, Dylan's weird, topsy-turvy perspective is apparent and apt: 'The empty-handed painter from your streets/Is drawing crazy patterns on your sheets/This sky, too, is folding under you/And it's all over now, Baby Blue'. Once the protean process has run its course and a new incarnation of the self settles into being, Dylan can put old matters to an end and leave the past behind, but for one last glimpse of that iconic folk protest image he once inhabited:

> Leave your stepping stones behind, something calls for you
> Forget the dead you've left, they will not follow you
> The vagabond who's rapping at your door
> Is standing in the clothes that you once wore
> Strike another match, go start anew
> And it's all over now, Baby Blue.
> (Dylan, 2004a: 159)

Though understandably blue from facing the loss of what once existed, and is now gone, in the flux of time, there is no doubt about how to proceed.

By striking another match, we ignite something else. As an artist, Dylan insists on looking ahead, lighting out for new territory until he reaches that last outpost at the world's end. 'Change of identity is a way of "seeing around the corner".... Such changes of identity occur in everyone. They become acute when a person has been particularly scrupulous in forming himself about one set of coordinates, so scrupulous that the shift to new co-ordinates requires a violent wrenching of his earlier categories' (Burke, 1984: 269). Burke's insight is especially pertinent in view of Dylan's dissociation from folk protest after he plugged in. In fact, during his 1965 San Francisco press conference (at KQED Studios on 3 December) he caricatured the folk movement as 'a constitutional replay of mass production'. Going electric enabled Dylan to be exuberant, rambling and spontaneous – to shift coordinates from 'finger-pointing songs' to frenzied social commentary with a blend of voice, lyric and sound unprecedented in American popular music.

'Like a Rolling Stone', the opening number of *Highway 61 Revisited*, kicks in with a vengeance, adding a screeching Hammond organ to the mix, clearly announcing that Dylan is now in his own orbit artistically. Along with the other tracks on the album, such as 'Tombstone Blues', 'Ballad of a Thin Man' and the title song, Dylan is venting the hostility, aggression and surrealism filtered out of folk music. In doing so, he expresses an attitude, a hip sneer. At times, his voice is full of bite, snarl and insinuation. But it is more complicated than that, for even in a harsh song such as 'Like a Rolling Stone', in which he chides someone who has taken a steep fall from social privilege and must now confront the naked realities of survival on the streets without any 'secrets to conceal', the refrain – 'How does it feel' – is tinged with pathos, as if he is singing beyond the object of chastisement to a whole generation cut loose from the secure trajectory of tradition. In a way, then, this song is a new kind of confrontational anthem for the unmooring of an entire counter-culture during the tumultuous mid to late 1960s. Perhaps the best acoustic example of this new 'set of coordinates' is 'Desolation Row', a *Götterdämmerung* ushering the Western pantheon of mythic, fictional and real heroes down into the underworld, where everyone is altered for the worse. One can also hear this reorientation throughout the next album, *Blonde on Blonde*, especially in 'One of Us Must Know', 'Stuck Inside of Mobile with the Memphis Blues Again' and 'Absolutely Sweet Marie'.

The integration of a new persona and aesthetic style attained in the electric trilogy clinched Dylan's assertion of authenticity and emotional subjectivity that defied simple folk sincerity. According to this more protean version, the self is seen as an experimental realm of possibility to explore. Therefore, the authentic person aims to pass beyond him- or herself, not simply to exist as a static entity: the self must be envisioned and created, not merely mined. And such a process always occurs within a distinct social context. Dylan's transformation was prescient, for it embodied the changing times and confirmed that rock'n'roll set the tone and terms for the cultural radicalism of the 1960s. Dylan was perceived by members of this generation as the seminal artist of the era. As such, he provided them with a cognitive map of cultural radicalism, a recalibrated moral compass, an edge without ideology and a soundtrack that could be heard in all the nooks and crannies of those who were decidedly anti-establishment – on the road to a new America. Of course, for Dylan this was provisional. His motorcycle accident in July 1966 catapulted him into a prolonged state of abeyance. Although he would never be the same again, his protean style would persist throughout the next four decades, propelling him forward to redefining the method and meaning of popular music.

Tangled up in motives

Throughout his career, Dylan's proteanism has served an existential imperative, fulfilling the Sartrean maxim that existence precedes essence. This has been Dylan's *modus vivendi*. Like anyone else, Dylan has experienced profound changes during his lifetime (perhaps accelerated at times). Yet being an artist – a 'musical expeditionary' – Dylan has used such upheavals to serve his musical art, making theatre out of this personal process of transformation, appearing and vanishing and reappearing into his various artistic forms and public images over the past fifty years. No doubt, the existential thrust towards becoming has sparked his many transitions, including his remarkable late period, marked by the release of *Time Out of Mind* in 1997 and continuing through *"Love and Theft"* (2001), *Modern Times* (2006), *Together Through Life* (2009) and *Tempest* (2012). Therefore, the protean style integrates both existential and aesthetic motives. In keeping with Pound's injunction, and from the beginning of his career to this day, Dylan has consistently made it new. His gifts – genius if you will – were spotted early on by Ellen Willis: 'as composer, interpreter, most of all as lyricist, Dylan has made a revolution. He expanded folk idiom into a rich, figurative language, grafted literary and philosophical subtleties onto the protest song, revitalized folk vision by rejecting proletarian and ethnic sentimentality, then all but destroyed pure folk as a contemporary form by merging it with pop. Since then rock-and-roll … has been transformed' (Willis, 1972: 220–1). As we know, Dylan did not stop there but has worked with a variety of musical forms: blues, country and western, gospel, jazz and traditional folk songs. And, of course, Dylan has always been interested in new combinations that merge poetry with song, not simply retaining the past, but – as Sean Wilentz notes in his book *Bob Dylan in America* – singing 'the present out of the past' (Wilentz, 2010: 302).

Yet it would be naïve to suppose that economic motives were not entangled with personal and aesthetic ones. From the very beginning, economic considerations were part and parcel of Dylan's predilection for reinventing himself. The early branding of Dylan as a protean artist is a case in point. Also, proteanism became a reliable vehicle with which to corner the market on novelty and thereby rise to the top in an intensely competitive industry and consumer-driven society. Over the decades, fame, celebrity and the cult of self fuelled the economic motive. Even so, Dylan's enigmatic legend lives on so stubbornly that historian Douglas Brinkley refers to him in a *Rolling Stone* interview as 'our great American poet of drifting', the personification of Whitman's open road (Brinkley, 2009: 48). But whereas Whitman might have proclaimed, 'Look for me loafing upon these leaves of grass', Dylan must respond, 'Search for me on the second-floor suite of the Amsterdam Intercontinental Hotel'. The meaning of the road itself has altered enormously, making it all the more difficult to discern the 'divine things more beautiful than words can tell' (Whitman, 2009: 322). For, on Whitman's road, rough prizes supplanted smooth ones: 'You shall not heap up what is called riches, / You shall scatter with lavish hand all that you earn or achieve' (Whitman, 2009: 323). Surely, things have changed.

According to the Recording Industry Association of America, Dylan has sold more than 35 million albums in the United States alone. He has been constantly touring since 1988, performing on average 100 shows per year. In the first decade of the millennium, he moved more than 3.7 million concert tickets and grossed over $192 million (Jurgensen, 2010). Dylan's music has enriched us all, but his own enrichment has been fabulous. At the low end, Dylan's net worth is estimated at $80 million; at the high end, $200 million (Sounes, 2001: 381, 411, 423–4). In the twelve years up to 2014, his music (and in a couple of instances his person as well) appeared in television advertising for the following companies: Apple Inc., Victoria's Secret, iTunes, Bank of Montreal, Cadillac Escalade and the Co-operative Group. A spokesman for Sony, the parent company of Columbia Records (Dylan's long-time record company), stated: '[Dylan] has a career based on surprising people, on people not being able to second guess him. He continues to embrace change in music' (Clements, 2009). Needless to say, proteanism is used here as a convenient explanation for a formidable economic impetus. The fact that it is wrapped up in a personal and aesthetic framework only reinforces the notion that the protean style is tangled up in motives.

In contemplating this entanglement, one is reminded that, during the 1960s, personal nonconformity by musical artists usurped the role of large-scale revolt. Cultural rebellion trumped social revolution. The cathartic expression of cultural radicalism may very well cause an altered state of consciousness (that is, a reframing of meaning, significance and lifestyle), but it never penetrates the core of economic and political power and the structures of inequality maintained by this insulated alliance. Cultural radicalism may push the First Amendment to its limits, circulating liberating forms of personal expression, but this does not necessarily translate into effective social movements. Subversive songs of freedom and empowerment seem to float above the enactment of fundamental change. In America today, cultural production – especially contemporary popular music – can be viewed as the new opiate of the masses. It seems that everything – even the most outrageous artistic or cultural achievement – is likely to end up in a TV advertisement. Like clockwork, the products of cultural radicalism get absorbed, processed and incorporated into American consumer capitalism. This co-optation is the new matrix: the neoliberal corporate Moloch of our postindustrial age. Working pragmatically from within the matrix, Dylan stands as the pre-eminent musical artist of our time. Yet, in the end, as in the beginning, one wonders: was he the shill or the con itself? The answer is blowing in the wind.

References

Brinkley, D. (2009) 'Bob Dylan's America', *Rolling Stone* (14 May). 43–9.

Burke, K. (1984) *Attitudes Toward History* (3rd edition) (Berkeley, CA: University of California Press).

Clements, J. (2009) 'Has Bob Dylan sold out? The answer is blowin' in the wind', *MailOnline* (28 January), at http://www.dailymail.co.uk (accessed 13 March 2014).

Cott, J. (ed.) (2006) *Dylan on Dylan: The Essential Interviews* (New York: Wenner Books).

Dylan, B. (2004a) *Lyrics, 1962–2001* (New York: Simon and Schuster).

Dylan, B. (2004b) *Chronicles: Volume One* (New York: Simon and Schuster).

Jurgensen, J. (2010) 'The no longer freewheelin' Bob Dylan: when to leave the stage', *Wall Street Journal* (3 December). D1–2.

Lifton, R. J. (1993) *The Protean Self: Human Resilience in an Age of Fragmentation* (Chicago, IL: University of Chicago Press).

Sounes, H. (2001) *Down the Highway: The Life of Bob Dylan* (New York: Grove Press).

Whitman, W. (2009) 'Poem of the road', in *Leaves of Grass, 1860* (Iowa City, IA: University of Iowa Press). 315–28.

Wilentz, S. (2010) *Bob Dylan in America* (New York: Doubleday).

Willis, E. (1972) 'Dylan', in C. McGregor (ed.), *Bob Dylan: A Retrospective* (New York: William Morrow and Company). 218–39.

7

'I don't believe you … you're a liar': the fabulatory function of Bob Dylan

Rob Coley

> do not create anything. it will be
> misinterpreted. it will not change
> …
> beware of bathroom walls that've not
> been written on. when told t'look at
> yourself … never look. when asked
> t'give your real name … never give it.
> (Bob Dylan, 1964)

No success like failure

It is dusk and the moon is already visible. People saunter in front of a large tent, partially lit by a web of lights that glimmer against the darkness of woods lying in the distance. Also in the sky is a man. Sporting Wayfarer shades and a tousled nest of hair, he flutters in the breeze like a kite, or balloon, his ankle tethered and secured by cord to a framework on the ground below.

Quickly, though, these images become unstable and begin to break apart. As they deform, disfigure and blister – the atomic solidity of the film emulsion from which they are projected rapidly dissipating – a voice proclaims: 'The only natural things are dreams, which nature cannot touch with decay.' And then … nothing. White light. Silence.

The scene, of course, is from Todd Haynes's film *I'm Not There* (2007), one of many scenes that allude to Fellini's *8½* (1963). The voice recounts words, almost exactly, that were spoken by Bob Dylan in an interview with Robert Shelton in 1966. And behind the voice, the shuffling, doleful song that gives the film its title is one previously heard only through bootleg recordings – copied, traded and passed from person to person. But to the audience at the Rialto cinema, where I first saw the movie, none of this mattered. For us, the sight of Cate Blanchett's Dylan-iteration, Jude Quinn, swaying in the monochrome evening's currents of air was the last image of the night: the film had melted in the projector.

For this audience, the screen's archival web of connections was more than just intertextual. The 'Dylan image' – constituted only in part by the film itself – was shown to function through a set of forces which escape boundaries of representation and resonate through a distributed assemblage of bodies. Despite being revealed by a 'failed' screening (in which the film narrative was prematurely aborted), the non-representational image of Dylan exhibited its performative power: it melts away the myth, it dissolves the fixity and coherency of a figure thoroughly circumscribed by the forces of history.

To explore this idea we will call in again at the Rialto later on; first, though, we need to consider what is at stake. This means avoiding the familiar temptation to pore over lyrics. It also means shifting the focus away from Dylan as an individual. Instead, it is necessary to consider the idea of performance more broadly, namely, as a performance in which we, his fans and critics, are equal players. This exploration will be assisted by calling upon what Henri Bergson and Gilles Deleuze have called 'fabulation', a concept which can be understood to operate in two modes, as two different aesthetics, two different ways of perceiving the world. Broadly, these can be described as, on the one hand, an 'intellectual' mode, functioning as the oft-cited Dylan myth, and, on the other, an activity that is more intuitive, a process which I will call the Dylan *mythos*.

In the Dylan myth, the young singer–songwriter leaves behind his native Minnesota for the hotbed of political bohemianism that is Greenwich Village, a community previously home to the jazz-inspired Beat poets and, in the folk scene of the early 1960s, the site of a burgeoning counter-culture. Underlying this culture are the first stirrings of a progressive youth movement, an emergence of political energies which sets out to criticise hegemonic social values and to find new, collective alternatives. To bring home a politics of truth. Dylan, so the myth tells us, provides the initial soundtrack to this movement. His earnest ballads were anthemic, his lyrics both witty and penetrating. His were songs that announced change, not as something on its way but as something at hand – as the movement progressed from Washington Square Park to the Great March on Washington it was recognised that historical change was taking shape in the present. And yet, while the myth confirms that Dylan's creative innovations were responsible for radical transformations to popular music, it also tells us that he renounced its political force, that in contrast to the forces which came to define the decade's social revolution, Dylan abandoned politics for rock'n'roll and the sex and drugs that came with it. When he plugged in, he disconnected.

By focusing on Dylan as *mythos*, I want to tell a different story. I want to suggest that Dylan has performatively manifested a certain fabulatory politics which explicitly seize hold of otherwise repressed powers of invention. Specifically, drawing upon these powers involves dispensing with the politics of truth in favour of the potential immanent to falsity. Deleuzian fabulation understands falsity as an affirmative, experimental power which replaces a political investment in *the* world with one directed towards bringing *a* world into being. Amid the turmoil of the times, Dylan seized upon what, in Bergson's terms, we might call their 'fabulatory function', thus illustrating that while such falsity is conventionally understood to be at odds with a valid picture of the world – the world as fixed object – it can also exploit processes of worlding – it can play with something which is, itself, already false.

Big ideas, images and distorted facts

As an image, as a consequence of a certain visuality, Dylan is a performative and productive fiction. To conceive this image, we first need to distinguish a lie from a lie, a falsity from a falsity. On one level, of course, 'Bob Dylan' is a name always enclosed within quotation marks, always a *mask*, as he famously put it one Halloween night. In this sense he has always employed the functional lie: in his new friendships, forged in the folk clubs and bars of the Village, and in his dealings with increasingly ubiquitous interviewers. In the spinning of a back-story which told of a life in New Mexico or of one spent with a travelling circus, he adopted another persona, substituted one image of the world for another. On another level, though, in their performance, to the extent to which they are played like an instrument, functional lies become detached from their functions. No longer employed by an individual, lies become constituent instead of complex, generative relations with each other – they exceed any enclosure, they produce the world rather than mask it. It is this worlding power which defines *mythos*.

For ancient cultures, the cycles of mythology served to assemble collective memory and shape a reflexive engagement with everyday experience (Sandywell, 1996: 9). Mythical tradition was central to social life and communality, and shared, mythical history operated as a medium for common discourse. It was through myth-making that collectivities 'told themselves about themselves' and so created 'the frameworks of symbolic self-interpretation and societal self-definition' (*ibid.*: 25). Accordingly, these activities had ethical, social value. But with the development of Socratic thought, these same activities became the subject of critique. The authority of *logos* came to oppose the speculative and 'open ended' *mythos*, instituting a universal truth value derived from rational reflection on 'the real' (*ibid.*: 7). Extrapolating from such rationality, our dominant contemporary relationship with mythical tradition is rendered in terms of what the Marxist critic Walter Benjamin called 'vulgar historical naturalism' (Benjamin, 1999: 461), our path of 'progression' determined by a transcendent truth.

America, of course, is a nation founded on myth: the land of the American dream, where any individual can achieve greatness, where life, liberty and the pursuit of happiness are enshrined. Initially, the cultural upheavals of the 1960s were all about confronting the enormous aporias to such ideals: racial and sexual inequality, political corruption, wars in foreign lands. But myth cannot be so easily smashed – one can easily be replaced by another. In the 1960s, the individuals who came to represent the artistic face of these transformations were quickly cast as new ideals, new idols, either on the basis of their virtuosity captured on tape, on screen or in print, or on the basis of other activity – a motorcycle crash, for example – precisely because such activity had escaped the recording devices of an increasingly global media. According to the logic of myth, the 'absence' of the event serves only to validate its presence, to confirm its authenticity.

So, the transcendent fabulation of myth functions by pinning down, documenting and archiving. It creates a situation where it is possible only to know or perceive a world that has itself been constructed in representational terms. On such a basis, interaction takes place with a world we already know; it operates according to an 'intelligent' mode of perception, commanding multiple viewpoints, that is, by 'going all around' an object (Bergson, 1946: 159). A perception of the world which is in line with myth works on the basis of calculation; it aims at perceiving the complex whole by identifying and combining the various parts which comprise it. This is what we are presented with at the beginning of *I'm Not There*. One of the first scenes takes place in a mortuary: the wheels of a gurney are adjusted into position, the bright light above it is switched on, two pathologists and a nurse stand around the body of Jude Quinn, the clinical gaze of these medical professionals targeted from all angles. For Bergson, this kind of perception 'will not have made you go one step *beyond* what you had perceived in the first place' (Bergson, 1946: 140); it merely 'stops at the relative' (*ibid.*: 159). It is, in short, closed off from the world's immanent *virtual* qualities – the fabulation of myth encloses perception.[1]

Myth enforces the impression that a rationalised, intelligent mode of perception is 'natural', thereby subjecting the powers of creative invention to self-discipline.[2] Perceptually blind to the virtual potential of the world, life becomes action-oriented, our sense of the world based purely upon ways that we can make use of its actual form. In Deleuze's terms, this is interaction as 'recognition', where life unfolds purely in order to reconfirm and re-present the world according to an existing series of fictional standards, values and systems of knowledge (Deleuze, 2004: 176). Clearly, then, the mythical structure of this stable, action-oriented and attentional form of perception is anything but 'natural' and it is precisely in response to such a structure that

Dylan has relentlessly sought to recapture the efficacy of *mythos*, to subvert naturalised truth value. As he said in the same interview later ventriloquised in *I'm Not There*: 'I am against nature. I don't dig nature at all. I think nature is very unnatural' (Shelton, 2011: 52). The unnaturalness of nature must also be conceived in aesthetic terms. In his early writing, Nietzsche examines the aesthetic duality of life's Apollonian and Dionysian tendencies, the opposing artistic powers which 'burst forth from nature itself' (Nietzsche, 2006b: 46). To the Greeks, Apollo was the deity of representational art, in which life's processes are fixed in aesthetic form, while Dionysus was the god of non-representational art like music, where aesthetic power can be experienced only by giving oneself up to life's affective drives.[3] So where the Apollonian aesthetic orders life on a transcendent level, the Dionysian impulse involves an aesthetic intoxication with the world's immanent, chaotic processes. Given the conventional images of the classical world, it might seem that the Apollonian drive was wholly triumphant. Indeed, in this context, unnatural naturalness describes the extent to which communicative practice and aesthetic practice operate according to *formal* laws of recognition, defending a predefined state of social cohesion. In such a world, any person who deigns to use 'valid descriptions ... in order to make something which is unreal appear to be real' (Nietzsche, 2006a: 115) is judged to have employed deception for dissimulation, to have actively threatened social stability in an attempt to elevate the individual. This person is, in short, a 'Judas!', a traitor, an enemy of the representational truths which preserve life and social stability. Yet, in such a world, 'truth' is nothing more than 'a sum of human relations which have been poetically and rhetorically intensified, transferred, and embellished, and which, after long usage, seem to a people to be fixed, canonical, and binding' (*ibid.*: 117). Truths are interactions as recognition, 'illusions which we have forgotten are illusions', perceptions aligned to pre-existing categories, 'drained of sensuous force'. Behaviour in such a world becomes little more than an expression of the myths, the fabulatory force, projected onto it.

What Nietzsche argues, though, is that any order or progress is constituted by its relation with Dionysian processes. For him, the genuine power of creative, artistic invention emerges only through the temporary and dynamic reconciliation of these opposing tendencies. Indeed, we might say that aesthetic activity which escapes the strictures of 'recognition' is possible only by means of what, in Deleuzian terms, can be called a 'disjunctive synthesis' of Apollonian and Dionysian powers, wherein their distinctions come together in a new relation, one of *immanent transcendence*.

Back in Haynes's strange mortuary scene, we see a gloved hand, in close-up, make a scalpel incision along pale flesh. The filmmaker seems to be announcing something forensic; he seems to be saying that it might be possible – by transversally cutting through sedimented, layered images – to get at something beyond myth, a 'beyond' which is not transcendent but 'situated in the here and now, in the very flows and encounters of everyday existence' (Shaviro, 2010: 9). Such a process cuts through the various cultural histories, social institutions and technical systems which constitute the myth; it reveals and forges new links between them, remaking them in the act. This is, then, a curious cross-sectional autopsy, one performed on a mythical body afflicted by a kind of *rigor vitae*, an operation that seeks to revive a living force which has become stratified and fixed. Its activity is, in opposition to 'recognition', immanent transcendent, an 'encounter' (Deleuze, 2004: 176) concerned with effects rather than causes, conducted to map out new connections and produce new relations rather than trace what already exists. Indeed, instead of a generic clinical expert, we might imagine that the gloved hand belongs to a collective force. Though, at his most vital, Dylan stages an 'autopsy' of his own image, this operation is most directly performed by an assemblage of individuals seeking to encounter the image – and, with it, the world itself – in newly productive ways, ways they do not recognise. It is this act of 'opening up' and cutting through the centralised notion of myth which characterises the Dylan *mythos*.

Mythos is experimental; it can reveal and generate *counter*-truths. Like Fellini, Dylan wields what Nietzsche calls 'powers of the false', fabulation as productive political force, a power which exceeds the definition of truth and falsity precisely because it does not 'correspond to a pre-existing reality' but is instead able to create something *new* in this world, to actualise that which has been previously rendered imperceptible (Deleuze, 1998: 119). He is a liar, but a truthing liar. Let there be no doubt as to the politics of this experimentality: it is a politics of 'untruth', extending from a refusal – as he puts it in his fabulated autobiography – to 'cough up some facts' (Dylan, 2004: 35, 7). Haynes illustrates this by restaging the supposed *vérité* of Pennebaker's 1967 documentary *Dont Look Back* in Fellini's surreal dreamscape, eating and regurgitating 'the document' by interweaving near-verbatim recitation with the imagined stuff of Dylanological legend, and channelling it all through echoes of a film director similarly pursued for an answer – perhaps *the* answer – which fits the form of the question. This is a politics unconcerned with progression towards wisdom or with 'changing the world' in any conventional sense; rather, it involves a new way of perceiving which undermines any claims to the truth to this world.

As you might expect, in the Rialto cinema that night there were a few disgruntled murmurs at the absence of closure, the lack of a resolution to Haynes's Dylan simulacrum. How did the story end? How was it all wrapped up? How did the various contradictory images come to be synthesised? Indeed, it is important to acknowledge that the powers which constitute *mythos* are necessarily precarious: the disjunctive synthesis is always in danger of falling back into a binary opposition, always in danger of becoming intellectualised. Such activity is most explicitly manifested as an archival Dylanology, an activity beset by passively nihilistic idolatry which aims only to fix the image, to better define the image by lashing it ever more securely to a grounding framework of truthful reality. Even to glibly celebrate the image's protean quality – Dylan as postmodern, hyper-real trickster – is to ignore its excess and focus instead on the extent to which 'meaning' endlessly flutters in interpretative, hermeneutic squalls, thus serving to endorse the further foundation of myth. For most of the audience, though, representational answers could not have compared to what they had just encountered. The sudden interruption, the rupture to the flow of narrative, seemed to reveal something more forceful about the open and processual nature of the Dylan image, seemed to unfold its heuristic powers.

While an Apollonian dream image is interpretively approached with 'measured restraint' in order to maintain coherent, individual subjectivity, and while the Dionysian impulse causes subjective states to become affectively engulfed, to 'dwindle to complete self-oblivion' (Nietzsche, 2006b: 45), a disjunctive synthesis of the two aesthetic powers – a relation of immanent transcendence – enables individuals to become collectively attuned, to forge a new nature, a single heterogeneous unity, a 'multitude'.[4] It is in assemblage with such a social body that an image resonates with non-representational force: the intoxicating affect of Dionysian music collectively perceived in dream images. As a multitude, the Rialto audience took the melted image, stretched to the point of disappearance, as a powerfully intuitive moment at which to bifurcate from the film's narrative continuum. It was clear to them, to us, that there is no stable framework through which to encounter Dylan, but rather a multiplicity of cultural and temporal entry points. But it was equally clear that such images express the transformative processes of the world, its virtual qualities, its future potential. Rather than bemoaning a ruined performance, then, the audience were roused to take up this performance themselves, to maintain its energy. Filing out of the screening, a series of intense, collective conversations sprang up; a surge of communication tapped into dynamic, living concepts which cross, cut through and extend from Dylan, concepts through which the audience ceased to be audience and became, themselves, inventors, perhaps even artists. Forging new, speculative connections as to what might be 'felt out', beyond the frame of filmic representation, the group probed and transformed Dylan's ontology of 'untruth' into a means of collectively and reflexively engaging with the world.

Weird visions

It is well established that the cultural experiments of the 1960s, while surging towards a revolutionary future, were powered by history and tradition. In Dylan's fabulatory perception though, the temporality of history becomes – as Greil Marcus (1998) has it – *weird*, a weirdness that becomes released from its enclosure in the past so that it might infect the present.[5] In the rest of this chapter I want to consider how this perception is constitutive of future potential. Indeed, what Nietzsche described as the 'untimely' quality of such weird histories can be understood to actively reject the stratification of myth through a political intervention in ongoing, worlding processes.[6]

In *Chronicles*, an account of his own untimely history, Dylan discusses a vast network of early influences which links together – among many others – the Beat poets, Arthur Rimbaud and Bertolt Brecht. In these discussions, the crucial temporal power of fabulation is frequently invoked in the figure of the prophetic *seer* (Deleuze and Guattari, 1994: 171). The Beats, for example, were roused by a philosophical doctrine (formulated by Lucien Carr and Alan Ginsberg), known as 'New Vision' – a rallying cry to reject the moral codes and social conformities of paranoid post-war America and to embark instead upon an exploration and expression of the *self*. This, as Ginsberg later confirmed, was a philosophy inspired directly by the poetry of Rimbaud (Watson, 1995: 35–40).[7] Accordingly, the New Vision was a movement of artistic romanticism, one in which the 'artist' as individual aims for a transcendent escape of the social. It was a notion centred on Rimbaud's insistence that, to arrive at the unknown, one must 'disorder' the senses and become, uniquely, a seer (Rimbaud, 2004: 236). Yet, in contrast to this myth of the seer as a 'great man' set aside from the rest of the world, Dylan invokes the power of the seer precisely for its collective quality. This is something that can be detected in his references to the blues musician Robert Johnson.

A compilation, released in early 1961 (the same year Dylan arrived in New York), which designated Johnson 'King of the Delta Blues Singers', retrospectively assigned him authorship of various blues standards. In life, though, decades previously, Johnson had recorded fewer than thirty songs, all of which had been a commercial failure. Dylan writes that he had never heard of Johnson before he was given an advance copy of the record by his producer at Columbia, and that playing it for the first time was like experiencing a 'panoramic story – fires of mankind blasting off the surface of this spinning piece of plastic' (Dylan, 2004: 282). For him, the music vibrated with sounds from beyond the obvious Mississippi delta influences and drew together a series of other ideas and images, arranging them in new and complex forms.[8] For him, the modernist bricolage of Johnson's song-writing joined up the bluesman's own time with one that had yet to come, and joined up, too, with a *people* yet to come: 'You have to wonder if Johnson was playing for an audience that only he could see, one off in the future' (*ibid.*: 285).

Dylan provides us with a further pointer as to the critical significance of this atemporal mode of perception. Reflecting on his own early undertaking to formulate a song-writing process, he states that: 'I needed to learn how to telescope things, ideas. Things were too big to see all at once, like all the books in the library – everything laying around on all the tables. You might be able to put it all into one paragraph or into one verse of a song if you could get it right' (*ibid.*: 61). Telescoping describes his conscious attempts to master the art of the seer, and to be a seer is to be a becomer, to enter into a becoming. Becoming is a Dionysian force, a force by which the creative artist seizes hold of the transmutative power of life itself: 'He carries the power of the false to a degree that is no longer effected in a form, but in a transformation' (Deleuze, 1998: 105; original emphasis removed). Becoming is – like a never ending tour – an ongoing performance, a *processual* activity, not a discrete action. As *I'm Not There* explores, the Dylan image always moves towards what Deleuze calls a 'becoming-other', always unfixed from discrete representations and linear narratives, always between categories and between fixed points in time, always moving though a 'zone of indetermination or uncertainty' (Deleuze and Guattari, 2004: 301).

Yet, the process of becoming is necessarily complex, even disorienting – to enter into this virtual zone is to come up against coexisting, contradictory potentialities. The natural response to such chaos is to fall back on myths of homogeneous historical 'progress', to view history posthumously, post-mortem. Telescoping is Dylan's strategy for avoiding such pitfalls. To telescope is to intervene in chronological time, to disrupt the machinery of historicisation, to cut into and engage with temporal heterogeneity, to construct a new image of time. What Deleuze makes clear is that artists cannot enter into such a becoming alone, they cannot fabulate alone – the activity of open invention, of mythopoiesis, can take place only in collective assemblage.

So, instead of Rimbaud, to grasp the way in which Dylan frames Johnson as a seer, we might consider his reference to Brecht instead. In the early 1960s, Dylan's then girlfriend and muse, Suze Rotolo, was working at a theatre which staged a performance of songs by Brecht and Kurt Weill. As he recalls, these songs – like 'Pirate Jenny' from *The Threepenny Opera*, an example of Brecht's 'epic' or dialectical theatre – were '[s]ongs with tough language. They were erratic, unrhythmical and herky-jerky – weird visions' (Dylan, 2004: 272). More broadly, Brecht's Marxist, avant-garde methodology responds to the danger of wholly submitting to Dionysian intoxication, doing so by safeguarding the *critical* relation of disjunctive synthesis. It is what might be called a theatre of intercession.

Intercession is crucial to the collective, creative process of becoming; indeed, communities and social assemblages are constructed and maintained through relations between intercessors. An intercessional relation is not simply based on rhythmical exchange. It is not constituted through acts of consumption, nor does it occur in a devotee's passive response to facts banally coughed up on demand. Rather, it is a relation of interplay, of 'creative interference' (Bogue, 2007: 13), a relation that interrupts the transmission of signal with noise, that tests a truth with other truths, that continually generates change: 'Intercession is a form of positive dissonance, made possible through an openness to interferences that disturb one's regular harmonic vibrations' (*ibid.*: 14).[9] We might consider 'telescoping' in similar terms, as a powerful source of vitality, generated by the sudden montage, of heterogeneous ideas being pulled together, sometimes violently. It is, then, through a disjunctive synthesis that telescoping clarifies, brings into focus and magnifies some elements, while refracting and foreshortening others, an intercessional relation that remains in continual flux.[10]

For Walter Benjamin, this kind of historical perception is an 'image-making medium', by which he means that activities which involve the '[t]elescoping of the past through the present' (Benjamin, 1999: 471) engage in political montage. Like Brecht, Benjamin understands the temporality of this relation as something that is dialectical rather than linear, that is to say, a relation in which history is perceived through its actualisation in the present moment, an event which brings about the recomposition of both. The virtual power of the historical past remains alive in the present – historical time is not homogeneous and empty but remains 'charged with the time of the now', a force which can be 'blasted out of the continuum of history' (Benjamin, 2007: 261). In other words, the creative movement involved in picking up the 'rags and refuse' (Benjamin, 1999: 460) – the weirdness of history – is not motivated by a desire to catalogue and archive but, rather, seeks to make new, critical use of such historical remainders in the present.

It is through this method of telescopic montage that Dylan can come to perceive 'it all' in a single image, that he can encounter – in a single, individual moment – what Benjamin (1999: 461) calls 'the crystal of the total event', a refractive relation that breaks with any naturalism. Such crystalline states do not just refract – they grow, they remain in a process of crystallisation. To telescope a crystal image is not simply to reveal the coalescence of virtual past and actual present (Deleuze, 2005: 123) but to continually disclose new ways in which the actualisation of this immanent history can change present becoming, can alter collective perception of our movement into the future.[11] This also means that the fabulation of weird histories, and the dissolution of formal myths concerning 'timeless truth', is an *antagonistic* process.

Accordingly, the difference between conventional dramatic theatre and Brecht's epic theatre is the latter's active dissent against the conventional 'witchcraft' involved in hypnotising the spectator; it continually resists fusing or integrating a passive audience into a pre-constructed process (Brecht, 2001a). Instead of the usual theatrical staging, where an audience is introduced to a carefully composed illusion and where aesthetics are employed for representational effect, here the audience is incessantly subject to alienation, to interruptive techniques of defamiliarisation, to an aesthetics of *affect*, the intention of which is to force an audience into reflexively perceiving the constructed falsity of forms, the unnaturalness of nature.

As Deleuze (1995: 125) suggests, such collective relations are essential to genuine creative expression, including that of an individual, meaning that – in their relation with an artist, *but also with one another* – readers, spectators and listeners become co-creators rather than consumers. It is equally important that such relations retain an antagonistic quality: artist, audience, fans, critics and detractors encounter each other in collective intercession. The development of Dylan's song-writing undoubtedly responds to such politics, seeking to avoid both the Tin Pan Alley assembly line of pop-song-as-commodity, and the emotive, 'authentic' appeal of the so-called 'protest' song, a form of recognition from which he rapidly retreated. In doing so, the 'voice of a generation' is replaced with a multiplicity of voices which, although tuned to each other, retain their singularity; by operating as 'fragile network' (Deleuze, 1998: 118) they avoid reduction to a chorus. Indeed, Dylan's performative transition to master of discordant electricity and lyrical absurdity exhibits certain Brechtian qualities, with a desire to provoke and tap into an audience's immanent potentialities. Just like Brechtian theatre, the Dylan image 'works against creating an illusion among the audience' (Benjamin, 1998: 99), acting instead as a reflection on its own medial power. But as intercessors who engage with the image, with the *mythos* of Dylan, we, too, are involved in a communally productive process, a process which works towards the creation of a collectivity exceeding that which exists in the defined space of the actual world, something we might describe as a collective becoming-other (Bogue, 2007: 104).

For this reason, the power of intercession is not restricted to a bourgeois world of creative expression but is fundamental to the 'constitution of a people' (Deleuze, 1995: 125–6), to the formulation of a multitude which has yet to take shape, yet to actualise its latent political power. It is in this respect that Brecht is not interested in the audience member of the present but, by creating a situation in which 'he' is compelled to perceive the power of difference immanent to his present, Brecht is interested in his *potential*: 'He does not have to stay the way he is now, nor does he have to be seen only as he is now, but also as he might become' (Brecht, 2001b). In the mid-twentieth century, this radical position was particularly in tune with the context generated by a newly virulent mass media, where hegemonic images testified to the existence of a certain people, a solidly coherent citizen, a people always-already in the world. What Dylan sought to call attention to was the fact that the people were 'missing', that a group subject, as opposed to a subjected group, did not (and does not) yet exist. The people are missing because their *true* potential defies representation. It is in the act of identifying this absence that a new politics becomes possible. To fabulate, instead, a 'people to come' is to enter into a process of collective self-invention (Deleuze, 2005: 209). According to Dylan, it is this people to come that Johnson, the seer, is able to perceive.

We ought to be wary, though, about a future observed by an individual seer; such utopia is too easily turned back against itself and converted into myth, to origins, to a transcendent ideal. After all, as with Rimbaud, the myth of the seer's transcendent power is invariably a tragic one. This includes the great myth of the blues, perpetuated in the 1960s by a generation of white British guitarists, which aligns the power of the music to demonic forces (Wald, 2004: 266). Johnson, of course, is at the centre of this, encapsulated in the much repeated tale of a Faustian pact: having gone down to the crossroads and exchanged his soul for the transcendent knowledge of blues power, the uncannily talented musician lives out the rest of his truncated days with a devil on his tail and suffers an agonising death. But in opposition to the temptations of such myth, a collective *mythos* performs the power of what we might call a '*collective* seer', a power which affirms the virtuality immanent to its own assemblage.

On its own, a dream of the future is nothing. Without intensity it quickly decays into a historical past and can be perceived only in a pre-existing, recognisable form, an extrapolation of present conditions. Yet, the power of the dream – its vital, worlding weirdness – is preserved. The resistance to historicising decay is therefore generated through vitality, in the *force* through which the lived fiction of an image is felt and performed, in the 'validity' of its intensity. Because, though such an image conforms to no pre-existing reality, it remains altogether real. At the same time, however, there is nothing 'behind' such an image; it exists only in assemblage. As a consequence, the force through which it is projected is always collective. The fabulatory function of Dylan's telescopic perception comes from aiming towards and constructing an image of this future people, a fictional image which becomes vital and takes on a 'life of its own'. This is a people who are always 'to come', always 'off in the future', precisely because the power of invention – the new – cannot be predefined: it can only be encountered. For Deleuze (1998: 118), such a process functions as 'a machine for manufacturing giants' but, rather than the singular, individual or unified giant of the great artist, it operates as a fragile network, a collective becoming-other, and so is a process over which 'Bob Dylan' has only contributory control.

Last thoughts on 'Bob Dylan'

As an affective encounter, the 'meaning' of the mythopoeic image is always second to what it does: affirm this world and new ways to live within it, rather than seek out a transcendent escape. One of the final scenes in *I'm Not There*, a scene which the Rialto audience did not get to see, has Blanchett's Quinn deliver a monologue in the back seat of a car as it speeds through the London night. Her words resonate off those Dylan spoke in an interview with Nat Hentoff in 1966. Tradition, history, is innately weird, s/he says. The music of such tradition is 'too unreal to die' (see Cott, 2006a: 98), which goes for the image as well. The only truth, the only fact of history, is its mystery. In this, Dylan tells us, in 'its meaninglessness', is where its purity lies.[12]

Yet, our own era is one in which malleable, transformational subjectivity has become central to systems of power which operate on the basis of flexibility, precariousness and reinvention. In such systems, virtual qualities prove to be ever more valuable and modulating the 'people to come' takes priority over moulding those in the present. Indeed, today the hegemonic institution of truth, a single reality, is increasingly abandoned in favour of an excess of immanent realities awaiting exploitation. As Dylan predicted, the ownership and control of meaninglessness is now in great demand.

Nonetheless, even as we find ourselves integrated within such systems, to respond by simply attacking counter-cultural idols with iconoclastic hammers (Judas!) not only maintains the naïve idea that it is possible to get at some inner truth but actively contributes to the cycle, adding yet further layers to the myth itself. Perhaps the myths of the 1960s are, in any case, indestructible. We need to remain focused on what such mythological images can *do*, rather than defining what they mean in ever greater detail. Instead of a hammer, then, we would do better to follow William Mitchell's reading of Nietzsche and approach such idols with a critical 'tuning fork', allowing us to ensure they are 'struck ... with just enough force to make them resonate, but not so much as to smash them' (Mitchell, 2005: 9).[13] Rather than destroy such images, we must 'play upon them as if they were musical instruments' (*ibid.*: 26). The trick, of course, is to play this image-instrument collectively, to ensure a multiplicity of heterogeneous resonances build towards a generative surge, towards encounters with new truths. And this means, as Dylan put it himself, that we should *play it fucking loud*.

Notes

1 The notion of the virtual employed here is that conceived by Henri Bergson and developed by Gilles Deleuze, namely a virtual that is not opposed to the real but is immanent to it – 'real but not yet actual'.

2 As Bergson (1935: 89) puts it: 'A fiction, if its image is vivid and insistent, may indeed masquerade as perception and in that way prevent or modify action. A systematically false experience, confronting the intelligence, may indeed stop it pushing too far the conclusions it deduces from a true experience'.

3 It is actually Apollo, in Greek tradition, who is generally considered patron of the art of music, but for Nietzsche this form of music is no more than 'Doric architecture rendered in sound' – it is a purely cognitive music, kept at a careful distance from the world. In comparison, the power of Dionysian music is that it works non-cognitively, affectively; it stimulates 'the faculties of man ... to the highest pitch of intensity' (Nietzsche, 2006b: 48).

4 Despite the fact that Spinoza opposes multitude to the homogeneity of 'people', my forthcoming reference to people, inspired by Deleuze's late writing, employs the term as an equivalent to multitude, as a heterogenous composition.

5 I am, of course, referring to Marcus's now defining characterisation of 'Old, Weird America', a title under which his book has been republished. Weirdness is also central to the idea of an open *mythos*, as for example in the 'Cthulhu mythos' associated with the writer of 'weird fiction', H. P. Lovecraft.

6 This is something – despite his ludic response to cross-examination – that is clearly expressed in various interviews Dylan gave during this crucial, revolutionary period. His relation to history opposed both the static monumentalisation of memory and the hierarchical power of the archive; as he said in 1965, 'It's not the bomb that has to go, man, it's the museums' (see Cott, 2006b: 54).

7 In *Chronicles*, Dylan (2004: 288) recalls the period in which Suze Rotolo introduced him to Rimbaud's work as being highly significant to his early life.

8 Dave Van Ronk, at whose house Dylan first heard the Johnson record, was unimpressed. He was quick to point out the echoes in Johnson's sound of what had come before, a technique of composition which Pete Seeger would less dismissively call 'the folk process'. Dylan, though, found something else in the music: 'The songs weren't customary blues songs. They were perfected pieces – each song contained four or five verses, every couplet intertwined with the next but in no obvious way' (Dylan, 2004: 282). The repositioning of Johnson as something of a modernist songwriter is certainly easier to accept in the era of remastering. His twenty-nine tracks are now joined by various out-takes and alternative cuts which add new insight to the sophistication of his process.

9 Despite the fact that the English translation renders Deleuze's term as 'mediator', I follow Ronald Bogue's (2007: 13) translation, which reads it as 'intercessor' (from the Latin *inter+cedere*, meaning 'go between'), which better emphasises a mediative relation that is also critical.

10 Here, I am also thinking of T. S. Eliot's use of the term. For him, the force of telescopic 'impeachment' specifically emerges from the '*failure* of the conjunction, the fact that often the ideas are yoked but not united' (Eliot, 1980: 283; my emphasis). This dynamic state is held together through intercessional relations, a disjunctive synthesis of forces from which a vital, creative power can emerge. Dylan's *Chronicles* is, of course, a document of telescoping itself, expressed (despite the lazy accusations of plagiarism laid against it) in its challenges to linear time and representational unity. Even the couple who own the Greenwich Village apartment in which Dylan was living where his 'telescoping' comment is situated, are, according to Sean Wilentz (2010: 299), 'almost certainly a fabrication, most likely a composite'.

11 Deleuze (2005) proposes the idea of the crystal image as part of his metaphysics of cinema, where it features in the explicit context of powers of the false.

12 This is also a good example of how Haynes's technique does not merely involve the repetition of these interview transcripts, but treats the words as a refrain which produces difference in the act of their repetition. Where Hentoff's transcript archives Dylan as having said 'Traditional music is based on hexagrams', Blanchett says 'What I'm talking about is traditional music – which is to say mathematical music, based on hexagons'. This idea of a circular refrain which generates difference in its process of circulation is something the film expresses directly, concluding as it does with footage from the 1966 documentary film *Eat the Document*, in which the resonances of Dylan's spiralling harmonica expand by falsifying its own refrain, generating difference in its eternal return.

13 In *Twilight of the Idols* – which is subtitled *How to Philosophize with a Hammer* – Nietzsche writes that idols are 'touched here with a hammer as with a tuning fork' (cited in Mitchell, 2005: 9).

References

Benjamin, W. (1998) *Understanding Brecht* (London: Verso).

Benjamin, W. (1999) *The Arcades Project* (Cambridge, MA: Belknap/Harvard University Press).

Benjamin, W. (2007) *Illuminations* (New York: Schocken Books).

Bergson, H. (1935) *The Two Sources of Morality and Religion* (London: Macmillan).

Bergson, H. (1946) *The Creative Mind: An Introduction to Metaphysics* (Secaucus, NJ: Citadel Press).

Bogue, R. (2007) *Deleuze's Way: Essays in Transverse Ethics and Aesthetics* (Farnham: Ashgate).

Brecht, B. (2001a) 'The modern theatre is the epic theatre', in J. Willett (ed.), *Brecht on Theatre: The Development of an Aesthetic* (London: Methuen). 37–8.

Brecht, B. (2001b) 'A short organum for the theatre', in J. Willett (ed.), *Brecht on Theatre: The Development of an Aesthetic* (London: Methuen). 193.

Cott, J. (ed.) (2006a) 'Interview with Nat Hentoff, *Playboy*, March 1966', in *Dylan on Dylan: The Essential Interviews* (London: Hodder and Stoughton). 93–111.

Cott, J. (ed.) (2006b) 'Interview with Nora Ephron and Susan Edmiston, *Positively Tie Dream*, August 1965', in *Dylan on Dylan: The Essential Interviews* (London: Hodder and Stoughton). 47–55.

Deleuze, G. (1995) *Negotiations 1972–1990* (New York: Columbia University Press).

Deleuze, G. (1998) *Essays Critical and Clinical* (London: Verso).

Deleuze, G. (2004) *Difference and Repetition* (London: Continuum).

Deleuze, G. (2005) *Cinema 2: The Time Image* (London: Continuum).

Deleuze, G. and Guattari, F. (1994) *What Is Philosophy?* (New York: Columbia University Press).

Deleuze, G. and Guattari, F. (2004) *A Thousand Plateaus: Capitalism and Schizophrenia* (London: Continuum).

Dylan, B. (1964) 'Advice for Geraldine on her miscellaneous birthday', in *New York Philharmonic Hall Concert Programme* (31 October 1964). n.p.

Dylan, B. (2004) *Chronicles: Volume One* (London: Simon and Schuster).

Eliot, T. S. (1980) *Selected Essays* (London: Faber and Faber).

Marcus, G. (1998) *Invisible Republic: Bob Dylan's Basement Tapes* (Basingstoke: Picador/Pan Macmillan).

Mitchell, W. J. T. (2005) *What Do Pictures Want? The Lives and Loves of Images* (Chicago, IL: University of Chicago Press).

Nietzsche, F. (2006a) 'On truth and lies in a nonmoral sense', in K. Ansell Pearson and D. Large (eds), *The Nietzsche Reader* (Oxford: Blackwell). 114–23.

Nietzsche, F. (2006b) 'The birth of tragedy from the spirit of music', in K. Ansell Pearson and D. Large (eds), *The Nietzsche Reader* (Oxford: Blackwell). 42–87.

Rimbaud, A. (2004) *Selected Poems and Letters* (London: Penguin).

Sandywell, B. (1996) *The Beginnings of European Theorizing: Reflexivity in the Archaic Age* (London: Routledge).

Shaviro, S. (2010) *Post-Cinematic Affect* (Winchester: Zer0 Books).

Shelton, R. (2011) *No Direction Home: The Life and Music of Bob Dylan* (revised edition) (Milwaukee, WI: Backbeat/Hal Leonard).

Wald, E. (2004) *Escaping the Delta: Robert Johnson and the Invention of the Blues* (New York: Amistad/HarperCollins).

Watson, S. (1995) *The Birth of the Beat Generation: Visionaries, Rebels and Hipsters, 1944–1960* (New York: Pantheon).

Wilentz, S. (2010) *Bob Dylan in America* (London: Bodley Head).

8

The ghost of Bob Dylan: spectrality and performance in *I'm Not There*

Susanne Hamscha

'There he lay: poet, prophet, outlaw, fake, star of electricity. Nailed by a peeping tom, who would soon discover: even the ghost was more than one person.' Thus begins *I'm Not There*, a highly intriguing and experimental 2007 motion picture by Todd Haynes based on the many lives of Bob Dylan. In this film, five actors (Christian Bale, Marcus Carl Franklin, Richard Gere, Heath Ledger and Ben Whishaw) and one actress (Cate Blanchett) play characters who embody different aspects of the musician's life and work: everyone *is* Bob Dylan, as the movie trailer tells us, and Bob Dylan is no one.

This apparent paradox laid out in the trailer is the incentive for my chapter, in which I am less interested in analysing who the American icon Bob Dylan is, or might be, than in investigating who Bob Dylan is *not* and *cannot* be. If I were to exaggerate, I would say that my aim here is to show that Bob Dylan actually does not exist at all. This is a provocative claim, but let me for a moment dwell on this possibility by drawing on Haynes's *I'm Not There*. As this film will be at the centre of my analysis, the chapter is, first of all, concerned with the various representations of Bob Dylan in *I'm Not There*, rather than with the living musician and his *œuvre*. An innovative and original biopic that does not actually want to fall into this genre, *I'm Not There* is based on the many lives of Bob Dylan but does not vouch for authenticity or truth, does not follow chronology or lived reality and does not distinguish between fact and fiction. As unusual as Haynes's undertaking to let a woman, a black boy and four men of various ages play Bob Dylan may seem, it is also a strangely familiar approach to capturing Dylan's shape-shifting persona: the inability 'to pin Dylan down to one mode, one category, or a clearly laid out trajectory is by now the common way in which his career and its numerous resurgences have been encapsulated and accounted for' (Danks, 2008).

To speak of him as a shape-shifter or multiple self has become a standard approach in analyses of Dylan;[1] however, such an approach presupposes an ontology, that is, the *being* of Bob Dylan, which I want to challenge in this chapter by taking a different route. In the following, I suggest a reading of Bob Dylan as a 'ghost' in the sense of Jacques Derrida. I read Dylan as a 'spectre', as a deconstructive figure that is a repetition yet an original, is neither absent nor present, is neither dead nor alive. In *I'm Not There*, 'Bob Dylan' is a signifier that defies ontology and authenticity while it invites appropriation and reinscription – indeed, the open-ended signifier 'Bob Dylan', it follows, can become meaningful only in its many appropriations and performances, which endow the spectre Bob Dylan with something like materiality and solid form. As Derrida argues, ontology is replaced by the logics of hauntology in the spectre's act of haunting, which forces us to acknowledge the non-being which precedes the being, that is, the imperfection and elusiveness inherent in all fleshly existence. In *I'm Not There*, Bob Dylan is the ghost that haunts the 'poet, prophet, outlaw, fake, star of electricity' – he is the spectre that is gone before he was even there.

I'm not there. Yet. Or, the search for Bob Dylan

When *I'm Not There* was released in 2007, it seemed to slip easily into a genre that had dominated the landscape of Hollywood in the last decade: biographical films, or 'biopics', proved to be immensely successful at the box office as well as with critics and at award shows. *A Beautiful Mind* (2001), *Ali* (2001), *Ray* (2004), *The Aviator* (2004), *Capote* (2005), *Walk the Line* (2005), *Frost/Nixon* (2008), *127 Hours* (2010), *The Social Network* (2010) and *J. Edgar* (2011) are just a few of the many examples that immediately come to mind and that all, quite typical of the genre, integrate 'disparate historical episodes of selected individual lives into a nearly monochromatic "Hollywood view of history"' through the construction of 'a highly conventional view of fame' and through the 'strategic use of star images in the creation of the stories of famous people' (Custen, 1992: 3). In his comprehensive study of contemporary biopics, Dennis Bingham has identified the biopic as a 'genuine, dynamic genre' which 'narrates, exhibits, and celebrates the life of a subject in order to demonstrate, investigate, or question his or her importance in the world; to illuminate the fine points of a personality; and for both artist and spectator to discover what it would be like to be this person, or to be a certain type of person' (Bingham, 2010: 10). While biopics are based on 'reality' and 'true' events in the life of a famous person, they generally dramatise actuality and frequently contribute to the mythification of their subject. However, as Bingham points out, the appeal of biopics lies in 'seeing an actual person who did something interesting in life, known mostly in public, transformed into a character' (*ibid.*: 10). A biopic, it follows, is not simply the recounting of the facts of someone's life, but rather an attempt to discover biographical 'truth' by delineating someone's journey and rise to fame. Most crucially, the subject of a biopic is therefore usually depicted as 'a visionary with a pure, one of a kind talent or idea who must overcome opposition to this idea or even just to himself' (*ibid.*: 7). In other words, the narrative of a traditional biopic is teleological, focuses on individual improvement and ends by emphasising the success and enduring importance of its protagonist.

Why *I'm Not There* is not a traditional biopic becomes most obvious when it is compared with, for instance, *Walk the Line*, in which Joaquin Phoenix plays Johnny Cash. *I'm Not There* and *Walk the Line* share the same motifs and plotline: both films follow the career of a singer–songwriter and his rise to the status of American icon. Both films contain episodes of a struggling marriage, of the abuse of drugs and alcohol and of conversion. However, a comparison of the films' titles alone graphically explains how very differently Bob Dylan and Johnny Cash are being approached. As the title *Walk the Line* already implies, Johnny Cash is depicted as an upright and authentic man, who overcomes all obstacles in a classic American success story in order to rise to superstar status. *Walk the Line* delineates Cash's journey from a struggling, young musician to an American icon, from his childhood in Arkansas to his famous performance at Folsom Prison. While Johnny Cash certainly evolves in the course of the film, *Walk the Line* very much holds on to the notion of an authentic self, of a 'true' Johnny Cash, whose life has a clearly definable origin and telos.

I'm Not There is completely different: no straight line is followed; rather, this film takes turns, skips and rewinds, and moves in circles. Haynes's concept underlines the impossibility of any individual, including Bob Dylan, ever completely knowing a subject and providing a comprehensive account of a subject's life.[2] As David Yaffe remarks, 'if anything has been constant in Dylan's career, it's change' (Yaffe, 2011: xvii) and Haynes has made a movie that follows this thought. *I'm Not There* does not want to tell a complete, comprehensive story but sells itself as a film inspired by the music and many lives of Bob Dylan. However, Dylan himself, as the title suggests, is not there. At the end of the film, we get the simple image of Dylan playing an acoustic version of 'Mr. Tambourine Man' on his harmonica, but throughout the film his image cannot be found, his name is never mentioned and his presence resonates only in the form of allusions and associations. Cate Blanchett, for instance, plays Jude Quinn, the Bob Dylan of the 1960s, who famously 'went electric' at the 1965 Newport Folk Festival and was infamously called 'Judas' at the 1966 Manchester Free Trade Hall concert. Ben Whishaw is Dylan's poetic self, Arthur Rimbaud, while Marcus Carl Franklin as Woody takes us back to Dylan's beginnings as Woody Guthrie's musical heir. 'He is everyone. He is no one', as we are told in the trailer – Bob Dylan is everyone and no one at the same time. Or, put differently, Bob Dylan is no one precisely *because* he is everyone. 'By now it's official: Bob Dylan is a multiple self' Adrian Martin had remarked before the release of *I'm Not There* (Martin, 2007: 57), alluding to the complexity and multi-layeredness of Bob Dylan, which makes it virtually impossible to contain Dylan in singular form. In *I'm Not There* Bob Dylan is 'officially' a spectral self, a haunting presence, that reverberates in each of the six Dylanesque protagonists but remains ungraspable throughout the film.

Most crucially, Bob Dylan's haunting presence in *I'm Not There* is marked by absence, by the gaping hole that the film's title has already produced and that eventually turns out to be its central motif. Let us take a closer look at the film's title: *I'm Not There* takes its name from the Dylan song 'I'm Not There (1956)', which was written in 1967 during the recording of the 'Basement Tapes' and for long circulated only as a bootleg. According to Greil Marcus, this song is unique in Dylan's *œuvre*, because it was recorded only once and then never sung again. It is a 'bottomless song', he argues (Marcus, 1997: 155); because of Dylan's poor enunciation, it is difficult to make sense of the half-finished lyrics, which makes it nearly impossible to properly analyse the song and to place it within Dylan's work. 'I'm Not There (1956)' is a haunting song, 'barely written at all' and composed of words 'floated together in a dyslexia that is music itself – a dyslexia that seems meant to prove the claims of music over words, to see just how little words can do' (*ibid*.: 199). Perhaps it is the song's enigmatic nature that makes it not only one of the most fascinating pieces of Dylan's work, but also one of the most timeless and enduring pieces, as it offers itself to continuous reinterpretation and develops new shape and form at every re-listening. In his book *Invisible Republic*, Marcus eloquently describes the sensation of listening to 'I'm Not There (1956)', as follows:

> The song is a trance, a waking dream, a whirlpool, a 'closing vortex,' as on the last page of *Moby-Dick*.... Very quickly the listener is drawn into the sickly embrace of the music, its wash of half-heard, half-formed words and the increasing bitterness and despair behind them. Just as quickly, the sense that music of this particular nature has no reason to end, a sense that this music can have no real exit, come into focus and fades away; for this music a sense of time is almost vulgar. (Marcus, 1997: 198)

In its essence, 'I'm Not There (1956)' is a confession of failure and a dramatisation of absence. The failure to articulate his words properly – indeed, some words Dylan supposedly sings are 'not there' – mirrors the song's story of a man who should have been there but has long left. He has failed to be present, to support and to accompany the woman he has abandoned, and he is very much aware of the pain and loss his absence has caused. The unfinished lyrics, the words that are missing in order for the song to make sense, point towards the unspeakable chaos and gap that are the effect of his absence. The words Dylan mumbles seem to dissolve before they even leave his mouth, as if he reluctantly confessed a crime or were unable to make sense of himself. Marcus calls the lyrics a 'phantom text' which 'disappears as soon as it is apprehended', just as the 'I' disappears and cannot reach the woman in the song, with his song (Marcus, 1997: 202). The raw emotions and the pain cannot be properly articulated but they resonate throughout the song. 'When I'm there she is alright but then she's not when I'm gone': Dylan puts the pain of abandonment into simple words, only to confess the prime failure of his lyrical 'I' in similarly painful clarity: 'I don't perceive her, I'm not there, I'm gone'.[3] As Yaffe writes, Dylan sings 'an open wound' in this song, 'but who is the wounded?' (Yaffe, 2011: 49). The inability of the lyrical 'I' to apprehend his former lover is peculiar, because it is not *her* absence that makes it impossible for him to see her but his *own*. *Where* he is remains unclear and seems to be unimportant; emphasis is put on his not-being, as he speaks from the vantage point of one who has vanished and will not come back. After all, the 'I' is not there and yet its voice is the only voice we hear. In 'I'm Not There (1956)' the listener thus becomes the witness of things falling apart: sentences, words, a relationship, a man and his life all crumble and may well turn into dust.

It certainly makes sense that Todd Haynes chose this obscure song as an inspiration for his film. The utterance 'I'm not there' is a particularly apt title both for Dylan's song and for the film because of its cryptic nature. If one says 'I am', then one confirms one's ontological presence and affirms one's awareness of one's own existence. The utterance 'I am' situates the self within time and space, as this utterance binds the self to a here and now from which the 'I' speaks. The utterance 'I'm not there' leaves us with a riddle that is solved neither in Haynes's film nor in Dylan's song. In reference to the song, Stephen Scobie has argued that the paradox of the title lies in the words 'claim[ing] that he is not "there"', while the voice 'overwhelmingly insists that he *is* there, even if "there" is "not there", even if it is absence, loss, betrayal, anguish' (Scobie, 2006). Both the song and the title of the film tell us that the 'I' is not 'there', but we do not get a clue as to where it *is*, where the *here* is from which it articulates its being. Dylan's voice in the song signifies his presence in a 'here' from which the 'I' speaks, but where this 'here' is remains obscure. All we learn is that the 'I' is 'not there' and that only its absence from that place, its not-being, is of relevance. The 'I' is thus permanently displaced and constitutes itself through the affirmation of its absence, which seems paradigmatic for the phenomenon and the signifier 'Bob Dylan'. Bob Dylan *is*, but he is *not there*, just like his song 'I'm Not There (1956)' *is* but is *not there*: like a ghost, its bootlegged version haunts the 'Basement Tapes' and Dylan's entire *œuvre*, incomplete and unreleased, never performed live on stage, but still reverberating.

In *I'm Not There*, it is Bob Dylan who resembles a ghost: his presence in the film is ephemeral and ungraspable, yet undeniable. His name is never explicitly mentioned, yet it is written everywhere between the lines. I suggest that a reading of *I'm Not There* and the presence-*qua*-absence of Bob Dylan in this movie through Jacques Derrida's concept of the spectre illuminates Dylan's ghostliness and provides new insights into Dylan's 'multiplicity'. The spectre, as Derrida defines it, is 'a paradoxical incorporation, the becoming-body, a certain phenomenal and carnal form of the spirit' (Derrida, 1994: 5). Flesh and phenomenality 'give to the spirit its spectral apparition', Derrida explains, but they 'disappear right away in the apparition, in the very coming of the *revenant* or the return of the specter' (*ibid.*; original emphasis here and below). The precise difference between spirit and spectre is difficult to determine, for it is impossible to know what they have in common, 'what it *is*, what it is presently' (*ibid.*). Indeed, Derrida points out, '*it is* something that one does not know, precisely, and one does not know if precisely it *is*, if it exists, if it responds to a name or corresponds to an essence. One does not know: not out of ignorance, but because this non-object, this non-present present, this being-there of an absent or departed one no longer belongs to knowledge' (*ibid.*). The spectre, this unnameable thing that lies outside the realm of our knowledge, defies semantics and ontology as it is invisible – or at least nothing visible – but constantly conjured up rhetorically and visually by emphasising its not-being. The film's title displaces Bob Dylan and writes him out of the narrative (he is not there) but, at the same time, through the act of displacing, Dylan enters the narrative from which he had already vanished. A conceptualisation of Bob Dylan in *I'm Not There* as a Derridean spectre thus means to conceive of Dylan's presence in the film as spectrality, as a shadowy existence between real and non-real, factual and fictional, being and non-being.

There he lay: the ghost of Bob Dylan

The very first sequence of *I'm Not There* alludes to Bob Dylan's ghostliness. Strictly speaking, *I'm Not There* begins with Bob Dylan's death: 'There he lay: poet, prophet, outlaw, fake, star of electricity. Nailed by a peeping tom, who would soon discover: even the ghost was more than one person', a voice-over tells us while we see Cate Blanchett's character, Jude Quinn, lying in a coffin. Quinn has died after a fatal motorcycle crash, which refers to Dylan's own motorcycle accident in 1966. After his accident, Dylan withdrew from the public eye and did not tour for almost eight years, apparently using his recovery to escape from the pressures of the business, as he implies in *Chronicles*:[4] 'I had been in a motorcycle accident and I'd been hurt, but I recovered. Truth was that I wanted to get out of the rat race' (Dylan, 2004a: 114). *I'm Not There* interprets Dylan's withdrawal from the public – the peeping tom – as a metaphorical death that marks the end of Jude Quinn, the film's embodiment of the rock'n'roll spirit: live fast, die young.

The voice-over meditation on Quinn's death is a variation of the two epitaphs Dylan wrote for himself in *Tarantula*, which was written in 1966 (the year of Quinn's death and Dylan's accident) and published in 1971:

> here lies bob dylan
> murdered
> from behind
> by trembling flesh
> who after being refused by Lazarus...
> was amazed to discover
> that he was already
> a streetcar &
> that was exactly the end
> of bob dylan
> ...
>
> here lies bob dylan
> demolished by Vienna politeness –
> which will now claim to have invented him
> the cool people can
> now write Fugues about him
> & Cupid can now kick over his kerosene lamp –
> boy Dylan – killed by a discarded Oedipus
> who turned
> around
> to investigate a ghost
> & discovered that the ghost too
> was more than one person
> (Dylan, 1971: 118–20)

The two epitaphs are united by the realisation that 'the ghost too/was more than one person', but what does that mean? Ghosts are commonly featured in Dylan's lyrics and are one of his most significant key images, standing for the self outside the self or identity at one remove. According to Scobie, the ghost is the 'proper name' referring both to the self and to the other – or, more precisely, to the parts of the self that have been repudiated or disavowed (Scobie, 2003: 53). We would like to believe that the proper name – our property – always refers only to one person, and is a signal of individual identity and personal presence, but a proper name is something handed down to us, something we inherited. It is the Name of the Father, a name given to us, and in some instances a burden we must carry. 'It is the name which comes back', is how Derrida explains the haunting quality of proper names, for 'names are revenants' (Derrida, 1987: 98). In both epitaphs, the act of naming is linked to death, and, in *Tarantula*, to the Oedipal scenario of the father's murder. Unlike Lazarus, who was raised from the dead, the murdered Bob Dylan is transformed into a streetcar and it is this transformation – not death *per se* – that marks the end of Bob Dylan.

It is the Oedipal scenario that has caused both his beginning and his end, as 'a rejection of the father's name, the adoption of a pseudonym always carries [the] Oedipal charge' (Scobie, 2003: 59). The rejection of his father's name invents Bob Dylan but it kills the boy, Abraham Zimmerman's son, and, by implication, it also kills the father, Abraham Zimmerman. Bob Dylan is thus haunted by the ghost of his birth name, Robert Zimmerman, and by the ghost of his father, whose name he has denied and discarded for his alias.[5] The multiplicity of the ghost he investigates lies in the proper name he has shed and the persons he has shed with it. However, Bob Dylan, Robert Zimmerman and Abraham Zimmerman's son all merge in the same person, or rather the same body, whose singularity cannot adequately express the multiplicity of the subject.

The question of identity has been at the core of Dylan's persona and his career ever since he assumed the alias 'Bob Dylan' in a gesture of (re-)invention. Numerous reinventions have followed this first, original re-invention, each and every assumption of a new pose questioning the previous pose and sketching a new hypothesis of Dylan's identity. 'Can we rightly say he has a self?', Lewis Hyde asks about Herman Melville's 'confidence-man' (from the 1857 novel of that name) and we may pose the same question with regard to Dylan (Hyde, 1998: 53). Of course, the answer to this question can only be 'no'. All that Dylan has presented to us, and all that we see of Dylan in *I'm Not There*, is a series of masks and moving surfaces that hide the self from the peeping toms who try to nail it down.

The 'peeping tom', the voyeur evoked in the film's epitaph, may be Todd Haynes, or the film's audience or Dylan himself, looking at himself through the film. In any case, *I'm Not There* plays with the notion of identity as images of the self once removed, the self 'which is itself but not quite itself – rather, identity is doubled, divided, or deferred' (Scobie, 2003: 35). These images of the self include, according to Scobie, 'alias, mask, mirror, shadow, brother, ghost, and all the echo-effects of allusion and quotation', that is, all the effects in which *I'm Not There* revels (*ibid.*). All of these images problematise identity, as they render the self never quite identical with itself: 'Identity is always something that comes back *from* the "other", reflection or shadow; identity is always constructed *for* the "other", mask or disguise' (*ibid.*).

As the master of disguise, Dylan has, throughout his career, played the role of the trickster, as Scobie suggests, of the border-crosser and the disrupter of order. According to Hyde (1998), the trickster is a transgressive force, and according to Scobie, 'the mythic embodiment of ambiguity and ambivalence, doubleness and duplicity, contradiction and paradox' (Scobie, 2003: 7). The trickster likes to play practical jokes and to disrupt stability; he or she is 'the element of the unexpected, of productive change, which any culture needs in order to avoid rigidity and stagnation' (Scobie, 2003: 31). The trickster is a figure of reinvention, shifts, changes, masks and aimless wanderings, found at the crossroads and on the border, in the liminal space

105

'between heaven and earth, and between the living and the dead' (Hyde, 1998: 6).

When Bob Dylan is named in the epitaph of *Tarantula* he is already dead; when Bob Dylan finally appears in the last scene of *I'm Not There*, he appears only as a shadow or ghost of himself. Having already died in the very first sequence as his alias Jude Quinn, Dylan's ghost returns at the end of the film he had haunted throughout. The ghost, the alias, the mask, the mirror, the shadow and the figure of the trickster are all metaphors which express the notion of the 'I' once removed, that is, the continuous deferral of the self and its inherent fluidity and instability. While tropes like the mask or the mirror seem to imply that there is an authentic self behind the mask or mirror image of Bob Dylan which can (or at least could) be exposed, metaphors like the trickster or the ghost seem to yield more fruitful results in an analysis of the shifting, fragmentary self in motion.

In 'Diamonds and Rust' (1975), a song which she has confirmed to be about Bob Dylan, Joan Baez sings 'Well, I'll be damned, here comes your ghost again', showing a sensitivity for the importance of the image of the ghost in Dylan's work but also displaying an acute sense for Dylan's own ghostliness, which, in Derridean terms, 'begins by coming back' (Derrida, 1994: 11). As the ghost or spectre always originates in and begins with the act of haunting, its comings and goings cannot be controlled and it cannot be pinned down or contained. The revenant is, paradoxically enough, both a repetition and an original apparition: 'he comes back, so to speak, for the first time', as Derrida explains (Derrida, 1994: 4). However, the revenant also comes back for the *last* time, since 'the singularity of any *first time* makes of it also a *last time*' (*ibid.*: 10). Each and every appearance of the spectre is a repetition yet an original, is a first and a last appearance at the same time. Derrida concludes: '*What is* a ghost? What is the *effectivity* or *presence* of the spectre, that is, of what seems to remain as ineffective, virtual, insubstantial as a simulacrum?' (*ibid.*). Signifying an always-already unrealised and un-realisable ontology, Derrida concludes, the spectre represents the inherent instability of reality and the fleeting modality of materiality. As Frederic Jameson explains:

> Spectrality does not involve the conviction that ghosts exist or that the past (and maybe even the future they offer to prophesy) is still very much alive and at work, within the living present: all it says, if it can be thought to speak, is that the living present is scarcely as self-sufficient as it claims to be; that we would do well not to count on its density and solidity, which might under exceptional circumstances betray us. (Jameson, 1999: 39)

The spectre is a deconstructive figure that is neither absent nor present, neither dead nor alive. Consequently, the priority of material existence and presence is supplanted by an existence that is inherently incomplete and indefinable. Ontology, in other words, is replaced by its quasi-homonym 'hauntology', which denotes an impossible state of being – impossible, because there is no materiality, no presence, no tangible proof of actual existence.

In *I'm Not There*, Bob Dylan appears abruptly and suddenly to the six protagonists and keeps coming back without ever manifesting according to a logic of ontology. Dylan haunts them all, the 'poet, prophet, outlaw, fake, star of electricity', blurring the boundaries between real and non-real, fact and fiction, self and other in his comings and goings. In *Specters of Marx*, Derrida asks whether the comings and goings of the spectre are 'ordered according to the linear succession of a before and an after, between a present-past, a present-present, and a present-future, between a "real time" and a "deferred time"' (Derrida, 1994: 48). If there is something like spectrality, then the 'reassuring order of presents' and the neat borders between present, actual 'reality' of the present, and absence or non-presence collapse, as the '*spectrality effect*', as Derrida calls it, undoes the opposition between an effective presence and an absence, between past present and future present, focusing instead on a politics of conjuration – on a constant process of negotiation between magical incantation and magical exorcism (*ibid.*).[6] The utterance 'I'm not there' follows a politics of conjuration, as it both evokes the 'I' and expulses it, renders it present and absent at the same time.

'I is someone else', Ben Whishaw's 'Arthur Rimbaud' Dylan declares at one point, putting the deferral of the self and the politics of conjuration into poetry. The 'I' is never one, but always split, always doubled, always deferred, always referring to something or someone else; it is always evoked, insisting on its existence, and it is always exorcised, transferred onto an other outside the self. As Dylan writes in *Tarantula*, 'it is not that there is no Receptive for anything written or acted in the first person – it is just that there is no Second Person' (Dylan, 1971: 134), pointing out that the instability of the 'I' always entails an instability of the 'you'. Scobie explains the consequence of this basic realisation: 'If there is no "I", there is no "you"' (Scobie, 2003: 60), no person from which one needs to set oneself apart in order to reaffirm one's own authenticity. If 'I' and 'you' are both cancelled out, the only party that remains is 'someone else', the impersonal third person whose appropriation and performance of one's self is as authentic as one's own. In other words, Cate Blanchett's 'Jude Quinn' is as authentic as Bob Dylan's 'Bob Dylan', who is as much an appropriation and performance as his six *doppelgängers* in *I'm Not There*. It follows that there is no 'real' or 'original' Bob Dylan; the 'original' Bob Dylan is not there, is absent, a ghost, and can find material existence only through proxies, or effigies, as Joseph Roach would say.

According to Roach, an effigy is inextricably linked to performance, as it fills the vacancy created by the absence of an original by means of surrogation, that is, by providing a satisfactory alternative. Effigies can be fashioned from cloth, wood or other inanimate material; however, there are also more elusive effigies, made from flesh, which come down to us in performances and 'provide communities with a method of perpetuating themselves through specially nominated mediums or surrogates' (Roach, 1996: 36). Effigies fill the vacancy produced by the absence of an original – by an original that has never existed in the first place. Living effigies 'consist of a set of actions that hold open a place in memory into which many different people may step', among them actors, dancers, orators, celebrities, statesmen, priests and corpses (*ibid.*).

The epitaph announcing Bob Dylan's death plays with fictions of identity and troubles the boundaries between self and other. Dylan's metaphorical death resembles ritualised public announcements such as 'The King is dead. Long live the King!', which is probably one of the most prominent methods of perpetuation. The implied declaration 'Bob Dylan is dead. Long live Bob Dylan!' is a 'symbolic immutability' which solidifies the signifier 'Bob Dylan' by immortalising Dylan in the form of a 'second body' (Roach, 1996: 38), an enduring, iconic, institutionalised performance of 'Dylan-ness'. Bob Dylan manifests himself through performances of 'Dylan-ness', through appropriations and incorporations of his gestures, his behaviours, his looks and his style. The 'real' and 'original' Bob Dylan, however, is not there. The multiplicity of actors portraying him in *I'm Not There* is an index of his presence in absence: no one portrayal can ever be enough to capture Bob Dylan. 'He is more, or less, than the sum of his images', as Scobie puts it (Scobie, 2006). No matter how many actors portray him, Bob Dylan is not there. He is always somewhere else, always someone else, and thus finds material existence only through effigies that fill the vacancy of his absence.

Conclusion: 'When I'm gone you will remember my name'

'I can change during the course of a day. When I wake I'm one person, when I go to sleep I know for certain I'm somebody else. I don't know who I am most of the time',[7] Richard Gere's incarnation of Bob Dylan as 'Billy the Kid' remarks as *I'm Not There* closes, clearly referencing the multiplicity of the film's subject. Gere's words also allude to the spectrality of the film's subject, as they recall Derrida's observation that the spectre is never wholly present nor material, can never *be* anything but always only 'almost-be', that is, approximate a state of being. The collapse of linear time and sequential order provoked by the spectrality effect causes chaos and disruption, continuous shifts and changes, which complicates the constitution of a coherent subject.

'The time is out of joint', Derrida quotes from William Shakespeare's *Hamlet* to emphasise the disarticulation and dislocation of time in the presence-absence of the spectre, which also resonates in *I'm Not There*: 'It's like you got yesterday, today, and tomorrow all in the same room. There is no telling what can happen', are the final words of Gere's 'Billy the Kid' as the film ends. Here, the film once again recalls the song it was named after – or, more precisely, Greil Marcus's interpretation of it. As Marcus suggests, 'I'm Not There (1956)' is filled with the presence of tragedy, in the sense that it is 'the sung and played embodiment of crimes that float in terms of argument and evidence, but are immovable as verdicts, in their weight' (Marcus, 1997: 192). These crimes, he elaborates, are 'sins committed, perhaps without intent, that will throw the world *out of joint*, crimes that will reverberate across space and time in ways that no one can stop' (*ibid.*; emphasis added). Marcus, too, here implicitly references *Hamlet* to underline the disruptive forces set free by the ghostly presence-absence of the 'I'.

'What language do you speak when you speak of things like this?' Marcus finally asks (*ibid.*). My answer would be that you speak the language of the spectral. The key to understanding this language, Derrida suggests (according to Wendy Brown), is to learn to live with the spectres, 'with the things that shape the present, rendering it as always permeated by an elsewhere but in a fashion that is inconsistent, ephemeral, and hence not fully mappable' (Brown, 2001: 145). In a Derridean reading of the spectral, phantoms and ghosts 'emblematise a postmetaphysical way of life', Brown writes, 'a way of life saturated by elements … that are not under our sway and that also cannot be harnessed to projects of reason, development, progress, or structure' (*ibid.*: 145–6). Ghosts wander freely, and resist mastering and subjection through knowledge, power, action, place or time. Ghosts come to us as effects, as traces of something that has been lost, that has been purposefully repressed or that cannot be properly articulated. When ghosts become spectres, that is, carnal spirits or embodiments of the unliveable that transfer from the realm of the immaterial to materiality, they disrupt and destabilise established structures and laws of time, knowledge and being.

'When I'm gone you will remember my name', Dylan sings in ''Til I Fell in Love With You', alluding to the haunting quality of names, which reverberate and linger on even though their bearer may be absent (Dylan, 2004b: 565). Just as Bob Dylan haunts *I'm Not There*, Bob Dylan also haunts Bob Dylan, and Bob Dylan is being haunted by his masks and aliases. His ghostliness may well be Bob Dylan's most enduring quality, a quality that renders him an unnameable thing, a thing that defies semantics and ontology, a thing that one cannot see but that still appears again and again. As I have outlined in this chapter, Bob Dylan is a spectral figure of the in-between, a multifaceted and ungraspable, infinitely mutable signifier that continually takes on new and different meanings. Every imagination, appropriation and performance of Dylan-ness contributes to momentary and ephemeral materialisations of Bob Dylan, revisiting Dylan through citations and recitations. In citations of himself, Dylan becomes his own ghost, his own spectre, and outlives himself in performance. Even though he may no longer be there, 'you will remember my name'; he insists on his own ghostly endurance. Bob Dylan may be gone, but he is still here, even if he is not there.

Notes

1 According to Adrian Danks, Dylan himself has in many ways promoted and fuelled such an approach. D. A. Pennebaker's film *Dont Look Back* (1967) or Martin Scorsese's documentary *No Direction Home: Bob Dylan* (2005) are fascinating precisely because Dylan deliberately and effectively evades both straightforward questions and answers, making everything seem both painfully simple and endlessly complicated. Also, various films that associate partly or fully with Dylan's image have reinforced this multifaceted and masked persona, from the aptly named Alias in Sam Peckinpah's 1973 opus *Pat Garrett and Billy the Kid* to Dylan's own projects like *Renaldo and Clara* (1978). As Danks (2008) argues, 'Dylan has himself been integral to the creation of this shifting cinematic image.... Dylan has worked to both discourage and reinforce critical interpretations of his own work (and life)'.

2 Commenting on Dylan's memoir *Chronicles*, Perry Meisel remarks that 'Dylan is not wholly conscious of himself either' and must 'take himself as his own subject' in his book. Even Dylan does not know who Dylan is, because 'there is no Dylan himself', as Meisel states. Therefore, Dylan's work 'both is and is about this dislocation within, or of, the self' (Meisel, 2010: 170).

3 As no official transcription of the lyrics to 'I'm Not There (1956)' is available, I am quoting from 'I'm Not There' as it was released on the 2007 CD *I'm Not There Original Soundtrack*. Many of the words of 'I'm Not There (1956)' are an incomprehensible and inaudible blur, as Dylan was improvising and free-associating the verses around a written refrain. The song remained sketchy and unfinished, but it was nevertheless released on the film's soundtrack, which features a cover version of the song by American rock band Sonic Youth and Bob Dylan's original recording from 1967. The parts I am quoting are my transcription of Dylan's recording.

4 It is interesting to note that the chapters of Dylan's memoir, *Chronicles, Volume One*, are not organised chronologically but thematically, which underlines that Dylan probably does not conceive of his personal history in linear and teleological terms, but rather in terms of themes, contexts and associations. 'In fact', David Yaffe writes, 'he overlaps, looking back, forward, then back again' (see Yaffe, 2011: xvi).

5 Stephen Scobie suggests that Dylan's writing contains repeated images and motifs that can be interpreted as textual traces of an Oedipal conflict. Such moments include the evocation of Oedipus in the epitaph quoted above, the figure of the failed or dying father, and Dylan's re-enactment, in performances of the song 'Highway 61 Revisited', of the patriarchal father Abraham trying to kill his son. As Scobie writes, 'this song, this journey, *has to* start with a lethal confrontation with the name of the father – "God said to Abraham, Kill me a son" – so that it can allow the son to continue, surviving in his pseudonym' (Scobie, 2003: 43).

6 The French noun 'conjuration' articulates two seemingly conflicting meanings, as Derrida points out. It signifies 'conjuration' (its English homonym), on the one hand, and 'conjurement', on the other. The English 'conjuration' may denote either 'the conspiracy ... of those who promise solemnly ... by swearing together an oath to struggle against a superior power' or the 'magical incantation destined to *evoke*, to bring forth with the voice, to *convoke* a charm or spirit'. 'Conjurement', by contrast, refers to the 'magical exorcism that ... tends to expulse the evil spirit which would have been called up or evoked' (see Derrida, 1994: 50, 58).

7 This remark is almost a verbatim quote from a *Newsweek* feature on Bob Dylan published in 1997. In his conversation with *Newsweek* senior editor David Gates, Dylan stated: 'I don't think I'm tangible to myself. I mean, I think one thing today and I think another thing tomorrow. I change during the course of a day. I wake and I'm one person, and when I go to sleep I know for certain I'm somebody else. I don't know *who* I am most of the time. It doesn't even matter to me' (Gates, 2004: 236).

References

Bingham, D. (2010) *Whose Lives Are They Anyway? The Biopic as Contemporary Film Genre* (New Brunswick, NJ: Rutgers University Press).

Brown, W. (2001) *Politics Out of History* (Princeton, MA: Princeton University Press).

Custen, G. F. (1992) *Bio/Pics: How Hollywood Constructed Public History* (New Brunswick, NJ: Rutgers University Press).

Danks, A. (2008) '… I'm gone; or, seven characters in search of an exit: some reflections on Todd Haynes' *I'm Not There*', *Senses of Cinema*, 46. Available at http://www.sensesofcinema.com/2008/feature-articles/im-not-there (accessed 17 March 2012).

Derrida, J. (1987) *The Post Card: From Socrates to Freud and Beyond*, trans. A. Bass (Chicago, IL: University of Chicago Press).

Derrida, J. (1994) *Specters of Marx*, trans. P. Kamuf (London: Routledge).

Dylan, B. (1971) *Tarantula* (New York: Scribner).

Dylan, B. (2004a) *Chronicles: Volume One* (New York: Simon and Schuster).

Dylan, B. (2004b) *Lyrics, 1962–2001* (New York: Simon and Schuster).

Gates, D. (2004) 'Dylan revisited', in B. Hedin (ed.), *Studio A: The Bob Dylan Reader* (New York: W. W. Norton). 235–43.

Hyde, L. (1998) *Trickster Makes This World: Mischief, Myth, and Art* (New York: Farrar, Strauss, and Giroux).

Jameson, F. (1999) 'Marx's purloined letter', in M. Sprinkler (ed.), *Ghostly Demarcations: A Symposium on Jacques Derrida's Specters of Marx* (London: Verso). 26–67.

Marcus, G. (1997) *Invisible Republic: The Basement Tapes* (New York: Picador).

Martin, A. (2007) 'Another kind of river', *Studies in Documentary Film*, 1:1. 53–8.

Meisel, P. (2010) *The Myth of Popular Culture: From Dante to Dylan* (Malden, MA: Blackwell).

Roach, J. (1996) *Cities of the Dead: Circum-Atlantic Performance* (New York: Columbia University Press).

Scobie, S. (2003) *Alias: Bob Dylan Revisited* (Alberta: Red Deer Press).

Scobie, S. (2006) 'I'm not there yet', unpublished paper presented at the conference 'Just a Series of Interpretations of Bob Dylan's Lyrical Works', at Dartmouth College, 11–13 August 2006. Available at http://www.dartmouth.edu/~2006dylancon/papers/Scobie-notthere.pdf (accessed 17 March 2011).

Yaffe, D. (2011) *Bob Dylan: Like a Complete Unknown* (New Haven, CT: Yale University Press).

9

Mr Pound, Mr Eliot and Mr Dylan: the United States and Europe, modernity and modernism

Leighton Grist

Almost midway through *Masculin Féminin* (Jean-Luc Godard, 1966), the film's protagonist, Paul (Jean-Pierre Léaud), is shown sitting in a Paris laundrette beside his friend, left-wing activist Robert (Michel Debord), who peruses a newspaper. Asked by Paul what he is reading, Robert replies, 'An article on Bob Dylan', whom he describes as a 'Vietnik'.

In the penultimate verse of 'Desolation Row', Bob Dylan makes reference to the poets Ezra Pound and T. S. Eliot. Pound and Eliot were both poets who were born in the United States but who moved to and passed much of their lives in Europe. Pound was born in Hailey, Idaho Territory, in 1885, and lived in London, England, 1908–21, Paris, France, 1921–24, and Rapallo, Italy, 1924–45. After a period spent back in the United States, 1945–58, he returned to Italy, where he resided, mainly in Rapallo, until his death in 1972. Eliot was born in St Louis, Missouri, in 1888. He migrated to Europe in 1914, and spent most of his time, until his death in 1965, living in London, becoming a British citizen in 1927. These physical and, in Eliot's case, legal relocations were consonant with both poets' turning to and embracing of European culture and traditions as a means of ameliorating the dislocations and un-certainties that were attendant upon a modernity with which, historically, the United States has been not insignificantly aligned.

Dylan was similarly born in the United States, in Duluth, Minnesota, in 1941. He is, however, someone who has embodied and affirmed the very modernity that Pound and Eliot abjured. Perhaps symptomatically, he has, in terms of residence, followed a peculiarly American itinerary, which has seen him at different times living in Hibbing, Minneapolis, New York, Woodstock and Malibu. Dylan has nevertheless been a quite regular visitor to Europe: visits that in the mid-1960s worked to underline the differences between Europe and the United States, tradition and modernity, and age and youth. Hence in part the fascination of *Dont Look Back* (D. A. Pennebaker, 1967), in which, as the film centres upon Dylan's brief 1965 English tour, the tousle-haired, wafer-thin, casually hip Dylan stands strikingly apart from the environment that he traverses – whether one considers the tired glamour of a record-company reception at London's Dorchester Hotel, the dingy urban surroundings of provincial 1960s Britain or the shabby datedness of numerous non-descript backstage areas. In turn, while the behaviour of Dylan and his tour manager-cum-sidekick Bob Neuwirth at times slides into self-conscious posturing, Dylan's confident, youthful insouciance correspondingly contrasts and increasingly comes into conflict with the stolid, often patronising attitudes of a residually hierarchical, unequivocally class-bound society. Apparent throughout in Dylan's encounters with the press, the collision of what he calls 'two different worlds' is encapsulated in the scenes shot backstage at Newcastle City Hall that represent Dylan confronting and being confronted by the science student and the High Sheriff's Lady, persons whose respective maladroit truculence and overbearing, privileged confidence bespeak their larger historical determination.[1] That noted, the film also evidences a gravitation towards Dylan by the young, for whom Dylan, the science student notwithstanding, would appear to be a figure of liberating emulation and desire, as witness the covers combo who play his songs with 'a big-band sound', the groups of teens and sub-teens who dog his movements, or Donovan.[2]

Of a piece with the generational dynamics of the 1960s, such investment in Dylan, and in the liberation that Dylan figures, further indexes the larger breakdown of established norms, structures and verities that is associated with modernity, which in the 1960s attained both its apotheosis and its end point. Complementing matters ideologically, Dylan's work, which in general partakes of a left-liberal perspective, was in the early to mid-1960s indivisibly connected with the civil rights movement and associated political protest. That in *Masculin Féminin* Paul and Robert should be represented discussing Dylan is, in turn, again testimony to the impact within Europe of his person and his music, but it is also appropriate to characters whom the film places as belonging to a generation that it dubs, with condensed political and cultural resonance, the 'children of Marx and Coca-Cola'. Similarly appropriate is that Paul and Robert should, in a film that, like much of Godard's 1960s film-making, conveys the tensions implicit to a developing French modernity, be shown as speaking in the *echt* modern setting of a laundrette. Moreover, while Robert's designation of Dylan as a 'Vietnik' may be semantically and empirically inexact, it has – within a film that was shot in late 1965 – a distinct extrapolative logic.

The left-liberal relation of Dylan and his work provides another point of contrast between him and Pound and Eliot. Both Pound and Eliot were

113

political reactionaries. Pound was a fascist who, apart from embracing, and being embraced by, the regime headed by Benito Mussolini in Italy, expressed support and admiration for Adolf Hitler and wrote for the newspaper, *Action*, run by British fascist figurehead Oswald Mosley. Having broadcast anti-American propaganda on Italian radio, Pound was arrested near the end of the Second World War and passed most of his time in the United States between 1945 and 1958 in a sanitorium, to which he was committed in lieu of being tried for treason. Eliot, who characterised his outlook as being 'classicist in literature, royalist in politics, and anglo-catholic in religion' (Eliot, 1928: ix), variously espoused a traditionalist, anti-liberal conservatism. Correlative to his fascism, Pound was virulently anti-Semitic; anti-Semitism has likewise been claimed of Eliot and his work.[3] It is, consequently, more than suggestive, given the divergent ideological implications of Dylan's work and his affiliations, not to mention his Jewishness, that in 'Desolation Row' Pound and Eliot, who enjoyed a close personal and professional relationship, are described, with knowing yet vengefully ironic kidding, as 'Fighting in the captain's tower'.[4]

That noted, the adduction of Pound and Eliot is also an acknowledgement of poetic forebears, and 'Desolation Row' has been widely compared to Eliot's *The Waste Land*, a poem that Pound edited.[5] Moreover, Dylan's work as a whole is formally and epistemologically consonant with the modernism that the poetry of Pound and Eliot differently instantiates. With respect to this, if modernity afforded emancipating opportunity, then it was likewise the site, coextensively and paradoxically, of systematised, oppressive rationalisation.[6] Modernism, in turn, as it emerges out of modernity, articulates modernity's underside, expresses what modernity disavows: the undecidedness, illogic and ambiguity that attend modernity's seemingly ordered, unequivocal progression and/or, reciprocally, the estrangement, anomie and inexpressible or unrealised impulses and desires that are resultant upon modernity's potentially or actually overwhelming development. Concordantly, within modernism there obtains an emphasis on the contingent rather than the essential, the relative rather than the absolute: an accentuation that finds an aesthetic correlative in the reflexivity of modernist representation, the foregrounding, across forms and media, of the signifier, of the (itself contingent and relative) fact of signification. Modernism's engagement with and refraction of modernity nevertheless carry contrasting representational and ideological connotations, with there being a variable weighting granted liberating possibility or disquieting disorder, alienated want or deadened purposelessness. There is, accordingly, a certain congruence apparent between Pound's and Eliot's politics and their poetic practice, the dense allusiveness of which not only augments its reflexivity but underpins a modernist mythopoeia that – divergently embodied otherwise in the work of, for example, W. B. Yeats, James Joyce and Thomas Mann, and evidenced not least in *The Waste Land* and Pound's *magnum opus* the *Cantos* – seeks to mitigate what they perceived to be the depredations and chaos of modernity through the evocation of a larger cultural and trans-historical order.[7]

An analogous structuration might be suggested by Dylan's recourse, especially within his initial, acoustic output, to folk and blues forms. Further, although the blues is not a modernist mode *per se*, as it vents individualised experience by means of a form that bespeaks cultural longevity, its mutual expression and amelioration of the uncertainties and dislocations of American black life post-Emancipation invokes, epistemologically, a distinctly modernist *Weltanschauung*.[8] However, while the blues thus partakes implicitly of that which is explicitly constructed within the canonical writings of the likes of Yeats, Pound and Eliot, Dylan's employment of folk and blues configurations less contains than provides a framework facilitating the development of his distinctive aesthetic vision. Indeed, if modernism is, in part, as Malcolm Bradbury and James McFarlane aver, 'less a style than a search for a style in a highly individualistic sense' (Bradbury and McFarlane, 1976: 29), then elements particular to Dylan's stylistic signature are apparent from early in his work. Note, for instance, the cited allusion to and reworking of folk and blues precedents, together with their infusion by and interpenetration with a latently Symbolic precision of diction and image and a concordantly intensive, contextually foregrounded utilisation of poetic devices (assonance, dissonance, rhyme, metaphor, enjambment and so on); or the elongation of song length and elaboration of internal involution, and the reflective extension of line and syntax to a point of near impossible verbal articulation. In turn, not only does Dylan's 'ability to sustain, without faltering, extremely long lyrical lines against a melody' comprise, as Neil Corcoran observes, another of his work's 'hallmarks' (Corcoran, 2002b: 173), but his vocals' emotional intensity, nuanced phrasing and accordant, precisely reverberant communication of meaning and affect, while drawing on folk and blues antecedents, significantly redefined what constitutes singing: this despite, or because of, what Biba Kopf lists as 'its commonly perceived shortcomings – abrasive tone, grating nasality, tunelessness, wayward pitching' (Kopf, 1998: 36). Referable to modernism's investment in newness and innovation, Dylan's singing also contributes to the sense of empowerment and potential that is conveyed throughout the early phase of his career, and that contrasts signally with the stress – formally and otherwise – within Pound's and Eliot's work on an innately unchanged, unchanging and unchangeable order of being.

That Dylan should declare that 'the times they are a-changin'' has, correspondingly, an amplitude that arguably exceeds the particular social and political situation that the song of the same title speaks to. The appeal of his work to his predominantly young audience is, hence, in terms of its modernist implications, possibly as much referable to formal and epistemological as ideological consonance: hence too, perhaps, supplementing the

115

connotations of Dylan's person and appearance, the appeal of that work outside of its immediate American context.[9] This is not to discount the context that informs Dylan's early, acoustic output, or that output's relation and indebtedness to its context. However, it also lends Dylan's work a positivism that is notably jettisoned as it enters the mid-1960s and undergoes significant changes, lyrically and musically. These changes have been much rehearsed, but gain, once more, from their formal and epistemological positioning. Lyrically, latent Symbolism becomes manifest, shading at times, like Symbolism itself, into the surrealist. In his sleeve notes for the album that confirmed his changed approach, *Bringing It All Back Home* (1965), Dylan writes: 'i accept chaos. i am not sure whether it accepts me'. Positivism and overt social and political reference are, accordingly, forsworn before the adduction of a more personalised realm of the ambiguous, confused, alienating, perversely generative and/or corrupt. Not that social and political reference disappears, but it is displaced within an open engagement with the extant complexities of modernity. For Richard Brown: 'Rather than the abandonment of politics, the new discourse inaugurates a more contemporary politics' (Brown, 2002: 205). In turn, as Pound and Eliot are ironised in 'Desolation Row', so, in the same verse, is everybody who is shouting the 1930s miners' union song, 'Which Side Are You On?' Musically, the switch from acoustic to electric instrumentation both underscores Dylan's (at the time contentious) break from the folk-protest grouping with which he had previously been associated, and for whom 'Which Side Are You On?' was a repertory staple,[10] and provides an apt sonic complement to the rendering of modernity that his lyrics contemporaneously purvey – 'electric music', as Michael Gray notes, with respect to the album *Highway 61 Revisited* (also 1965), 'as the embodiment of our whole out-of-control, nervous-energy-fuelled, chaotic civilization' (Gray, 2000: 5). Or, as Dylan puts it, 'my songs are pictures and the band makes the sound of the pictures' (in interview with Nat Hentoff, 1966 – see Cott, 2006: 97).

Symbolism, with its reflexive emphasis on word and phrase, on writing in and of itself, has been regarded as being foundational to literary modernism.[11] Its influence upon Dylan's work provides another connection with that of the similarly Symbolist-influenced Eliot, as well as with the European culture that Eliot extolled. Nevertheless, if in his mid-1960s output the specificities of Dylan's language and expression remain unequivocally American, then those of his music, which maintains its folk and, especially, blues underpinnings, are brashly, forcefully, even impolitely so. Further, as Dylan's work of the period compounds and fulfils the empowerment and potential of his acoustic material to produce a thrilling, intellectually and emotionally complex whole, so it is a whole that, while possessing no illusions concerning modernity's brutalities and oppressions, continues to function to fundamentally liberatory effect in as much how as what it expresses – regarding which its very 'American-ness' is intrinsic.

116

So, too, is, epistemologically, its exemplary modernist purport. A key bridge between Dylan's early and mid-1960s output is 'My Back Pages', a song on his 1964 album *Another Side of Bob Dylan*. A farewell to folk-protest and its attendant positivism, it concordantly heralds a movement from a situation in which terms could be defined as 'Good and bad', 'Quite clear, no doubt, somehow', to an acceptance of contingency and undecidedness in which, as in 'Visions of Johanna' (from *Blonde on Blonde*, 1966), 'Louise holds a handful of rain, temptin' you to defy it'. It is also a movement that is suggestively reflected in the differences, formally and epistemologically, that are apparent between *Dont Look Back*, which represents what turned out to be Dylan's last fully acoustic tour, and *Eat the Document*, which represents his 1966 European tour, during which Dylan's concerts comprised two sets, one acoustic, and solo, and one electric, with Dylan being accompanied by the Hawks.[12] *Dont Look Back* is an example of direct cinema, a documentary approach that developed within the United States in the late 1950s and 1960s. However, while the contemporaneous documentary practice of *cinéma vérité*, which emerged out of France, reflexively acknowledges the motivating and manipulative intervention of the filming process, within direct cinema this is dissimulated – as *Dont Look Back* demonstrates – through a recourse to indirect address and 'a modified form' of continuity editing (Nichols, 1981: 210). The result is an approximation of (inherently positivist) classical realist narrative, wherein the potentially disruptive markers of signification – unsteady handheld camerawork, grainy visual texture, uneven sound quality – are recuperated as validating the immediate capture of contingent actuality. Reciprocating this, through its long association with reportage, is, in *Dont Look Back*, the use of black-and-white film stock. *Eat the Document* is, in contrast, shot in colour. Presenting a fragmented and elliptical assemblage of shots, scenes and sequences, the film further invokes and can be aligned with the modernist, avant-garde filmmaking of the likes of Ken Jacobs, Jack Smith and Robert Frank, which has been corralled as part of the New American Cinema that transpired synchronously with, although divergent from, direct cinema. It is a connection that is implied both visually – for instance, during the film's concert footage, with its frequent decentred framing, and flaring of lighting and colour – and through the delineation of incident that is variously, and at times ambiguously, documentary, staged and/or improvised.[13]

Among Frank's films is *Pull My Daisy* (1959), which he co-directed with Alfred Leslie. Written and narrated by Jack Kerouac, and based on his unproduced play *The Beat Generation*, *Pull My Daisy* is one of the comparatively few examples of Beat cinema, a cinematic embodiment of a movement that Dylan has openly admitted as an influence.[14] Yet if this further reflects upon Robert's characterisation of Dylan as a Vietnik in *Masculin Féminin*, then he may well have revised his opinion in the light of Dylan's electric set during his Paris concert on his 1966 tour. *Masculin Féminin* premiered in Paris on 22

April 1966; on 24 May Dylan and the Hawks played before a large Stars and Stripes. The upshot, with the Vietnam War ongoing, and being contested by the European left, was a compounding of the vehement discontent that had been expressed towards Dylan's shift in musical direction by disaffected folk-music dogmatists throughout the tour. However, with the United States itself becoming increasingly polarised ideologically and politically with respect to the Vietnam War, the flag – which Dylan chose, markedly, to unveil on his twenty-fifth birthday – can be regarded as being less a signifier of pro-war or broader establishment support than of, as Sean Wilentz notes, 'his own version of "America"' (Wilentz, 2010: 262), of, with due implication of the paradoxes of the modernity that American imperialist aggression in South-East Asia otherwise instantiated, the different 'America' that had diversely underpinned the appeal within Europe of Dylan and his work. Concordantly, both the loud, confrontational implacability of the tour's electric sets in general and the displaying of the Stars and Stripes in particular intimate another aspect of the modernism that likewise shapes that work: 'the shock, the violation of expected continuities, the element of de-creation and crisis' that Bradbury and McFarlane cite as being, apropos of modernism, 'crucial' (Bradbury and McFarlane, 1976: 24).[15] Moreover, Dylan's mid-1960s output can be seen to mediate that which in *Masculin Féminin* is represented as being mutually irreconcilable and problematically gendered – (masculine) left politics and (feminine) popular music and culture. Its 'more contemporary politics', its correlation of the resonantly personal and the implicitly political, as well as its unfettered acceptance of complexity, accordingly foreshadow somewhat the personalisation and expansion of what constitutes politics that animated and resulted from *les événements* of May 1968: the worst rioting of which occurred, as Wilentz observes, exactly two years after Dylan's concert (Wilentz, 2010: 261), and that Godard's filmmaking, as it continued during the 1960s, proceeded contrastingly to presage, to chart and to be informed by.

From a left perspective, the longer-term consequences of May 1968 have been unfortunate, as the relativising and fragmentation of progressive positions has seen a leeching of motive force, and their easy containment and recuperation within the consummation of modernity, the mutual expansion of apparent liberties and totalising systemisation that is postmodernity. In turn, while modernism, whatever the ideological connotations of its particular embodiments, partakes of an if not always oppositional, then at least oblique perspective with respect to the reality that it relays, not only does postmodernism, as what has been termed postmodernity's 'cultural dominant' (Jameson, 1984: 56), lack any such expository imperative, but as it maintains and elaborates upon the allusiveness and reflexivity familiar to modernism, so there is at best a deferred and at worst a short-circuiting of any functional relation to, much less engagement with, the context from which it issues.

Yet while modernity has shifted, epochally, into postmodernity, Dylan's work has remained resolutely modernist, and has correspondingly continued to refract and invite reflection upon its encompassing actuality, no matter what its designation. Further to this, we might turn again to *Eat the Document*. Described by Wilentz as 'a chaotic film that appears to be about chaos' (Wilentz, 2010: 158), it is considered by C. P. Lee more prosaically to show 'what life is like on the road' (Lee, 2000: 42), and certainly much of the film's off-stage footage represents a seemingly endless round of travelling, press conferences and attempts to pass the time, within which Dylan cuts an increasingly isolated and/or disconsolate figure. Noteworthy is the scene in which a stoned and tired Dylan rides in a car with an unnaturally perky John Lennon. This culminates – upon Lennon's attempts to enliven Dylan, which conclude with a crass, nominally ironic assertion of financial incentive: 'Another few dollars, eh? That'll get your head up ...' – with a cut to a close-up of a wearily impassive Dylan, his head resting on his hand.[16] However, the scene also cuts, via a (spatially and temporally unrelated) shot through a car windscreen of a dreary, rain-spattered British cityscape, to the representation of an enthused and energetically involved Dylan playing a characteristically intensive electric version of 'One Too Many Mornings' on stage with the Hawks. The suggested differences between Dylan, and existence, on stage and off are, in this instance, as throughout the film, stark. *Eat the Document* concordantly educes, with larger, implicit reference to Dylan's work overall, a pair of vestigial, supplementary premises regarding modernist artistic practice. On the one hand, such practice is considered to redeem the artist, to 'set the artist free to be more himself', to 'let him move beyond the kingdom of necessity to the kingdom of light'; on the other, it redeems as it elucidates reality, which 'is discontinuous till art comes along', but 'within art' becomes 'vital' – 'discontinuous, yes, but within an aesthetic system of positioning' (Bradbury and McFarlane, 1976: 25).

If this brings us back to and more broadly contextualises the modernist mythopoeia of Pound and Eliot, then it also takes us to the ongoing modernist extravaganza that, commencing in 1988, has been called Dylan's Never Ending Tour. Further, while the allusion to and reworking of musical forms and precedents have continued, and even proliferated, in Dylan's newly written work during this period, he has likewise continued in performance his tendency, following 1966, to submit his own earlier output to the same operation. Complemented by the 'ever inventive', and at times demanding, phrasing of his 'singular voice' (Kopf, 1998: 37), not only does the resultant interplay of familiarity and difference, as it highlights the specificities of signification and expression, maintain the reflexivity indivisible from the modernist mode, but the songs' revision works to foreclose the reification, and attendant, potential co-optation, formally and ideologically, of art and artefacts that – consonant with the processes of postmodernism – is another concomitant of postmodernity. For as such reworking both serves, in Corcoran's words, 'the original text' and acts 'to reintroduce it to the contemporary moment', bringing it 'newly alive' (Corcoran, 2002a: 15), so it enables what Fredric Jameson describes as the reality of 'the work-in-situation, the work-in-performance' to bridge, meaningfully, if only 'for a brief moment', 'the gap between producer and consumer' that reification and co-optation occasion (Jameson, 1976: 177).

The Never Ending Tour has not infrequently passed through Europe. In Lyon, France, 20 June 2010, Dylan's set concluded with a rendition of 'Ballad of a Thin Man'. A song whose performance has been contrastingly accusatory, vindictive, haunting, jaunty and self-implicating, in this instance – with Dylan standing centre stage, his shadow projected massively on the backdrop and the song's blues inflections foregrounded – it partook of a confrontational, recriminatory menace. Moreover, if the rendition constituted modernist potential realised, then the modernist challenge that the song mutually embodies and expresses remained: 'Because something is happening here / But you don't know what it is / Do you, Mister Jones?'

Notes

1 An obverse, negative reflection of Dylan's 'difference' is arguably embodied by his manager, Albert Grossman. A notoriously ruthless operator, Grossman is in *Dont Look Back* shown in a scene with British booking agent Tito Burns attempting to finagle the best possible fee for some television appearances by Dylan, during which, to cite Michael Gray, Burns's 'wily bully-boy' is made to 'look a bumbling fraud alongside Grossman's genuine article' (Gray, 2006: 188).

2 Or even, as well, the science student himself. One Terry Ellis, he not only proceeded to form a band called the Science Students (Bauldie, 1987: 14) but 'went on to found Chrysalis Records, manage Jethro Tull, and become a millionaire' (Heylin, 2011: 188).

3 See, for example, Julius (1995).

4 John Gibbens offers a different interpretation of the line, arguing that Pound and Eliot 'could be fighting side by side to seize the "captain's tower"', an interpretation that he proposes is 'more biographically accurate' (Gibbens, 2001: 228).

5 In the first volume of his autobiography, *Chronicles*, Dylan admits that he 'liked T. S. Eliot', whom he considered to be 'worth reading', but states that he 'never did read' Pound, whom he dismisses, pointedly, as 'a Nazi sympathizer in World War II' who 'did anti-American broadcasts from Italy' (Dylan, 2004: 110). It is, however, perhaps indicative of the uncertain truth status that has been claimed of *Chronicles* that in the interview conducted by Cameron Crowe which is published in the booklet that accompanies the 1985 box set *Biograph*, Dylan, talking about his time in Minneapolis, lists the work of 'Pound, Camus, T. S. Eliot, e. e. cummings' as being among that which 'left the rest of everything in the dust' (p. 5). Regarding the comparisons made between 'Desolation Row' and *The Waste Land* see, for example, among numerous other, often offhand likenings, Gibbens (2001: 206–9, 230–2) and Wilentz (2010: 82–3). For a more general consideration of the relation of Dylan and Eliot's work, see Gray (2000: 71–4; 2006: 206–7).

6 Thus, maybe, the contrasting difference embodied by Dylan and Grossman as they are represented in *Dont Look Back*.

7 As Eliot notes, addressing what he terms 'the mythical method' in relation to Joyce's

Ulysses: 'It is simply a way of controlling, of ordering, of giving a shape and a significance to the immense panorama of futility and anarchy which is contemporary history' (Eliot, 1923: 178, 177).

8 With respect to this, see Grist (2007).

9 For a similar argument regarding the blues in terms of the British blues boom, see Grist (2007).

10 The song was written in 1931 by Florence Reece, and was in the years following the Second World War performed by the left-wing group the Weavers, whose members included Pete Seeger.

11 See, for example, Wilson (1931).

12 Although first screened publicly in 1971, *Eat the Document*, which was putatively completed in 1967, had initially been shot as a programme for the 1966 ABC television series *Stage 66*. It was directed by Dylan, largely shot by Pennebaker and officially released in 1972.

13 According to Pennebaker, the flaring was in part encouraged by the film stock that was employed: 'We were using this new colour stock – the first of the new Ektachrome, the high speed ... if you shot into a concert hall ... and you picked up some of the spotlights and just flared ... the effect was fantastic' (Bauldie, 1987: 24).

14 Apart from the involvement of Kerouac, *Pull My Daisy* features, of those involved with the Beat movement, writers Allen Ginsberg, Gregory Corso and Peter Orlovsky, and painters Alice Neel and Larry Rivers. For Dylan's admission of the influence of the Beats, see, for example, the *Biograph* booklet (p. 5); for an extended discussion of Dylan's relation to the Beats, see Wilentz (2010: 47–84).

15 The electric sets also comprised, in Clinton Heylin's words, 'totally integrated, inspired rock music' (Heylin, 2011: 246).

16 Lennon has attributed his behaviour in the scene to a combination of anxiety and drugs: 'I was always so paranoid.... So in the film I'm just blabbing off, just commenting all the time like you do when you're very high and stoned.... It was [Dylan's] movie. I was on his territory. That's why I was nervous' (Lee, 2000: 56).

References

Bauldie, J. (1987) 'Eye to eye: a conversation with D. A. Pennebaker', *Telegraph*, 26(spring). 10–26.

Bradbury, M. and McFarlane, J. (1976) 'The name and nature of modernism', in M. Bradbury and J. McFarlane (eds), *Modernism: 1890–1930* (Harmondsworth: Penguin). 19–55.

Brown, R. (2002) 'Highway 61 and other American states of mind', in N. Corcoran (ed.), *Do You Mr Jones? Bob Dylan with the Poets and Professors* (London: Chatto and Windus). 193–220.

Corcoran, N. (2002a) 'Introduction: writing aloud', in N. Corcoran (ed.), *Do You, Mr Jones? Bob Dylan with the Poets and Professors* (London: Chatto and Windus). 7–23.

Corcoran, N. (2002b) 'Death's honesty', in N. Corcoran (ed.), *Do You Mr Jones? Bob Dylan with the Poets and Professors* (London: Chatto and Windus). 143–74.

Cott, J. (ed.) (2006) 'Interview with Nat Hentoff, *Playboy*, March 1966', in *Dylan on Dylan: The Essential Interviews* (New York: Wenner Books). 93–111.

Dylan, B. (2004) *Chronicles: Volume One* (London: Simon and Schuster).

Eliot, T. S. (1923) '*Ulysses*, order, and myth', in F. Kermode (ed.), *Selected Prose of T. S. Eliot* (London: Faber and Faber, 1975). 175–8.

Eliot, T. S. (1928) 'Preface', in *For Lancelot Andrewes: Essays in Style and Order* (London: Faber and Gwyer). ix–x.

Gibbens, J. (2001) *The Nightingale's Code: A Poetic Study of Bob Dylan* (London: Touched Press).

Gray, M. (2000) *Song and Dance Man III: The Art of Bob Dylan* (London: Cassell).

Gray, M. (2006) *The Bob Dylan Encyclopedia* (New York: Continuum).

Grist, L. (2007) '"The blues is the truth": the blues, modernity, and the British blues boom', in N. A. Wynn (ed.), *Cross the Water Blues: African American Music in America* (Jackson, MI: University Press of Mississippi). 202–17.

Heylin, C. (2011) *Bob Dylan: Behind the Shades* (20th anniversary edition) (London: Faber and Faber).

Jameson, F. (1976) 'Modernism and its repressed; or, Robbe-Grillet as anti-colonialist', in *The Ideologies of Theory: Essays 1971–1986 (Volume 1: Situations of Theory)* (Minneapolis, MN: University of Minnesota Press, 1988). 167–80.

Jameson, F. (1984) 'Postmodernism, or the cultural logic of late capitalism', *New Left Review*, 146 (July/August). 53–92.

Julius, A. (1995) *T. S. Eliot, Anti-Semitism, and Literary Form* (Cambridge: Cambridge University Press).

Kopf, B. (1998) 'The singer not the song ...', *Wire*, 178 (November). 36–7.

Lee, C. P. (2000) *Like a Bullet of Light: The Films of Bob Dylan* (London: Helter Skelter).

Nichols, B. (1981) *Ideology and the Image: Social Representation in the Cinema and Other Media* (Bloomington, IN: Indiana University Press).

Wilentz, S. (2010) *Bob Dylan in America* (London: Bodley Head).

Wilson, E. (1931) *Axel's Castle: A Study in the Imaginative Literature of 1870–1930* (London: Fontana, 1971).

Part IV

Dylan critics

10

Time out of mind: Bob Dylan and Paul Nelson transformed

John Frederick Bell

> I have a hunch the people who feel I betrayed them picked up on me a few years ago and weren't really back there with me at the beginning. Because I still see the people who were with me from the beginning once in a while, and they know what I'm doing.
> (Bob Dylan, 27 November 1965; see Haas, 1972: 110)

Labelling Bob Dylan a sellout has become something of an American pastime. Maureen Dowd's conspicuous April 2011 rebuke in the *New York Times* is a recent example in a long line of criticisms extending back to the 1960s. Dowd lambasted Dylan for submitting his set-list for a Beijing concert to Chinese government censors. 'The idea that the raspy troubadour of '60s freedom anthems would go to a dictatorship and not sing those anthems is a whole new kind of sellout', she wrote (Dowd, 2011). To Dylan watchers, it was a familiar censure. Over the course of his musical career, he has routinely been castigated for pursuing selfish ends over political ones. At least one commentator, however, made it a point to do just the opposite.

In the formative years of Dylan's career, journalist Paul Nelson (1936–2006) implored the artist to ignore social causes and pursue his own creative vision. The interactions between the singer and the critic from 1960 to 1966 prompted dramatic evolutions in each man's perspective on artistic expression and folk music performance. Through their exchanges in person, print and song, Dylan and Nelson enriched each other's understanding of authenticity in the folk tradition. Tracing the development of their relationship illuminates the aesthetic and personal circumstances that brought folk and rock together in the mid-1960s, forever transforming American popular music and music criticism.

Like Robert Zimmerman, Paul Nelson grew up in a small town in northern Minnesota. While a college student in Minneapolis, he befriended

Jon Pankake, with whom he developed a passion for folk music. Pete Seeger was an early favourite, but after listening to Harry Smith's 1952 six-album compilation *Anthology of American Folk Music*, they grew to prefer old-time fare (Avery, 2011: 19–20). In March 1960, they started a folk fanzine called the *Little Sandy Review*, supposedly as a means of obtaining free recordings from Folkways and other record labels (Ward, 2000). Through their often trenchant album reviews, the two developed a reputation for being rabid traditionalists who reserved special scorn for so-called commercial folk-singers like Harry Belafonte and the Kingston Trio (Lightbourne, 2009). In response to one record executive's criticism of their editorialising, they articulated the philosophy of the *Little Sandy Review*: 'Folk music should and can only be performed by people in the folk tradition or by people who have taken the trouble to learn it' (Cohen, 2002: 166).

One performer eager to learn was Bob Dylan, who arrived on the Minneapolis folk scene around the time the *Review* began. The editors were not initially impressed with the young folksinger, who had hoped Nelson and Pankake would use their magazine to promote his local concerts (Avery, 2011: 13). Dylan later recalled how Pankake, in particular, went out of his way to disparage Dylan's performances of Woody Guthrie songs (Dylan, 2004a: 248–50). Though Dylan did not especially enjoy Pankake's company, the young folksinger was enamoured with his and Nelson's prodigious col-lection of rare folk albums. The editors invited Dylan to listening sessions in Pankake's apartment, where they attempted to disabuse the performer of some of his loftier aspirations. But their purist pretensions had the opposite effect. In short order, Dylan incorporated into his act the styles and techniques of the artists he heard. Pankake was as disparaging of these appropriations as he was of the earlier Guthrie routine, but Nelson saw the change as indicative of something greater: Dylan's extraordinary precocious-ness as a musician (Dylan, 2004a: 251–3; Shelton, 2011: 61). 'He came back in a day or two at the most', Nelson recalled, '… [and he] had this whole system down that quickly … that was really impressive. He did what it took [Ramblin' Jack] Elliot ten, fifteen years [to do] in two days, and it was really convincing' (see Heylin, 2001: 48). In fact, Dylan was so eager to learn and absorb that he once helped himself to some of the *Review*'s best records when the editors were out of town (Heylin, 2001: 48–9; Shelton, 2011: 61).

But hearing the greats live was preferable to listening to their records. In January 1961 Dylan left Minneapolis for New York City, the nerve centre of the ascendant folk revival. After several months honing his craft on the Greenwich Village scene, Dylan returned to Minnesota brimming with con-fidence. As Pankake told it, 'He was pretty much transformed by the time he got back to town.… When he had been here, he had been as inhibited as the rest of us but now he was howling and bobbing up and down. He picked up his freedom before he had gotten his technique' (see Heylin, 2001: 65). Pankake was right. Dylan was substituting bravado for proficiency, and he knew it. Even as he accumulated accolades and a recording contract with Columbia that autumn, he grew preoccupied with his perceived inadequacies as a folk musician. By 1962, the folk movement's standards for interpreting traditional music were more rigorous than they had ever been. Self-taught and inexperienced, Dylan began to fear that he could never measure up.

Watching folk virtuosos like Mike Seeger perform in the Village made Dylan realise that his future might lay in composing new songs rather than interpreting old ones:

> It dawned on me ... that I would have to start believing in possibilities that I wouldn't have allowed before, that I had been closing my creativity down to a very narrow, controllable scale ... that things had become too familiar and I might have to disorient myself ... it could take me the rest of my life ... to be as good as [Mike Seeger].... The thought occurred to me that maybe I'd have to write my own folk songs, ones that Mike didn't know. (Dylan, 2004a: 71)

From the start, Dylan knew that his move to song-writing would come at a price. By becoming a composer rather than an interpreter of folk music, Dylan would have to ask more of himself artistically than he ever had. While he had written a few songs since arriving in New York and included two on his first album, his compositions were, in style and substance, more homages to Guthrie than original creations. To accomplish his new goal, he would have to find his own voice rather than borrowing from those of the past. In his judgement, it was a difficult but necessary move. 'If I wanted to stay playing music', he later wrote, '... I would have to claim a larger part of myself' (Dylan, 2004a: 72).

Dylan's decision to compose his own songs coincided with a revival of topical folk music. The sub-genre had lain more or less dormant in the folk community since the McCarthy years, when some of its most accomplished practioners such as Josh White and Pete Seeger ended up on the blacklist. In February 1962, the first issue of *Broadside* appeared. The topical song magazine promised 'a handful of songs about our times', including Dylan's 'Talking John Birch' (Cunningham and Friesen, 1962). The magazine quickly became the vehicle for the spread of Dylan's songs and celebrity. Compositions like 'The Ballad of Emmett Till' and 'Masters of War' first appeared in *Broadside* and represented significant departures from his earlier Guthrie-esque stylings. The folk community marvelled at his combinations of traditional melodies and contemporary, socially conscious lyrics. But not everyone was impressed with his new direction. The *Little Sandy Review* had been one of the few publications to even review Dylan's first album, let alone review it favourably. Nelson and Pankake had applauded his LP as a 'fantastic debut' and congratulated their acquaintance for '[hoisting] himself up by his bootstraps to single-handedly conquer the folksong big time'. Their glowing review did, however, conclude with a caveat. 'We sincerely hope', they wrote, 'that Dylan will steer clear of the Protesty people, continue to write songs near the traditional manner, and continue to develop his mastery of his difficult, delicate personal style' (see Cohen, 2002: 182).

Dyed-in-the-wool traditionalists, Nelson and Pankake had no patience for political folk singing, which to them posed as great a threat to the authenticity of folk music as commercialism. As Nelson later explained, he and Pankake represented 'the anti-topical people' who agreed with the political sentiments of protest songs but felt that they were 'shitty art', too 'obvious' to have any kind of artistic merit (Heylin, 2001: 123). For them, timelessness was folk music's greatest virtue; it was the enduring mystery of old ballads that made them appealing, accessible and authentic. They believed the role of the folk performer was to interpret and advance this tradition. By writing and performing songs about *current* political issues, the 'Protesty people' of *Broadside* were introducing an unwelcome degree of self-consciousness and temporality to folk performance. For Nelson and Pankake, genuine folk songs had both contemporary and historical relevance. As Nelson would later write, 'time invariably vindicates form over topicality, and poetry always outlives journalism' (Nelson, 1972: 105).

Because it omitted traditional material and focused on contemporary issues, Dylan's second album, *The Freewheelin' Bob Dylan*, was a great disappointment to the *Little Sandy Review*. In a June 1963 review entitled 'Flat tire', the editors railed against the 'absurd concoctions' on the record, which they considered 'not particularly folk-derived', 'melodramatic and maudlin'. Its biggest failing was in its concessions to the present; the traditionalists wrote that the album laid its 'foundations in nothing that isn't constantly shifting, searching, and changing'. 'What Dylan needs to do', they advised, 'is to square the percentages between traditional and original ... to give some anchor of solidarity to his work'. As it stood, Pankake and Nelson deemed the album 'a failure, but a most interesting one' (see Hedin, 2004a). Dylan read their review and when he returned to Minneapolis that July he challenged them to a debate on the merits of topical folk songs. Pankake bowed out, leaving Nelson to face Dylan and his entourage alone.

At the apartment of a mutual friend, Dave 'Tony' Glover, they argued the merits of political versus traditional folk singing for hours. With his ponderous Midwestern drawl, Nelson was no match for the then fast-talking Dylan. By Nelson's own admission, Dylan won the debate, but the critic was proud of himself for scoring one body blow. Whenever Dylan repeated the worth of social issues as lyrical material, and even after he played Nelson some of his latest topical compositions, the editor maintained a consistent refrain: 'You're way too talented to be in this blind alley. You can only express A through B by writing [like] this. Why would you want to stay there?' Having witnessed the growth of Dylan's artistic prowess, Nelson predicted: 'You won't' (see Heylin, 2001: 122).

128

The two left that evening with newfound respect for each other. As Nelson later explained, 'I felt I owed it to him to show up and defend what was written in *Little Sandy* and I kind of wanted to get to know him better a little bit also' (see Avery, 2011: 22). From the critic's perspective, they had 'sorta made friends that night' because Nelson 'did *argue* and ... didn't cave in' (Heylin, 2001: 123, original emphasis). Dylan was fast becoming the golden child of the folk revival, and Nelson's willingness to confront and critique him must have been disquieting for the rising star. If Dylan admired Nelson's tenacity, it was in part because he sympathised with his argument. As Dylan would later explain, folk songs had always appealed to him because they were 'evasive' and 'transcended the immediate culture'; 'a folk song might vary in meaning and it might not appear the same from one moment to the next' (Dylan, 2004a: 71). Dylan could not say the same of his topical material, which, as Nelson put it, 'only express[ed] A through B'. Songs about contemporary issues came readily to Dylan, perhaps too much so. Nelson was challenging him to forsake the familiar and further disorient himself for the sake of authenticity in his art.

A week after the debate, Dylan was asked to compose a prose poem for the Newport Folk Festival programme (Wilentz, 2010: 89). He used the opportunity to publicly reiterate his defence of topical song-writing from the Minneapolis debate. '– for Dave Glover' was ostensibly directed at that evening's host, but in retrospect the poem appears equally intended for Paul Nelson.[1] Reprinted in *Broadside* the following November, the poem expresses Dylan's indebtedness to the folk tradition as well as his craving for topical relevance. 'The folk songs showed me the way', Dylan wrote, but he was determined to 'make my own statement 'bout this day' (Dylan, 1963: 5–6). Despite Dylan's unequivocal insistence on contemporary, politically conscious products, there is a tone of regret in his poem, which begins and ends with apologies. Over the course of the autumn and into the winter, these subtle misgivings about his artistic purpose grew into full-on anxieties as Dylan's fame increased in kind. Upon receiving the Tom Paine Award from the Emergency Civil Liberties Committee in December, a drunken Dylan told the distinguished audience that theirs was 'an old people's world' and went on to belittle their ageing Old Left politics (Shelton, 2011: 143). In a January 1964 open letter to *Broadside* editors Sis Cunnigham and Gordon Friesen, he distinguished himself and other commercially successful folk singers from the more committed topical singers like Tom Paxton and Barbara Dane, implying that he, at least, could not sustain the same conscientiousness in his convictions. His mind, he wrote, was beginning to 'run like a roll of toilet paper' (Dylan, 1964: 11).

In the months that followed, Dylan came around to Nelson's position, fulfilling the critic's prediction. By June, he had foresworn 'finger-pointin' songs' (according to Nat Hentoff; see Hedin, 2004b: 25). His new material traded commentary for introspection and factuality for surrealism. As he told Nat Hentoff in an interview for *The New Yorker* that month: 'From now on, I want to write from inside me' (*ibid.*). At the Newport Folk Festival that summer, he introduced some of his new material to the assembled folk community. Appearing at a topical song-writing workshop, he sang two decidedly non-topical songs – 'It Ain't Me, Babe' and 'Mr. Tambourine Man' – and replayed them in his main stage set along with 'All I Really Want To Do', 'To Ramona' and 'Chimes of Freedom'. These songs followed what Dylan later deemed 'a new set of ordinances': intimate, existential verses replete with imagery and symbolism distinct from his prior work (Dylan, 2004a: 67). The lyrics of 'Mr. Tambourine Man' reflected the songwriter's new approach and attitude: 'Take me disappearin' through the smoke rings of my mind.... Let me forget about today until tomorrow' (Dylan, 2004b: 153).

Critics at the folk revival's premiere magazine *Sing Out!* were divided in their opinions of the new Dylan. Nelson had left Minneapolis for New York earlier in the year to become the publication's managing editor. Dylan was pleased to learn of his new post and enquired after 'good critic Paul' in a May letter to the magazine's editor-in-chief, Irwin Silber (Heylin, 2001: 124). Dylan's performance at Newport in July sparked disagreement between the two editors. Silber objected to the artist's new 'inner-probing, self-conscious' style in a patronising 'open letter to Bob Dylan' (Silber, 1964: 22), while Nelson quietly welcomed Dylan's change in approach. Reviewing the festival for the *Little Sandy Review*, of which he remained co-editor, Nelson characteristically maligned the topical songwriters but concluded by commending Dylan for choosing 'to show off his more personal, introspective songs rather than shoot the obvious fish in the barrel'. Perhaps reminiscing on prior critiques, Nelson wrote that Dylan was 'taking his first faltering steps in a long time in a productive direction for himself as an artist' (see Cohen, 2002: 221).

The album *Another Side of Bob Dylan*, a testament to those faltering steps, was released in August 1964. The same month, another consequential record debuted on the American charts. 'House of the Rising Sun' had appeared on Dylan's first album, but this new rendition by the Animals was something altogether different. With its signature guitar arpeggio and hypnotic background organ, their electric version breathed new life into the traditional lament. Dylan took notice (Heylin, 2001: 173). The Animals' rendition achieved sonically what he had been aspiring to do lyrically: extend the boundaries of the folk song through an infusion of personality and creativity. 'House of the Rising Sun' posed an electric imperative to match Nelson's artistic challenge of the previous summer. By 'going electric', Dylan was not abandoning the folk tradition but instead, like the Animals, transforming it. As Clinton Heylin has suggested, it was 'a sound that lent meaning to the words' (*ibid.*: 202). Dylan's initial electric forays simply added an R&B beat to what could otherwise stand as acoustic material (Hadju, 2001: 236). It was not until June 1965 that he achieved his coveted amalgamation of sound and lyric with 'Like a Rolling Stone'. Five days after that song was released, Dylan appeared at the Newport Folk Festival and performed his magnum opus, along with two other songs. Apart from a cameo appearance with the Byrds that spring in West Hollywood, it was his first live electric performance since high school. Nelson was at Newport to cover the festival for *Sing Out!* Unlike many in the audience who famously booed the performance, Nelson was enthralled by Dylan's electric metamorphosis. He shot a dozen rolls of film during the set to capture the moment (Avery, 2011: 30).

The folk critic recognised the significance of Dylan's achievement: a union of sound and substance in fulfilment of the folk tradition. The founder of Elektra Records, Jac Holzman, stood alongside the photo-snapping Nelson and recalled the moment years later: 'We just turned to each other and shit-grinned. This was electricity married to content. We were hearing music that had meaning, with a rock beat.... All the parallel strains of music over the years coalesced for me in that moment' (see Heylin, 2001: 212). In *Sing Out!* Nelson wrote that 'Dylan, doing his new ... stuff knocked me out' and two weeks after Newport he remained spellbound (Nelson, 1965: 6). In a letter to Pankake, Nelson praised Dylan as effusively as he had in the *Little Sandy Review* three years earlier: 'Before I wouldn't have given much of a damn what happened to him at Newport. But, by God, he was so great in those three numbers! ... I'll bet my critical judgment I'm right (and particularly so because Irwin [Silber] hated it) and I'll stand by Dylan and his new songs. He's made it back to Hero with me' (see Cohen, 2002: 238).

As his tone suggested, Nelson was not shy about his enthusiasm for Dylan's new approach. In *Sing Out!* he defied Silber and defended Dylan as 'an angry, passionate poet who demands his art to be all', chastising those who booed him at Newport for choosing 'suffocation over invention and adventure' and 'the safety of wishful thinking rather than the painful, always difficult stab of art'. As for his own position, Nelson was unequivocal: 'I choose Dylan', he wrote, 'I choose art' (Nelson, 1965: 8).

Opponents just two summers before, Dylan and Nelson were now united in their philosophy of authenticity in contemporary folk music. Articles that appeared within weeks of each other demonstrated their shared perspective. In an interview with Hentoff for *Playboy* conducted in the autumn of 1965 and published in March 1966, Dylan portrayed topical songs as unimaginative and inimical to the folk tradition for their basis in a fleeting historical present. 'Songs like "Which Side Are You On?" ... they're not folk-music songs; they're political songs', he said. 'They're *already* dead'. He contrasted the effervescence of political songs with the immortality and universality of 'traditional music', whose 'just plain simple mystery' made it 'too unreal to die' (see Cott, 2006: 98).[2] Nelson applied the same vocabulary of eternality to what he called Dylan's 'New Music' in his review of the artist's most recent album for the February/March 1966 issue of *Sing Out!* '"The Hammer Song" and "Banks of Marble" are already dead', Nelson argued, 'while "Mr. Tambourine Man," "Lay Down Your Weary Tune," and "Chimes

131

of Freedom" become more impressive with each passing year'. Against those 'historical-political adversaries' who criticised Dylan's non-topical music, Nelson argued that 'unless the personal is achieved, the universal cannot follow'. From the start, Nelson had encouraged Dylan to make this leap, and the critic was astonished by how ably he had done so: 'He has, in effect, dragged folk music, perhaps by the nape of the neck, into areas it never dreamed existed and enriched both it and himself a thousandfold by the journey'. The consummate connoisseur of folk music went as far as to label Dylan's 1965 album *Highway 61 Revisited* 'one of the two or three greatest folk music albums ever made' (Nelson, 1972: 104–5). The thief who once pilfered Nelson's finest records had finally given one back.

Nelson was willing to label the artist's innovation 'folk music', but Dylan could not. 'Folk music is a word I can't use', he told Hentoff. 'Everybody knows that I'm not a folk singer'. The designation was too reminiscent of topical song-writing and the Old Left. 'Folk music is a bunch of fat people', Dylan joked, in a manner redolent of his Tom Paine Award speech. And he could not countenance 'folk-rock' as a label, either: 'I don't think that such a word ... has anything to do with it' (see Cott, 2006: 98). The hyphenated term suggested synthesis, but Dylan considered the reconciliation redundant. He may have apologised to Glover and Nelson for embracing topical song-writing over traditional folk music in 1963, but advancing the folk tradition by going electric in 1965 did not elicit his contrition. When Hentoff asked if he had erred in changing his style, Dylan challenged the question itself. 'A mistake is to commit a misunderstanding', he explained. 'There could be no such thing, anyway, as this action' (*ibid.*: 99).

Dylan knew exactly what he was doing with his electric material. Like Nelson, he could contextualise his artistic turn within the larger trajectory of the folk tradition. The better question for Dylan was whether his audience could do the same. 'Either people understand or they *pretend* to understand – or else they really *don't* understand', he explained to Hentoff (*ibid.*: 99). Nelson certainly comprehended Dylan's 'New Music' in the artistic spirit it was intended. He was comfortable calling it 'folk' and evaluating the move as progressive rather than aberrant. Dylan, fed up with labels of any sort by 1965, was willing to go a step further and claim that terminology itself had become irrelevant. 'It doesn't matter what kind of nasty names people invent for the music', he said. 'It could be called arsenic music' (*ibid.*: 98–9).

In the years that followed, Paul Nelson left *Sing Out!* to become a rock critic at *Rolling Stone*, where he continued reviewing Dylan albums into the 1980s. Though he partly inspired Bob Dylan's artistic transformation, he never took credit for it. His reticence reflects more than a Midwesterner's modesty. Dylan converted Nelson from traditionalism to modernism, and the critic was grateful for it. 'The folk music just turned into rock for me', Nelson told an interviewer in 2000, 'When I heard "Like A Rolling Stone" it changed everything' (Ward, 2000). With his 'New Music', Dylan had proven what Nelson had always hoped: folk could be modern without being indebted to the moment. Introspection was as worthy as retrospection. 'Now, for the first time, I think … we have finally progressed out of Then and into Now', Nelson wrote in March 1966. 'With a Minnesota gypsy leading us, we have truly become contemporary' (see Nelson, 1972: 105). Thanks to Bob Dylan, folk authenticity was no longer beholden to tradition, and neither was Paul Nelson.

Acknowledgement

For their support and encouragement of this chapter, I would like to thank Kevin Avery, Robert S. Leventhal, Charles McGovern and, especially, Eugen Banauch.

Notes

1 I am grateful to Clinton Heylin for sharing this observation with me.
2 In 1976 Hentoff revealed that Dylan had rejected the text of their original interview. The version which was published is actually his and Dylan's more amusing rewrite. See Heylin (2001: 229–30).

References

Avery, K. (2011) *Everything is an Afterthought: The Life and Writings of Paul Nelson* (Seattle, WA: Fantagraphics Books).

Cohen, R. (2002) *Rainbow Quest: The Folk Music Revival and American Society, 1940–1970* (Amherst, MA: University of Massachusetts Press).

Cott, J. (ed.) (2006) 'Interview Nat Hentoff, *Playboy*, March 1966', in *Dylan on Dylan: The Essential Interviews* (New York: Werner Books). 93–111.

Cunningham, A. and Friesen, G. (1962) 'Introducing … *Broadside*', *Broadside*, 1 (February). 1.

Dowd, M. (2011) 'Blowin' in the idiot wind', *New York Times* (9 April). Available at http://www.nytimes.com/2011/04/10/opinion/10dowd.html (accessed 22 March 2014).

Dylan, B. (1963) '– for Dave Glover', *Broadside*, 35 (November). 5–6.

Dylan, B. (1964) 'Letter from Bob Dylan', *Broadside*, 38 (January). 9–14.

Dylan, B. (2004a) *Chronicles: Volume One* (New York: Simon and Schuster).

Dylan, B. (2004b) *Lyrics, 1962–2001* (New York: Simon and Schuster).

Haas, J. (1972) 'The Panorama interview ("Bob Dylan talking")', in C. McGregor (ed.), *Bob Dylan: A Retrospective* (New York: Morrow). 108–13.

Hajdu, D. (2001) *Positively 4th Street* (New York: Farrar, Straus and Giroux).

Hedin, B. (ed.) (2004a) 'Paul Nelson and John Pankake. Flat tire'. In *Studio A: The Bob Dylan Reader* (New York: W. W. Norton). 16–19.

Hedin, B. (ed.) (2004b) 'Nat Hentoff. The crackin', shakin', breakin' sounds'. In *Studio A: The Bob Dylan Reader* (New York: W. W. Norton). 22–40.

Heylin, C. (2001) *Bob Dylan: Behind the Shades Revisited* (New York: Harper Collins).

Lightbourne, D. (2009) 'The *Little Sandy Review* and the birth of rock criticism', *New Vulgate* (29 July). Available at http://newvulgate.blogspot.com/2009/07/issue-4-july-29-2009.html (accessed 23 May 2013).

Nelson, P. (1965) 'What's happening', *Sing Out!*, 15 (November). 6–8.

Nelson, P. (1972) 'Bob Dylan: another view', in C. McGregor (ed.), *Bob Dylan: A Retrospective* (NewYork: Morrow). 104–7.

Shelton, R. (2011) *No Direction Home: The Life and Music of Bob Dylan* (Milwaukee, WI: Backbeat Books).

Silber, I. (1964) 'An open letter to Bob Dylan', *Sing Out!*, 14 (November). 22–3.

Ward, S. (2000) 'What ever happened to rock critic Paul Nelson?', *Rockcritics.com* (January). Available at http://rockcriticsarchives.com/interviews/paulnelson/paulnelson.html (accessed 23 May 2013).

Wilentz, S. (2010) *Bob Dylan in America* (New York: Anchor Books).

11

Greil Marcus and Bob Dylan: the writer and his singer

Jean-Martin Büttner

'Let me tell you why I hate critics', Julian Barnes writes in *Flaubert's Parrot*.

> Not for the normal reasons: that they're failed creatures (they usually aren't; they may be failed critics, but that's another matter); or that they're by nature carping, jealous and vain (they usually aren't; if anything, they might better be accused of over-generosity, of upgrading the second-rate so that their own fine discriminations thereby appear the rarer). No, the reason I hate critics – well, some of the time – is that they write sentences like this: ... (Barnes, 2009: 74)

Now feel free to insert any piece of criticism you can't stand. Mine would sound something like this (and anyway probably come from Paul Williams): 'Ultimately, I don't identify with "Joey" or with the person singing about him, whereas I identify fiercely with Hurricane and, particularly, with the narrator of Hurricane's story' (Williams, 1992: 45). Julian Barnes's book, by the way, is a novel about a grieving doctor who is obsessed with Gustave Flaubert. Fans are obsessed and have every right to be – even though they can be really annoying when they are talking or writing about their object of obsession, as we will discover. After all, 'fan', as Theodor Adorno gleefully pointed out, is short for fanatic. But are critics obsessed, too? Should they be? They probably shouldn't. Obsession is not a good state of mind if you want to be fair, if you want to be accurate, if you want to be published, if you want to get reasonably old. Obsessions narrow the mind. Also, obsessive people, like revolutionaries, have no sense of humour.

So what does it mean when the world's best-known rock critic and, to many, the world's best rock critic tells you that he is obsessed? True, Greil Marcus says 'intellectually obsessed'. Or at least he said it to me on a sunny January afternoon in 2011 when I visited him at home in his large, quiet house in Berkeley, California.

If you have ever met or heard Greil Marcus, you will agree that 'obsession' is not the first word that comes to mind. Even though he writes and talks a lot about feelings that he experiences when hearing music, he does not really come across an overtly emotional man in conversation or during his public lectures. He very rarely laughs and seldom smiles, even when he is joking. He looks at you unflinchingly, and it is a concentrated and yet guarded look.

Considering that he is someone who writes about the feelings of destruction he experienced during the last ever Sex Pistols concert in San Francisco's Winterland (14 January 1978, as recounted in his *Lipstick Traces*: Marcus, 1989: 27ff.) it is odd that – in conversation – you have no idea what he is thinking at any given moment.

In other words, I have rarely met someone who is so intellectually curious and seems to be so withdrawn. I have also never met someone who talks at such length and seems utterly quiet even while talking. And talking is something that Marcus does with relish, style and great accuracy. Actually, he talks a bit like he writes. He loves language, loves the sound the words make and loves to look for different ways of saying something. Also, he is an exhaustive listener who likes all quotes to be correct, including his own.

So when I mentioned that he had written that Bob Dylan made him want to be a writer, he immediately corrected me:

> No, I said that he was one of the several things that made me a writer. Rather than want to be a writer. I mean, I never wanted to be a writer, whatever that means. I just wanted to write, and I did write. By 'made me a writer' I meant someone that both gave me something to write about and gave me a sense of language and a sense of what writing is. And what the possibilities are for writing. And what it means to write in your own voice – you know, whether it's a voice you discover or that you invent. There are many, many ways in which people find their voice.[1]

Anyway, he went on, the main inspiration for him as a writer had not been Bob Dylan, but Pauline Kael, the film critic. To him, it was all about being alive and being even more alive by writing. He had read her first collection of reviews, *I Lost It at the Movies*, in 1965 (its year of publication), when he himself was twenty years old.

> But I'd never read anything where the person behind the words seemed so alive, seemed so present. And I had the feeling that I wanted to know how it feels to be so alive. And for me, the way to do that was to write. She was a writer; I had tendencies in that direction, and so I could do that. A lot of people, you know, when they listen to music, they're so moved, they're swept away, they're lifted up, and they want to have that feeling even more intensely. And the way they can do that is when they play the instrument themselves. Some people have affinity for that, and I didn't have any musical abilities. At the very end of Keith Richards' biography[2]

136

there's one thing I really do like: where he says that music and particularly performing for him is about trying to communicate emotion, sometimes desperately. And he says, 'what I'm saying is: can you feel that?' And that's what happens when people listen to music: 'yes, I feel that, I never felt this way before. I have never felt this so powerfully.' And I wanted to feel that even more powerfully; I wanted to affect other people the way it affected me.

When I mentioned that I felt the common thread between him, Kael, Richards and Dylan was the radical subjectivity of their approach, he said:

> I never really thought about it that way in terms of subjectivity. It has never occurred to me; maybe I learned this from Pauline or other people. It's never occurred to me that any kind of writer – be it a novelist or political speechwriter, anyone – should be objective. The point is to figure out what is it that you want to say, and then try to understand how to say it. What's the best, the most honest, the most effective way to say it?

As a journalist who covers both political and cultural events, I am aware of false objectivity, but I am also weary of self-proclaimed subjectivity. Obviously, you can fake objectivity; just by deciding whom you are going to quote last, for instance, and whom you will call an expert as opposed to a lobbyist, or which expert you will call in the first place. I am saying all this because although I greatly enjoy Greil Marcus's books, talks, columns, liner notes and lectures, I can understand why his approach has met with some controversy. To be more precise, I understand the criticism, but not the hostility. Greil Marcus is not only famous as a writer, he is also controversial. This has to do with the way he works. Instead of talking about a song, a performance or an album, he uses them as starting points for his personal associations, for his travels through American history and politics. He is the echo chamber, so to speak, of the material and the artists he writes about.

First let him explain how he proceeds. When I ask him for an example of the way he was working, Marcus refers to his book *Invisible Republic* (Marcus, 1997), a book which is officially about Dylan's 'Basement Tapes' but unofficially about all the songs preceding them – which has been both applauded and criticised for this very reason. He uses the material more than actually writing about it. As he himself relates (and I would like to let him speak a bit longer about it, because he gives a good example of his way of working, and of writing about Dylan):

> In *Invisible Republic*, the first chapter that focuses on the 'Basement Tapes' themselves is after this long chapter called 'Another country', which is about Dylan and the Band's touring of America and Europe in '65 and '66. And then the curtain kind of comes down, you turn the page and now we're in the basement in Big Pink in 1967, Dylan sitting at the piano, doing 'Lo and Behold'. And in that chapter, the whole chapter is about Dylan's

tone of voice in that song. And my trying to get a fix on where that tone of voice comes from and what it suggests, what the tone of voice itself communicates, not the individual words this voice carries. And I go back to William Burroughs making his own records in the early '60s in Paris, reading from *Junky* and *Naked Lunch*; with this very determined, flat Kansas accent. And I say, yeah, but…. And then there's Frank Hutchinson, a white blues singer from the West Virginia mountains in the 1920s. And I go back and start to talk about his tone of voice in his records. And then I say, what is it about this tone of voice that says there's nothing new under the sun, you can't surprise me, I've seen it all before, I know how the story's going to end, you don't even have to tell me. This kind of laconic, amused, bitter, fuck-it-all tone of voice. And I start thinking about Frank Hutchinson, where he lived and what he saw. And what he did to make a living other than play music. And I start to talk about the West Virginia mine war of 1921. And what happened right where Frank Hutchinson lived four, five, six years before he started making records. How and where he lived was completely torn apart by, in essence, a mini civil war between miners and owners. I talk about what it means to talk after a war like that, what it means to keep your mouth shut, what you can talk about, what you can't. And that whole chapter was there for a reason: that's me letting 'Lo and Behold' and my fascination for that particular song, which to me is an absolute perfect recording, remind me of everything else. But it's also there to tell the reader that this is the way the book's going to work. If you don't like it, get off the train now. Because this is how the book's going to go. It's going to go from one thing to another to another, and then if I'm able to, it's going to come back to where it started, and the starting place's going to look a little different. So that chapter was there as a warning.

This approach has angered Dylan fans the world over, at least judging from the insults you come across on the internet. Why these people are always so abusive in their forums is a subject which I will not go into here, because it is so depressingly uninteresting. But I have never read such spiteful remarks directed at a specific critic as the reaction Greil Marcus gets for his work, especially *Invisible Republic* and *Like a Rolling Stone (Bob Dylan at the Crossroads)* (Marcus, 2005). Basically, what makes Dylan fans angry is that Marcus is not talking enough about Bob Dylan.

I think it was the *New York Post* that summed up this criticism in a wonderfully bitchy line: 'Everything reminds him of everything else'. Greil Marcus knows the line, too. He reacts to it, as we have seen, by confessing his interest in music and the fact that Bob Dylan is, for him, an emotional obsession.

> Well, I mean, I remember whoever it was that said 'everything reminds him of everything else'. And that's a valid criticism. But when you're in the throes of an obsession, an intellectual obsession, that's what happens. It isn't that everything reminds you of everything else. But if you're obsessed with a fascination with, let's say Hank Williams or Cary Grant for that matter, or, you know, Huckleberry Finn, Franklin Roosevelt: you just

become obsessed with this thing, this person, every aspect of this phenomenon, whatever it might be, you know, the way it looks, the way it sounds, the way it smells, whatever people say about it. If you're in the throes of that kind of fascination, everything will remind you of that. You'll be walking down the street, and somebody will say something, and say it with the same inflection than in such and such a song, or scene in this movie. And that's the great gift of being intellectually obsessed, because then you are able to begin to construct a world, a whole new frame of reference around the object of your fascination. And it's a question of whether you succeed or whether you fail.

Considering his intellectual obsession, you wonder why Greil Marcus has never wanted to interview Bob Dylan. It would have been easy for the writer to contact the singer. After all, Marcus is the only critic Dylan name checks in his *Chronicles* (Dylan, 2004: 34–5). All the other writers and critics have to make do with their dubious claim to be the inspiration for Mr Jones in 'Ballad of a Thin Man'. Marcus could easily have met and interviewed Dylan; he also knows his manager, Jeff Rosen, quite well. And since he has written two extended books on Dylan, mentioned him in most of the others and has published many articles and columns about him, you would expect Marcus to be keenly interested in asking Dylan the questions he has pondered for so long. But he apparently is not.

> But I never interviewed him, no. When I was writing the 'Basement Tapes' book I tried to interview him simply to ask him what and where, you know: 'When was this recorded? Where was this recorded?' Stuff like that. I didn't want to ask him what his songs were about, who's this song really about. And his manager, Jeff Rosen, said, 'No, he doesn't really remember that. He doesn't want to talk about it.' Okay, fine. So I talked to Robbie Robertson and Rick Danko and Garth Hudson about those things and got the information the best I could.

But even though he got great material out of the three musicians – Marcus has known them since their very first gig as the Band, back in 1969 – he still thinks that it does not really help to interview musicians if you want to know something about songs:

> And often they would say things that were just really so colourful or interesting or would throw something into relief or give a perspective that I would never have had. But what I was asking was really nuts and bolts stuff. Because, ultimately, I don't care what the artist thinks he or she was doing. I'm not really interested.

Greil Marcus hasn't interviewed Bob Dylan, but he has met him on two occasions. First in 1963, the second time in 1997. The first meeting, as he remembers in the foreword to his latest book, did not go well.

Because I've thought about it so many times in the past thirty-four years, I remember very clearly the first time I saw Bob Dylan perform. It was in the summer of 1963, in a field somewhere in New Jersey. I'd gone to see Joan Baez.... She sang, and after a bit she said, 'I want to introduce a friend of mine,' and out came a scruffy-looking guy with a guitar. He looked dusty. His shoulders were hunched and he looked slightly embarrassed. He sang a couple of songs by himself, and then he sang one or two with Joan Baez. Then he left and she finished her show ... I barely noticed the end of it. I was transfixed. I was confused.

When the show was over, I saw this person, whose name I hadn't caught ... and so I went up to him. He was trying to light a cigarette, it was windy, his hands were shaking; he wasn't paying attention to anything but the match. I was just dumbfounded enough to open my mouth. 'You were terrific', I said brightly. He didn't look up. 'I was shit', he said. 'I was just shit.' I didn't know what to say to that, so I walked off. (Marcus, 2010: xiii–xiv)

The second time they met was decades later, when Dylan was awarded with the Gish Prize[3] for his lifetime's work; *Time Out of Mind*, Dylan's 1997 album, had just come out. Marcus remembers:

And the board decided that it had to go to someone who had made a great contribution but who was still creative. Not to someone whose best days are behind him or behind her. And not to someone who's showing great promise. To someone who already made a huge difference but whose features were not closed. And so when I was asked to give a talk at the awards ceremony I agreed because I knew for $300,000 even Bob Dylan would show up, you know, and I'd get a chance to meet him. And so I did; I met him at that ceremony. We talked a little bit. In fact he said something that was as good a critique of what I've written as I've ever gotten. We're talking, and, you know, what do you ask a writer? You say, 'Well, what are you working on next?' And I said, 'I don't know, I don't have a subject, I just published *Invisible Republic*, and I haven't another subject right now'. And he said, 'Why don't you write Part Two? You only scratched the surface.' Now that from somebody who really knows what's under the surface, that's a great compliment, I thought. And he was completely right. I knew he was right; of course I'd only scratched the surface. That was what was so exciting for me about writing the book: knowing that I was only drawing a bare outline of what somebody else could make and do, a full portrait. So that was my encounter with Bob Dylan.

With feedback like that, who needs interviews?

So on the one hand you have the fans who complain that the author writes too much, or that he writes too little about Bob Dylan. And on the other hand you have the artist who wishes the author would write even more, but not necessarily about him. And the artist does not seem to care that the author is using the artist's work to talk about other artists. I think

Dylan's reaction says a lot about his artistic focus and his self-conception as a writer: that by going back to musical traditions and keeping them alive, he becomes part of the tradition itself. Anyone who has heard Dylan's *Theme Time Radio Hour* broadcasts (2006–10) will agree how keenly aware Dylan is of the music that has inspired him. Marcus loved the shows, too – not least because he learned so much from them while at the same time having so much fun:

> What thrilled me about that programme was – and this was less so as it went on and he would play the same people over and over again or very frequently – but the first year I couldn't believe how much I didn't know. I mean I am not wholly ignorant in the realm of American popular music [he smiles], but half of the songs he played I'd never heard. And a quarter of the people I'd never heard of. I remember in a very early show he played a song called 'Big Guitar' [that starts with]: 'I've got a big guitar'…. It was one of these really stupid songs that just sound great and unlikely. You can't believe anyone had the nerve to put it out. And I don't remember right now who it was by [Bill Watkins, my comment]; it was certainly someone I'd never heard of. Where did this record come from?

Great artists are also great fans. The same seems to apply to great writers, as Greil Marcus has shown. The problem is that while all great writers are fans, not all fans are great writers. This is the main reason why I grew tired of Paul Williams's *Bob Dylan: Performing Artist* trilogy of books. It is not his findings that irritated me but the way he went on about them.

First of all, I do not like declarations like '"Blind Willie McTell" is a stunningly brilliant composition that we could analyse needlessly and ecstatically for hours' (Williams, 1992: 233). And I certainly do not like confessions of his like 'I'm babbling'. Babbling is not a graceful way to communicate, and babbling from a guy who is doing it and saying so is not honest – it is ridiculous. One could argue that Paul Williams really knew what he was talking about. But as a writer, you have to know when to shut up, and what to leave out when. There are few writers who can get away with babbling. I am thinking of the best stuff Hunter S. Thompson wrote and the better stuff of Lester Bangs. But even Bangs sometimes lost the plot in a way that not even his irony and humour could save.

As I acknowledged earlier, I know how misleading the demand of being objective can be. And I do not like the habit of American newspapers to almost ritually talk to the other side of any issue, even if the other side is the Flat Earth Society, just so that they appear objective. But I think there is a distinction between subjectivity and narcissism. Subjective writers will tell you interesting things the way they see them, evaluate and judge them. Narcissists will use the pretext of any given subject to talk about themselves and nothing else in particular. My point is: the main reason so many hardcore Dylan fans rail against Greil Marcus is because he excels at what

Jean-Martin Büttner

they are trying to do as well – making themselves interesting by talking about someone else, in this case Bob Dylan.

Which really brings us to Bob Dylan's fans, and I am talking about the obsessive kind here, the ones of whom Dylan himself once said they should get a life. One of the things that irritates me no end is some of the fans' babbling after any given show Dylan has just played. It is a strange combination of all-inclusiveness and exclusiveness. They speak in codes and references and at the same time scream their exclamation marks at the world. Michael Gray said it best when he wrote, in his *Song and Dance Man III*: 'the fans are maintaining an élite inner circle while using a populist tone' (Gray, 2000: 257).

And when the fans are not babbling, they are collecting facts and so-called facts, hunting for absurd details like virtual A. J. Webermans. So you have the exuberant fans or the anal-retentive fans all over the net; they are equally difficult to bear, in my view. I asked Marcus why the most obsessed Dylan fans also were the worst. He replied:

> There is no question you're right. Not just the worst, they're the stupidest. I think it's because something in Dylan's writing leads people to believe that there is a secret behind every song. And if you can unlock that secret then you'll understand the meaning of life. Like every song is this treasure chest, and nothing is what it seems.

He then mentioned a symposium about Dylan in New York in December 2010, with panelists like Christopher Ricks, the filmmaker D. A. Pennebaker, the novelist Dana Spiotta, Matt Friedberger of the Fiery Furnaces and the musician John Wesley Harding:

> So Christopher Ricks is giving this very interesting talk, very subtle as almost everything he does is, but with great enthusiasm, and this guy stands up to ask a question. And he's about my age, so he's an older guy. And he says, in just this way, in just this tone of kind of abject seriousness: 'It's always been said that "Don't Think Twice" was really about Suze Rotolo. But I've heard recently that it might have been about Joan Baez. What do you think?' And how do you respond to something that intellectually dead? You know, Christopher Ricks very wonderfully said, 'That's not the point. No song is about any one thing. Where a song begins says nothing about where a song goes and what it ultimately turns into. And ultimately it doesn't matter if the inspiration of a song is really big like the Second World War – it still has to be a good song, or nobody will care.' So of course he [Christopher Ricks, my comment] didn't try to answer that question. But I heard this guy and suddenly felt so depressed, I just felt like 'Why bother?' If that's the way people want to view the world then everything interesting has to have a one-dimensional reality.... Is that what you mean about Dylan fans being the worst? They want to take something or can't help themselves from taking something that is infinite and making it inert.

142

So how can you talk about Dylan's work without making the infinite sound inert? Every good Bob Dylan song has its moments, what the German writer Diedrich Diederichsen aptly calls 'die guten Stellen', the good bits in the song, the chicken-skin music bits, the ones that will always get you, however often you hear them. The great thing about these bits is that they can be completely unrelated to the lyrical content; and they can emanate from songs not often talked about. One of my favourite best bits, to give you an example, is Dylan's way of singing, in 'Highlands' (on *Time Out of Mind*, 1997): 'Somebody just asked me/If I registered to vote'. The sad way he says it, with his voice falling at the end of the line as if trailing off, tells you that his character has abandoned all hope of changing the times with the help of politics. Asking the question gives the answer by the way the question is sung. Another of my personal best bits is an even smaller detail in a song. It is the first line of the third stanza in 'It Takes a Lot to Laugh, It Takes a Train to Cry' (on *Highway 61 Revisited*, 1965) which goes: 'Now the wintertime is coming/The windows are filled with frost'. There is sadness in the voice but there is also some experience of peace in the lyric, like the feeling you get when you wake up and the snow has fallen overnight covering everything, and all is quiet outside, while you are looking out. I decided to ask Marcus why he thought that line did so much to me. Also, I wanted to see how he would work with something he probably had not thought about in great depth yet. This is what he came up with:

> You know, that is a lovely image. But isolated from the song when you say the windows are filled with frost; well, here's what's happening. First of all there is the laconic swing of the music, just this easy back-and-forth in the saddle rhythm that is carrying that [line, my comment]. So everything seems just moving along so naturally. You know, 'the windows are filled with frost' – yet that's not the obvious, ordinary way to say what he's saying. You'd say the windows are covered with frost, you wouldn't say they're filled with frost. So that immediately, when you're thinking about it, without noticing throws you off a little bit, it highlights the image and makes the image a little bit mysterious. But then what follows after that is 'I tried to tell everybody, but I could not get across'.[4] So that makes the image of the windows filled with frost even more mysterious. Because it's meant to signify something, and the singer wants to tell everybody what it is. But he can't. So right in this moment when the singer hits you so hard he's describing how he cannot tell you what it's all about. So he creates a whole drama within just a couple of lines and with an image that for you could be an indifferent image, [but] for somebody else it is what focuses everything.

A whole drama being created out of a seemingly indifferent image. So Marcus got it right. He managed to talk about the song with passion and insight; he told me something I was not aware of, and in doing so he made me like the song even more. This is what critics should do; this is the reason we like them.

Few fans should become critics, but critics are always fans. The same is true for musicians. Every great musician has always been a fan. Think of Elvis Presley, Johnny Cash, Keith Richards, Robert Plant, David Bowie, Scott Walker, Tom Waits, Elvis Costello, Pete Townshend and all the others. The biggest fan of them all, of course, is Bob Dylan – proving it in every song he covers, in every interview in which he mentions another artist, in every piece he has written about somebody else, in every one of his radio shows. So being a fan can be an intellectual obsession, it can be an inspiration, it can be a nuisance. But being a fan in itself is enough only as long as you do not plan to publicly write about it. You might tell everybody, but you will not get across.

Notes

1 All quotes from Marcus are from the interview conducted by the author at Marcus's home in Berkeley, California, on 7 January 2011, unless noted otherwise.
2 *Life*, Keith Richards' (2010) autobiography, had just come out, and we had been discussing the book before the interview, since Marcus was reviewing it at the time. He was greatly disappointed by it, by the way.
3 Established in 1994 by the Dorothy and Lillian Gish Prize Trust and administered by JPMorgan Chase Bank as trustee, the Prize is given annually to 'a man or woman who has made an outstanding contribution to the beauty of the world and to mankind's enjoyment and understanding of life'. In her will, Lillian Gish stated: 'It is my desire, by establishing this prize, to give recipients of the prize the recognition they deserve, to bring attention to their contributions to society and encourage others to follow in their path'. The Dorothy and Lillian Gish Prize is one of the largest awards in the arts. See https://groups.yahoo.com/neo/groups/NIgerianWorldForum/conversations/topics/61878.
4 According to Dylan's official website (http://www.bobdylan.com) the lyrics actually read: 'I went to tell everybody / But I could not get across'.

References

Barnes, J. (2009) *Flaubert's Parrot* (London: Vintage).
Dylan, B. (2004) *Chronicles: Volume One* (New York: Simon and Schuster).
Gray, M. (2000) *Song and Dance Man III: The Art of Bob Dylan* (London: Cassell).
Marcus, G. (1989) *Lipstick Traces: A Secret History of the Twentieth Century* (Cambridge, MA: Harvard University Press).
Marcus, G. (1997) *Invisible Republic: Bob Dylan's Basement Tapes* (New York: Henry Holt and Company).
Marcus, G. (2005) *Like a Rolling Stone: Bob Dylan at the Crossroads* (New York: PublicAffairs).
Marcus, G. (2010) *Bob Dylan by Greil Marcus: Writings 1968–2010* (New York: PublicAffairs).
Richards, K. (2010) *Life* (New York: Little, Brown and Company).
Williams, P. (1992) *Bob Dylan: Performing Artist (The Middle Years: 1974–1986)* (Novato, CA: Underwood-Miller).

Part V

Dylan appropriated

12

Tell-tale signs: self-deception in Dylan

Paul Fagan and Mark Shanahan

A central concern of Bob Dylan's song-writing is the attempt to test the terms, stakes, and politics of truth and representation, as conceived through the significant moral, ethical and cultural issues of twentieth-century America. Depending on the label applied, his songs are read either as evolutions of the Wobbly tradition of 'revealing' objective moral truths that demand social justice,[1] or as engagements with the American (post-)modernist tradition of encountering subjective truths that demand a recalibration of personal ethics. When Dylan is given the tag 'protest singer', his complex and often opaque songs have been read for their moral propositionality on issues such as civil rights struggles ('Oxford Town'), the threat of nuclear warfare ('Talkin' World War III Blues'), America's history of war ('With God on Our Side') and the Cold War arms build-up ('Masters of War'). When he is given the tag 'avant-garde innovator', his provocative and often socially oriented songs have been read for their engagement with the problems of knowing and representing objective truths, taking up Dylan's cue that the answers to these questions of morality and justice were 'blowin' in the wind'. Rather than argue for one side or the other in this debate, in this chapter we mean to embrace as programmatic such conflicts between *what* is said (or implied) and *how* it is said (or implied) in Dylan's *oeuvre*. We claim that in contemplating the relativity of truth and the problems of its representation, Dylan began to develop an aesthetic that introduced into twentieth-century song-writing a way of representing the clash between subjective and objective perspectives by exploring the tension between the moral and ethical dimensions of song-writing. In particular, we conceive of Dylan's handling of these themes as resting upon an encounter between a folk romanticism which 'locates authenticity principally in the direct communication between artist and audience' and of modernist artistry, which 'manifests its concern with authenticity more indirectly, at an aesthetic level' (Knightly, 2001: 138–9).

In order to unpack and address this claim, we relocate from the geo-political to the personal, by prioritising Dylan's representation of the event of 'lost love' as a fruitful site for investigating the stakes of such attempts to obscure the lines between direct and indirect dealings with his audience. In particular, our intention is to read the central and pervasive trope of self-deception as the index that renders accessible Dylan's reflections upon what is owed in the representation both of a former lover and of the spurned self. Towards these ends, we first take a closer look at the most indirect articu-lation of the difficult processing of a failed relationship in Dylan's early work, 'Don't Think Twice, It's All Right' (on *The Freewheelin' Bob Dylan*, 1963). Comparing the intersubjective encounter staged in this song with previous representations of lost love in popular music, we call on Paul Grice's model of inferential pragmatics to illuminate the strategies of indirect proposition-ality (or implicature) that Dylan applies to his subject. We then turn to Adam Zachary Newton's theory of 'narrative ethics' to highlight what is at stake in ethical terms in the different representations of self-deception employed by Dylan and his contemporaries. Having established 'Don't Think Twice, It's All Right' as an important laboratory in which Dylan tests the representa-tional and ethical problems of subjectivity, self-knowledge and alterity, we finally assess how these strategies are expanded and complicated in *Blood on the Tracks* (1975), Dylan's most extended meditation on the conflict of sub-jective and objective truths necessitated in the considered representation of a failed relationship.

She thinks I still care

'Don't Think Twice, It's All Right'[2] stages the bitter end of a relationship to a melody taught to Dylan by folk singer Paul Clayton.[3] Yet, despite its overt folk genre markings, 'Don't Think Twice' presents the listener with a very different proposition from the album's other folk laments, such as 'Girl from the North Country' ('Remember me to one who lives there/She once was a true love of mine'), or the blues stylings of 'Down the Highway' ('My baby took my heart from me/She packed it all up in a suitcase/Lord, she took it away to Italy, Italy'). While the song evokes the discourses of folk, country, blues and the lamenting ballad as known to the crooners of the Great American Songbook, the cumulative effect remains oddly jarring in relation to the usual conventions of each of these genres. 'A lot of people', Dylan notes, 'make ["Don't Think Twice"] sort of a love song – slow and easy-going. But it isn't a love song' (*Freewheelin'* liner notes). Indeed, 'Don't Think Twice' not only treats the bitter aftermath of a failed relationship but also assumes the unusual perspective of the party who has ostensibly ended the affair, rather than that of the spurned lover. Even more distinctively, the song's lyrical 'I'[4] seems almost perversely phlegmatic about the whole affair: 'I ain't sayin' you treated me unkind/You could have done better but *I don't mind*/You just kinda wasted my precious time/But *don't think twice, it's all right*' (emphasis added).

Barbara O'Dair contends that throughout 'Don't Think Twice' 'Dylan limns a well-worn male–female dynamic ... where, in the guise of a needy girlfriend, the woman really just wants to change him' (O'Dair, 2009: 82); however, by our analysis this reading is too literal. In a telling 1985 interview with Scott Cohen, Dylan revealed how his song-writing works to obscure such clear distinctions between self and other, and thus to trouble the romantic sense that the authenticity of his songs is to be found in their direct communication of an unproblematically accessible subjective experience or attitude:

> Sometimes the 'you' in my songs is me talking to me. Other times I can be talking to somebody else.... It's up to you to figure out who's who. A lot of times it's 'you' talking to 'you.' The 'I' ... also changes. It could be I, or ... it could be another person who's saying 'I.' When I say 'I' right now, I don't know who I'm talking about. (Cohen, 1985: 40)

In this context, it is telling that Dylan describes 'Don't Think Twice' as 'a statement that maybe you can say to make yourself feel better. It's as if you were talking to yourself' (*Freewheelin'* liner notes). This notion of a split in the integrity of the 'self' is an important one to which we will return. For now, it is worth underlining that if the song bears emotional resonance beyond its detached professions of aloofness upon ending a relationship with a needy, controlling woman (not an obviously sympathetic or marketable perspective for a popular song) and beyond its potential as a self-help seminar for its author (not particularly fertile ground for artistic integrity), this is because this pep-talk with the singer's own hurt pride is not open and frank but riddled with indices of self-deception.

The impression that the song reveals an 'off-record purpose' that remains inaccessible to the lyrical 'I' is echoed by a number of Dylan critics. As Howard Sounes observes, 'the greatness of the song was in the cleverness of the language. The phrase "don't think twice, it's all right" could be snarled, sung with resignation, or delivered with an ambiguous mixture of bitterness and regret. Seldom have the contradictory emotions of a thwarted lover been so well expressed' (Sounes, 2002: 152). Addressing these strategies of indirection, Paul Williams wonders at the myriad potential emotions communicated by them:

> 'Don't Think Twice' is about the transmuting of pain into something not only bearable but actually attractive.... The singer of the song conveys a tremendous dignity, and an authentic lightness, even while also

> communicating pain, bitterness, confusion, and more than a hint that he
> would get down on his knees and beg if he thought it'd do any good. He
> also communicates love. There is no 'way' to put all this into a simple
> song, four verses, that can be understood and sung by anyone. Dylan has
> done it. (Williams, 2004: 57)

In considering the 'way' in which the relation of the song's text to its
performance gives expression to a voice that both explicitly renounces its
responsibility in the failure of the relationship (and denies that anything
is owed in the exchange with the former lover) and implicitly betrays its
anxieties and culpabilities, we can posit a continuum of potential emotional
stances to the failure of a love affair that the lyrical 'I' might take up. At one
end, we find a stance of candid and cathartic 'self'-awareness, expressed in
the belief that the jilted lover has full and clear access to her or his own
feelings, desires and culpabilities, as well as her or his responsibilities to
the other party. 'Don't Worry 'Bout Me' (a song recorded by Billie Holiday
in 1938) insists upon this possibility of overcoming narcissism through self-
reflection, as the lyrical 'I' proposes mutual acceptance of the affair's natural
end in order to preserve the friendship.[5]

Moving along this continuum we find songs written from the perspective
of the cast-off lover: yielding to the former lover's account of the reasons
for the relationship's failure as objectively true, accepting full culpability, pleading to be taken back. Examples are legion, from the Righteous
Brothers' 'You've Lost that Lovin' Feelin'' (1964) to the Temptations' 'Ain't
Too Proud to Beg' (1966), in which the lyrical 'I' casts aside dignity and
begs to be taken back. By contrast, elsewhere we find songs that inhabit
the perspective of the jilted lover through the trope of self-pity. In Burt
Bacharach's 'I Just Don't Know What To Do With Myself' (1962), for example,
the intersubjective positioning is not focused on a radical willingness to
abandon the integrity of the self in order to reclaim the affections of the
other, but rather in a paralysing narcissistic gaze that lingers obsessively on
the feelings of the self. Each of these modes of representation is aligned with
Knightly's definition of a romantic tradition which 'locates authenticity …
in the direct communication between artist and audience' (Knightly, 2001:
136) and which implies that not only can the feelings and desires of the
self be fully and unambiguously known, but also that the 'song' offers an
ideal vehicle for the subjective representation of this coherent, stable and
transparent self. These are some of the most enduring devices and stances of
twentieth-century song-writing – and yet, despite its overt genre markings,
'Don't Think Twice' cannot be easily aligned with any of them.

Another strategy for representing the event of a failed love affair is to
call upon the trope of deception, inhabiting the stance of the jilted lover
who would deceive others about his or her pain, but cannot deceive him-
or herself. This stance is most representatively articulated in Caroline

Crawford's 'My Smile is Just a Frown (Turned Upside Down)' (1964) and the Miracles' 'The Tracks of My Tears' (1965), both composed by Smokey Robinson.[6] When this stance is expressed, the narrative situation is evolved to create two audiences – one to which the lyrical 'I' is direct and sincere, and another to which he or she is indirect and guarded. While 'Don't Think Twice' similarly inhabits registers of deception and indirection, it belongs to a farther end still of our posited continuum, at which we find a stance of total *self*-deception. In a further evolution of the narrative situation, at least three audiences can be conceptualised: two intratextual audiences to which the lyrical 'I' is indirect and insincere (his former lover, himself) and a third, extratextual audience, who intuit or infer an off-record message.

There is some precedent for complicating the representation of 'lost love' through the trope of self-deception and, as we shall see, Dylan taps into this vein of song-writing in 'Don't Think Twice', even as he distinguishes his approach by subtly tweaking the formula. 'I Get Along Without You Very Well (Except Sometimes)' (1939) is exemplary of this approach. Between repeated protestations that she gets along well without her former lover the lyrical 'I' lets her mask slip when she lists numerous exceptions to this rule.[7] As Richard M. Sudhalter points out, the singer's continued insistence serves only 'to shore up flagging resolve' and foreground the trope of self-deception, as '[t]he listener knows what the speaker won't admit: she does *not* get along without him very well' (Sudhalter, 2003: 210).

'I Get Along Without You Very Well (Except Sometimes)' offers us an illustrative model for investigating how such off-record messages are broadcast in Dylan's song. Towards this end, we can briefly call upon Paul Grice's 'co-operative principle', a model for demonstrating how language users violate the conceptual rules of communication to create a propositional force not encoded in what is actually said, but inferable from the relation of text to context. Grice proposed the existence of four 'conversational maxims': *quality* (only say what you believe to be true), *quantity* (do not offer more or less information than is required for the particular purpose), *relation* (contribute in a manner that is relevant to the interlocution) and *manner* (avoid ambiguity) (Grice, 1989: 26–8). Grice further argues that pragmatic 'implicatures' of meaning are created when speakers wilfully flaunt these maxims. As H. G. Widdowson elaborates, 'non-adherence [to the maxims] is marked and taken to imply some significance, an extra dimension of meaning not directly signalled by what is actually said' (Widdowson, 2008: 508). In order for an inference to be made, then, the interpreter must consider not only the form or semantic meaning of a text but also the relevance of speech acts that give too much or too little information, offer non-sequiturs, or are inappropriately contradictory or ambiguous in relation to their context, discourse or purpose.

As such, the 'off-record' inferences of self-deception in 'I Get Along Without You Very Well (Except Sometimes)' and 'Don't Think Twice' might be conceived, and accessed, as a series of signalled violations of the Gricean maxims. 'I Get Along Without You Very Well (Except Sometimes)' signals the singer's self-deception through her repeated declarations of nonchalance about the affair ('of course I do'), which violate Grice's *quantity* maxim through their excessive reiteration. The solicited inference indicates a deeper violation of the *quality* maxim through the double exposure of two incompatible claims about the self (indexed in the song's full title): that she gets along/does not get along very well without her lover.[8] Sounes (2002: 152) describes 'Don't Think Twice' similarly as 'a yearning for and a resenting of the object of his affection', a contradictory set of emotions that flout the *quality* maxim and solicit inferences as to the violation's relevance. As with 'I Get Along Without You Very Well (Except Sometimes)', 'Don't Think Twice' solicits 'implicatures' by a primary violation of the *quantity* maxim. As with Gertrude, of whom Hamlet says 'The lady doth protest too much, methinks', the lyrical 'I' of 'Don't Think Twice' insists so passionately, and at such length, about not minding that the relationship has come to an end, that one is compelled to suspect that something might be rotten in the state of Dylan. Beyond such overwrought declarations of professed nonchalance, the song exhibits a number of telling contradictions between the charges levelled against his former lover and the tone of his condemnation. For example, despite the charge of immaturity – that the former lover is 'a child' (or so he's told) – his harsh, narcissistic dismissal 'you just kinda wasted my precious time' displays no more maturity, thus undermining his studied attempts to portray himself as the unprejudiced speaker of truths.

Both songs employ the mechanism of indirection, then, in order to inhabit another identifiable perspective along the continuum of heartbreak songs: the compulsion towards self-deception about both the degree of emotional investment in a failed relationship and one's culpability for its failure, necessitated by the anxiety of losing the integrity of the self. Confronted with the possibility that firmly held subjective truths might not stand up to scrutiny, the romantic self, which is 'unitary, stable over time and able to suppress desire' (Macías and Núñez, 2011: 258), is in danger of being revealed as decentred, opaque and driven by alien desires. Yet beyond the fact that 'Don't Think Twice' bears a strain of vitriol and self-righteousness absent from 'I Get Along Without You Very Well (Except Sometimes)', the self-deception in the latter song, and in most of the best performances thereof, is so palpable and knowing, and there is such sustained daylight between the semantic and pragmatic levels of meaning, that while the essential mechanisms may be the same as in 'Don't Think Twice', the execution is something quite different.

In this sense, 'Don't Think Twice' is closer still to our final example, of George Jones's country hit 'She Thinks I Still Care' (1962), which also takes an ostensibly phlegmatic approach towards a former lover: 'If she's happy thinkin' I still need her/Then let that silly notion bring her cheer'.[9] Once again, such bravado is signalled, through Gricean violation, as a form of self-deception. As Aaron A. Fox underlines, Jones is here tapping into the 'heartbroke [sic] tore-up fool' trope, as the lyrical 'I' 'insist[s] that even though he still talks about his ex-lover, mentions her name, and calls her phone number by mistake, she's crazy to think that he "still cares"' (Fox, 2004: 149). Fox describes this discursive strategy of the split self riddled by self-deception – as opposed to a unified self projecting self-awareness – in more detail: 'Jones packs two identities into the "I" of this song. One is falling "all to pieces" ... and the other ... the "I" that can say "she thinks I still care", wavering between objectifying poetic mastery of the moment and the abject subjectivity of the fool, caught up in the grip of memory' (ibid.). In the last verse, however, the lyrical 'I' lets his guard slip: 'Just because I saw her, then went all to pieces/She thinks I still care'. In this final move, 'Jones is suddenly unable to keep up his façade of cool, poised disdain, and like the "fool" he sings of, he explodes in excessive display, as his voice suddenly goes wildly swooping over its full range' (ibid.).

Dylan's take on this technique of inhabiting the seemingly unified 'I' voice to project a split self – a form of narcissistic 'self-echo' in which the lyrical 'I' is simultaneously obsessed with and distanced from him- or herself – distinguishes itself from 'I Get Along Without You Very Well (Except Sometimes)' or 'She Thinks I Still Care' to the extent that no such slips of the mask occur. The opposing truths and untruths are encoded in the same string of words, without recourse to a moment of insight by the 'authentic' romantic self. By introducing this split in the lyrical 'I' exclusively through indirect Gricean 'implicature' – rather than in a direct statement, knowing contradiction or moment of romantic insight – Dylan not only deepens the emotional complexity of the song, but also complicates the representation of the event itself, as the usual alignment of the fool's dual selves to subjective (false) and objective (warranted) truths is not clearly delineated.

In staging an intersubjective encounter – positioning a lyrical 'I' against both a former lover and an audience in negotiating the claims to objective truth about his culpability and responsibility – 'Don't Think Twice' signals its engagement in 'a realm of ethical confrontation' (Newton, 1995: 4). In his *Narrative Ethics*, Adam Zachary Newton makes an important distinction 'between moral propositionality, or the realm of the "Said" and ethical performance, the domain of "Saying"' (ibid.: 5), and argues that texts that foreground the latter dimension by emphasising *form* over *content* are primarily interested in the ethical problem of how to represent an intersubjective encounter with an other. By these lights, a song such as 'Masters of War' (on the 1963 album *The Freewheelin' Bob Dylan*), with its direct proposition of condemnation, can be said to operate on a *moral* register, regarding the objectively 'right' or 'true', while a song such as 'Visions of Johanna' (from Dylan's 1966 album, *Blonde on Blonde*), with its opaque and shifting staging of a set of relationships between Louise, Johanna and the 'little boy lost', functions on the *ethical* level regarding what is owed in 'the reciprocal claims binding teller, listener, witness, and reader' in the process of creating narratives (*ibid.*: 4).

Clearly, with the strategies outlined in 'Don't Think Twice' we have moved into a modernist realm that 'manifests its concern with authenticity more indirectly, at the aesthetic level' and which is marked by 'irony, sarcasm, obliqueness', as opposed to a romantic authenticity founded in 'sincerity, directness' or self-insight (Knightly, 2001: 136–7). At stake, then, in the song's tension between 'message' and 'vehicle', between *product* and *process*, is the attempt to draw a distinction between 'Saying' and the 'Said' in order to stage an encounter between these moral (propositional) and ethical (intersubjective) domains. In exploring the human bias towards thinking dishonestly about one's own feelings and motivations, and even the accessibility of one's own desires, the song hints at the difficulty of seeing oneself simultaneously as both as deceiver and deceived. This implication speaks to a broader concern in Dylan's 1960s work, which is marked by simultaneous attempts to uncover 'truth' by exposing those who 'lie and deceive' (the 'Masters of War', to whom the lyrical 'I' charges: 'I can see through your masks'), and challenges the integrity of such 'truth' by laying bare the speaker's own self-deceptions and biases. As the distinction between deceiver and deceived – and, concomitantly, between subjective and objective truth, between self and other – upon which so much twentieth-century song-writing is based becomes untenable, Dylan looks to develop an aesthetic that can stage an ethical representation of an intersubjective experience in which there is at once an identifiable other and in which the motivations of the decentred and relational self – or, as he would put it a few years later, of 'The Man in Me' – remain opaque. Establishing a dialogue between the voices of the Wobblies (with their attention to the register of the 'Said') and the Beats (with their attention to the register of 'Saying'), Dylan progressively explores the relation between formal and ethical concerns in considering what is owed to the parties (other, self) involved in the representation of failed love. And in eliding the direct moral propositionality of positioning either lover in relation to an objective 'truth', Dylan starts to open up a paradigm that implies 'fundamental ethical questions about what it means to generate and transmit narratives, and to implicate, transform, or force the persons who participate in them' (Newton, 1995: 7).

She might think that I've forgotten her, don't tell her it isn't so

Twelve years after the release of 'Don't Think Twice', Dylan would achieve the acme of this aesthetic project with the release of the ten songs of *Blood on the Tracks* (1975). To Michael Gray, the album as a piece is primarily concerned with 'a profoundly felt understanding of our fragile impermanence of control,

154

so that in dealing with the overlay of past upon present Dylan is dealing with the inexorable disintegration of relationships, and with the dignity of keeping on trying to reintegrate them against all odds' (Gray, 2000: 182). Throughout the album, Dylan subtly expands and complicates his exploration of tropes of self-insight and self-deception, testing the representation of lost love between 'romantic' moral and 'modernist' ethical planes. Here we will explore this evolved aesthetic for ethically representing 'the inexorable disintegration of relationships' not by way of comparison to the example of Dylan's contemporaries, but rather through the album's interrelated strategies of creating intertextual, auto-citational networks with Dylan's earlier songs ('the overlay of past upon present') and its wilful, polyphonic employment of shifting pronouns and perspectives (exposing 'our fragile impermanence of control'). Each of these auto-referential strategies will be considered to foreground *Blood on the Tracks*' engagement with the problems of representing the encounter between the self and the other and of asking what is owed to each in the representation: as Gray puts it, the question of 'dignity' in the exchange.

The album's eighth track, 'If You See Her, Say Hello',[10] treats a love affair gone bad from the perspective of the spurned male, some time since the lovers had had 'a falling-out, like lovers often will'. The song has drawn comparison from Dylan's biographers with two of his earlier songs: 'Girl from the North Country' (from Dylan's 1963 album *The Freewheelin' Bob Dylan*) and 'Mama, You Been on My Mind' (an out-take from Dylan's 1964 album *Another Side of Bob Dylan*, subsequently released on volume 2 of the Bootleg Series). The resonances and implications of these narcissistic auto-citations cast light upon the distinctions between Dylan's 1960s and 1970s handling of the trope of self-deception, and demonstrate Dylan's attempt to draw together previous stances and representational modes into a more complex whole.

'Girl from the North Country'[11] establishes a narrative situation in which the lyrical 'I' addresses an off-stage figure (rather than his audience directly) with the instruction to 'remember' him to his former lover, the longing and despondency of the appeal expressed with unambiguous candour: 'She once was a true love of mine'. In the fourth verse, the lyrical 'I' openly wonders 'if she remembers [him] at all', a contemplation which serves as an enlightening counterpoint to the opening verse of 'If You See Her': 'Say for me that I'm all right though things get kind of slow/She might think that I've forgotten her, don't tell her it isn't so'.[12] The later song complicates the original's sincerity by cloaking its central concern (whether the ex-lover remembers him, fondly or otherwise) in the air of cool detachment and feigned indifference evoked in 'Don't Think Twice' ('Oh, whatever makes her happy, I won't stand in the way'), in the process implying that traces of bitterness still remain ('If she's passin' back this way, I'm not that hard to find/Tell her she can look me up if she's got the time').

This complicated stance evokes 'Mama, You Been on My Mind',[13] which Clinton Heylin describes as an early attempt at the professed nonchalance of 'If You See Her' (Heylin, 2001: 159). Again, the self-representation in 'Mama' of a 'modest and undemanding admirer' (Marqusee, 2003: 175) who stresses that 'it don't even matter to me where you're wakin' up tomorrow', wilfully exploits the trope of self-deception through indirection and Gricean violation: 'Rather than envisaging his messenger making love to her, he professes not to care who strokes her skin.... Methinks he doth protest too much' (Heylin, 2001: 159). 'Mama' opens: 'Perhaps it's the color of the sun cut flat/An' cov'rin' the crossroads I'm standing at,/Or maybe it's the weather or something like that,/But mama, you been on my mind'. This pathetic fallacy is economically echoed in the final verse of 'If You See Her': 'Sundown, yellow moon, I replay the past'. Indeed, in evoking this earlier song, replaying the past is exactly what Dylan is doing, and this self-reference is integral to what Andy Gill pinpoints as the turn throughout *Blood on the Tracks* to 'view narrative not in such strictly linear terms, but to telescope past, present and future together to attain a more powerful, unified focus' (Gill quoted in Tucker, 2007). Beyond further strengthening the implication of self-deception, and moving us into a modernist domain of intertextuality and multi-temporality, the echo with 'Mama' indexes the complex entanglements of self-awareness and alterity that are at the heart of *Blood on the Tracks* in its piercing question: 'I'd just be curious to know if you can see yourself as clear/As someone who has had you on his mind'.

And yet, 'If You See Her' contains a subtle but crucial representational difference from both 'Girl' and 'Mama' with the direct acknowledgements that 'our separation, it pierced me to the heart' and that 'the bitter taste still lingers on from the night I tried to make her stay'. Such admissions are far removed from the absolute exemptions from blame or emotional investment to be found in 'Don't Think Twice', yet even if there is an ostensible maturation of perspective, the lyrical 'I' remains too emotionally involved and continues to shelter his self-integrity through self-deception. By invoking simultaneously the directness of 'Girl' and the indirectness of 'Mama', 'If You See Her' recalibrates the emotional stance to allow for sorrow-tinged moments of romantic self-insight into the singer's own responsibilities, emotions and culpability, which coincide and clash with the fog of modernist indirection and self-deception. For example, even as the lyrical 'I' realises and admits that 'I've never gotten used to it, I've just learned to turn it off', the wilful ambiguity of the pronoun 'it' in each clause leaves the confession shrouded in ambiguity. Consequentially, 'If You See Her' introduces a space for considering simultaneously what is owed to the former lover and the spurned self in their representation. From this perspective, one can conceive that beyond its initial impression of bravado and male pride, the line 'She might think that I've forgotten her, don't tell her it isn't so' offers, in fact, a sophisticated articulation of a range of emotions. Indeed, why raise the issue of memory if it should remain unspoken? From this flouting of the *relation* maxim, we might infer that it is, in fact, the lyrical 'I' who is wondering whether she has forgotten him. And yet, the indirection of the phrasing in which the lyrical 'I' admits that he has not forgotten his former lover suggests a number of alien or inarticulable desires that trouble the implication in 'Mama' that 'someone who has had [her] on his mind' could see his lover's true self more clearly. That the echoes of 'Girl' evoke this question in its previous direct formulation ('I'm a-wonderin' if she remembers me at all') highlights the ways in which Dylan is testing a mode of song-writing in which the direct and indirect avowal, the self-aware and self-deceived lie, challenge (and perhaps contaminate) each other.

'Simple Twist of Fate', another song of failed love, is exemplary of the album's strategies of pronoun confusion and perspectival blending towards an ethical consideration and representation of these problems, as it sees Dylan employ the conceit of a one-night stand potentially to describe the course of his disintegrating relationship and ongoing separation from his then wife, Sara. Dylan breaks with his usual first-person perspective to sing in the third person, as though establishing the pretence (which he maintains to this day) that the songs on *Blood on the Tracks* are in no part autobiographical.[14] The song's lyrical 'I' betrays himself, however, in the second verse: '*They* walked along by the old canal/A little confused, *I* remember well' (emphasis added). Gill perceptively characterises the effect of such wilful shifts and slips in perspective throughout the album as one in which 'temporality, location and viewpoint shift back and forth from verse to verse, rather in the manner of montaged jump-cuts in a movie or the fictions of Thomas Pynchon and Don DeLillo, allowing [Dylan] to reveal underlying truths about the songs' characters while letting them remain shadowy, secretive figures' (Gill in Tucker, 2007). In the fourth verse, we see the culmination of this split narratological perspective as a means of representing the decentred self, as the protagonist deceives himself in a way that is revealed almost immediately by the omniscient narrator: 'He woke up, the room was bare/He didn't see her anywhere/*He told himself he didn't care*, pushed the window open wide/*Felt an emptiness inside* to which he just could not relate' (emphasis added). The third-person conceit, however, is dropped entirely in the final verse, when perspective shifts to the first-person singular. 'People tell *me* it's a sin/To know and feel too much within/*I* still believe she was my twin, but *I* lost the ring/She was born in spring, but *I* was born too late/Blame it on a simple twist of fate'. Collapsing the third-person conceit, the lyrical 'I' hints at a collapse of the self/other distinction by positioning his fleeting lover as his 'twin', and acknowledges that he is not completely blameless for the disintegration of the marriage ('but I lost the ring'). Most importantly, Dylan here introduces a new element to the narrative situation that offers the potential to exculpate both parties, as the overwhelming cause is the one thing over which neither has any control – fate. However, as revealed in

157

the album's centrepiece, 'Idiot Wind', this promise of mutual acquittal by re-linquishing culpability to powers outside of the lovers' control is ultimately found to be unethical, if not impossible.[15]

Idiot wind

In 'Idiot Wind' we see the culmination of these various strategies of auto-citational echoes, multitemporality, kaleidoscopic perspectives, pronoun shifts and the co-mingling of direct and indirect articulations of self-deception and self-awareness as means of 'reveal[ing] underlying truths about the songs' characters while letting them remain shadowy, secretive figures' (Gill in Tucker, 2007). However, as we shall see, the introduction here of a self-awareness inaccessible in 'Don't Think Twice', and hinted at in 'If You See Her', is cast in terms that are ambivalent at best.

At the centre of the long, often digressive, first-person narrative of 'Idiot Wind' is a failing relationship. The lyrical 'I' claims that fate played a part in the couple's break-up ('It was gravity which pulled us down and destiny which broke us apart'); however, this ostensible abdication of blame provides little emotional cover, and ultimately proves to be untenable. While the song's tapestry is woven with strands of self-loathing ('Every time I crawl past your door, I been wishin' I was somebody else instead'), his accusations ('You hurt the ones that I love best') and insults ('You're an idiot, babe/It's a wonder that you still know how to breathe') imply that he (at least also) blames the sarcastically dubbed 'sweet lady' for their separation. The lyrical 'I' details his former lover's 'corrupt ways' and failings through-out, including, significantly, the charge that she has failed to know him ('I couldn't believe after all these years, you didn't know me better than that'). Perhaps the most damning accusation is that she has committed the same crime as Dylan's earlier protagonists, who haunt the album's margins through its numerous intertextual echoes, by 'cover[ing] up the truth with lies'. However, recalling Dylan's declaration that 'Sometimes the "you" in my songs is me talking to me' (Cohen, 1985: 40) (an assertion we hope to have substantiated in our readings thus far), a clear distinction between self and other, between deceiver and deceived, is elided here, as 'you' can be read to refer to either the lover, as 'other', or the 'enemy within'. By the last verse it appears that the lyrical 'I' has convinced himself that he is glad the relationship is at an end, representing the break-up as a moment of liberation from an intersubjective event conceived of as a confusion of the distinction between self and other: 'I been double-crossed now for the very last time and now I'm finally free/I kissed goodbye the howling beast on the borderline which separated you from me'.

'Ballad in Plain D', released eleven years previously, is the only song in the Dylan canon that bears comparison with 'Idiot Wind' in terms of the unrestrained bitterness and rage directed towards its target, and by comparing the resonances and differences between the two songs we might find what is at stake in the latter's representational ambiguities. Like 'Idiot Wind', 'Ballad in Plain D' (on *Another Side of Bob Dylan*, 1964) concerns the end of a relationship, and the invective is aimed at the person whom the lyrical 'I' believes to be the main cause of the break-up – in this case, his former lover's 'parasite sister'. At one stage in the song, it appears that the lyrical 'I' is prepared to accept some of the blame: 'Myself, for what I did, I cannot be excused/The changes I was going through can't even be used/For the lies that I told her in hopes not to lose/The could-be dream-lover of my lifetime'. Here the violation of Grice's *relation* maxim is even more pronounced than in 'If You See Her': if 'the changes' the singer was going through 'can't even be used' as an excuse, then why bring them up, except as a backhanded attempt to absolve himself of blame? Similarly, the attempt to recast his 'lies' with noble intentions supports the inference that the lies he is telling are to himself.

'Idiot Wind', however, elevates itself above this duplicity and rancour when, having transgressed 'the borderline which separated you from me', the mask of self-deception slips, and the lyrical 'I' recognises, for the first time in the song, his lover's humanity: 'You'll never know the hurt I suffered, nor the pain I rise above/And I'll never know the same about you, your holiness or your kind of love/And it makes me feel so sorry'. With that 'sorry' – which Dylan delivers with particularly poignant emphasis – it appears that the lyrical 'I' finally recognises at once the inaccessible opacity of the other, as inaccessible as his own desires and feelings, and his shared culpability in the break-up, as acknowledged by a powerful pronoun change in the final chorus: 'Idiot wind, blowing through the buttons of *our* coats/Blowing through the letters that *we* wrote/Idiot wind, blowing through the dust upon *our* shelves/*We*'re idiots, babe/It's a wonder *we* can even feed ourselves' (emphasis added). The maturity to implicate oneself in the failure of the relationship – a maturity the protagonist of 'Ballad in Plain D' had attempted but failed to achieve[16] – amid all the rancour of the song is not only surprising, but also devastating. In his recognition that he will never know, and perhaps has never known, the love and 'holiness' of his partner, the relationship becomes an empty and foolish endeavour in its entirety, with the 'idiot wind' blowing even through the love letters they had written each other in presumably happier times.[17] That Dylan had once referred to Sara as one of the only two 'holy people' he had ever met only adds to the poignancy of this recognition that he has never truly known his lover's 'holiness', nor his own true feelings and desires.[18] In this way, one might consider 'Idiot Wind' not only a powerful testing of the possibilities of an ethical representation of Dylan's own lost love, but also a beautiful and tragic exposure of the conceit that had underpinned the catalogue of heartbreak songs he had written up to that point: that at stake in his sustained staging of the trope of self-deception is not only the problem of the ethical representation of the other party in the break-up, but also the ethical representation of the 'other' within oneself. Thus Dylan briefly exposes that which lies beyond the protective self-deception of an 'I' who experiences himself as an 'other' – who acknowledges that 'when I say "I" right now, I don't know who I'm talking about' (Cohen, 1985: 40) – is not a potential for self-learning and epiphany, as presented by the romantic tradition of songs such as Billie Holiday's 'Don't Worry 'Bout Me', but rather an alienation and self-loathing too painful to bear.

Conclusion

Dylan would return to this trope a number of times, although perhaps never as powerfully as he had done throughout *Blood on the Tracks*. In the sessions for 1976's *Desire*, he composed 'Abandoned Love', a song that explicitly picks up on this theme of the self as other, complicit in the failure of a relationship: 'I've been deceived by the clown inside of me/I thought that he was righteous but he's vain/Oh, something's a-telling me I wear the ball and chain'. Likewise, 'Where Are You Tonight? (Journey Through Dark Heat)', which closes *Street Legal* (1978), exemplifies the fact that when confronted with a realisation that 'The truth was obscure, too profound and too pure', Dylan's spurned lovers often resort to self-deception rather than encounter directly the ethical problem of what is owed in the representation of the failed relationship, given the alienating inaccessibility of his lover's or his own desires: 'I fought with my twin, that enemy within/'Til both of us fell by the way'.[19]

Dylan's most successful return to the technique of a phlegmatic treatment of a clearly less than casual emotional investment with the event of lost love is to be found in 1989's 'Most of the Time' (on *Oh Mercy*). Evoking Dylan's many impassioned declarations protesting his dispassionate feelings regarding a former lover, the song implicitly tackles a spurned lover's need to 'learn to turn it off' through a web of self-deception about his feelings and responsibilities, before reinforcing the stance that 'I don't even think about her/Most of the time'. Here Dylan returns to the traditional moves that we had seen in 'I Get Along Without You Very Well (Except Sometimes)', with the phrase 'most of the time' serving the function of projecting a split self, as the parenthetical '(Except Sometimes)' had done in Hoagy Carmichael's 'I Get Along Without You Very Well'. 'Most of the Time' also offers one of the best examples of Dylan's exploitation of delivery and phrasing to alter the potential meaning of a phrase; as Williams observes, 'at the start of each verse [the phrase "most of the time"] means "usually" or "more often than not". But the way he sings it at the end of each verse it means "but not always"' (Williams, 2004: 194). Ultimately, however, the song illustrates the extent to which, in Dylan's hands, indirect self-deception takes on the form of a simultaneous confessional: 'I don't cheat on myself, I don't run and hide / Hide from the feelings that are buried inside / I don't compromise and I don't pretend / I don't even care if I ever see her again / Most of the time'. Even if the lyrical 'I' is not to believed on a semantic level here, the fact that Dylan crafts his songs in this way means that his personae are not, in fact, running or hiding, compromising or pretending, but rather presenting the listener with a double exposure of self-opacity and self-awareness, in which the boundaries between truth and dishonesty are ephemeral and perhaps even impossible to draw – a double exposure perceivable to anybody who 'can follow the path' or read the tell-tale signs.

Notes

1   'Wobblies' were members of radical labour union the Industrial Workers of the World, which had a strong tradition of songs (famously collected in the *Little Red Songbook*) that protested against social inequality, parodied capitalist discourse and attempted to organise workers into the One Big Union. Dylan's most prominent point of access into this tradition would have been through the influence of Woody Guthrie and, to a lesser extent, Pete Seeger. An example of Dylan's unique invocations of Wobbly tropes can be seen in 'I Dreamed I Saw St. Augustine' (on *John Wesley Harding*, 1967), the first two lines of which rework the opening of Wobbly anthem 'I Dreamed I Saw Joe Hill Last Night' (lyrics by Alfred Hayes, music by Earl Robinson, 1936) in a religious context.

2   Hereafter, 'Don't Think Twice'.

3   In the song Dylan signals this debt through intertextual references to a number of lines from Clayton's 'Who's Goin' to Buy You Ribbons When I'm Gone?'

4   Throughout this chapter, the term 'lyrical I' has been chosen in order to emphasise the necessary distinction between the singer and the voice of the character inhabited or performed, and as distinct from a narrative voice. As we argue, in part, that Dylan calls upon, and challenges, the romantic concept of creation as a mark of pure subjectivity in his song-writing, we feel that the choice is warranted.

5   B. Holiday, 'Don't Worry 'Bout Me', *Last Recordings* (MGM, 1959). Composed by Rube Bloom, with lyrics by Ted Koehler.

6   In each song, the lyrical 'I' discloses to the listener that the smile is solely for the benefit of others, a mask to conceal the 'real' inner heartbreak. Interestingly, Dylan exploits this trope in 'Can't Escape from You', a cut from *Tell Tale Signs* (2008, vol. 8 of Dylan's Bootleg Series of albums): 'I'll be here 'til tomorrow / Beneath a shroud of grey / I pretend I'm free of sorrow / My heart is miles away'.

7   See Sudhalter (2003: 209–10). Composed by Hoagy Carmichael in 1939 and set to a poem by Jane Brown Thompson (*ibid.*: 212), the song is most usually sung from a 'female' perspective – by noteworthy jazz singers such as Rosemary Clooney, Nina Simone and Billie Holiday – although it is malleable enough to be amenable to a 'male' perspective, as when Chet Baker covered the song for his 1956 album *Chet Baker Sings*.

8   While one needs to be careful to allow for genre-specific scripts of repetition, such as choruses or refrains, when applying Grice's model to song-writing, we contend that violations can be justifiably distinguished from convention through considerations of performance (phrasing, timbre, key, hesitations, etc.) and of the specific propositional import of such potential violations.

9   G. Jones, 'She Thinks I Still Care', *The New Favorites of George Jones* (Liberty, 1962). Composed by Dickey Lee and Steve Duffy. Hereafter, 'She Thinks'.

10 Hereafter, 'If You See Her'.

11 Hereafter, 'Girl'.

12 The correspondence between the two songs is further supported by the 'Say for me' line in 'If You See Her, Say Hello', in which Gray hears the echo of the 'see for me' refrain of 'Girl from the North Country' (Gray, 2008: 60).

13 Hereafter, 'Mama'.

14 In an interview with Bill Flanagan, Dylan said 'A lot of people thought … that album *Blood on the Tracks*, pertained to me. Because it seemed to at the time. It didn't pertain to me' (Flanagan, 1986: 96). On the other side of the ledger, his son, Jakob Dylan, has stated that 'The songs are my parents talking' (Sounes, 2002: 333). For our purposes here, we are not interested in taking a definitive stance on what is, essentially, an irreconcilable issue. However, we likewise find any critical standard that forecloses considerations of an autobiographical dynamic to *Blood on the Tracks*, through the clear-cut distinction between Bob Dylan the flesh-and-blood person (Robert Zimmerman) and 'Bob Dylan' the character, to be reductive with regard to what we perceive as the album's paradigmatic conflation of the registers of 'fictional' and 'autobiographical' in testing the ethical and representational problems of self-knowledge and alterity.

15 In a rewritten version of 'Simple Twist of Fate' that Dylan has played live since the initial release of *Blood on the Tracks*, there are more indications that fate alone was not to blame, though in this version the singer appears to absolve himself (there is no mention of lost rings). In the final verse, Dylan sings 'she should have caught me in my prime, she would have stayed with me'. The first claim implies that it is in some way her fault that she did not catch him in his prime. The second claim is unequivocal: had she done so, she would have stayed with him.

16 In fact, when discussing 'Ballad in Plain D' in interview with Bill Flanagan, Dylan admitted: 'That one I look back and I say, "I must have been a real schmuck to write that"' (Flanagan, 1986: 97).

17 Not only this, but in a grand narcissistic flourish, the entire United States of America is contaminated with this futility, 'From the Grand Coulee Dam to the Capitol'.

18 'I know just two holy people, Allen Ginsberg is one. The other, for lack of a better term, I just want to call "this person named Sara". What I mean by "holy" is crossing all boundaries of time and usefulness' (Dylan quoted in Shelton, 1997: 353).

19 It is worth noting the recurrence of the twin/lover confusion introduced in 'Simple Twist of Fate' as an index of the problem of negotiating and representing the ambiguous self/other, deceiver/deceived divide in relationships.

References

Cohen, S. (1985) 'Bob Dylan: not like a rolling stone interview', *Spin*, 1:8 (December). 37–42, 80–1.

Flanagan, B. (1986) *Written in My Soul: Rock's Great Songwriters Talk About Creating Their Music* (Michigan, MI: Contemporary Books).

Fox, A. A. (2004) *Real Country: Music and Language in Working-Class Culture* (Durham, NC: Duke University Press).

Gill, A. (1998) *Classic Bob Dylan 1962–1969: My Back Pages* (Zurich: Edition Olms).

Gray, M. (2000) *Song and Dance Man III* (New York: Continuum).

Gray, M. (2008) *The Bob Dylan Encyclopedia* (New York: Continuum).

Grice, P. (1989) *Studies in the Way of Words* (Harvard, MA: Harvard University Press).

Heylin, C. (2001) *Behind the Shades: Take Two* (London: Penguin).

Knightly, K. (2001) 'Reconsidering rock', in S. Frith, W. Straw and J. Street (eds), *The Cambridge Companion to Pop and Rock* (Cambridge: Cambridge University Press). 109–42.

Macías, J.S. and Núñez, R.V. (2011) 'The other self: psychopathology and literature', *Journal of Medical Humanities*, 32:4 (December). 257–67.

Marqusee, M. (2003) *Chimes of Freedom: The Politics of Bob Dylan's Art* (New York: New Press).

Newton, A. Z. (1995) *Narrative Ethics* (Cambridge, MA: Harvard University Press).

O'Dair, B. (2009) 'Bob Dylan and gender politics', in K. J. H. Dettmar (ed.), *The Cambridge Companion to Bob Dylan* (Cambridge: Cambridge University Press). 80–6.

Shelton, R. (1997) *No Direction Home: The Life and Music of Bob Dylan* (New York: Da Capo Press).

Sounes, H. (2002) *Down the Highway: The Life of Bob Dylan* (London: Black Swan).

Sudhalter, R. M. (2003) *Stardust Melody: The Life and Music of Hoagy Carmichael* (Oxford: Oxford University Press).

Tucker, T. (2007) 'Defying time in Bob Dylan's *Blood on the Tracks*', *The Culture Club* (2 January). Available at http://www.thecultureclub.net/2007/01/02/defying-time-in-bob-dylans-blood-on-the-tracks (accessed 2 July 2013).

Widdowson, H. G. (2008) 'Language creativity and the poetic function: a response to Swann and Maybin (2007)', *Applied Linguistics*, 29:1 (September). 503–8.

Williams, P. (2004) *Bob Dylan, Performing Artist: The Early Years, 1960–1973* (Reading: Omnibus).

13

'Yes, it's a very funny song': spoken intros and the seriousness of Bob Dylan's Halloween show

Paul Keckeis

Accounts of Bob Dylan's five-decade career as a performing artist could be abbreviated in many ways but, certainly, all would include his first electric appearance at the Newport Folk Festival on Sunday, 25 July 1965. While most focus on questions regarding Dylan's intentions for going electric, as well as the audience's reaction to their former folk hero and now electrified band leader, it has proven impossible to come to consensus, either about Dylan's 'true' motives, or, despite its being taped, about the public's reaction (see Light, 2009: 59). Paul Williams, a chronicler of Dylan's performance art, is 'not sure' whether the audience 'booed all that much' (Williams, 2004: 156); with respect to the sound quality, Michael Gray concludes 'people weren't anti electric … people were just anti bad sound' (Gray, 2008: 497); and, on a different note, biographer Robert Shelton observed, 'What happened … depended on where you were, but I heard enormous vocal hostility all around me' (Shelton, 2011: 210).

Regardless of which narrative one finds most plausible, Dylan's legendary appearance at Newport is inscribed into US cultural history as an epochal transformation. Compared with the myth, according to which in 'a single, galvanizing instant, Dylan plugged an entire generation in',[1] the protagonist's own representation of the lead-up to Newport might read as uninspired:

> I was doing fine, singing and playing my guitar. It was a sure thing, don't you understand, it was a sure thing. I was getting very bored with that. I couldn't go out and play like that. I was thinking of quitting. Out front it was a sure thing. I knew what the audience was gonna do, how they would react. It was very automatic. Your mind just drifts unless you can find some way to get in there and remain totally there. It's so much of a fight remaining totally there all by yourself. It takes too much. (Dylan, 1965, in Cott, 2006a:52)

The long-established narrative, according to which Dylan's renunciation of protest begins at Newport, is itself aligned to the 'actual' scandal of the performance, the mere event of electrification. However, Dylan's explanation for going electric, together with his remarks on the challenge of performing solo, points to the importance of investigating prior indications of dissonance between Dylan and his audience.

From the start, the appeal of Dylan's writing drew from social conflict and impending threats to the American society of the 1960s. For Dylan, however, it seems that even when he has exploited matters of most urgent interest, the poetic potential of the real world has always outweighed the political implications of his songs. 'Dylan's genius of American tongue'[2] emerged from the concurrence of an outrageously gifted individual and the cultural and political upheavals of the 1950s and early 1960s. But as soon as Dylan was chosen to be the 'voice of his generation', it was too late for him to tone down the topical relevance of his songs.

This chapter analyses some of the more subtle deviations of Dylan's acoustic era. The first part points to early manifestations of conflict between Dylan and his audience. It concentrates on Dylan's Halloween show at the Philharmonic Hall in New York City on 31 October 1964, outlines the dramaturgy of the concert and, contextualised within a whole series of acoustic performances, focuses on Dylan's use of spoken intros as an effort both to entertain and to challenge the crowds. The second part reflects on the significance of his ambivalence towards the crowd's expectations and traces the miscommunication between Dylan and his audience to the contemporary appeal of American folk music in the 1960s.

The acoustic renegade

Dylan's performative impulse uncovers a continuity that transcends the common acoustic/electric periodisation of his early career. As Dylan recalls, when he arrived in New York City in late January 1961, he felt a strong urge to perform in front of an audience, any audience really: 'I could never sit in a room and just play all by myself. I needed to play for people and all the time. You can say I practiced in public and my whole life was becoming what I practiced' (Dylan, 2004: 16). Soon after, he performed at places like the Gaslight, the Café Wha? and Gerde's Folk City. Dylan became a protagonist of the folk scene in Greenwich Village and rapidly gathered a rich body of stage experience. When he appeared at the Newport Folk Festival for the first time in 1963 he had the repertoire, the tools and the charisma to conquer his audience; after Newport, wherever he performed, Dylan already owned the crowds, so much he could only deliberately push them away. And, indeed, by the time he was recording his fourth studio album *Another Side of Bob Dylan* (recorded in June, released in August 1964) he was about to leave behind his old material; as Dylan told Nat Hentoff during a recording session for *Another Side*, 'There aren't any finger-pointing songs in here, either. Those records I've already made.... Me, I don't want to write *for* people anymore.... From now on, I want to write from inside me' (see Cott, 2006b: 15). As Hentoff observes, Dylan had 'transcended most of his early influences and developed an incisively personal style' (*ibid*.: 22); moreover, he could no longer bear the burden of finding himself constrained to live up to the expectations of any movement or generation whatsoever. Dylan's 'fierce heavy feeling'[3] in the face of all the expectations led to the scandalous acceptance speech for the Tom Paine Award from the National Emergency Civil Liberties Committee in December of 1963.[4] While winning qualities, such as entertaining the crowds, the ability to create a dramaturgy for his concerts and to charmingly fill the gaps between songs, seemed to come naturally to Dylan, his conceptual efforts in trying to distance himself from his audience in the years to come should not be underestimated. Even before the visual provocations of the album cover of *Bringing It All Back Home* (March 1965), with its allusion to bourgeois decadence, or D. A. Pennebaker's *Dont Look Back* (filmed on the England tour in April–May 1965), when Dylan was on the verge of going electric, he developed strategies to question certain political narratives which were of eminent relevance to his politicised audience. Dylan frequently tried to subvert their expectations and to legitimise his aesthetic freedom.

From the extemporaneous speech at the Bill of Rights Dinner (the occasion of the Tom Paine Award), to his *Another Side* album of 1964, which 'contained Dylan's specific recantation of the protest phase' (Gray, 2008: 21), to *Bringing It All Back Home*, which was 'enough to gain him a new notoriety and to lose him even more devotees' (*ibid*.: 88): the electric set at Newport only summarises an insurmountable gap between what Dylan was willing to give and what the Irwin Silbers of *Sing Out!* wanted to hear from their prophet – to them, Dylan was 'losing his left wing credentials' (Lee, 1998: 39).[5]

Dylan's repulse of the crowds' claim is documented in a remarkable series of acoustic shows at the Philharmonic Hall in New York City (31 October 1964), at the San Jose Civic Auditorium (25 November 1964), at the Masonic Memorial Auditorium in San Francisco (27 November 1964) as well as at the Civic Auditorium in Santa Monica (27 March 1965) and the Manchester Free Trade Hall in Britain (7 May 1965). Dylan's new songs and old material merged into a hybrid repertoire which could no longer be easily brought into service of the civil rights and anti-war movements. Also, Dylan's deliberate use of spoken intros prevented the audience from embracing him as the messenger bringing some hidden truth or from identifying the singer with the song; his audience, then, had to rise to the challenge of an acoustic renegade in the making.

Sean Wilentz, in his comprehensive study *Bob Dylan in America* (2010), attaches particular significance to Dylan's concert at the Philharmonic Hall:

'The show was in part a summation of past work and in part a summons to an explosion for which none of us, not even he, was fully prepared' (Wilentz, 2010: 87). Wilentz appreciates the Halloween show 'not just in what Dylan sang, but in what he said, and in the amazing audible rapport he had with his audience' (*ibid.*: 92). To start with, a short description will be given of Dylan's performance, at the peak of his stage intelligence.

The set-list of the concert at the Philharmonic Hall consists of eighteen songs: three from *The Freewheelin' Bob Dylan* (May 1963), three from *The Times They Are A-Changin'* (January 1964), five from *Another Side*, three from the yet-to-be-released *Bringing It All Back Home* and four songs Dylan never recorded or released on a studio album. Contrary to what the occasion suggests, with its selection and sequence of songs the Halloween show is a rather exemplary concert of Dylan's late 'folk hero' period. He opens the concert with 'The Times They Are A-Changin'', as he had been doing for quite some time and would continue to do until Newport, and he presents a basic choice of songs that he would more or less stick with in the months to come. Aside from speculating about Dylan's potential benefit from 'having a familiar structure to work within, a script to fall back on or embellish or play around with' (Williams, 2004: 119), there might be more significant implications to take away from Dylan's routine, especially with regard to his interaction with the audience.

The following sequence illustrates some of the challenges posed to Dylan's Halloween audience:[6] in the middle of the first set Dylan announces the yet to be released 'Gates of Eden': 'This is called a sacrilegious lullaby in D minor ... that's the D minor ... [laughing] now in all seriousness ... this is a love song and it's called "The Gates of Eden"'. With the cryptic eight-minute song still echoing, Dylan allays his somewhat overcharged audience with the often cited masquerade: 'Don't want that scare you ... it's just Halloween ... I have my Bob-Dylan-mask on ... I'm masquerading'. Dylan then carries forward with the permissive comical song 'If You Gotta Go, Go Now', which is far from any serious, let alone engaged political song-writing. Dylan with his cockiness cuts across the expectations of the audience, which prompts somebody to shout, 'What do you do for a living?' Dylan responds, 'Anything you say ... I hope I never have to make a living'. He then introduces his next song: 'This is called "It's Alright Ma, It's Life and Life Only"'. His introduction of the song turns into a joke, as a result of its position within the set-list (as a follow-up to 'If You Gotta Go'), his phrasing and what, roughly, must have been the economy of emotions of a common Dylan crowd in late 1964. Dylan comments on the crowd's timid laughter: 'Yes, it's a very funny song'. Of course, there is nothing funny about 'It's Alright Ma', or Dylan's performance of it here, but most of the audience do not know any of the sequenced songs. 'Gates of Eden' and 'It's Alright Ma' are featured on Dylan's fifth album, *Bringing It All Back Home*, which was released only on 27 March 1965; 'If You Gotta Go' was recorded during the first session for the album, but was not released as a single until 1967 (in Holland). The unfamiliarity of the material and its complexity come as an excessive demand on the audience. Dylan's arrangement additionally exposes them to a series of fast, sharp changes of mood, from the visionary 'Gates of Eden' to the frivolous 'If You Gotta Go', to the disorienting spoken intro and the colossal 'It's Alright Ma', which, with its 'plummeting energy' and 'demonic drive' (Shelton, 2011: 195), is as far from being a funny song as Dylan is from accepting any restrictive affiliations to the New Left and its normative aesthetics – anybody who attended the show must have felt quite baffled.

But Dylan's seemingly unpredictable volatility is not to be ascribed to some exceptional Halloween mood; in San Jose and San Francisco, within a few weeks of New York, in Santa Monica, and in Manchester only a few months later, Dylan follows the path of the Philharmonic Hall and performs the exact same sequence of songs: 'Gates of Eden', 'If You Gotta Go' and 'It's Alright Ma'. Each time, Dylan introduces 'It's Alright Ma' with the more or less same phrase, each time to the same effect and each time he comments on the crowd's laughter.

Within the whole series of acoustic concerts of late 1964 and early 1965 there are dozens of other examples of such spoken intros, to a greater or lesser extent revelatory remarks between songs, which correspond to both Dylan's repertoire and the crowds' expectations. Another example: the introduction of 'Love Minus Zero/No Limit' in Santa Monica goes, 'This song is love minus zero … a … slash no limit … end of quote … it's kind of like a painting – the title … painted in purple'; at the Manchester Free Trade Hall it goes, 'The name of this song is, it is a fraction … Love minus Zero is on the top and underneath is no limit … I made the title before I made the song'.

All these spoken intros refer to songs which were released on *Bringing It All Back Home*. None of them are protest songs, topical songs or 'finger-pointing songs', but rather song poems, (anti-)love songs and songs that become comprehensible by contemplating not the possibilities but rather the impossibility of social criticism.

The most fascinating aspect of this period in Dylan's career, however, is that his renunciation of the protest genre is not yet complete. With the set-list quantitatively still dominated by Dylan's old material, some spoken intros refer to typical Dylan protest songs or topical songs. 'Who Killed Davey Moore?' is based on the death of the Afro-American featherweight world boxing champion Davey Moore, who died in 1963 in the aftermath of a title fight against Sugar Ramos. Dylan is not so much accusing somebody in particular of being responsible for Moore's death, but on another level he offers a commentary on the exaggerated politicisation of the event instead: Dylan infiltrates the naïve political sense of some of his audience. The song was first performed at the Town Hall in New York City on 12 April 1963 and then at Newport 1963; afterwards, it was absorbed into the repertoire. It is therefore likely that most of Dylan's audience at the Philharmonic Hall already knew the song. It was, though, the last time he would ever play the song, and on this occasion Dylan's introduction brings something new to it: 'This is a ... this is a song about a boxer ... a boxer ... it's got nothing to do with a boxer, it's just a song about a boxer ... [laughter] ... and, uh ... it's uh ... it's not even havin' to do with a boxer really ... it's got nothing to do with nothing ... [laughter] ... but I fit all these words together, that's all, this is, uh, taken out of the newspapers, nothing has been changed, except the words ... [laughter]'. Dylan's introduction to the song is amusing, but different from the other examples in that it weighs heavier this time, as it substantially refers to the theme of the song. The first part of Dylan's intro-duction undermines some of the more shallow political implications of the song. The coda of the intro, which Dylan uses to introduce 'The Lonesome Death of Hattie Carroll' as well – 'This is a true story ... right out of the newspapers again ... just the words have been changed around ... it's like conversation really' – reconciles the audience to their expectations. Dylan's ambivalence, then, is erased with the almost frenetic applause to the first line of 'Who Killed Davey Moore?' Its source, however, the underlying conflict, remains acute; before Dylan performs the last song of the show, 'All I Really Want To Do', somebody shouts a request for the nursery rhyme 'Mary Had a Little Lamb'. Dylan bluntly jokes 'God, did I record that? That's "Mary Had a Little Lamb" ... is that a protest song?'[7]

One crucial observation about Dylan's performance is the repetitiveness of certain intros in connection with certain songs; it suggests Dylan's calcu-lated use of spoken intros, at least to some extent. Besides that, the frequent use of spoken intros creates a rather erratic atmosphere; shifting from the monologic space of a song to the dialogic space in between dissolves the narratives of Dylan's songs into the fact of their performance by an artist whose attitude is not exactly one of a dedicated civil rights activist. Together with other manifestations of conflict, Dylan's spoken intros can be read as an indication of the gap between the crowds' expectations and Dylan's programme long before the scandal of Newport.

Dylan and the complex legacy of American folk music

Similar to Newport, there are different opinions about the relevance of Dylan's Halloween show. Paul Williams registers a 'sheer beauty' of the performance and observes Dylan's 'pure affection' (Williams, 2004: 121) for some of his classics such as 'The Lonesome Death of Hattie Carroll'. He completely misses Dylan's ambivalence and thus inadequately offers a har-monious reading of a much more complex performance. For Clinton Heylin, on the other hand, Dylan's ambivalence is reason to firmly disapprove of the concert. According to his assessment, the Halloween show 'was a real landmark ... in the negative sense'; since Dylan was 'completely and totally

169

bored' with his old material, and 'clearly stoned', Heylin 'never rated [the Halloween show] as a performance' (see Pelusi, 2004).

Rather than taking sides, the question is, what leads to such a range of judgement? Aside from personal opinion, Williams and Heylin seemingly prioritise different aspects of Dylan's performance: whereas Williams draws attention exclusively to the songs – and surely there is nothing to find fault with in Dylan's singing – Heylin takes notice of Dylan's wandering focus instead, his kidding around, everything which distorts the intensity of a song. Still, Heylin's marginalisation, the general dismissal of the seriousness of Dylan's performance, is rather arbitrary – Dylan might well have been 'clearly stoned', but that is hardly the scale on which to measure the quality of a Dylan performance.

The interpretive challenge of a live concert compared with that of a studio album among other things lies in the fact that it is not just a sequence of songs: the space in between shapes its unique character. As Williams's and Heylin's reactions indicate, however, we as listeners seem to be used to treating these units as if they were different realms of a performance. Sean Wilentz, in his account of Dylan's concert at the Philharmonic Hall, suggests rethinking our habitualised reception and with regard to Dylan's introduction of 'It's Alright Ma' concludes: 'The joke was serious' (Wilentz, 2010: 103). Indeed, far from being a unique feature of that particular night, Dylan's jokes were aimed to further undermine certain notions of solidarity between the artist and his fans. Dylan's crowds, however, showed astonishing persistence in ignoring his many efforts to distance himself from their expectations. In what follows, I will try to historicise this remarkable constellation and trace some of the miscommunication between Dylan and his audience to both the complex legacy of American folk music and its contemporary appeal in the 1960s.

The mythification of Dylan as 'the voice of his generation' sometimes corresponds to what his songs offer. The apocalyptic imagery of 'A Hard Rain's A-Gonna Fall' (written and recorded in 1962 and featured on the 1963 album *The Freewheelin' Bob Dylan*) anticipates the threat of nuclear annihilation, a threat which was real during the Cold War and became imminent during the Cuban Missile Crisis of October 1962. Within the context of these real historical events it is irrelevant whether Dylan intended the song to refer to nuclear fallout or not. During the cultural and political upheavals of the 1950s and early 1960s, when folk became a catalyst to the civil rights and anti-war movement, with his fingers firmly on the pulse of time, Dylan almost inevitably became the golden child of folk.

Whereas Dylan might not have been genuinely interested in folk as a mode of social criticism – as he told Nat Hentoff, 'some of that was jumping into the scene to be heard and a lot of it was because I didn't see anybody else doing that kind of thing' (Cott, 2006b: 15–16) – his ability to exploit the political possibilities of folk was exceptional. Paul Simon suggests that with his early compositions Dylan had 'so enlarged himself through the folk background that he incorporated it' and 'defined the genre for a while' (see Fong-Torres, 1973: 424). It was too late for him, then, to dissociate from the Village context he emerged out of; it was too late to convince the crowds of the 'real' Dylan, since they had already run away with 'their' Dylan.

In order to further investigate the increasing gap between Dylan's programme and the crowds' expectations, which culminated in the 'scandal' of Newport, we shall refer to Dylan's autobiography, *Chronicles*, one more time. At the early height of his popularity, when asked about his opinion or definition of folk, Dylan would always try to evade the question.[8] In *Chronicles*, however, Dylan chooses a generic perspective to position himself within the cultural field of the early 1960s and thus gives a detailed representation of his attraction to American folk music:

> The madly complicated modern world was something I took little interest in. It had no relevancy, no weight. I wasn't seduced by it. What was swinging, topical and up to date for me was stuff like the *Titanic* sinking, the Galveston flood, John Henry driving steel, John Hardy shooting a man on the West Virginia line. All this was current, played out and in the open. This was the news that I considered, followed and kept tabs on. (Dylan, 2004: 20)

What I find most interesting here is Dylan's emphasis on the timeless urgency of folk song; they figure as a way he 'explored the universe' (Dylan, 2004: 18). 'Gutenberg could have been some guy who stepped out of an old folk song, too. Practically speaking, the '50s culture was like a judge in his last days on the bench. It was about to go. Within ten years' time, it would struggle to rise and then come crashing to the floor. With folk songs embedded in my mind like a religion, it wouldn't matter. Folk songs transcended the immediate culture' (Dylan, 2004: 27).

From these quotes we can read a complexity of folk which is incompatible with the purist claim of the traditionalists and 'preachy folksters' who 'were sermonizing' (Shelton, 2011: 181) against Dylan's 'sellout'. Dylan's definition of folk might be read as deliberately aimed to put aside any foundation to him ever having been called to the responsibility of being the voice of his generation. His reflections are counterintuitive with regard to a more conventional notion according to which in the 1960s, folk songs, as a means of understanding the world, presented us with an alternative to the hermeticism of some French symbolists or the vanguard of the Beat generation. In this view, supposedly, folk songs were oriented to a framework of values that appeared to give an answer to the urgent questions of the present. However, this would be 'to underestimate the strangeness of the cultures that spoke through folk-lyric fragments' (Marcus, 1997: 116).[9]

Dylan's representation of folk in many ways heavily corresponds to Greil Marcus's take on the 'Old, Weird America'. In *Invisible Republic* (1997) Marcus describes how Harry Smith's six-album *Anthology of American Folk Music* (1952) was essential to both the folk revival in general and to the young Dylan in particular: the *Anthology*, as Marcus puts it, was 'Dylan's first true map of a republic that was still a hunch to him'. Smith's definition of American folk music, however, was rather intuitive. He 'ignored all field recordings, Library of Congress archives, anything validated only by scholarship or carrying the must of the museum' and he even deliberately 'constructed internal narratives and orchestrated continuities'. With the *Anthology*, Marcus concludes, Smith 'made his own country'. It is precisely the synthetic, genuine composition of the *Anthology* that seems to have satisfied Dylan's appetite; not the 'madly complicated modern world', not Vietnam, not Martin Luther King, but the *Titanic*, the Galveston flood, John Henry and John Hardy piqued Dylan's curiosity.

In the quote above, Dylan ties his own poetic ability to the generic possibilities of folk music. Indeed, Marcus demonstrates how Dylan, on different levels, drew from the poetics of folk. Handed down in 'verbal fragments that had no direct or logical relationship to each other', folk offered a 'floating pool of thousands of disconnected verses, couplets, oneliners, pieces of eight'. According to Marcus, folk songs 'dissolve a known history of wars and elections into a sort of national dream, a flux of desire and punishment, sin and luck, joke and horror – and as in a dream, the categories don't hold'. In such configuration, the worldliness of folk did not come as a restriction, but rather allowed Dylan to inscribe into folk, to write his own folk songs and to become himself one of these figures which are of timeless appeal. Dylan's productive reception of American folk music might be illustrated by the correspondence of the both fictional and factual sceneries of Dylan's songs with the cover art of the *Anthology* volumes – as represented by Marcus: 'It was as if they had something to do with each other: as if Pythagoras, Fludd, and the likes of Jilson Setters, Ramblin' Thomas, the Alabama Sacred Harp Singers, Charlie Poole and the North Carolina Ramblers, and Smith himself were calling on the same gods'. Just like Smith, inscribing into the tradition of American folk music, Dylan made his own country, too.

Dylan's genuine understanding of folk, however, is different from the rather exoteric perception of most of his audience; somewhere along the emergence of 'Dylan's genius of American tongue' and the recognition of Dylan as the foremost songwriter of his generation, the crowds became insensitive to the nuances, strangeness and some of the complexity of American folk music. Dylan, of course, was quick to realise the nature of the problem:

> There is – and I'm sure nobody realizes this, all the authorities who write about what it is and what it should be, when they say keep things simple, they should be easily understood – folk music is the only music where it isn't simple. It's never been simple. It's weird, man, full of legend, myth, Bible and ghosts. I've never written anything hard to understand, not in my head anyway, and nothing as far out as some of the old songs. They were out of sight. (Cott, 2006a: 50)

172

Because of the politically exploited misconception of folk during the early 1960s, it became more and more difficult for Dylan to get the ambiguity of his songs over to the crowds. When he realised that he could not control what the audience would do with them, he tried to put things in perspective and started to throw in some serious obstacles to the embarrassing notion of his redemptive powers. His new songs were of an unequivocally different kind; his repertoire merged into more obvious incoherencies and with the use of spoken intros he dissolved some of the misconstrued narratives of his songs into the real presence of his performance. Nonetheless, up until Newport and sometimes beyond, Dylan's audience persistently ignored his efforts to escape their expectations.

Bob Dylan's Halloween show at the Philharmonic Hall in New York City, on 31 October 1964, is a valuable document for today's rediscovery of Dylan's early versatility. As the highlight of a remarkable series of acoustic shows in late 1964 and early 1965, it caught Dylan in transition. Long before going electric, Dylan's repertoire and his appearance had already transcended most preconceived notions about himself. With 'Masters of War' Dylan never aimed for a leading role in the anti-war movement and with 'Girl from the North Country' he never aimed for a reputation as the foremost writer of non-kitschy love songs; he was just capable of writing these songs (both from *The Freewheelin' Bob Dylan*, 1963). The seriousness of the Halloween show is that it gives evidence of the fact that Dylan, in different ways, tried to prevent himself being dissolved into the political turmoil of Vietnam or being identified with a brand of criticism which was about to be fully absorbed by the culture industry. The significance of Dylan's early work rests in its ambiguity, which might help to preserve a sense of the complexity, polyphony and worldwide appeal of American culture during both an unnecessary neocolonial war and the truly liberating social upheavals of the 1960s.

Notes

1 Such reads Sony's advertising to the release of Murray Lerner's video footage of Dylan's performance at Newport. See the back cover of the DVD package for M. Lerner's 2007 film *The Other Side of the Mirror: Bob Dylan – Live at the Newport Folk Festival 1963–1965* (Sony BMG Music Entertainment).

2 Allen Ginsberg coined the phrase in his approval of Williams's *Performing Artist* series (see the back cover of Williams, 2004).

3 Cited from Dylan's letter (early 1964) to the National Emergency Civil Liberties Committee (NECLC); transcript at http://www.corliss-lamont.org/dylan.htm.

4 Dylan's acceptance speech is reprinted in Shelton (2011: 143).

5 In November 1964, Silber published 'An open letter to Bob Dylan', criticising Dylan's new songs and complaining about him turning into a 'different Bob Dylan from the one we knew' (see Silber, 1964).

6 The following quotes are transcribed from the recording; for the most part they are in line with Sean Wilentz's transcription in *Bob Dylan in America* (see Wilentz, 2010: 87–114).

7   Coincidently, when the BBC in 1972 censored Paul McCartney's 'Give Ireland Back to the Irish', the former Beatle released 'Mary Had a Little Lamb' as a sign of protest.
8   See for instance Dylan (2004: 7).
9   All unreferenced quotations from the following two paragraphs are taken from the fourth chapter of *Invisible Republic* (Marcus, 1997: 87–126, respectively at 88, 102, 104, 92, 116, 107, 93).

References

Cott, J. (ed.) (2006a) 'Interview with Nora Ephron and Susan Edmiston, *Positively Tie Dream*, August 1965', in *Dylan on Dylan: The Essential Interviews* (New York: Wenner Books). 47–55.

Cott, J. (ed.) (2006b) '"The crackin', shakin', breakin', sound": Nat Hentoff, the *New Yorker*, October 1964', in *Dylan on Dylan: The Essential Interviews* (New York: Wenner Books). 13–28.

Dylan, B. (2004) *Chronicles: Volume One* (New York: Simon and Schuster).

Fong-Torres, B. (1973) *The Rolling Stone Interviews: Volume Two* (New York: Warner Paperback Library).

Gray, M. (2008) *The Bob Dylan Encyclopedia* (corrected and updated paperback edition) (London: Continuum).

Lee, C. P. (1998) *Like the Night: Bob Dylan and the Road to the Manchester Free Trade Hall* (London: Helter Skelter).

Light, A. (2009) 'Bob Dylan as performer', in K. J. H. Dettmar (ed.), *The Cambridge Companion to Bob Dylan* (Cambridge: Cambridge University Press). 55–68.

Marcus, G. (1997) *Invisible Republic: Bob Dylan's Basement Tapes* (New York: Picador).

Pelusi, M. (2004) 'Shall I be released? Just how good is Bob Dylan's Bootleg Series?', *Philadelphia Citypaper* (25–31 March). Available at http://archives.citypaper.net/articles/2004-03-25/music.shtml (accessed 27 March 2012).

Shelton, R. (2011) *No Direction Home: The Life and Music of Bob Dylan* (revised and updated edition edited by E. Thompson and P. Humphries) (London: Omnibus Press).

Silber, I. (1964) 'An open letter to Bob Dylan', *Sing Out!*, 14 (November). 22–3.

Wilentz, S. (2010) *Bob Dylan in America* (New York: Anchor Books).

Williams, P. (2004) *Bob Dylan, Performing Artist: The Early Years, 1960–1973* (London: Omnibus).

14

Surplus and demand *or* too much to ask: (in)appropriating Dylan

Robert McColl

The opening to the song 'Workingman's Blues #2' on Dylan's *Modern Times* (2006) is both amusing and audacious:

> There's an evenin' haze settlin' over the town
> Starlight by the edge of the creek
> The buyin' power of the proletariat's gone down
> Money's gettin' shallow and weak
>
> The place I love best is a sweet memory
> It's a new path that we trod
> They say low wages are a reality
> If we want to compete abroad[1]

Firstly, it seems unusual, even inappropriate, for a song to field explanations of economic conditions – especially to repeat the prognoses of economists ('They say low wages are a reality') and in their own intractable jargon ('The buyin' power of the proletariat'). Secondly, there is the odd juxtaposition of economy with nature. Our instinct is to say that the sufficiency of the latter compensates for the insufficiency of the former – and no doubt there is something in this. But it is not the whole story. The contradiction we expect between nature and economy risks becoming a correlation. Note how the 'shallow' money recalls the creek; how the going down of buying power evokes the settling haze. The economy seems to be an extension of a natural phenomenon, here; a settling down in the affairs of men. This is a fanciful notion – knowingly so – part of the song's lyrical impressionism and melodic levity; but it would seem one-eyed to call the song sentimental. Like many of Dylan's late songs, it smartly contrasts sentimental and satirical perspectives.

Nor is nature the only compensation – and comparison – available. Language, too, displays a curious plenitude in its treatment of dearth. The singer can take as long as he likes to sing 'The buyin' power of the proletariat's gone down', can indulge in the elaborations of reported speech ('They say…'), can allow a careless slip from present to past tense ('It's a new path that we trod'), which itself occasions the nonchalant half-rhyme of *trod/ abroad*. None of these conforms to what we would call poetic economy. Yet, as with nature, the poetics here are at least as like the economy as they are different. While money is getting 'shallow and weak', the use of two words, when one will do, supports the notion that the 'weakness' is occasioned not by shortage but by superfluity. There is too much money, just as there are too many words. Poetry and economy are both suffering from inflation. We do not have a dearth so much as a devaluation of our properties.

If the singer can be at ease with these conditions, he appears to have a longer-term view in mind, one perhaps the economist, or the proletariat, are not at leisure to entertain: what exposes us in the short term may toughen us in the long. Song, like other oral expressions, is both evanescent and tenacious. Indeed, the latter in some sense depends on the former. Evanescence (and invisibility) makes it harder to penetrate, or appropriate, than, say, page poetry. In Walter Ong's terms, while sight 'isolates' and 'dissects', sound 'incorporates' and 'unifies' (Ong, 2009: 71). Evanescence also makes necessary, even guarantees, song's repetition. Indeed, oral expression is peculiarly well suited to survive, even flourish, in hard times. Witness 'Motorpsycho Nightmare' (from the 1964 album *Another Side of Bob Dylan*), in which 'freedom' depends on the recklessness of 'speech'.

Perhaps it should not surprise us, then, that what may destabilise page poetry may work to song's advantage. Wasted words, for example, as vital sounds, are more likely to be useful to song than to page poetry. 'Oral expression', writes Ong, 'carries a load of epithets and other formulary baggage which high literacy rejects as cumbersome and tiresomely redundant because of its aggregative weight' (*ibid.*: 38). Whether in spendthrift albums (like *Bringing It All Back Home*, 1965, and *Desire*, 1976) or more Spartan productions (*John Wesley Harding*, 1967, *World Gone Wrong*, 1993), Dylan – always a singer first and writer second – privileges and exploits what is peculiar to song. In a line like 'Her mouth was watery and wet', in the song 'I Don't Believe You (She Acts Like We Never Have Met)', on *Another Side of Bob Dylan*, the tautology celebrates the sensuous generosity not only of *her* mouth but of mouths generally.

But if the emphasis on the vocal and musical moment *is*, first and foremost, a privilege, it is also, as in 'Motorpsycho Nightmare', a lucky escape. Where song becomes too stable ('in the swamp' in the terms of 'Motorpsycho Nightmare'), it loses the power of renovation and subjects itself to ownership. For Ong, this process takes place in the transition from oral expression to print. Citing Elizabeth Eisenstein's (1979) point, that print was a significant agent in the 'development of modern capitalism', Ong argues that capitalism generally, like print locally, seeks 'control of position' (Ong, 2009: 119); hence, the buying (and selling) power of a song is what undermines it *as* song. And if we fix, or anthropomorphise, capitalism (controlling *its* position, as it were), then this is hard to dispute. But if we characterise capital not as fixed but as fluid, if we think of it not as stabilising property but as destabilising it, we find it easier to reconcile to orality. As in 'Workingman's Blues #2', song may require something of the economy's fragile phenomenality.

Of course, the possibility remains that this economic discourse is 'only' a metaphor, or a metaphor with clearly separable vehicle and tenor. But Dylan customarily refuses such clear distinctions. We could start with the episode in 'I Shall Be Free' (from *The Freewheelin' Bob Dylan*, 1963), when President Kennedy asks his friend Bob for advice on economic growth and is supplied with a list of sex symbols. From the beginning, Dylan offers us a broad, if not buxom, interpretation of what constitutes economic conditions. Following his line, then, I want to suggest that, from the mid-1990s onwards, what we might call 'late Dylan' displays a particular interest in the problem of linguistic and pictorial inflation. I argue that, via a verbal and visual flooding of the market, Dylan confounds appropriation of himself or his songs. In this sense, his notorious inscrutability is due less to self-protection than to an almost strategic overfreighting of the self. It is this confounding of appropriation which, peculiarly, even perversely, enables his songs' repeatability.

Hence, what is true of his late songs is equally true of his late live performances of early songs – not always to everyone's taste. Christopher Ricks famously argues that 'The Lonesome Death of Hattie Carroll' (from Dylan's 1964 album *The Times They Are A-Changin'*) should not be 're-performed', appearing to centre his argument upon the fact that it is a song peculiarly dependent upon a historical event: 'His art, in such a dedication to historical facts that are not of his making, needs to set limits (not *too* expanded) to its own rights in honouring hers'.[2] As the event cannot be repeated, so the song should not be. To repeat it, implies Ricks, is to dilute and devalue both event and song. 'The historical songs', he says, 'can't be re-created in the same way as the more personal ... songs of consciousness'. Certainly, 'The Lonesome Death of Hattie Carroll' establishes a period of mourning. 'Bury the rag deep in your face/For now's the time for your tears' is a call for silence, beyond the overly literary 'philosophising' and 'criticising'. We have that Nietzschean sense that awful historical events require digestion, must be allowed to speak for themselves before the work of interpretation, or appropriation, begins.[3]

To say that the song prohibits repeatability is too much, however. The problem lies, in part, in Ricks's use of 're' in 're-perform'. After all, we cannot, as Ricks asks us to do, conceive of performing, or even re-performing, as similar to a page poet's revision of texts, particularly after Ricks himself has drawn our attention to Larkin's nice distinctions between reading and hearing a poem (Ricks, 2002: 17, 13–14).[4] Furthermore, the song is not a mere catalogue of historical events. Ricks notes the jarring *you/who* rhyme at the beginning of the chorus, comparing it with a 'tank turning in threat'. Certainly, it represents a rotation of kinds. It is an apparently superfluous, but actually repositioning, rhyme, initiating the chorus's dramatic shift in perspective. That chorus removes us from the relentless historical dependency Ricks alludes to and addresses the question of appropriation. The chorus represents public assimilation of, and implication in, the event. That this is a painful removal goes without saying, but it can hardly be said to represent a dilation of focus, or divestment of the song's responsibilities. If the verses, in their 'newspaper item' monotony (*ibid.*: 221), argue for the intransigence of fact, the chorus argues for the necessity of recognition. There *is* no easy assimilation, it asserts.

It is, then, to use Ricks's (2002: 16) somewhat evasive (but fittingly legal) word, 'legitimate' to ask whether this question of appropriating historical events may not be extended to the song's 're-performance'. And yet, since the most vexing question that the song raises is directed not at Hattie's killer, William Zanzinger, nor the justice system, but to the audience, it becomes certainly an apposite, with luck a discomfiting, question each time the song is performed. If this, implicitly, requires that the singer, too, be not an appropriator, this makes it as hard a song to sing as to hear – not an intrinsically fixed product, an artefactual terminus, inimical to vocalisation. While certainly giving place to the historical event, the song could not be said to derive all its energies from it; nor does knowledge of the event make the song unnecessary.[5] Indeed, Dylan's recent performances of the song tally with what appears to be a wider argument in his late work, that to resist appropriation by refusing access is, finally, as self-defeating as it is precious. If Ricks's vaunted assertion, that 'The Lonesome Death of Hattie Carroll' is 'perfect' were itself appropriate, the song, at least in Dylan's terms, would be a failure: less a song than a 'record', in both senses of the word.

The song's 'performance', then – not 're-performance' – puts to the test both its own tenacity and our power to appropriate, and something of the same strategy applies to Dylan's late songs. It is possible to detect a shift of emphasis at some point in the mid-1990s from an economical Dylan, rarely interviewed, austere in his musical and lyrical habits, having a defined, defiant sense of self, to a proliferate, profligate Dylan, promiscuous with possession (or – as in 'Bye and Bye' from the 2001 album *"Love and Theft"* – repossession), more content, seemingly, with the public eye, musically various, lyrically extravagant, vocally playful, whose voice remains forceful, but whose personae are so various, or – since the term 'personae' may itself be too distinctive – whose personality is so opaque, that he becomes invisible.

If the difference between *World Gone Wrong* (1993) and *Time Out of Mind* (1997) was marked, however, *"Love and Theft"* represented a shift again, combining the narrative minimalism, and nursery-rhyme idioms, of *Under the Red Sky* (1990) with a linguistic hyperbole. While in 'Highlands' (on *Time Out of Mind*) Dylan sings 'I don't want nothing from anyone, ain't that much to take', *"Love and Theft"*, which seems to me to be Dylan's most radical (perhaps *eradicate* would be a better term) statement so far about appropriation (or theft), is full of images of surplus; there is *too* much to take, and take in. The singer has, he tells us, a 'house on a hill, I got hogs all out in the mud' ('Summer Days', on *"Love and Theft"*), in which the superfluous 'all' articulates the sloppiness of both hogs and mud. He has (in the same song) 'eight carburetors, boys', he's 'using 'em all', and the apostrophe to the 'boys' – standard in sea-shanties and rebel ballads – is exploited for all its macho excess. It is a world where poor boys not only stay in palatial hotels, in which absence and presence, demand and supply, overlap ('Poor boy, in the hotel called the Palace of Gloom/Calls down to room service, says send up a room'), but travel sadly in first-class trains. (It is hard to imagine this fact being a matter of pathos in the precursory 'Po' Boy', or 'Poor Boy', songs, or those which use the phrase as a floater.) It is also a world which, unexpectedly, tolerates the following advice: 'She says, "You can't repeat the past." I say, "You can't? What do you mean, you can't? Of course you can."' ('Summer Days') and 'Plenty of places to hide things here if you wanna hide 'em bad enough' ('Sugar Baby', on the same album). If, for Dylan, the past and the hiding place are usually synonymous and illusory, swiftly exposed to the unstable present, here both are too easily available – and it should be no surprise that *"Love and Theft"*, an album which advertedly toys with the autobiographical, was the last album to come out before Dylan's memoir, *Chronicles* (Dylan, 2004a). Avoiding the south side of New York, where Dylan flourished in the early 1960s, the singer comments: 'These memories I got, they can strangle a man' ('Honest with Me'). In 'Lonesome Day Blues', the singer wishes his mother were still alive and, of course, Beattie Rutman, previously Zimmerman, died in January 2000, a year before the album was released. On the other hand, the Po' Boy's father 'was a traveling salesman' – he 'never met him' – which serves to conflate the autobiographical with the fictitious. As in 'Highway 61 Revisited' and 'Queen Jane Approximately' (both on the 1965 album *Highway 61 Revisited*), the family figures come at us rather too thick and fast: 'When my mother died, my uncle took me in – he ran a funeral parlor/He did a lot of nice things for me and I won't forget him' ('Po' Boy' on *"Love and Theft"*). In the first line, the 'funeral parlor' afterthought is anecdotal rather than essential. In the second line, the phrase 'a lot of … things' is an oddly detached expression for attaching unforgotten deeds. It is typical of the album. Above all, in *"Love and Theft"*, there is too much stuff. Cherries fall off plates ('Po' Boy') just as 'things' fall off shelves ('Lonesome Day Blues'). If Fat Nancy's shelf is probably well stocked ('High Water'), the singer, too, has more than he knows what to do with. 'The man says, "Three dollars." "All right," I say, "Will you take four?"' he sings ('Po' Boy'), as if it were all the same to him. He catches a lot of bullheads, 'sometimes too many' ('Floater'), as if it were not so much a boast as a puzzle. '*Lot of things* can get in the way when you're tryin' to do what's right' ('Honest with Me', emphasis added), he tells us, proving it, too, with the periphrasis, of which there is, indeed, a lot here. Indeed, in the overspill of 'things are fallin' *off of* the shelf' ('Lonesome Day Blues') and '*For* whom does the bell toll *for*, love' ('Moonlight', emphasis added), we find his usual colloquial careless-ness, in which the distinction between verbal style and slip is nicely elided. Like Tweedledum and Tweedledee, words are located side by side with their doubles, as in: 'I gave it to *you, you* drank it' ('Po' Boy', emphasis added). If 'pain' pours down instead of rain ('Mississippi'), the pun seems overdone, like the pain itself, which is indiscriminate and futile.

We notice, too, the abundance of dialogue on the album. Spoken words abound and lines usually lengthen when they do. A politician sucks the blood out of the 'genius of generosity' ('Summer Days') and the allitera-tion is as overgenerous as the phrase is overlapping, this being a version of Abraham Lincoln's 'the blood of genius *and* generosity' (emphasis added). Note how Dylan exchanges the 'and' for an 'of', conflating the ideas, where Lincoln kept them separate. Quotations are rife and, at times, inseparable from original words. 'Poor boy – where you been?/I already tol' you – won't tell you again' ('Po' Boy') is amusing not only for its spiky, anti-climactic refusal to supply an answer or punchline, but also because there have been so many 'poor boy' songs, we *do* know where he's been. It is a world where quotation, proverb and advice 'ooze' out of the ears ('Honest with Me'), not so much because they are unheeded as because they are overheeded.

It seems inappropriate, not to say banal, to call this kind of heeding 'plagiarism', just as it is to call the current proliferation of Dylan's products, identities and voices 'selling out', and we assume that these fears are hurled by the same people, because they are related. In the one scenario, he is stealing something that, self-evidently, belongs to someone else and pretend-ing that it is his own. In the other scenario, he is taking a product that is his own and selling it, injudiciously, to an audience the accuser does not feel is worthy of the product and its carefully cultivated sense of the occult. 'Selling out' implies that, first, there is property, and, second, that this property should not be sold, or should be sold only under certain conditions, sold *in*, as it were, both of which make the concept of a 'floater' a problematic one.

What is a floater? A floater, to folklorists, is a word, phrase, line or verse which is adaptable, transferring freely from one song to the next.[6] The blues in particular, not precious when it comes to property, makes great use of them. Lines flow between songs as easily as lovers. This is perhaps best expressed in the linguistic and narrative disjunctions natural to the blues. Narrative depends on a certain sense of property. Aristotle might say that narrative events should derive 'probably' (or appropriately) one from another. There is a sense in which an effect is owned by a cause in this Aristotelian preference for coherent narratives. The blues, generally, has no such investment in causation. Blues is content with a verse like: 'Well, they're doing the double shuffle, throwin' sand on the floor/They're doing the double shuffle, they're throwin' sand on the floor/When I left my long-time darlin'/She was standing in the door' ('Lonesome Day Blues' on *"Love and Theft"*). 'There is no line that has to be there to get to another line', Dylan tells *Newsweek*, referring to *Time Out Of Mind*.[7] No sooner have we been sold the image – double shuffle, sand on the floor – than it is swept from under us. We are back with standards, floaters even: women standing in the door. The blues moves on, unsentimentally refusing narrative possession. 'Well, the road's washed out – weather not fit for man or beast/Yeah the road's washed out – weather not fit for man or beast/Funny, how the things you have the hardest time parting with/Are the things you need the least' ('Lonesome Day Blues'). Contrary to popular belief, we often find a breadline *necessity*, or probability, downplayed in the blues. Instead of cause and effect, we find not only contradiction but digression – the redundancy, or fluency, Ong finds more natural to oral cultures than 'sparse linearity' (Ong, 2009: 40–1). 'Funny', muses the singer of 'Lonesome Day Blues', as if the thought itself were superfluous – one of those 'needless' but obdurate 'things'. The song, here, and *"Love and Theft"* generally, is concerned with the propriety of the superfluous and, conversely, with the impropriety of the necessary, hence the recurrent images of flood. It should not surprise us that an album dominated by such images has a floating approach to property.[8]

'Floater', like that other song about flotation, 'High Water', has a paren-thetical appendage to its title. These are often pedantic looking – after all, titles are usually read, not heard[9] – drawing attention to the extraneously textual.[10] In the case of 'High Water', of course, we have '(For Charley Patton)', the kind of reference which those who accuse Dylan of plagiarism would be happier (or, one suspects, disappointed) if he included more often. Except that it is not quite citation – it is homage: referencing is a matter of legitimacy; it is *necessary*, whereas homage is impressively not so. For these are not subtitles exactly; they do not so much belong to as exist alongside. In the case of 'Floater', '(Too Much To Ask)' points us to the governing principle of the song: surplus. '(Too Much To Ask)' is itself too much because we have a title already, yet, at the same time, in its carelessness and dissonance, it suggests that one should not ask too much of the song, as its repetition at the end confirms. 'Floater' comprises floaters, with only floating convictions.

This spirit pervades the song: 'Down over the window/Comes the dazzling sunlit rays' Dylan sings, as if both of the first two words were necessary; as if, indeed, 'over' were not a word over, as if the sun's rays could themselves be 'sunlit'. Of course, this could be a slip of the tongue in performance – although, if so, it is compounded by the *Lyrics* book (Dylan, 2004b) and official website (http://www.bobdylan.com) – but this would only add to our sense of surplus here. It is the excess of light that Dylan is evoking, both slanting

181

and overrunning. Since the song is to make copious references to copious waters – squalls, cold rain, rebel rivers, tears – as well as to fishing and duck trapping, we may well imagine the interplay, or conflation, of light and water as central to the song's effect. As are 'Sugar Baby' and 'Moonlight', in particular, the song is interested in the various sources and outlets of light, and the way in which light may confound, rather than merely mark, time. 'Through the back alleys – through the blinds'. In the spillage, of the *b* and *l*, from back alleys to blinds, we have the sense of a singer luxuriating in sound. The conflation of back alleys and blinds lends a sense of similitude to these separate objects, one effected, rather than disassembled, by light. Light, in these songs, makes surfaces complementary, even indistinguishable, as limits are blended and overleapt.

Listening on, we find the same sense of surplus in the languid, unnecessary rhyme of 'buzzin'' and 'cousin':[11] 'Honey bees are buzzin'/Leaves begin to stir/I'm in love with my second cousin/I tell myself I could be happy forever with her'. I say 'unnecessary' for several reasons. If, for the sake of argument, we divide the song up into quatrains (as the *Lyrics* book and website do), it is one of only three times in the song when lines 1 and 3 of the quatrain rhyme, and the other two occasions are half-rhymes only (footsteps/bullheads and get/weight). Like the first of these, it is also a feminine rhyme, lacking urgency, a notion reinforced by the elongating removal to 'second' cousin, which puts us further than we need be merely to accomplish the rhyme, although sufficiently far not to confuse excess with incest. Rather than rhyme serving the needs of narrative, we have the sense that the song is luxuriating in rhyme here; so long as it gets there in the end, it doesn't matter how long it takes to do so. This is implied to be what happens in love. Direction becomes dalliance.

Finally we hear 'I tell myself I could be happy forever with her'. We can separate this line into three parts, as follows:

I tell myself   I could be   happy forever with her

The verse could have made do with the last part only ('I'm in love with my second cousin/Happy forever with her'), in which case it would have suggested achievement. It could likewise have made do with the second two parts ('I'm in love with my second cousin/I could be happy forever with her') which would suggest possibility: *possible* achievement and *possible* self-deception. But, of course, what we have is 'I tell myself' and this wanton preamble to both possibility and achievement becomes *most* telling. Of course, there is still the suggestion of wilful self-deception ('I tell myself, even though it isn't true') but, given the comically lugubrious attitude of the singer ('It doesn't matter in the end'; 'We'll just have to see how it goes'; 'Things come alive or they fall flat' and so on), and given the transience that suffuses both song and album, we might have assumed that anyway. Of more importance is the telling. Speech is superfluous, drawing attention to the distance between the end and the means; but the superfluous, paradoxically, becomes the essence of the thing. Telling bears no responsibility to the told, here. It is able to say one thing one moment and another thing the next, and, of course, to spend as long as it likes doing so. 'I tell myself I could be happy forever with her' comes in a long, jazz tradition of long, extravagant lines, in this case five syllables longer than the next longest in the verse. If the line gives us a sense of the cloying repletion of love, its predominant sense is of the largess of speech.

One could go on forever in this vein, and the song seems to think so, abounding as it does with alliterative conflations ('All the rest of them rebel rivers'), overlong lines ('"You got a poor complexion/It doesn't give your appearance a very youthful touch!"'; 'To go along/With all the ring-dancin' Christmas carols on all of the Christmas eves'), reckless enjambements ('The old men 'round here, sometimes they get/On bad terms with the younger men'), lush evocations ('I left all my dreams and hopes/Buried under tobacco leaves'), sprawling boasts ('If you ever try to interfere with me or cross my path again/You do so at the peril of your own life'), staunch hendiadys and glorious tautologies ('dazzling sunlit rays'; 'interfere with me or cross my path'; 'dreams and hopes'; 'heartaches and strife'), needless interpolations, either jolting rhythmically ('The old men 'round here, *sometimes* they get/ On') or inessential to meaning ('But I ain't *ever* hearing any'; 'I had 'em once though, *I suppose*'; emphasis added in each case), while verses taper off in lines which gesture to proverbial wisdom, but so halfheartedly as to become directionless ('Sometimes it's just plain stupid/To get into any kind of wind'; 'It doesn't matter in the end'; 'We'll just have to see how it goes'; 'Things come alive or they fall flat'). The fiddle, when it comes, only adds to this impression, dreamily becalming the song's rhythms. This is a world in which it is hard to achieve anything by exertion ('It has the opposite effect'), yet where, as in an early version of the Dylan song 'Jokerman' (released on the 1983 *Infidels* album), good things 'fall in your lap'. Even when the singer grudgingly withholds, his own tongue contradicts him: 'Sometimes somebody wants you to give something up/And tears or not, it's too much to ask'. There is no sense of tension, of withholding, about the line, even as it asserts privacy. It seems to have as much time as it desires ('Sometimes somebody … something'), can introduce and withdraw qualifications ('tears or not'), claim that to give something up is 'too much' and yet express it in such a way that is too much to give.

We find similar effects throughout *"Love and Theft"*. But, 'Floater' aside, 'Moonlight' is perhaps the best example of a song offering us more than we bargained for. 'The seasons they are turnin'', we are told, and the plural is appropriate, for it is hard to say which season we are in. Spring? ('[M]asquerades of birds and bees'; 'petals, pink and white'; 'purple blossoms'.) Summer? ('Orchids, Poppies, Black-eyed Susan'; 'earth and sky that melts with flesh

183

and bone'; 'the air is thick and heavy'; 'yellow fields'.) Autumn? ('[T]he leaves fall from the limbs'; 'petals … the wind has blown'.) Or winter? ('[Y]earnin'/To hear again the songbird's sweet melodious tone'.) To call this a description of the seasonal cycle would be a little coercive. The song gives us no such sense of order and, on those terms, would constitute a failure. But the song is a quiet success and one of the things it succeeds in is not seasonal cycle but conflation. Via its dense assemblages, the song gives us a sense of the instability and fluency of seasons and, more, the acute experience of that fluency (attesting, as it does, that natural, emotional and linguistic processes are symbiotic). Hence: 'The trailing moss and mystic glow/Purple blossoms soft as snow/My tears keep flowing to the sea'. We note, or hear, how 'moss' becomes '*bloss*om', how 'glow' and 'snow' become 'flowing'. We hear the justice of the latter, as, via its gerund, it transitions into 'sea'. We wonder how clearly we are to distinguish the glow from either moss or blossoms; we marvel at how, through that 'soft', alliterative simile (wherein not only 'soft' and 'snow' are conjoined, but the *os* of 'blossom' slips easily into the *so* of 'soft'), 'blossom' becomes 'snow' and how, via the release from 'snow' to 'flowing', the snow melts to tears, itself a continuation of other meltings in the song ('earth and sky', 'flesh and bone'). The singer's bodily responses become inseparable from the seasonal expressions. Perhaps I should say bodily *expressions* become inseparable from seasonal ones, and emotions from motions, because the sense of causation is subsumed here. Instead of progressing linearly from season to season, action to reaction, in Ong's terms, the song 'incorporates' these processes.

Of course, emotion, if not a trite word, can be used tritely; but the song justifies the term in its insistence on bodily movement, the sense that emotion is an agitation or moving out: 'My pulse is runnin' through my palm – the sharp hills are rising from/The yellow fields with twisted oaks that groan'. The yellow fields extend, via enjambment, the premise of the palm. Once again, there is a lengthening of body into landscape, suggesting mortality. Where is the centre of the verse? The repeated adjective–noun formula ('sharp hills', 'yellow fields', 'twisted oaks') necessitates constant re-positioning. Instead of composition, we have sequence, or 'running through'. Yet the great stress this places upon the words 'with' and 'that', to bear the weight of connection, conversely extends the manual motif. Emotional, then, but there is nothing trite about this. There are sinews to nature, here.

How long can the singer sustain this climax, we wonder? The song lives on the build and release of tension. The two long lines, rhythmic, internally rhyming, move fluently towards the crucial, and overcooked, rhyme words ('tone', 'bone', 'flown', 'stone' and so on) and, just when we think that this cannot last much longer, the 'moonlight' chorus, or 'floater', resolves the problem. The less it has to do with the rest of the song, the better. The song's emotional costs are defrayed by the floater, which belongs to nothing, that which has no party or colour, or particolour, only light.

To return to Larkin's 'false analogy' between the eye and ear, it is a false analogy that 'Floater' and 'Moonlight' do not so much suffer from as exploit. Light, ordinarily 'dissecting', becomes organic and elastic, unreliable to sight. Multiplying to excess, images become unfixed and hard to own. Yet it is not so much that vision cannot cope with the *copia* of the landscape as that orality 'incorporates' its spatial (and temporal) disparities. Dylan's songs organise themselves primarily through sound, not sight.

If Dylan is always viscerally present in the words he sings, then the linguistic and pictorial surpluses we find in *"Love and Theft"* comprise not just an analogy for, but a recompositioning of, his public image, too. Responding to the (nonsensical) notion that *Time Out of Mind*, *"Love and Theft"* and *Modern Times* represent a trilogy, Dylan had this to say: 'Time Out of Mind was me getting back in and fighting my way out of the corner. But by the time I made *"Love and Theft"*, I was out of the corner. On *this* record, I ain't nowhere, you can't find me anywhere, because I'm way gone from the corner' (Lethem, 2006). It is an extraordinary claim for one who, whether '*In Show & Concert!*' as the posters tautologically trumpet, or via a variety of media, has never been more ubiquitous, more consumable, more available on demand. Like the word which stretches over the entire map, in Edgar Allan Poe's 1844 short story 'The Purloined Letter', Dylan is *too* visible. Surfeiting with floaters and confessions, products and performances, the appropriator finds he can do nothing with them. He is forced back to the vivid ephemera of song. When Ricks argues, or suggests, that Dylan should not re-perform 'The Lonesome Death of Hattie Carroll' (for the appropriation he works upon both song and event), he hoists himself by his own petard, seeking, too soon, to anticipate and appropriate the event of the song, as if he underestimates its accusatory power. Fortunately, as with all of Dylan's work, it sees through such infringements because, unlike Ricks, it does not set parameters about itself, recognises no private, or elite, sphere from which it can sell itself 'out'. Ricks's suggestion may be 'legitimate' but, finally, it is inappropriate rather than the reverse.

Notes

1 In quoting Dylan's songs in this chapter, I have adopted a compound approach, sometimes referring to http://www.bobdylan.com, sometimes to my ear, but, at all times, attempting to reproduce the words, and sometimes the units of phrasing, that one hears in the song at hand, and keeping punctuation to a minimum. Exactitude, of course, is impossible in quoting Dylan, which is partly what this chapter is about.

2 For the following discussion of 'Hattie Carroll', see Ricks (2002: 15–18, 221–33). The phrase quoted here has some of Ricks's characteristic, and unfortunate, ambiguity. I assume the primary sense is 'set limits ... to its own rights, in order to honour her [i.e. Hattie Carroll's] rights', although there is a latter sense of 'its right to honour her rights'. In the first, the song is capable of honouring Hattie Carroll; in the second, this is something song itself can only partially, compromisingly, achieve. Ricks, ever alert

to ambiguity, should be more ingenuous with his readers. It is possible – and could be plausible – that he is saying both of these things are true, but they mean very different things.

3 See, for example, Nietzsche's 'On the uses and disadvantages of history for life' (1874), in Breazeale (2003: 83–5).

4 See also Larkin (1982).

5 Presumably, this is one reason why, from the outset, Dylan distances himself from topical or protest songs which subordinate song itself to a historical event (past or to come). As A. L. Lloyd says, 'in most cases the more important the event the worse was the ballad' (Lloyd, 2008: 271).

6 See, for example, Lloyd (2008: 190–4). An example of a floater would be 'I wish, I wish, I wish in vain' (cf. 'Bob Dylan's Dream', from *The Freewheelin' Bob Dylan*). The whole of the traditional song 'The Water Is Wide', as Dylan sings it (cf. for example, *The Bootleg Series, Vol. 5: Bob Dylan Live 1975*), is said to be composed of floaters. The traditional ballad 'The Butcher Boy (Railroad Boy)' is replete with them. In blues lyrics, we could point to 'The woman I love, stoled from my best friend', variations of which appear in Skip James ('Devil Got My Woman') and Robert Johnson ('Come on in My Kitchen'), among others.

7 *Newsweek*, 6 October 1997. I have taken the quotation from Ricks (2002: 233).

8 Of course, a floater is also a person with no fixed political allegiance, employment or location. Anglers will also know that floater fishing means using floating bait, useful for carp, chub and orfe, though I don't know whether it works on bullheads, which, in America, usually signifies a kind of catfish – perhaps the kind caught in Woody Guthrie's 'Talkin' Fishing Blues', sung by Dylan on the *The Minneapolis Party Tape* (2012). Interestingly, bullheads are rarely targeted, Wikipedia informs me (http://en.wikipedia. org/wiki/Ameiurus). They tend to be caught *accidentally*, while trying to catch other fish, except in Minnesota, where commercial fishing harvests about one million pounds a year. This, according to the Minnesota Department of Natural Resources (2012), is because bullheads are plentiful in the prairie regions, where other species are scarce. Plenty, in Minnesota at least, seems inseparable from scarcity.

9 Unless the singer chooses to draw attention to it, as in: 'This is called "It's Alright Ma, It's Life and Life Only"'. Eheh. Yes, it's a very funny song, ha ha ha' (at the Philharmonic Hall, 1964). Dylan is, typically, as little precious, or possessive, about his titles as he is about his lyrics.

10 Examples would be 'I Don't Believe You (She Acts Like We Never Have Met)'; 'It's Alright Ma (I'm Only Bleeding)'; 'One of Us Must Know (Sooner or Later)'; 'Senor (Tales of Yankee Power)'; 'Where Are You Tonight (Journey Through Dark Heat)'; and 'Tight Connection to My Heart (Has Anyone Seen My Love)'.

11 This, itself, may well be a languid recall of Tom Waits's buzzin'/cousin rhyme in the song '(Looking for) the Heart of Saturday Night' (on Waits's 1974 album *The Heart of Saturday Night*), which Dylan includes on the play list of the 'Days of the Week' episode of his broadcast *Theme Time Radio Hour*.

References

Breazeale, D. (ed.) (2003) *Nietzsche. Untimely Meditations* (trans. R. J. Hollingdale) (Cambridge: Cambridge University Press).

Dylan, B. (2004a) *Chronicles: Volume One* (New York: Simon and Schuster).

Dylan, B. (2004b) *Lyrics, 1962–2001* (New York: Simon and Schuster).

Eisenstein, E. L. (1979) *Press as an Agent of Change: Communications and Cultural Transformations in Early-Modern Europe* (2 vols) (New York: Cambridge University Press).

Larkin, P. (1982) Interview, 'Philip Larkin: the art of poetry, no. 30', *Paris Review*, 84 (summer

1982). Available at http://www.theparisreview.org/interviews/3153/the-art-of-poetry-no-30-philip-larkin (accessed 22 March 2014).

Lethem, J. (2006) 'The genius of Bob Dylan', *Rolling Stone*, 1008 (September). 74–80.

Lloyd, A. L. (2008) *Folk Song in England* (London: Faber).

Minnesota Department of Natural Resources (2012) 'Catfish management'. Available at http://www.dnr.state.mn.us/fish/catfish/management.html (accessed 30 March 2012).

Ong, W. J. (2009) *Orality and Literacy* (London: Routledge).

Ricks, C. (2002) *Dylan's Visions of Sin* (London: Penguin).

15

Plagiarism, Bob, Jean-Luc and me

Stephen Scobie

Why must I always be the thief?
(Bob Dylan, 'Tears of Rage', 1968)

Bob Dylan's reach is too wide, too deep and too long for any book about him to cover it all. He's a senior citizen. His career spans forty-five years of American history, and that history has intersected with his prolific song-writing, recording, touring, acting, filmmaking, TV appearances and interviews. He has published a novel and a book of drawings, composed for film soundtracks and written a best-selling first volume of memoirs. He has found a place in the world of literature and academic study as well as in popular music. He is important to the history of the times, having given voice to a generation at a time of huge social change and political struggle; his songs are enmeshed in the story of the US civil rights movement as well as the Folk Revival movement. His busy life has embraced everything from bohemian excess to being Born Again.

But here let me pause. Does this opening paragraph strike you as an adequate, even eloquent, introduction to Bob Dylan? I certainly hope it does. Or are you bothered by a couple of slight discrepancies: that what I am introducing here is not a book but a chapter; that the forty-five years are now over fifty; that the one book of drawings has now become a few? Because, in fact, the whole paragraph does come from a book, published in 2006: Michael Gray's *Bob Dylan Encyclopaedia* (xv). I did not write a word of it.

But I have presented it here, as the first paragraph of this chapter, without quotation marks or any other sign of attribution. If I were to leave it like that, without the qualification of the second paragraph, it would be a clear and flagrant case of plagiarism. Within an institutional academic context, it would be punishable by anything from failure to expulsion; if Michael was of a litigious nature, he could sue me for breach of copyright.

Cases of plagiarism, however, are not always so clear cut; nor is the rigour of academic discipline necessarily the best context within which to consider artistic texts. As many of Bob Dylan's defenders against accusations of plagiarism have put it, 'He's writing a song, not a term paper!' Well, maybe. Some of Dylan's songs are so replete with quotation that they seem a lot like term papers, or at least like the footnotes to one; and the category of 'plagiarism' begins to drift, through a series of very hazy distinctions, into associated terms such as tribute, parody, allusion, citation, appropriation and intertextuality.

Plagiarism, however, is the most loaded term, the most pejorative accusation. In the last few years, it has been bandied about in discussions of Dylan ranging from internet chat groups to the august pages of the *New York Times*. He has been denounced as a cheat and a charlatan. Joni Mitchell declared in an interview, 'Bob is not authentic at all. He's a plagiarist, and his name and voice are fake. Everything about Bob is a deception.'[1]

A good starting point for considering these questions may be the following stanza from 'Nettie Moore', the finest song on Dylan's 2006 album *Modern Times*: 'The world of research has gone berserk/Too much paperwork/Albert's in the graveyard, Frankie's raising hell/I'm beginning to believe what the scriptures tell'. The first two lines provide a slightly aggrieved commentary on the current state of Bob Dylan scholarship – and, indeed, on scholarship generally. Every source, every hint of an allusion, every line even vaguely susceptible to a charge of plagiarism has been tracked down, documented and publicised. The lines might well be understood as an indication that Mr Dylan feels himself to be under siege, or under a microscope. But, in a surely deliberate gesture of irony, the next two lines positively sit up and beg to be subjected to 'research' and 'paperwork'. 'Frankie and Albert' is a traditional murder ballad, recorded by Dylan on *Good As I Been to You* (1992); 'I'm beginning to believe what the scriptures tell' is an almost direct quotation from Blind Lemon Jefferson's 'See That My Grave Is Kept Clean', recorded by Dylan in 1961 for his (eponymous) debut album released in 1962. And the lines occur within a song, 'Nettie Moore', which takes both its title and its chorus from a nineteenth-century sentimental song about slavery.

So when Dylan quotes Jefferson's line, without any attribution or acknowledgement, but within the context of a 'world of research' that has 'gone berserk', is he guilty of plagiarism? Is he indulging in a sophisticated postmodernist game of allusion and intertextuality? Or is he merely taking part in the time-honoured and universally accepted folk music tradition of using older singers' material and adapting it for his own purposes?

Traditional folk songs were 'traditional' precisely because they had no single author. Songs were passed from mouth to mouth, from ear to ear, by a cumulative body of singers, making up a collective authorship for which the categories of 'plagiarism' and 'copyright' are simply irrelevant. Many, even most, of Dylan's early compositions use lines or melodies from previous songs, and the borrowings are often richly relevant and suggestive. 'Bob Dylan's Dream' (on *The Freewheelin' Bob Dylan*, 1963) uses both the tune and some of the words of the British ballad 'Lord Franklin'. His tribute to Woody Guthrie, 'Song to Woody', on his debut album uses a tune Guthrie had previously used for one of his own songs: this is clearly *not* plagiarism, but rather a respectful and traditional tribute. Working within the folk tradition of assimilation and adaptation, the young Dylan produced a stunning body of work, which richly deserves to be called 'original'.

The collection of forty-seven songs which comprise Dylan's 2010 *The Bootleg Series: Volume 9*, however, appears under the title *The Witmark Demos* – a title which strongly asserts Dylan's claim to individual authorship. Witmark was a music publishing company and these demonstration recordings were made precisely to enable Dylan, who could neither read nor write sheet music, to register his copyright. If the invocation of the folk tradition renders the notion of copyright irrelevant, then *The Witmark Demos* rather make it relevant again. Indeed, in two cases, the copyright claims made by the demos were legally challenged. Both cases were settled out of court and the two songs are stated on their most recent releases to be 'written by Bob Dylan'.[2] And Dylan has continued, throughout his career, to enter copyright claims on material which is sometimes only partially his.

The Dylan line most often evoked in defence of this cavalier attitude is 'To live outside the law, you must be honest'. But, ironically, this line itself is of dubious provenance. The teenage Bobby Zimmerman was an avid movie fan, aided by the fact that the cinema in his hometown of Hibbing, the Lybba, was owned by his family, so he got in free. It therefore seems altogether probable that he had seen a 1958 film by Don Siegel, *The Lineup*, in which one of the characters, a rather sinister criminal, says: 'When you live outside the law you have to eliminate dishonesty'. Other movie quotes in Dylan songs are more precise. The 1985 album *Empire Burlesque* is especially full of lines lifted from film dialogue. For example, the song 'Never Gonna Be the Same Again' contains the line 'I don't mind leaving/I'd just like it to be my idea', word for word as it is spoken by Alan Ladd in the 1953 film *Shane*. In other words, the singer's wish to act according to his own idea is expressed in words which are not his own idea. In the 1986 song 'Brownsville Girl', deeply indebted to a 1950 Gregory Peck movie, *The Gunfighter*, Dylan sings: 'If there's an original thought out there, I could use it right now'. In other words, he would like to 'use' someone else's 'original' thought, thus rendering it no longer original, yet still claiming it as copyright 1986 via his music publisher, Special Rider Music.[3]

The use of quotations from movie dialogue already takes us one step beyond a purist definition of 'the folk tradition', in which songs borrow primarily from other songs. And, indeed, the range of source material for Dylan's borrowings is both eclectic and incredibly wide.[4] He has quoted extensively from Jack London and selectively from Robert Louis Stevenson;

he has squeezed a whole sentence of F. Scott Fitzgerald into one implausibly long line; he has even adapted the crepuscular prose of Marcel Proust. Dylan's album *Time Out of Mind* (1997) shares phrase after phrase with the contemporary American writer Henry Rollins. The 2001 album *"Love and Theft"* borrows its title from John Lott's academic study of minstrelsy and is shot through with unacknowledged quotations from *Confessions of a Yakuza*, a contemporary Japanese book by Junichi Saga. *Modern Times* is presided over by the nineteenth-century American Confederate poet Henry Timrod. The title of his 2009 album, *Together Through Life*, comes from a letter by James Joyce. In his 2012 album, *Tempest*, Dylan makes brilliant use of quotations from the American poet John Greenleaf Whittier. He also seems to have been an assiduous reader of *Time* magazine and the letters of Thomas Wolfe. These are not the naïve adaptations of an anonymous folk tradition: these are the deliberate and sophisticated appropriations by a well read and highly self-conscious mind.

The point is still clearer in the case of the Roman poet Ovid, whose work is even more evident on *Modern Times* than that of Timrod. Classical scholars have identified as many as twenty-eight references to Ovid on this one album.[5] Especially interesting is the case of the song 'Ain't Talkin''. An early version of the song, later released on *Tell Tale Signs* (2006), contains no Ovid quotations at all, whereas the later version, released on *Modern Times*, contains about a dozen.[6] This suggests that the addition of these quotations was completely conscious and deliberate.

Not only does Dylan borrow from sources other than traditional songs: he does so in texts other than his own songs – for example, in his autobiographical *Chronicles*. The question of how a reader reacts to autobiography is a complex one. On the one hand, the reader grants to the autobiographer the privilege and authority of insider information: not just an eyewitness but an I-witness. On the other hand, the reader implicitly allows for authorial bias and for a good deal of retrospective self-justification. Only the most naïve reader would take *Chronicles* as a reliable source of factual information. But the reader's reaction to a text which proclaims itself as non-fiction – autobiography, memoir or chronicle – is still, surely, subtly different from the reaction to a poem or song. Take, for example, the following passage from *Chronicles*: 'One night when everyone was asleep and I was sitting at the kitchen table, nothing on the hillside but a shiny bed of lights … I wrote about twenty verses for a song called "Political World" and this was about the first of twenty songs I would write in the next month or so' (Dylan, 2004: 165). This seems to be a very specific recollection, pinpointing the beginning of the creative process that was to become the 1989 album *Oh Mercy*; and surely even the most sceptical reader might be entitled to assume that some such moment of inspiration did happen, and that it happened in the location described by that striking phrase 'a shiny bed of lights'. The only problem is that that striking phrase (closely coupled with 'everyone was asleep') comes directly from Mark Twain's *The Adventures of Huckleberry Finn*.[7] So does the quotation invalidate the memory? Is the use of 'shiny bed of lights' a graceful allusion to an American classic or is it a breach of the implicit promises and conventions of autobiography? Or is it the trickster's move, a sly undermining of the authoritative voice?[8]

Dylan's defenders have noted that the vast majority of his borrowings consist of a single line or phrase; he never appropriates whole paragraphs or arguments. While some come from obscure sources (like a Japanese book on gangsters), the vast majority come from very obvious, even classic sources. Dylan knows that all his work is subject to intense scrutiny; he must surely have expected that his 'sources' would sooner or later be revealed. There is no intent to deceive: rather, there is an invitation to join in the game.

Thus, Dylan's defenders have attempted to shift the discussion away from the loaded word 'plagiarism' to more neutral terms, such as allusion, intertextuality or collage. In the *New York Times*, Jon Pareles (2003) wrote: '[Dylan] was simply doing what he has always done: writing songs that are information collages. Allusions and memories, fragments of dialogue and nuggets of tradition have always been part of Mr Dylan's songs, all stitched together like crazy quilts.... His lyrics are like magpies' nests, full of shiny fragments from parts unknown.' The idea of 'collages' is taken up forcefully by Robert Polito (2006), in an article on the website of the Poetry Foundation. Dylan's recent songs, he writes, 'can probably best be apprehended as Modernist collages ... verbal echo chambers of harmonizing and clashing reverberations ... where we are meant to remark on the discrepant tones and idioms of the original texts bumping up against one another'. And he cites, as primary examples of the collage method, Ezra Pound's *Cantos* and T. S. Eliot's *The Waste Land*.[9]

Eliot, of course, did famously footnote his sources for *The Waste Land* – though the notes can be read just as easily as being a spoof of academic convention as being serious acknowledgements. Pound didn't even bother. The *Cantos*, relentlessly citational, left all that to the camp followers. It is Eliot, however, who provides the practice not only with its model but with its motto. In 1922, writing on the minor Jacobean dramatist Philip Massinger, Eliot wrote: 'One of the surest of tests is the way in which a poet borrows. Immature poets imitate; mature poets steal; bad poets deface what they take, and good poets make it into something better, or at least something different.' This passage has itself been widely borrowed – usually in the over-simplified form 'Good poets borrow; great poets steal' – and has often been attributed, aptly enough, to Picasso.[10] Note that Eliot still, defiantly, uses the word 'steal'. Unacknowledged quotation is still a crime: it's just that the genius of a great poet makes it a justifiable crime. 'Yes', Dylan wrote in '11 outlined epitaphs',[11] as long ago as 1963, 'I am a thief of thoughts'.

If unacknowledged quotation is indeed a crime, then it is an offence against what, in recent years, has been defined, in increasingly strict terms, as 'intellectual property'. Major battlefields have included bootleg music recordings and pirated movies; and Dylan is of course the primary instance of the extent and significance of bootleg recordings. But the issue is also becoming increasingly problematic in literary studies.

Personally, I was educated and trained at a time when the standard practice of criticism involved an extensive use of quotation, both from the original text being discussed and from secondary critical commentary. If you were making an argument, you were expected to back it up with supportive evidence, which took the form of quotation. Such quotations were, of course, to be acknowledged, but the right of the critic to quote extensively was never in question. Recently, however, the holders of legal copyright have become much more aggressive in the assertion of their intellectual property rights, both in terms of demanding permission fees for quotations and in terms of giving permission at all. The estate of James Joyce is notorious for throwing up roadblocks in the way of critics, biographers and anthologists (see Hyde, 2010: 4, 239–40).[12] (Dylan's office, in the person of Jeff Rosen, was also difficult to deal with twenty years ago, but it has lightened up substantially.) Writing and publishing criticism have become more difficult (and more expensive). Even in writing this chapter, I notice that I am using far fewer direct quotations than I would have a decade ago.

In an academic context, the acknowledgement of sources for quotations is governed by an elaborate system of punctuation, footnotes, bibliographies, lists of 'Works cited' and so on. The details of this system are conventional and often arbitrary. (Where do you put the commas? When do you use italics rather than quotation marks?). It has been argued that the whole notion of 'plagiarism' is similarly conventional and arbitrary. One leading scholar who has advanced this point of view is Stanley Fish, who in August 2010 published an article in the *New York Times* under the title 'Plagiarism is not a big moral deal'. Fish does not see plagiarism as a crime, either morally or legally, but rather as the breaking of a highly specialised set of rules, such as the laws which govern a sport.[13] Plagiarism, Fish writes, is 'no big moral deal; which doesn't mean, I hasten to add, that plagiarism shouldn't be punished – if you're in our house, you've got to play by our rules – just that what you're punishing is a breach of disciplinary decorum, not a breach of the moral universe'. In other words, Fish is suggesting that the word 'plagiarism' can be meaningfully defined and used only within a limited and largely arbitrary set of conventions and rules. The corollary is that, in contexts outside these limits, such as poems or songs, this particular word, 'plagiarism', may be neither useful nor relevant.

The online reactions to Fish's article, however, were overwhelmingly negative. 'How is [plagiarism] not a moral lapse?', wrote one respondent. 'If cheating for self advancement vis-à-vis one's non-cheating peers is not immoral, then I think you do not have a useful definition of morals'. Another response made explicit the commercial implications: plagiarism is 'primarily

193

a property crime against an author's copyright and the inability to enforce it "as a crime" would mean that publishers have nothing exclusive to sell to people who buy books' (see the 'comments' accompanying Fish, 2010).

This frankly financial view holds that there is no difference between 'intellectual' property, such as an idea or the text of a book, and more concrete forms of property, such as a house or a car or one particular copy of a book. The property right inheres in the individual author and in the absolute discreteness and originality of his or her work. Such a view is a very modern one: earlier ages set much less store on the individual and on the possibilities of originality. Knowledge – ideas and their expression – was seen not as the exploitable property of a private individual but as the common inheritance of a whole culture. In the first century AD, the Roman dramatist and essayist Seneca put the matter at its bluntest, writing: 'Whatever has been well said by anyone is mine'.

This topic has recently been explored in great detail by Lewis Hyde in his book *Common as Air: Revolution, Art, and Ownership* (2010). Hyde is much concerned with what he sees as recent and alarming shifts in attitudes towards copyright, especially the 1976 revisions to American copyright law:

> Until 1976, the point of departure was the assumed common nature of creative work; everything belonged to the commons and the exception, 'intellectual property', was a small set of things removed from the commons by consent, by an overt and public action, for a short term, and for a good reason. Now the point of departure is the assumption of exclusive ownership and those who think they have a right to common are greeted by FBI warnings at the start of every movie. (Hyde, 2010: 58)

Hyde traces the history of copyright and notes that the Founding Fathers of the American Revolution saw copyright as a kind of monopoly and were deeply distrustful of it. Copyright might be useful, and beneficial to the common good, as a means of encouraging and rewarding authors and inventors, but it was not seen as a moral right. The history that Hyde cautiously endorses 'begins by asserting that art and ideas, unlike land or houses, belong by nature to a cultural commons, open to all. It then allows for certain chosen exceptions: in the interest of the public good, government sometimes graces artists and thinkers with monopoly power over their work and lets them thereby enclose parts of that commons' (*ibid.*: 214–15). That is, Hyde still believes in individual rights of 'intellectual property', which may manifest themselves in issues such as copyright and plagiarism, but he sees such rights not as fundamental but as exceptions to a rule – the rule, that is, of common ownership of knowledge, ideas and art.

Hyde's book does include a brief section on Dylan, but he confines himself to the early work and its use of the folk tradition. There is no indication of what he might make of the wholesale quotations in *"Love and Theft"* and *Chronicles* of Henry Timrod and Peter Green's Ovid. In pursuing this

194

argument further, I now want to shift direction and introduce the example of another artist much given to quotation: the Swiss/French film director Jean-Luc Godard.

Indeed, before this chapter got mightily sidetracked into the question of plagiarism, it began life, in the proposal I first sent to Eugen Banauch, as a study of relations between Dylan and French *Nouvelle Vague* (New Wave) cinema. Dylan's closest professed affinity with the *Nouvelle Vague* is to François Truffaut, as is seen in his admiration for Truffaut's second film, *Tirez sur le Pianiste* (1960), and for its leading actor, the singer Charles Aznavour, one of whose songs, 'Les Bons Moments'/'The Times We've Known', Dylan has performed in concert. Dylan's '11 outlined epitaphs'[14] concludes: 'there's a movie called/<u>Shoot the Piano Player</u>/the last line proclaimin'/"music, man, that's where it's at"/it is a religious line'. Well, it may be a religious line, but it is *not* the last line of *Tirez sur le Pianiste*. Dylan's only direct quote from the New Wave is, actually, a misquote.

But for all Dylan's professed admiration of Truffaut, I think that his closer affinity may be to Godard. Both of them burst on the scene in the early 1960s as the *enfants terribles* of their arts; both of them survived motorcycle accidents, Dylan in 1966 and Godard in 1971; both of them went through periods of extreme ideological rigidity, Godard with Maoism and Dylan with evangelical Christianity; both of them are problematic, to say the least, in their depiction of women; both of them emerged to produce some of their finest work in the fourth or fifth decades of their careers. Consider this description: a long, basically non-linear film, in which plot elements are sketched in with little regard for coherence; which is organised primarily by associations of ideas and collages of images; and which depends heavily on quotations, largely unacknowledged, from previous sources. It is a description of just about any Godard movie. It is also, surely, a description of Bob Dylan's film *Renaldo and Clara* (1978). (Godard is reported to have seen *Renaldo and Clara* and found it 'sympathique': see Brody, 2011.)[15]

Godard mentions Dylan in several of his films. One of the central characters in *Masculin Féminin* (1966) is a pop singer called Madeleine Zimmer. It is not clear whether Godard knew that Dylan's original name was Zimmerman but Madeleine and her friends certainly know Bob Dylan. They discuss a magazine article entitled 'Who are you, Mister Bob Dylan?' This may be the quintessential Dylan question, identity, but the answer given here is, somewhat inaccurately, a 'Vietnik' – defined as 'a Yank word, a cross between "beatnik" and "Vietnam"'. We are told that he sells 10,000 records a day and comes out ahead of Madeleine on the Japanese hit parade!

Le Gai Savoir (1968) shows the well known Jerry Schatzberg photograph of Dylan (which also appears on the cover of Dylan's novel, *Tarantula*), with one side of his face in deep shadow; Godard then replicates the lighting in a subsequent shot of the lead actor, Jean-Pierre Léaud. In *Sauve Qui Peut (La Vie)* (1980), a voice-over by Isabelle Huppert ascribes to one of the other characters a list of 'heroes', including Al Capone, Che Guevera, Malcolm X, Ghandi, Castro, Van Gogh, Sartre and Bob Dylan, then scornfully adds: 'You see he identifies with all the losers'. The 1986 film *Grandeur et Décadence d'un Petit Commerce du Cinéma* features the Dylan song 'When He Returns'.

In a 1988 interview, Godard said of Dylan: 'I have a great deal of sympathy for him when I read critics who eviscerate him, who call him a "has-been". Sometimes I read *Rolling Stone* to get news of him. I want to see whether he's on the charts.' Godard tried unsuccessfully to get Dylan to appear in his 1987 film *King Lear*.

The favour has only once been returned. In an interview with Jonathan Cott in 1978, Dylan said: 'I figured Godard had the accessibility to make what he made, he broke new ground. I never saw any film like *Breathless*, but once you saw it, you said: "Yeah, man, why didn't I do that, I could have done that". Okay, he did it, but he couldn't have done it in America' (see Cott, 2006: 189). As far as I know (and I happily stand open to correction), Dylan has never mentioned Godard in any of his other writings or interviews.[16] Godard does, however, feature prominently in a film *about* Dylan: Todd Haynes's *I'm Not There* (2007), which is also, like Godard's own films, a movie made up of quotations.

Most of Haynes's quotations come, of course, from Dylan himself – in the songs on the soundtrack and in lines or phrases incorporated into the dialogue. But Haynes also draws on a wider variety of sources, and most of his quotations are without attribution. He does acknowledge many of his sources in the 'Director's Commentary' soundtrack on the DVD, but not in the movie itself. The first-time viewer is left without footnotes.[17]

For example, the lines spoken in the boxcar by the young Hobo Dylan, Woody (Marcus Carl Franklin), are taken partly from Dylan's 1966 *Playboy* interview, but also draw heavily on the 1957 movie *A Face in the Crowd*, directed by Elia Kazan, written by Budd Schulberg, about a hobo who gains overnight fame. In another scene, Claire (Charlotte Gainsbourg) quotes Rimbaud's seminal line 'Je est un autre'/'I is another', which could be seen as a variant on 'I'm not there'. In both cases, the source is acknowledged in the 'Director's Commentary', but not in the movie itself.

Claire quotes Rimbaud's line by reading it to Robbie (Heath Ledger): there is a close-up shot of the book page and a shot of Claire reading from it. These devices are highly typical, indeed quintessential Godard, who has filmed more shots of people reading aloud than any other ten directors combined. It is the Claire/Robbie thread of Haynes's film in which the Godard references are concentrated. The scene of the two of them in a café is richly reminiscent of several early Godard films; the one that Haynes cites on the DVD is *Masculin Féminin* (1966). Later in the film, during Claire's long monologue after Robbie leaves her, the lines 'I must listen. I must look around me more than ever' are taken directly from Godard's *Deux ou Trois Choses Que Je Sais d'Elle* (1967).

196

The most extended quotation, however, does come from *Masculin Féminin*. In the scene directly following the Rimbaud quotation, Robbie and Claire attend a premiere of his latest film. As the lights go down, we see both of them watching the film. And Robbie's voice on the soundtrack says: 'But the movie disappointed her [Claire]. The more they tried to make it look youthful, the more the images on screen seemed out of date. It wasn't the film they had dreamed, the film they had imagined and discussed, the film they each wanted to live.' This passage is adapted from a scene in *Masculin Féminin* in which the main character, Paul (Jean-Pierre Léaud), goes to the cinema with his girlfriend Madeleine (the same Madeleine Zimmer whose record falls behind Bob Dylan in the Japanese charts). As in Haynes's film, there is a shot of them watching the screen as the lights go down. And Paul's voice on Godard's soundtrack says: 'But more often than not, Madeleine and I were disappointed. The pictures were dated, they flickered. And Marilyn Monroe had aged terribly. It made us sad. This wasn't the film we'd dreamed of. This wasn't the total film that each of us had carried within himself – the film that we wanted to make, or, more secretly, no doubt, that we wanted to live.'

This scene has long been one of my favourite moments in Godard – and, evidently, the same is true for Todd Haynes. The problem is that, while he makes strikingly original use of these words, Godard didn't write them. They come from the contemporary French novelist Georges Perec, who was a leading member of the experimental Oulipo group, and is perhaps best known for his novel *La Disparition* (1969), which contrives to omit entirely the letter 'e'. Perec's first novel, which appeared in 1965, is *Les Choses: Une Histoire des Années Soixante*. It is a striking dissection of the growing consumer culture in France; and its analysis of the pervasiveness of the language of advertising is close to several Godard films, notably *Une Femme Mariée* (1964). The book's two central characters, Jérome and Sylvie, work in market research, as does Paul in *Masculin Féminin*. They are also cinema buffs and eagerly seek out screenings of old classics in obscure cinemas. But, writes Perec:

> Alas, quite often, to tell the truth, they were horribly let down.... The screen would light up, they would feel a thrill of satisfaction. But the colours had faded with age, the picture wobbled on the screen, the women were of another age; they would come out; they would be sad. It was not the film they had dreamt of. It was not the total film each of them had inside himself, the perfect film they could have enjoyed for ever and ever. The film they would have liked to make. Or more secretly, no doubt, the film they would have liked to live. (Perec, 1990: 57)

Godard's use of Perec is perfectly consistent: the characters in both novel and film suffer from a similar social malaise, from a persistent nagging disappointment. And the novel was so well known in France – it had been a huge success, had won several prizes and was adopted for school curricula – that he may simply have assumed that the quotation would readily be recognised. Nevertheless, he does quote it without any attribution or acknowledgement.[18] As for Haynes, he does acknowledge, again on the DVD Director's Commentary, that his scene is taken from *Masculin Féminin*; but he makes no mention of Perec. It is, however, thoroughly fitting that this high point of his film about Bob Dylan should be the unacknowledged quotation of an unacknowledged quotation.

Godard's unacknowledged borrowing from Perec is also entirely consistent with his practice throughout his career. Godard is a compulsive borrower – or, in Eliot's terms, a great thief. In *Une Femme Est une Femme* (1961), the central couple conduct their quarrels by plucking books off their shelves and reading insulting quotations at each other. In *Alphaville* (1965), Eddie Constantine seduces Anna Karina by reading to her passages from Paul Eluard's *Capitale de la Douleur*. In *Weekend* (1967), the leader of the hippy/revolutionary group plays a drum solo to a pond, apostrophised as 'Old Ocean', while declaiming the words of the French decadent poet Lautréamont. Godard's idiosyncratic version of *King Lear* (1987) constructs a deeply moving collage between Shakespeare's play and the final paragraph of Virginia Woolf's *The Waves*.

There is a story, possibly apocryphal, about Godard's 1990 film *Nouvelle Vague*. The film's marquee star, Alain Delon, became impatient with Godard's habits of improvisation and demanded a written script. So Godard sat down and wrote a script – made up entirely of quotations. A 'written' script indeed.

Godard's practice, like Dylan's, has been somewhat erratic in relation to acknowledging sources. Often, he will show on screen the front cover or title page of the work being quoted – as in the Eluard book cited in *Alphaville*. Just as often, there is no acknowledgement at all – as in the lines from Lautréamont cited in *Weekend*. In recent years, Godard's practice of unacknowledged quotation has been complicated by his extremely odd publication of scripts from his work. That is, for his most recent films, Godard has published scripts which consist, simply, of every word spoken in the films – but with no indication of who is the speaker or of any of the actions shown. And with, of course, no quotation marks.

For *Film Socialisme* (2010), Godard slightly altered this presentation. The published script again contains every line of dialogue spoken in the film – but whenever that line is a quotation, it is accompanied, on the page, by a photo of the author (Godard, 2010). These photos are not, however, captioned or identified – which is fine if you happen to know what Heidegger or Blanchot looks like – but if not, too bad. (Of course, for every French intellectual who identifies Martin or Maurice, there may well be one who is stumped by Joan Baez or Patti Smith.)

Godard's love of quotation reaches from the earliest to the latest stages of his career. As early as 1962, he wrote (in what might be a career manifesto for Dylan):

People in love
quote as they please

so we have the right
to quote as we please. Therefore,

I show people quoting,
merely making sure

that they quote what pleases me.[19]

As late as 2010, he came out publicly in defence of James Climent, a photographer accused of breaching copyright laws by downloading images from the internet. In a May 2010 interview, Godard stated: 'There is no intellectual property.... An author has no right. I have no right. I have only duties.' Acknowledging his own use of shots from a film by Agnès Varda, Godard said: 'I'm not quoting [her] film: I'm benefiting from her work. I'm taking an excerpt, which I'm incorporating somewhere else, where it takes on another meaning' (Lalanne, 2010).

Again, the defence is Eliot's: 'Immature poets imitate; mature poets steal'. Godard and Dylan steal all the time, but they incorporate their thefts 'somewhere else, where it takes on another meaning'. Or, in Eliot's words, 'good poets make it into something better, or at least something different'. The test is not in the mere fact of the theft itself but in the context, the use to which it is put. And, thus, some critics of Dylan have argued that the problem with his borrowing in recent years is not the borrowing itself but that he does not do anything particularly interesting *with* the quoted words. Such judgements would then have to be made on a case-by-case basis (does this one work? does this one?), rather than as a matter of general principle.

In concluding this chapter, I would like to allude briefly to some of my own poetic work. I know that there are many people, among them the subscribers of the Austrian Dylan magazine *Parking Meter* and veterans of the annual Dylan fan conventions at Schloss Plankenstein, who have kindly over the years followed my own poems about and around Bob Dylan.

Now, I would not want, arrogantly, to rank myself with artists as great as Godard and Dylan. But I have, modestly, employed the same tactics. My most recent work has been a series of poems inspired by the work of Jean-Luc Godard (Scobie, 2013). It begins with Godard's first feature:

À bout de souffle/Breathless
1960

At the edge, at the limit of breath,
time for a new sensation –
the gun abrupt and clumsy in his hands.

199

Thumb tracing the line of his lip,
sun-dazzle over trees, and then the bridge,
the river flowing under Notre-Dame.

Her T-shirt on the Avenue, tribune:
herald of a new wave rising.
Tonight I will be with you in Paradise.

What you believe in the long conversation,
Matisse and Renoir on the wall, the tiny room
filled by a bed and William Faulkner.

The man on the street pointing him out, and
pointing you the way to go. A phonecall's betrayal –
dégueulasse.

Trying to reach the intersection,
rue Campagne-Première:
staggering, falling, falling again.

What does it mean?
What does that strange word mean?

This poem, of course, includes many references to Godard's original movie. It also quotes quotations in the movie: images by Matisse and Renoir, lines from a novel by William Faulkner. These quotations are openly acknowledged. Less open is the reference to an incident in the film in which a bypasser on the street identifies the criminal fugitive (Jean-Paul Belmondo) and points out to a law officer the direction he has taken. From Godard's point of view, the incident is a quotation and *hommage* to Alfred Hitchcock: that is, the bypasser is played by Godard himself, in the same manner in which Hitchcock so often played walk-on parts in his own films. From my point of view, the quotation comes from a song written some seven years after the film: the line 'we pointed out the way to go' from the 1967 'Basement Tapes' Dylan song 'Tears of Rage'. And of course I fully intend that quotation, and intend it to be recognised.[20]

But if the reader does not recognise the quotation, what is lost? The line does still have its force (perhaps as an unspecified resonance) but it works, as itself. At least I hope it does. If not, the fault is mine, not the method's. Quotation from an unacknowledged source is not, to my way of thinking, a fault. It is a time-honoured practice of great poets.

Thus the title of this chapter, which I hope now makes more sense: Plagiarism, Bob, Jean-Luc and Me. Plagiarism is a serious matter, a serious charge. But so is its defence. When Dylan uses lines from other sources, he may or may not have intended the borrowing to be spotted. But he certainly makes the implicit claim that the borrowing enriches, rather than diminishes, his own text. Plagiarism attempts to steal credit; Dylan and Godard attempt to incorporate and extend credit. They may, in strictly legalistic terms, live outside the law; but their art remains honest.

Postscript 1

After the above text was written, the controversy surrounding Dylan and plagiarism resurfaced in an even more pronounced form, in relation to the paintings of his 'Asia Series' exhibited at the Gagosian Gallery in New York in 2011. (It should be noted that the word 'Series' already recalls its use in Dylan's 'official' releases of *The Bootleg Series* – as if 'Series' should already evoke, in the alert reader, the word 'bootleg'.)

Dylan's paintings in this exhibition were purported to be a 'visual journal' of his travels in Asia. The exhibition catalogue claimed that Dylan paints 'mostly from real life.... Real people, real street scenes, behind the curtain scenes, live models, paintings, photographs, staged setups, architecture, grids, graphic design. Whatever it takes to make it work' (Dylan, 2011). In this description, 'photographs' and 'staged setups' are buried deep within a list which gives its major priority to the word 'real'. Yet, as has amply been demonstrated, most, if not all, of the paintings in Dylan's exhibition are modelled directly on photographs of staged setups, taken by photographers as well known as Henri Cartier-Bresson and Léon Busy.

There seems to be no legal question here. Reportedly, Dylan secured and paid permission fees from the photographers and/or their heirs (though whether he did so before or after the controversy arose remains unclear). But the ethic and aesthetic questions remain. Despite the equivocation of its wording, the implication of Dylan's original statement remains clear: the claim is made that these paintings derive from the artist's personal observation. And this claim is patently false.

Moreover, the 'borrowing' in these paintings is not partial but wholesale. In the main part of the chapter, I noted that: 'the vast majority of his borrowings consist of a single line or phrase; he never appropriates whole paragraphs or arguments'. This point remains valid, I believe, for most of Dylan's quotations in his songs, and even in *Chronicles*: but it cannot be maintained in relation to these paintings.

What Dylan 'borrows' here is not simply an incidental phrase or image: it consists of the entire content and composition of the paintings. Every detail of the narrative setting – the dress, the gestures, the setting, the background decor – is taken from the original photograph. Every detail of the subject matter – the character's pose, gesture, clothing, action – is taken from the original photograph. Every detail of the composition – the angle from which the subject is viewed, the relation between background and foreground – is taken from the original photograph.

What remains? What area is left in which the painter Dylan may assert his individual vision, his unique contribution to an existing image? Two obvious answers are: his choice of colour; and his handling of the paint, individual brush strokes. And here, I must confess, I simply cannot judge. I did not go to the Gagosian Gallery; I have not seen Dylan's paintings in, as it were, 'the flesh'. All I have seen are online reproductions – a medium that reproduces inadequately, and thus obscures the very qualities here at issue.

Even so – given the most generous interpretation possible of the colour and the brush work – would that be enough to justify the patent theft of the entire content and composition of these images? I am compelled to think not. In my chapter, I attempt to argue in favour of Dylan's citational practice in recent songs and writings. And I still stand by that defence. But I cannot extend it to these paintings.

Postscript 2

In the 27 September 2013 issue of *Rolling Stone*, Bob Dylan gave an extended interview to Mikal Gilmore. It is in many ways a bizarre conversation, with all Dylan's insistence on a hazily conceived notion of 'transfiguration'; but it also contains Dylan's most direct response to accusations of plagiarism.

Some of what he has to say is perfectly reasonable: 'And as far as Henry Timrod is concerned, have you even heard of him? Who's been reading him lately? And who's pushed him to the forefront? Who's been making you read him? .... And if you think it's so easy to quote him and it can help your work, do it yourself and see how far you can get.' These are excellent comments, which seem to me well in line with the arguments I have been advancing throughout this chapter, from Eliot to Godard.

But the following comments are not quite so reasonable: 'Wussies and pussies complain about that stuff.... All those evil motherfuckers can rot in hell.' These comments rather align themselves with a strain of violent vengefulness which has become quite common in recent Dylan (*Tempest* is by far his most bloodthirsty album). If the violence of this reaction seems uncomfortably defensive, maybe it is because, at some level, Dylan realises there are things he ought to be defensive about. So let me in conclusion claim my status as an honorary wussie and pussie, and go find some quiet corner of hell in which I can cozily rot.

Notes

1   See, for example, Roberts (2010). Even if you disagree with this assessment, there is no denying that Mitchell cuts right to the heart of Bob Dylan: his name and his voice.
2   The two songs are 'Baby, Let Me Follow You Down' and (for the tune, not the words) 'Masters of War'. I am grateful to Clinton Heylin for information on this point.

3 In this case, the matter is further complicated by the fact that 'Brownsville Girl' is co-credited (and co-copyrighted) to Dylan and Sam Shepard.

4 Many of the borrowings which I cite here were first documented by Edward Cook in his blog 'Ralph the Sacred River', http://ralphriver.blogspot.com, an invaluable source.

5 My thanks to Richard Thomas for information on the Ovid quotations, derived from Peter Green's recent translations in a Penguin series. See also Thomas (2007).

6 This reading assumes that the *Tell Tale Signs* recording does indeed predate the version on *Modern Times* – which seems likely, but is not (yet) proven.

7 Again, this example is taken from Edward Cook's blog 'Ralph the Sacred River'.

8 For a fuller discussion of Dylan as trickster, see Scobie (2003: 31–5).

9 Both of them, in Dylan's words, 'fighting in the captain's tower' of the *Titanic* as it goes down ('Desolation Row', on the 1965 album *Highway 61 Revisited*).

10 Picasso may well have used some variant of the phrase. It's not clear whether or not he knew the Eliot quotation.

11 To be found as liner notes to his 1964 album *The Times They Are A-Changin'* (discussed in Chapter 5).

12 Hyde (2010) spends over two pages (235–8) listing instances of such obstruction.

13 The example he gives is golf, where professional players are scrupulous about invoking penalties against themselves for even the slightest breach of the most arcane rule.

14 See note 11.

15 Brody's blog (see Brody, 2011) is also the source for the 1988 interview quoted below.

16 There is a distant echo, in Dylan's 'The next sixty seconds could be like an eternity' (in the song 'Things Have Changed', 1999), of Godard's 'A real minute of silence can last for an eternity' (*Bande à Part*, 1964), but I don't think it qualifies as a deliberate quotation.

17 It is of course difficult to footnote a movie! The commentary track on a DVD is, however, an ideal site for acknowledgements.

18 Perec himself was not averse to unacknowledged quotation. His novel *Un Homme Qui Dort* (1967) ends in a veritable orgy of quotations. The last four pages are saturated in lines from Herman Melville, Malcolm Lowry and James Joyce.

19 This quotation is adapted from Godard (1972: 173). In the original, the first couplet reads 'People in life/quote as they please'. I mistyped 'life' as 'love' (no doubt a significant slip); but when I eventually discovered my error, I had grown so fond of the misquoted version that I decided to let it stand.

20 My sequence also includes yet another reworking of the Haynes/Godard/Perec quotation.

References

Brody, R. (2011) 'Bob Dylan in correspondence', *New Yorker* blog (25 May). Available at http://www.newyorker.com/online/blogs/movies/2011/05/bob-dylan-in-correspondence.html (accessed 1 April 2014).

Cott, J. (ed.) (2006) 'Interview with Jonathan Cott, *Rolling Stone*, 26 January 1978', in *Dylan on Dylan: The Essential Interviews* (New York: Wenner Books). 171–98.

Dylan, B. (2004) *Chronicles: Volume One* (New York: Simon and Schuster).

Dylan, B. (2011) *The Asia Series* (exhibition catalogue) (New York: Gagosian Galleries).

Eliot, T. S. (1922) 'Philip Massinger', in *The Sacred Wood: Essays on Poetry and Criticism* (London). 49.

Fish, S. (2010) 'Plagiarism is not a big moral deal', *New York Times* (9 August). Available at http://opinionator.blogs.nytimes.com/2010/08/09/plagiarism-is-not-a-big-moral-deal (accessed 2 April 2014).

Godard, J.-L. (1972) *Godard on Godard*, trans. T. Milne (New York: Viking Press).

Godard, J.-L. (2010) *Film Socialisme: Dialogues Avec Visages Auteurs* (Paris: POL).

Gray, M. (2006) *The Bob Dylan Encyclopaedia* (London: Continuum).

Hyde, L. (2010) *Common as Air: Revolution, Art, and Ownership* (New York: Farrar, Strauss and Giroux).

Lalanne, J.-M. (2010) Jean-Luc Godard interviewed by Jean-Marc Lalannein *Les Inrocks* (18 May). Available in translation by C. Kellar as 'Jean-Luc Godard interviewed by Jean-Marc Lalanne', on the *Cinemasparagus* website, at http://cinemasparagus.blogspot.co.at/2010/05/jean-luc-godard-interviewed-by-jean.html (accessed 2 April 2014).

Pareles, J. (2003) 'Plagiarism in Dylan, or a cultural collage?', *New York Times* (12 July). Available at http://www.nytimes.com/2003/07/12/books/critic-s-notebook-plagiarism-in-dylan-or-a-cultural-collage.html (accessed 8 November 2014.)

Perec, G. (1990) *Things: A Story of the Sixties*, trans. A. Leak (London: Collins Harvill).

Polito, R. (2006) 'Bob Dylan: Henry Timrod revisited'. Available at http://www.poetryfoundation.org/article/178703 (accessed 2 April 2014).

Roberts, R. (2010) 'Joni Mitchell on Bob Dylan: "He's a plagiarist, and his name and voice are fake"', *Pop and Hiss: The L.A. Times Music Blog* (22 April). Available at http://latimesblogs.latimes.com/music_blog/2010/04/joni-mitchell-on-bob-dylan-hes-a-plagiarist-his-name-is-fake-his-voice-is-fake.html (accessed 2 April 2014).

Scobie, S. (2003) *Alias Bob Dylan Revisited* (Calgary: Red Deer Press).

Scobie, S. (2013) *At the Limit of Breath* (Edmonton: University of Alberta Press).

Thomas, R. F. (2007) 'The streets of Rome: the classical Dylan', *Oral Tradition*, 22:1. 30–56.

Part VI
Outro

16

The evolution of fan culture and the impact of technology on the Never Ending Tour

Clinton Heylin and Michelle Engert

This chapter presents the transcript of a talk at the Refractions of Bob Dylan conference, Vienna, May 2011, on which this volume is based.[1]

Clinton Heylin

I am going to briefly explain the format my part of the session will take. I will look at the Never Ending Tour, which began in June 1988, specifically the first five years, from the point of view of the relationship that Dylan created, or recreated, with his audience. Michelle will then give you the perspective of a fan experiencing that same period. We will also both talk about how the history of this tour has been saved and shared from our distinct perspectives and how that has changed over time due to technology.

One of the issues that has been raised throughout the conference is the question: how does someone find an entry point into Dylan's work and career, especially at this late stage? Of all what I would call the A-list artists in 20th-century pop culture, Dylan's canon is the largest. The sheer scale of the body of work that he has created is vast, and it has more highs and lows than any other artist of similar stature; and that is a huge challenge for us to sort through. The Never Ending Tour throws that into high relief because those highs and lows often have happened in the blink of an eye. In the same show Bob could be murdering some classic song and five minutes later would pull out a song he had not played in thirty-five years, maybe even a song written 200 years ago, and give a performance of the kind of quality and depth that sticks with a person for years. I cannot think of any other musician where that has happened so consistently – and has been so fastidiously documented. Assimilating such a body of work throws up enormous challenges.

While preparing for this discussion, Michelle and I were talking about the spring 1991 shows. For many fans this was considered the nadir of the Never Ending Tour. Dylan was in a very bad way physically; he was visibly drinking to excess and his mental state was unfocused. And it was a period where he was not putting out any original songs which would give us an insight into what might have been going on inside. Night after night, he would get up on stage and slaughter masterpiece after masterpiece, live and in person.

There is a famous concert in Stuttgart[2] that spring, which was voted by a small fraternity of tape collectors the worst Dylan show of all time. The opening song was 'New Morning'; it went on for eight minutes and the words were simply unintelligible. After the concert, a friend of mine who had been to a considerable number of live Dylan shows, and was intimately familiar with all his material, was in a discussion with a hard-core German fan who had written down the songs played at the show. This fan came up to my friend and asked, 'Can you tell me what the opening song was?' He replied, '"New Morning"'. The German said, 'No, I know this song, it was not "New Morning"'. It almost got to fisticuffs as the fan would not accept that the first song was 'New Morning'. It was, of course; just played in a way unrecognisable even to someone who knew the song well.

But there were some brilliant moments, if no brilliant shows that spring. For instance, only days before this Dylan played in Budapest,[3] where he had started to do something he had not done for a long time, which was play one song of the show completely solo and acoustic. He generally played the song 'Barbara Allen', the well known Child ballad. In Budapest, though, he did a song called 'When First Unto This Country', a beautiful traditional song which Dylan used to sing at Gerdes Folk City in 1961. He actually once wrote his own song called 'Liverpool Gal' to the same tune of 'When First Unto This Country'. He suddenly pulls out this song and produces a quite extraordinary moment. At this moment, I would argue that everything came together and the Never Ending Tour – which had threatened to go permanently off the rails – returned to the straight and narrow. It is one of the defining moments of the Never Ending Tour, and I would put it among my favourite Dylan performances, from an artist who has more than 50,000 song performances captured on tape.

By the time Dylan got to the United States in October 1991, he had turned the corner. People were calling me, raving about the shows, saying I should come over. But based on what I had heard and seen earlier in the year, I did not go. Later, when I heard the tapes, I realised just how great that transformation had been. But this was pre-internet. One could not just click a button for a download, open an attachment in an email, or go to YouTube and see what was played the night before. Physical tapes had to be copied and mailed.

'When First Unto This Country' at Budapest is but one example of a continual process of reinventing the Never Ending Tour. The tour has constantly thrown up such highs and lows. There are very few Never Ending Tour shows – even early on – that are consistently brilliant. Clive James, the Australian critic, once said that Dylan never wrote a song which did not have a verse better than the rest, or a line better than its immediate kin. I don't agree, but on the Never Ending Tour you often have songs that transcend the whole of the concert and verses that transcend the rest of the song. I refer interested readers to the version of 'Queen Jane Approximately' at New York's Beacon Theater on 12 October 1989 for the most apposite example of a song that teeters on the brink of genius and chaos simultaneously. But they still have to be understood in the context of the tour as a whole in order to fully appreciate them. If you divorce 'When First Unto This Country' in Budapest from the rest of the concert you will still appreciate the performance, but what you really need to do is hear that one moment in context, the way that he works up to, down from and around the song. This requires the time, energy, expense required to sift through the material.

If, like me, you consider Dylan to be the most important popular artist of the twentieth century, it is imperative to sift through this vast volume of material. He is not Nick Drake, who had a body of work comprising three albums, no concerts and a bunch of home demos. One can easily absorb the full body of Drake's work. Dylan is the polar opposite. It is not just a question of scale but of endurance. Of the three original Dylan collectors who started in the '60s, A. J. Webberman, Sandy Gant and Simon Montgomery, there was only one of them, Sandy, who was still collecting by 1979. The others had given up. Dylan had played approximately 200 concerts between 1974 and 1978, which seemed at the time like a huge body of work. If only they had known what the next generation would have to do to keep up....

From 1981 and on, people were regularly videoing the shows. Indeed, I'd like to show two examples from the early part of the Never Ending Tour. These two videos are, by any production standards, terrible. They were not recorded on modern digital equipment. The cameras are constantly being jostled. The people filming are doing something that was not permitted, that was possibly illegal, and therefore were constantly on the lookout. Yet these people, and others like them, preserve these moments, believing them important enough to save. And God bless them. These two performances are so transcendent we would be poorer if they did not exist.

It is moments like this that inspire me to do what I do. It is why I write the books and articles. I believe that as long as Dylan remains a moving target, we need to get it down, document it, get the facts straight. We all like to pontificate now and again – me more than most – but the most important thing at this stage is to document it all, to make sure that if Bob turns up in a small *Ratskeller* in Vienna, someone is there to tape it – even if it is lousy. That is why the fan network grew up and why at this time certain people

209

were even sent on tours to document them, with fellow fans chipping in to pay their expenses. Truly, the best of times.

I once wrote a book ostensibly about Shakespeare's sonnets (*So Long as Men Can Breathe*). It is not about Shakespeare in and of himself, but about the bootlegging of these exquisite poems. In it I suggest that there should be a statue erected to the charlatan who stole the manuscript, because if he had not done that deed, the greatest love poems in the English language – well, excepting perhaps *Blood on the Tracks* – would not have survived. Dylan, like Shakespeare with his sonnets, was not remotely interested in making sure the Never Ending Tour shows were thoroughly documented on tape. Thankfully, some of us remembered to not trust the artist, but trust the tale.

There is a video of Dylan performing 'There'll Be Peace in the Valley' by Thomas Dorsey on 13 June 1989 in Frejus, France. I chose it partly because it is a one-off performance of a song Dylan would certainly have known from a young age, probably as performed by Elvis Presley. It is one of two songs that were played at Elvis's mother's funeral, the other of which was 'Precious Memories', which Dylan recorded for *Knocked Out Loaded* and also performed powerfully in 1989. Ever the music historian, Dylan doubtless knew by then that Thomas Dorsey was also Georgia Tom, a wildcat blues pianist from the 1920s.

'Peace in the Valley' was rehearsed, but this was the first and last time that it was played for an audience, and it seems clear he is making up the arrangement as he is going along. The lovely harmonica solo at the end was another Never Ending Tour afterthought, and listening to it reminded me just how much Dylan owes G. E. Smith, who is playing on this performance, and whose feel for the songs made those Never Ending Tour gigs between 1988 and 1990 so special.

I first heard this performance probably one week after the show. At the time, I had no idea if it was, or would become, a regular feature of the shows, but I believed even then that Dylan's heartfelt vocal and whole performance was giving us an insight into where he was 'at' spiritually at the time. After hearing it I wanted to say, 'So this is a guy who is no longer a Christian, but is singing this way because he likes the tune? I don't think so.' And the most important line for me (and him) is when Dylan sings 'Yes I'll be changed from the creature that I am', which he enunciates precisely, determined to get across the meaning. It is a specific reference to the Rapture, straight from Corinthians. He is telling us he still believes the same thing he believed in 1979, when he wrote the apocalyptic 'Ye Shall Be Changed'.

I am prepared to state with a degree of certainty that there was no official tape made of that show by Dylan's people. So the people who were taping that show did as much of a public service as Thomas Thorpe when he published Shakespeare's sonnets.

The other clip that I want to play and discuss is a performance of 'Idiot Wind' from 5 May 1992, at the Warfield in San Francisco. This was the first time that I had ever got to hear this epic song live. Indeed, I was one of those who got on a plane and flew 6,000 miles to California just hoping to see it. I learned he was doing it thanks to a long-distance phone call from Glen Dundas in Canada, in March of 1992. Later, when I heard the tapes from Australia of those early performances, they were tentative if still extraordinary. And not just because of 'Idiot Wind'. So, I went to California and took my chances on hearing it for myself. And I got to see it the one night Jerry Garcia joined Bobby D on that particular tour.

When Jerry Garcia came on, the gentleman who was making the video, who was a big Grateful Dead fan, did not realise he was on stage for about three minutes. Anyone watching the video will see the moment when he pans across to Garcia. Well, he has only just realised he is there. But he holds his nerve, as does Dylan, and the performance just gets better and better until, at the end of it, after the harmonica solo, the video shows for a split second a rare expression on Dylan's face, a broad grin. I remember thinking at the time, Dylan was saying to us all, 'I know how good that was'. Tony Bennett was once asked if he thought Bob Dylan could sing, and he responded, 'Well, he may not be able to sing, but he sure can *phrase*'. This performance of 'Idiot Wind' perfectly exemplifies Bennett's astute distinction.

Another show in 1990 in Toronto also comes to mind. A few rows behind me, a friend, a serious Dylan fan, yells out a request for 'Tomorrow Is a Long Time' to a man renowned for never doing requests. Oh, and who had already started playing 'It's All Over Now Baby Blue'. I turned around to my friend to laugh in his face but just as I was about to, Dylan said, 'It sure is, awfully long', and went straight into one of the best live performances of the Never Ending Tour era.

The people who followed the shows then knew how special a Dylan concert really could be. In contrast, you can go to a Paul McCartney concert, and it is not that he does not play with heart and soul, or that the fans are not savouring the experience, but I can say, from having recently seen one of them, that the experience was nothing like going to a Dylan concert, good night or bad. The McCartney audience have come to relive the past, not reinvigorate it.

The post-1993 shows represent an entirely different kind of Never Ending Tour – the No End In Sight Tour. I check in now and then, but these days it is more out of a sense of duty than embracing the aesthetic. Still, I can say I lived to see the chimes at midnight.

Michelle Engert

Throughout the conference we have been discussing multiple aspects and eras of the huge body of Bob Dylan's art, including the songs, the albums, the music, the performances, the books, the films and the paintings. He has released a diverse body of work that spans almost 50 years. There is no other popular artist who has successfully explored, mastered and influenced so many different forms of music and performance. Even after the enormous output of released 'official' material, a significant number of his fans are not satisfied with only the official releases; instead, we have wanted more, out-takes, live performances, rehearsals – anything that gives us additional insight into Bob Dylan the artist, Bob Dylan the person and the context for what was perfected and published. The performances of the Never Ending Tour are one sliver of that 'unofficial material'. These performances document Bob Dylan in the modern era.

Before talking about the Never Ending Tour, I should acknowledge that this is a loaded term. I use it as a shorthand for the period of live Dylan concerts that have taken place from 1988 until today. But we acknowledge that Bob himself said in 1993 in the liner notes to *World Gone Wrong*, 'there was a Never Ending Tour but it ended in '91 … that one's long gone but there have been many others since then. The Money Never Runs Out Tour (fall of '91) Southern Sympathizer Tour (early '92) Why Do You look At Me So Strangely Tour (European '92) … & others too many to mention each with their own character & design'.

In the last twenty-five years, from the start of the Never Ending Tour until today,[4] Bob has played by my rough count 2,324 public concerts. For me personally, the most meaningful segment of the Never Ending Tour was between 1990 and 1996. This was because I bore witness to a great deal of it, by making it a priority to see as many of the concerts as I possibly could. And it was being there as it unfolded, as opposed to hearing it on tape or watching it on video, that made it special to me. Going night after night, month after month and year after year allowed those who went to come to understand the tour in context, how one song related to an entire show and how one show related to the segment of the tour and how each year related to the ones before and after. The recordings of these shows that were painstakingly made helped to document the sounds that came alive for those fleeting moments on stages all over the world.

In the early '90s, there were about two dozen or so fans who went out on the road and travelled to experience and record Dylan's performances. Today there is a similar group of different people out following the tour and taping the shows and maintaining the records of them. I will share parts of my own story to shed light on how I believe that fan culture evolved during the Never Ending Tour and how it has changed from being relationship-based to technology-based and also how the digital machinery has made it both easier and also more complicated to understand Dylan as a live performer in the era of the Never Ending Tour.

I went to see Dylan for the first time in 1988 in Alpine Valley, Wisconsin, and for the second time in 1990 in Hoffman Estates, Illinois. Both of these shows took place before I had turned eighteen years old. The early '90s incarnation of Bob Dylan was my Bob Dylan, not the relic of the past, the guy who did his best work in the '60s, but the modern Dylan, live and in person. So, fifteen years after the fact, it deeply moved me to read his thoughts about who he was trying to reach at that time in the 'Oh Mercy' chapter of *Chronicles* (Dylan, 2004: 154). Bob wrote: that he set out on the Never Ending Tour consciously hoping to cultivate a new, younger audience of people who would come to understand him as a live performer, people who would come and see him multiple times; that he set up the tour to go back time and again to the same cities, so that the new audience could understand his development as a live performer in the present; and that he sought a new audience who had not grown up on his records, who did not know what yesterday was about. I suppose he was talking about trying to reach people like me and I was part of that new audience Dylan imagined when he conceived and set out on the Never Ending Tour in 1988. And by 1994, when he was touring the college campuses, this audience had been realised: the halls were filled with young people who knew the songs and had a real connection to what he was doing on the stage. This was Dylan acknowledging that the performances were not created to be experienced only once; instead, they were part of an evolution of reinvention and he was willing to come back to the fans time and again to be understood.

It was at my second Bob Dylan concert, in 1990, where I first learned about concerts and studio material that existed on tape which had not been officially released but had made it into the hands of the fan network. There, in a crowd of maybe 10,000 people, I happened, by circumstance, to be sitting next to a very enthusiastic Dylan fan – Tim Delaney. He asked me if I had any rare Bob Dylan recordings. Not understanding the exact nature of the question, I responded, 'I have *Shot of Love*', an official studio release from 1981 available in all record stores. I thought, because it was not along the lines of *Greatest Hits* or *Highway 61 Revisited*, that it was rare and only a real fan would have it. He took some pity on me and continued to talk with me anyway. He explained that people made recordings of the concerts, put them on cassette tapes and traded them with other fans. What he was looking for was someone new to trade tapes with, to grow his collection. This was how the casual network of tape collectors grew. Not in today's chatrooms, or online forums, or in the autonomy of the internet, but at the concerts or other Dylan-related events that people would attend hoping to meet other fans. Even though I had nothing to trade with him, Tim gave me my first ten unofficial Dylan cassettes. Among them were the New York sessions of *Blood on the Tracks*, Toronto 1980, the out-takes to *Infidels*, Rolling Thunder shows from '75. I listened to these until the tape strips wore out for the whole summer in which Tim became one of my very dearest friends.

I have here a piece of paper which I found that illustrates the old-school way of obtaining information about the tour. It is a *handwritten list* of the cities of where Bob would be playing in 1991. Back then, if you did not know who to call, or were not part of the fan network, it was difficult to see Bob Dylan far away from home. There were no easily accessible lists of concerts or tours before they happened, outlining where and when they would be or how to buy tickets. Figuring out the where and the when of the tour in order to follow it took some work. People who were travelling to see multiple shows learned where he was playing from fans in other cities, maybe *Rolling Stone* magazine or a Dylan fan publication. The information was not instantaneous.

One group of fans in the United States formed a long-distance phone chain at the start of the Never Ending Tour, back when calls were expensive, to keep track of where Bob was going to be playing and then what songs he played. When preparing for this talk I found a pamphlet called *Look Back*, which was started in Chicago in 1984 and was published through 1990 by a group of Dylan fans who wanted to be in a conversation about his work and share information about the shows. *Look Back* was produced by hand on a photocopy machine, hand-stapled and mailed out, before the days when people had computers and printers at home. In some issues, photographs were pasted into each copy one by one. It had tour information, set-lists and essays written by fans. There were classified ads in the back where people sold books about Dylan, posters and other memorabilia. Looking at this now in the age of the internet one gets a sense of how little information there was and how much effort, time and money it took to share it.

Today, if someone wants to know where and when Bob is going to play, from the comfort of home they can go to Bill Pagel's website, http://boblinks. com. He started the page in 1995 in the early days of the internet and has kept it running ever since. The site counter showed the page had been accessed close to 30 million times as of May 2011. This is the most reliable and up-to-date repository of information about the Never Ending Tour. It provides information about rumoured shows before they are confirmed, how to buy tickets, the capacity of the venue, sometimes even a seating chart. It allows for a person in Maryland to get the information they need to buy a ticket for a show in California, Iowa, Australia or Germany months in advance of the concert and know exactly where the venue and the seat inside will be without knowing another Dylan fan, without making a call, without talking to anyone. This is a phenomenon that was unimaginable in the early days of the Never Ending Tour. Many of us would consider ourselves lucky just to know when and where he was playing, to get to the right city and venue in time for the show and to get a ticket at the box office or on the street when we got to the show. Years after Bill started organising the tour information on the internet, Sony made the tour information official through its own website, http://www.bobdylan.com.

In the early days of the Never Ending Tour, Dylan's touring company and management were certainly not publishing advance information about each city and date in a comprehensive and centralised list. In fact, they could at times be secretive or coy when asked where the tour was going next. Fans were not encouraged to follow the tour. At one point on the 1991 tour, Dylan's management commented that Bob was tired of seeing the same people in the front row night after night, going so far as to request that the small core group of followers, myself included, stay back a little and give the locals a chance to be front and centre. The request was honoured, albeit be-grudgingly, and, after a few nights, management approached again, saying people were not getting up and dancing, the energy was off and maybe that the group should come on back to the front to help get people more enthu-siastic towards the end of the show. This became a pattern and for years the real fans, the repeat show-goers, learned that local security would be told to stand off after a certain point in the concert so that people could come up to the front of the stage and dance.

While there are hundreds of videos of Bob Dylan performances now widely available on the internet and others that have remained in the hands of collectors, watching a video of a performance is not the same as being there. Clicking on a YouTube link cannot provide the watcher with the whole of the experience of being in the hall when Dylan sings and plays. How much one enjoys a show is always a matter of perspective, which is separate and apart from the actual output of the performer. It depends on the energy in the hall or, even more particularly, where one is standing or seated, close to or far from the stage, who is standing next to you, if you are with your friends or alone, if someone is smoking next to you, or talking, clapping or drunkenly singing along, if the crowd responds accordingly when the performance is special, and a whole lot of other things. Watching a video does not allow for interaction with the artist or the audience; it is not possible to really have a feel for the energy of the concert. Still, these audio and video recordings supplement the official releases, they are enjoyable to listen to and watch, and they are necessary in order to understand Dylan as a live performer, today and for the sake of history. I was overcome, as were many others like me, by the magic that was being made, enough to spend considerable amounts of time and money to be out on the road and see the concerts as they were happening. The collateral rewards were many in terms of considerable travel to places we would have never seen, and even more in terms of the characters and friends that were met along the way.

Apart from the thrill of the performances, I want to say something more about what it meant to document the information on where, when and what Dylan played before the days of the internet. Michael Krogsgaard's (1991) book *Positively Bob Dylan* lists the songs played at Dylan concerts worldwide, from the first known Dylan performance up through 1991. It required centralising a huge amount of information, which came from multiple sources around the world. After 1991, but before the age of internet, if someone wanted to know what songs or where Dylan had played, you had to know who to ask, or wait for the next publication of a fanzine such as *Look Back* or *Isis* or *Judas!* over in England. There were also Glen Dundas's editions of *Tangled Up in Tapes*, which documented the set-lists and concerts through the listing and quality rankings of the known audio and video recordings throughout Dylan's entire career. Today, all of this historical concert information is centralised, free and available to anyone who wants it over the internet from multiple sources, including on the official website, http://www.bobdylan.com.

At one time, I kept handwritten updates to Krogsgaard, my own personal partial supplement, set-lists from concerts played after early 1991. The set-lists came from people I knew who were at the concerts, or concerts I was at myself. Today, learning what Dylan played at a show no longer requires someone to have any relationships within the Dylan fan community. Technology has totally changed the access to the information and the way that people experience Dylan as a result. It has created a new kind of autonomous serious Dylan fan. With the internet, it is no longer necessary to actively seek information about the concerts in advance, or what he played, after the fact, by forming relationships, subscribing to magazines or buying books. This is not to say that compiling the current information for the 100 or so Dylan concerts each year does not require some form of personal relationship and action. Anyone can write into Bill Pagel at Boblinks.com with the set-list, or post it in a chatroom on http://expectingrain.com or http://www.bobdylan.com. The information makes it onto the internet somehow. But there was, and still is, some level of organisation among the most serious of fans to be sure that each show will be documented and recorded – those recordings will be centralised among a few fans worldwide, whom we call completists – and that someone will get the set-list over to Bill shortly after the end of every show.

The internet has also changed the way people experience the concerts when they go to them. The most casual concert-goers can now see and hear what Dylan is currently doing in concert from the comfort of their own living rooms if they choose. This means, for example, that before a person goes to their first Dylan concert, without talking to anyone, they can quickly look up what songs he has been playing and easily download recordings to prepare for the live Dylan experience.

However, due to the mass of material out there, of various quality, someone who randomly downloads a recording of a concert based on a given date or by random chance cannot properly evaluate what they are seeing or hearing in context. The way many people used to prepare for the live Dylan experience was to listen to his most recent official material, with the expectation that this would be what he would perform in concert. This was often disappointing, as Dylan might ignore his most recent release. But the element of surprise and suspense was there for someone who had never seen a show, or who had not been to one for some time. At this point in the Never Ending Tour, the set-lists are usually quite predictable, so if someone looks up what he has played the previous nights before attending a live concert, they will have a relatively good sense of what it is they will be hearing when they go to see him and, thus, even having never seen Dylan before, they have the ability to know for the most part what songs he will play; they will have an outline of the concert in advance.

However, one of the things many of us enjoyed most about seeing multiple concerts in the early years of the Never Ending Tour was precisely that the song choices were not predictable. The set-lists and arrangements varied from night to night, leg to leg and year to year. Those who wanted to be there to experience these changes and surprises followed the tour, suffering the anxieties of travel and uncertainties of getting tickets, waiting for the payoff, hoping to be there when the gems were put on display.

Many of us went to the shows not knowing exactly what was to come, and hoping to be there on the nights that Bob was playing the songs that we liked but thought we might never see or hear him perform: 'bucket list' songs, so to speak. I remember the first time I saw Bob perform 'Visions of Johanna', in Wichita, Kansas, on Halloween night in 1991. While he plays it often now, he had played it only nine times in the three years before that. I had friends who were at a show in Texas five days before Halloween who told me that he had played it there. I was kicking myself for not joining that tour earlier and thought I had missed my chance. So when he did play it, to my great joy and surprise, the pain of driving over 700 miles to be there in an unseasonable snowstorm was all but forgotten.

He did not play 'Visions of Johanna' again until the Australian leg of the tour in 1992, almost five months later. He went on to play it seven more times in 1992, once in '95, twice in '96 and then did not play it again until 1999. My friend Bev, a very dedicated long-time Dylan fan, was not there, but she knew how much I wanted to see Bob perform that song. And when I saw her some days later at a show and she learned I had seen it she smiled and hugged me, saying 'Michelle you got your Visions!'

Another example of getting lucky and catching a gem was when Dylan played at Wolf Trap in Virginia in the summer of '93. During rehearsals on that tour we could hear from outside of the gates the band practising 'Series of Dreams', which he had never played live. My friend Peter and I were down in the front row and shouted for it so loud and so often that Dylan said 'I heard you already', with considerable annoyance in his voice. You can even hear this exchange on the tape. But then he did the song. Peter and I grasped onto each other for the first few lines while also jumping up and down, blood rushing into our hearts in disbelief and happiness that he responded to our request. Sharing these moments with people who understood their power solidified them in my memory and made them even bigger in terms of meaning, a meaning I get to experience time and again because someone went to the effort to make a tape that was shared.

To use Bob's line and to speak for others as well, we were searching for the gems, and there were a lot of gems in the first fifteen or so years of the Never Ending Tour. And the definition of gems changes over time. For me, the gems come from the quality of the performances, the song choices, the surprise elements, the energy on the stage and in the audience. To use a literal example about striking gold in song, in 1992, on the night Bill Clinton was elected, Dylan played 'Miners Song', in Youngstown, PA, for the first and only time. I remember being there in the front row with Andy G, a real deal Dylan fan, who was recording it with microphones hanging from these dime-store glasses without any lenses in them, his personal taper's disguise. We had no idea what the song was, but we were blown away by it in all of its unexpectedness; lines sung about the pursuit of gold and the futility of 'lady luck blaming' came out of nowhere. No one had any information on which they could predict that Bob was going to come out and play that song; this was part of the excitement. And because Andy G was there, we all have a record and a memory for every note that was played. That happened a lot in the early years of the Never Ending Tour: someone else's song would be played one night and never again performed. At some of the shows in 1990 he was opening with a song that related to the city he was playing in. For instance, he did the only live performance of 'Oxford Town' when he played in Oxford, Mississippi, the year before. In Cleveland in 1991 Dylan sang 'Pancho and Lefty' by Townes Van Zandt and proclaimed at the end, 'That's the only song in my repertoire with "Cleveland" in it'. Those surprises were wonderfully exciting.

The historical records of the tour have improved over time in terms of quality. The new digital technologies have allowed for both better and more photos and audio and video recordings over the years. The availability and the size of the equipment have changed. It was difficult to get into many of the concert halls with recording equipment and Dylan's management had local security on the lookout. This was before it was commonplace for people to carry mobile phones, let alone phones that record sound and take photos. Back then, the people making audio tapes did not position themselves at the best visual vantage point; instead they positioned themselves as close as possible to where the audio was the clearest but also where they were least likely to be spotted by security guards. Tapers who had gone to great expense and effort to be at the shows had the nagging worry of being spotted and thrown out during the performance. So they experienced the show stoically and silently. Dancing jeopardises the quality of the tape, so a serious taper does not move to the music or rush the stage, and does not share the joy of the performance during the concert because it scars the tape. So at the end of a heartwarming harmonica solo or an amazing turn of phrase, the taper does not give back to the performer in cheers of glee, but stays silent so we can all enjoy that moment later. So, yes, we absolutely owe a debt of gratitude to the people who made and shared these tapes; without them, most of the performances would have existed only in the air of the moment and we would not have them to relive or to memorialise the art.

The developments in technology have also changed the way people share and disseminate the pictures and recordings. Before the digital era, to get a good recording of a concert you would have to be connected to the inner circle of tapers to get a tape as close to the original analogue source as possible. People would use the conventions to meet new fans and grow their collections, staying up all night making tapes in real time, running multiple tape decks in crowded hotel rooms; each show would take as long to copy as the concert lasted. Booze and conversation were involved in that. This was also true after the concerts once the Never Ending Tour began; people would meet up on the road bringing their VCRs and tape decks with them. I remember being in hotel rooms with people running several tape decks at a time recording the show from the previous night or others along that tour, with stereo equipment and wires all over the floor.

The live or unreleased material made from a cassette that was made from a cassette that was made from a cassette could start to sound pretty terrible. The same was true for videotapes. So, the inner network had the better tapes; that is, if you knew the person who taped the show and got a copy from that master, your copy would be of much higher quality. For this, relationships mattered. Now, digital copies are made in an instant, often right off the internet; human relationships are not required. The degrees of separation do not change the quality of the recording, save for the compression of data. People who did not know other people with tapes of live shows or unreleased studio material could buy bootlegs, first records and later CDs, but sales were limited to a few stores in large cities, or at record conventions. Today, anyone who wants to take the time to find high-quality digital recordings can go on the internet and find them without any human contact with fans or collectors. If you want a quality unofficial photo of Bob performing, you no longer need to know someone who snuck a camera into the concert. Now hundreds of people hold up digital cameras or phones to take pictures and videos at the shows and post them online immediately. These recordings, photographs, videos of the shows are available in large part to anyone who wants them, whereas they used to be concentrated in the collections of a much smaller number of serious fans.

These are but a few examples to support the assertion that the technology has changed the way that fans interact, or do not interact, with each other. The question is, now that we have had twenty-three years of the Never Ending Tour, and well over 2,000 live shows from this period alone, how can we deal with this mass of information? Where is the inroad to it all?

How can this be experienced in a meaningful way when it is so voluminous, multiplicitous and difficult to sort out? It takes time to understand how one performance or concert relates to another and to the whole. And along with the mass of information, we have so many commentators upon much it and we no longer know who they are. What weight can we give to the comments on the performances when there are so many of them, and how are they going to be understood far into the future? In essence, where is the quality control? This is an issue outside of the Dylan fan community on nearly any given subject in the digital age. People used to talk to each other, they knew each other, there were fewer commentators, and this helped us to assess what weight to place on someone's opinion about the quality of a show or a performance in comparison to the whole. And with this volume of material from the Never Ending Tour, those secondary sources matter, to be able to sort through it in a meaningful way.

There is a difference between expressing enthusiasm about being at a show and that same show actually being a quality concert with quality performances. The ability to discriminate between the two is becoming increasingly rare, as people communicate over the internet with those they have not met and with the mass of amateur reviews, which become part of the massive record of the tour. What is all of this information going to do to how people will understand history when those of us who were there are gone? If you agree that Bob Dylan is the most important popular artist of the last century, the way people understand the material today and in the future matters a great deal.

A lot has changed over the last two decades or more, including the venues that he plays. He is far too often playing in sports arenas now, baseball or hockey stadiums, much bigger places and with famous opening acts who attract their own fans and with whom Dylan fans compete for tickets. It makes it more difficult to be close to the stage and being far away in these venues detracts from the magic of the show. Also, with the internet, there is more competition for the best tickets from people from all over the country and with ticket brokers. Internet technology has made things both easier and harder for fans in this respect.

The shows follow much tighter patterns today and have few, if any, surprises; there is not a real chance of a big payoff for going night after night if one is going hoping for the thrill of surprise. I have no insider informa- tion as to why the concerts have gone in that direction. Dylan plays what he wants and how he wants, and he has not commented publicly about the structure of the show in many years. We can see that he has forgone spontaneity for polish. Despite the predictability in the modern era of the Never Ending Tour, I still go when I can, even travelling to see Dylan almost always a few times every year, but I do not go out for weeks at a time like before, in the early years of the Never Ending Tour. The same is true for those who were out on the road in the years that I was there. However, there are several people who do go night after night who have replaced the early tour followers, and they are taking down and reporting the set-lists, making the tapes and maintaining the record. As I see it, Bob is and remains the master of live performance. Those gems are still in the performances; if they are not inside the elements of surprise, they are inside an inflection, a move, an energy that overtakes the room; even if they are rough diamonds compared with yesteryear, they are diamonds nonetheless which cannot be fully understood from a video, audio and a photo. To get the real experience of the mastery of the performances, one still has to show up, to come out from behind the computer screen and experience it unfold, live and in person, in show and concert. Don't you dare miss it!

Notes

1 The transcription of Clinton Heylin's and Michelle Engert's largely extemporised lecture was reconstructed for publication from an audience recording. Michelle Engert's section was partly also reconstructed from her initial notes. Michelle Engert dedicates her memories to Ed 'Coach' Wynne (24 January 1950–20 February 2015), the shoeless hunter who made the shows blast into our ears and who will always be deep in the fabric of the Never Ending Tour. Both authors thank David K for his tape. Further notes (below) have been provided by the editor.
2 On 17 June 1991, according to Dundas (2003).
3 On 12 June 1991, according to Dundas (2003).
4 Referring to the Refractions of Bob Dylan Conference in May 2011.

References

Dundas, G. (2003) *Tangled Up In Tapes: A Recording History of Bob Dylan* (5th edition) (self-published, available at http://www.tangled.ca).
Dylan, B. (2004) *Chronicles, Vol. 1* (London: Pocket Books).
Heylin, C. (2009) *So Long as Men Can Breathe: The Untold Story of Shakespeare's Sonnets* (Cambridge, MA: Da Capo Press).
Krogsgaard, M. (1991) *Positively Bob Dylan: A Thirty-Year Discography, Concert and Recording Session Guide, 1960–1991* (Ann Arbor, MI: Popular Culture, Ink).

Copyright information

She Thinks I Still Care, by Dickie Lee
Copyright © 1962 and 1978 by Glad Music Co. and Blackjack Music, Inc. Used with permission of the publisher.

Bob Dylan songs

All quotations from Bob Dylan songs are used with permission of the publisher. In accordance with this permission, throughout the book Dylan's lyrics are quoted from http://www.bobdylan.com.

Abandoned Love
Copyright © 1975 by Ram's Horn Music; renewed 2003 by Ram's Horn Music

Absolutely Sweet Marie
Copyright © 1966 by Dwarf Music; renewed 1994 by Dwarf Music

A Hard Rain's A-Gonna Fall
Copyright © 1963 by Warner Bros. Inc.; renewed 1991 by Special Rider Music

Ballad in Plain D
Copyright © 1964 by Warner Bros. Inc.; renewed 1992 by Special Rider Music

Ballad of a Thin Man
Copyright © 1965 by Warner Bros. Inc.; renewed 1993 by Special Rider Music

Blowin' in the Wind
Copyright © 1962 by Warner Bros. Inc.; renewed 1990 by Special Rider Music

Bob Dylan's Dream
Copyright © 1963, 1964 by Warner Bros. Inc.; renewed 1991, 1992 by Special Rider Music

Brownsville Girl
Copyright © 1986 by Special Rider Music

Bye and Bye
Copyright © 2001 by Special Rider Music

Can't Escape from You
Copyright © 2008 by Special Rider Music

Desolation Row
Copyright © 1965 by Warner Bros. Inc.; renewed 1993 by Special Rider Music

Don't Think Twice, It's All Right
Copyright © 1963 by Warner Bros. Inc.; renewed 1991 by Special Rider Music

Down the Highway
Copyright © 1963, 1967 by Warner Bros. Inc.; renewed 1991, 1995 by Special Rider Music

Floater (Too Much To Ask)
Copyright © 2001 by Special Rider Music

Girl from the North Country
Copyright © 1963 by Warner Bros. Inc.; renewed 1991 by Special Rider Music

Highlands
Copyright © 1997 by Special Rider Music

Highway 61 Revisited
Copyright © 1965 by Warner Bros. Inc.; renewed 1993 by Special Rider Music

Honest with Me
Copyright © 2001 by Special Rider Music

Idiot Wind
Copyright © 1974 by Ram's Horn Music; renewed 2002 by Ram's Horn Music

I Feel a Change Comin' On
Copyright © 2009 by Special Rider Music and Ice-Nine Publishing

If You See Her, Say Hello
Copyright © 1974 by Ram's Horn Music; renewed 2002 by Ram's Horn Music

I'm Not There
Copyright © 1970, 1998 by Special Rider

It's All Over Now, Baby Blue
Copyright © 1965 by Warner Bros. Inc.; renewed 1993 by Special Rider Music

It's Alright, Ma (I'm Only Bleeding)
Copyright © 1965 by Warner Bros. Inc.; renewed 1993 by Special Rider Music

It Takes a Lot to Laugh, It Takes a Train to Cry
Copyright © 1965 by Warner Bros. Inc.; renewed 1993 by Special Rider Music

Jokerman
Copyright © 1983 by Special Rider Music

Like a Rolling Stone
Copyright © 1965 by Warner Bros. Inc.; renewed 1993 by Special Rider Music

Lonesome Day Blues
Copyright © 2001 by Special Rider Music

Mama, You Been On My Mind
Copyright © 1964, 1967 by Warner Bros. Inc.; renewed 1992, 1995 by Special Rider Music

Masters of War
Copyright © 1963 by Warner Bros. Inc.; renewed 1991 by Special Rider Music

Mississippi
Copyright © 1997 by Special Rider Music

Moonlight
Copyright © 2001 by Special Rider Music

Index